The
SACRIFICE
of
TAMAR

Also by
NAOMI RAGEN
Sotah

Jephte's Daughter

The
SACRIFICE
of
TAMAR

NAOMI RAGEN

Crown Publishers, Inc.
New York

Published by Crown Publishers, Inc., 201 East 50th Street, New York, New York 10022. Member of the Crown Publishing Group.

Random House, Inc. New York, Toronto, London, Sydney, Auckland

CROWN is a trademark of Crown Publishers, Inc.

Manufactured in the U.S.A.

Design by Nancy Kenmore

Library of Congress Cataloging-in-Publication Data

Ragen, Naomi.
    The sacrifice of Tamar / Naomi Ragen.
        p.   cm.
    1. Jewish women—New York (N.Y.)—Fiction. 2. Rape victims— New York (N.Y.)—Fiction. 3. Blacks—Relations with Jews—Fiction. 4. Family—Israel—Fiction. I. Title.
    PS3568.A4118S23   1994
    813'.54—dc20   94-20497
                                                               CIP

ISBN 0-517-59561-3

10 9 8 7 6 5 4 3 2 1

First Edition

This book is dedicated to
Manny and Shirley Ragen,
and to Shanie,
whose courage inspired me
and whose brave retelling
brought me closer
than I ever dreamed possible
to understanding.

✦ ACKNOWLEDGMENTS ✦

I would like to express my appreciation to the following people: To Betty Prashker and Erica Marcus, my gifted editors, for their insightful reading and invaluable guidance. To my agent, Jean Naggar, for encouraging me to pursue this project and for continuing to be a writer's fairy godmother. To the many former Bais Yaakov and other yeshiva girls who grew up in Brooklyn in the fifties, for agreeing to be interviewed and for providing such valuable insights. And last, but not least, to my husband, Alex, for his continued generosity and dependable wisdom.

Consider the work of God:
for who can make straight, which
He has made crooked? In thy
days of good fortune be joyful, and
in thy days of adversity consider;
God has made the one as well as the other,
and man cannot know what lies
in store for him.

ECCLESIASTES 7:13–14

❧PART ONE❧

❈1❈

Orchard Park, Brooklyn, 1970

A few hours before it happened, Tamar Finegold stood smiling at herself in her bedroom mirror. With the shades drawn and her husband gone, she stomped around the room doing the "mashed potato," like a sixties teenager or an Indian, right there, a dance of happiness and excitement.

She was humming an old Neil Sedaka song to herself as she brushed her pretty, curly blond hair toward her high cheekbones, giving herself what she believed to be a seductive look, at least as seductive as a very devout rabbi's wife from Brooklyn imagined she could look. And as she studied herself, her lovely gray eyes began to sparkle and her cheeks grew warm.

It was mikvah night, the night the *halacha*, religious law, permitted her to go to the ritual bath and bathe away the spiritual uncleanness of menstrual blood, sending her back into her husband's arms after two maddening weeks of total physical estrangement. It was more than not sleeping with him, she often thought while suffering through the long days of separation. It was being forbidden to touch him, to feel the casual brush of his hand against hers as he handed her a cup or sat companionably beside her on the couch, reading.

And even though she knew Josh was simply following strict rabbinical decrees meant to prevent casual contact from turning into uncontrollable passion, still, irrationally, his distance made her feel unloved. But there was nothing to be done. She might as well have tried to convince him to commit murder as seduce him to hold her hand.

They had never touched at all before their wedding night. Under the wedding canopy he'd looked so severe in his dark black suit and hat, his austerely trimmed beard and mustache reminding her of old pictures of Prussian generals. It had terrified her a little. But soon enough she had experienced the startling revelation that men, deprived of their outer trappings, in the secret sexual cosmos of their relationship to their women, were as vulnerable as the frailest baby. In that cosmos, the wrong word, the smallest hesitancy on her part, could utterly crush him. And once she had learned this, she understood the mysterious smiles of women secreted behind the synagogue partition as they watched the men bluster and propose and direct the service to G-d like kings.

This was not to say that nothing of the Prussian general remained in Josh. As several minor but frightening incidents in their short marriage had taught her, when it came to adherence to *halacha*, he could be as harsh and uncompromising as any sergeant lambasting a raw recruit. Quite aside from her own sincere religious convictions, there was nothing Tamar Finegold had come to dread more than being found out in some infraction of religious duty by her husband.

This quality in him didn't overly disturb her. Women were not taught the *halacha* the way men were, and it was the men's responsibility to steer them straight, to ensure no hint of sin blemished the family's good name. Had not her father and grandfather been the same?

But tonight, sanctioned by *halacha*, she would unwrap herself to him once again like a bride. Fresh, desirable, and immaculately clean, she would reach out to him, and he would lay aside his Talmud and devote himself entirely to pleasing her.

She was twenty-one years old and very eager for the night to begin. She loved him.

She loved his hands, eager and considerate; his temperate voice; his unending compassion for friends and neighbors. She loved his intelligence and uncompromising righteousness that had earned them both success and status in the yeshiva world. She loved him and had never ceased to be amazed at her incredible luck in meriting such a husband. After all, he could have done so much better.

A little thrill went through her, remembering the unbearably dainty scrounging for husbands that had gone on among her classmates at the Ohel Sara Seminary for Young Women. A scholar of Josh's caliber, with the potential to one day head his own Talmudical academy, was the Lincoln Continental of matches, a genuine commodity. He was the kind of son-in-law for whom Orthodox parents were eager to burden themselves with serious debt so that his learning might continue unimpeded by material cares.

Josh could have had any one of her classmates—and a free apartment in a two- or three-family house in Orchard Park, a new Pontiac, and four years of uninterrupted, fully financed yeshiva studies.

Instead, he'd chosen her. "I don't want the spoiled daughter of the rich. I want a woman who is willing to sacrifice to reach the highest levels of holiness. A woman who will share my life and not complain of the hardships," he'd told her frankly. "A woman who'll let me learn in peace."

Yes, any one of her classmates would have been thrilled to accept such a proposal, to share the life of such a man! A life that ensured the most elevated status imaginable in the ultra-Orthodox world of Orchard Park and a golden reward in the World-to-Come. Any one of them, she breathed deeply, proudly, with a secret little smile.

Well, almost any one of them.

She rubbed the bridge between her eyes reflectively, her pleasure tarnished, as it always was when she thought of Hadassah. But then, no one had been good enough for Hadassah. She thought of her friend/enemy with love/hate and, finally, pity. So many years later, her story was still sending shock waves through the community. Her father—the Kovnitzer rebbe, heir to the century-old Hasidic dynasty founded in Kovnitz, Czechoslovakia—had nearly died of a heart attack, and her mother—always such a youthful, pretty rebbetzin— had grown haggard and old overnight.

Who would have imagined such a fate for Hadassah?

She gave an involuntary cringe. Then she smiled again into the mirror. And who would have predicted such a fate for herself, the pretty, plump child of financially strapped Orthodox immigrants who had survived Hitler's nightmare? The shy, self-deprecating young woman who had grown up in the shadow of a dazzling older sister who got everything perfect? Even the matchmaker, her own aunt, had been shocked that things had worked out.

But from the first moment, Josh had never made her feel that he was doing her a favor, overlooking things he had a right not to overlook. She remembered the young men who had turned over her parents' china to read the brand name, who had asked her point-blank if their home was rented or owned.

Josh had never asked. He had always treated her like some precious, rare find. He had been looking for a modest, sincerely devout young woman of impeccable reputation, a woman with no taint on her character or activities or desires. And he had found her.

She looked over her nails, taking out a manicure scissors and paring them down mercilessly until her fingertips were almost raw. She had no choice. Either she could cut her nails off, or the mikvah lady—that powerful inspector of female bodies who ruled the ritual bath, without whose approval no female flesh was allowed to enter its purifying waters—would cut them off for her. Besides, not preparing yourself properly for the mikvah was a sure way to start tongues wagging. This thought, more than any other, slapped her into submission. For despite all the noble *halachic* restrictions against gossip, gossip was the lifeblood of Orchard Park. People were quick to judge and incredibly slow to forgive and forget.

She sighed, vowing once again that the moment she got pregnant and thus liberated herself from a year's worth of mikvah inspections, she would let her nails grow and grow and grow, polishing them with shiny lacquers with names like Passionate Red, Tropical Dream, and Tawny Amber.

When she got pregnant. . . .

Every single time she'd gone to the mikvah in the last two

years, she'd prayed she wouldn't have to go again for nine months. She wanted a baby so badly, so badly. . . . It was something almost physical, a yearning that came up from her bowels and stomach and heart like a wave of purest desire. She had hailed prayers on G-d, begging, pleading, demanding, making rash promises, and proposing various deals. She'd received blessings from numerous rabbis and purchased amulets. She'd visited numerous gynecologists. Everyone had promised she would have a child.

But when . . . when . . . when?

Every time she saw a woman with a baby carriage, every time she saw a mother cat with kittens, her heart gave that wretched little skip of despair and envy. But the worst part was watching Josh's face at the circumcision ceremonies of friends and relatives as yet another son of some G-d–favored couple was welcomed into the Jewish people. For the past two years, she'd seen his wistful longing grow sadder and more desperate. Sterility was a curse; fertility a blessing. To be childless, according to the Talmud, was akin to being dead. It was also a sign that G-d was not pleased with the union of a certain man to a certain woman.

A chill crept up her spine. What wouldn't she give to hand her husband the most powerful proof of all that G-d approved of their marriage—a son for him to teach everything he had learned, a *kaddishul* to pray for his soul when he died? Or a daughter, she thought reluctantly. She had nothing against girls. Just—every religious couple looked forward to a *bechor*, a firstborn son. Let it be a healthy child, she told herself. That would be more than enough.

She rubbed her forehead, feeling tension crease the smooth young skin between her brows. "Relax," she could almost hear her friend Jenny say in that serene, strangely decisive and encouraging way of hers. "Just relax. G-d in his own good time will answer your prayers. You've been to doctors. There's nothing physically wrong with either of you. Just trust. He will bless you. . . ." Such calm, beautiful faith. From Jenny, of all people. . . .

She bit her lip, aware that it was wrong to question such

7

things. Tamar Finegold believed, at that moment and long afterward, that when the wind blew, G-d's hand was personally involved in turning every leaf on every tree in the direction He desired. And so, she should not have found it remarkable that Jenny Douglas, daughter of two assimilated Jews—an Ethical Culturalist mother who liked bacon with her eggs and an atheist-Communist father—had become—next to Josh—the most deeply faithful, scrupulously observant Jew she knew.

But would her faith be quite so perfect if she were married and childless? Tamar comforted herself with uncharacteristic cynicism. A moment later, though, her mood changed. For as long as she could remember, Jenny had been her best friend and a really good person. Her faith was solid and real. And perhaps she was right. Relax, just relax. Have faith.

She brushed her hair back and twisted it into a tight knot that she pinned down as flatly as she could. Then she took out an elegant new wig of almost identical color and pulled it carefully over her head, mercilessly concealing every errant wisp bent on escape. Turning her head from side to side, she admired it, feeling her heart once again stir with joy.

This was surprising. For of all the many religious laws she was bound to obey as an Orthodox Jewish woman, she found covering her hair the hardest, and harbored a secret resentment toward the wigs, *tichels*—head scarves—and hats that hid the glory of her own sunlit mane. Besides, it never failed to remind her of one of the worst "incidents" with Josh.

After three months of marriage and constant wig wearing, she'd noticed her beautiful hair going as dull and matted as an old doll's. In a panic, she'd run to the hairdresser and had it washed, rinsed with blond highlights, and blow-dried.

"I wish my husband could see it this way just once before I put the wig back on and ruin it," she'd told the hairdresser wistfully.

"Why not put on a hat instead?" the sympathetic woman had suggested.

She'd hesitated. Even though she'd been scrupulously careful to hide all her hair since her wedding day, she knew the *halacha* had a more lenient interpretation. Many religious women, including her own mother, believed it was enough to cover most of, not all, your hair. Her mother always wore hats. With this in mind, she'd tried on a little hat and looked at herself. What harm could it do? she'd wondered. After all, it was just a few minutes' walk to the house. Besides, everyone would probably think it was the wig underneath, not her own hair. It looked exactly the same. She'd walked home with the wig in a bag, feeling pleasantly wicked and joyfully young.

Of course, some yenta had immediately informed Josh.

His reaction had been terrifying. "How could you defy the *halacha* that way?!" he'd said, his face frighteningly red. "How could you be involved in such a display of *pritzus*, such wantonness, like some cheap shiksa!!!"

His harshness had stunned her. "But the *halacha* isn't so clear. . . . My mother always wore hats!" she'd defended herself weakly.

"*The* halacha *is perfectly clear!!*" he'd roared—he, who had never once raised his voice. "*It says to cover your hair! If G-d tells you to do something, you do it completely, with all your heart and soul. And if you're not sure, you always do more, never less than the letter of the law!! Our parents' generation was lax. This is no excuse. . . .*"

"I just wanted to be pretty for you. . . ."

"Pretty! How could you be so incredibly *stupid?!* Don't you know that if I want to be a *rav* in this community, it is not enough for people to look up to me. They have to look up to you as well! One thoughtless act . . . I can't understand it! You could *ruin our lives!*"

She'd wept hysterically, full of remorse, demolished more by the unrelenting unhappiness in his suddenly hard eyes, his offended air of having been undeservedly wronged, than by anything he'd said. Indeed, what had broken her heart most of all had been the realization of his capacity to be so unkind.

With the wild exaggeration of a young bride after her first fight, she'd imagined divorce, disgrace, banishment. But three days later, she'd come back from the mikvah, and his passion had been overwhelming. "You're young and foolish, but you meant no harm. I've been unfair to you," he'd whispered tenderly. "Forgive me." And a great wave of relief had washed away the soft newlywedded bliss, replacing it with a warmer, more tempered passion that included a wariness and a clearer understanding of limits: she had learned that it was not only G-d who was to be loved and feared. And that her marriage should never be taken for granted.

She adjusted the new wig, admitting to herself that most of her joy was not in how flattering it looked, but in how cheaply she had purchased it. Sixty percent off! Better than wholesale!

For Tamar Finegold, every bargain-basement sale, closeout, or discount properly exploited was a victory not only in making ends meet on her husband's ridiculously low salary, but also in showing all of Orchard Park that the brilliant, esteemed young Rabbi Finegold's dubious choice of bride had been the right one. It proved that he had been right to overlook the small dowry, the undistinguished family name—that he had married a true prize, a genuine *eshes chayil*, as tightfisted and shrewd as she was pious.

She kept in mind, however, that it was a minor victory in a never-ending war to reconcile two opposites. For in the world of ultra-Orthodox Brooklyn Jews into which she had been born, nothing was more disdained than the pursuit of material wealth—except the appearance of poverty. It was a world where learning, good character and spiritual growth were held as supreme goals; and where not having nice clothes, a fine home and the ability to provide a dowry and support a son-in-law were indelible black marks. A world where no one looked beneath the surface, as long as the surface looked right. A world where appearances were everything.

She started to get dressed, buttoning an exquisite long-sleeved white blouse, struggling with the little pearl buttons. It was pure silk. She had found it on a rack in Lord & Taylor where some careless salesperson had accidentally mismarked the price. She remembered the long, fierce argument with the manager, who'd had no choice but to let her have it at the ludicrously low price. As every talented New York shopper knew, that was the law. Her chest tightened pleasurably at the memory.

She packed her mikvah bag, putting in clean towels, combs, makeup, expensive shampoo, perfumed soap, cotton swabs to clean her ears and navel, everything she might need to totally cleanse her body before immersion and beautify it afterward. She drew back the living room curtains and stared restlessly at the rim of the sun, still bright and high in the late afternoon sky, apparently not sharing her impatience. The mikvah would open in about an hour, but she'd be permitted to immerse only after sunset. These long spring days, she thought, exasperated. They were killers to mikvah nights.

The phone rang. It was her sister, Rivkie.

"You've got to come over right away and watch the baby for me! Just for an hour or so. It's only the baby, not Moishe. He's at *Mameh's*. . . ."

"Just . . . I. . . ," she stammered, as she always did when being bulldozed by Rivkie.

"What's the big *giddeleh?* It'll just be for an hour. The driving teacher can't come any other time, and Menachem won't be home from the yeshiva for at least four hours. I don't want to ask my neighbors again. I asked them so much this week, and I'm new in the building. . . . I really hate to cancel my lesson. Besides, the baby's asleep. He won't be any bother," she said, her tone growing peevish and aggressive.

Just a stupid driving lesson, Tamar thought resentfully. The only way to beg off would be to tell her sister the truth. It's my mikvah night, she tested out the words silently. I don't want to be distracted. I want to get to the mikvah early. . . . But she couldn't bring herself to break the strong taboo against revealing such information. Mikvah night was a secret closely guarded by pious women out of deep modesty. Even one's own children were never told; their parents' relations had nothing to do with them. And so excuses always had to be found to explain where Mommy was going and why she was coming back with wet hair. . . . Even the mikvah entrance was always unmarked and off the street, concealed in shadows.

Besides, to have said no to her sister Rivkie's request for help would have been possible only if she had not been the child of Ruth and Aaron Gottlieb, the kindest people in the world. If she had not grown up in Orchard Park surrounded by Orthodox Jews who believed that doing favors was a religious duty. If she had not been instructed by rabbis and religious women of the Ohel Sara School for Girls in the unshirkable obligation of doing kind deeds for all askers. . . . She could only have said no to Rivkie if she had not been the person everything in her world had conspired to make her.

"Please. . . ," Rivkie wheedled, changing tactics, using her big sister I'll-be-your-best-friend-if-you'll-only irresistible tone of voice. "I've got to get out of the house before I go nuts. Menachem's brother's wedding has been so much work to arrange—I did most of it. And now Menachem's father is demanding we change caterers because someone in shul told him Hartner's isn't kosher enough anymore! Imagine—two days to the wedding to change caterers! And Menachem's aunt Sara called from Israel and said she's bringing her daughter and the two children, so now I have to find them a place to stay. . . ."

Tamar closed her eyes and gritted her teeth. G-d treated you the way you treated others. "All right."

"Great! I'll see you in ten minutes."

Tamar felt the moist breeze of thundershower weather curling her hair under the wig, helping the captive strands escape. She pushed them back in with deft furtiveness, anxiously searching the street for a pair of observant eyes. You were never alone in Orchard Park. Every minute detail of your clothes, your hair, your attitude was noted and recorded in some unwritten record book that rivaled—if not surpassed in sheer relentless detail—FBI and CIA files. Who you were, and how acceptable you and your children were to the community were made up of those accumulated details. Hair sticking out of your wig was a very bad mark in that record book.

She looked down, checking her clothes, feeling a little surge of confidence. It was a beautiful outfit meant for the Sabbath and holidays. One always wore Sabbath clothes to the mikvah, for one never knew whom one was likely to meet there. One time, she had even sat next to the great rebbetzin of Kovnitz herself, Hadassah's poor beleaguered mother.

Besides, not dressing "properly" was a sure way to arouse the suspicions of the mikvah lady and to find oneself cornered and relentlessly grilled on the embarrassing minutiae of preparing the body for the ritual bath. "Have you inserted the cloth deeply enough? Have you counted exactly seven days? Are you sure the cloth came out perfectly clean with no black or yellow spots? . . ." As if she needed reminders! As if the bride class hadn't made her an expert, stuffing her with enough rules to choke a hippopotamus! It was disgusting enough to have to stand there naked while she looked you over and over, but being grilled on top of it. . . !

She stood still, frightened and amazed at her rebellious thoughts. G-d, please don't punish me, she prayed. How could she, tonight of all nights, risk angering Him when so much depended on His goodwill? She bent her bewigged head humbly.

She walked past Orchard Park's neat one- and two-family houses with their manicured shrubbery; past newsstands selling Hebrew and Yiddish newspapers; rows of butcher shops selling strictly kosher meats; groceries vying with each other on prices for rabbinically supervised milk and cheeses. She crossed streets full of kosher bakeries with signs in Hebrew letters, shops selling Hebrew books and festive Sabbath candlesticks and tablecloths, until she reached the lone gentile's house that marked the unofficial end of Orchard Park. She averted her eyes from the front lawn, where a plaster Madonna defiantly greeted the pious Jewish interlopers who had stolen the neighborhood from its Italian founders.

She glanced under the elevated train tracks to where the Polish grocery displayed its canned hams and ropes of blood sausages, hurrying past the graffiti-covered steel safety doors of shops long shut down. Once or twice, she glanced at the odd symbols and slogans, which were mostly meaningless to her. Something to do with Vietnam, she thought, that strange, faraway war that evoked no interest in Orchard Park, whose young men were all safe from the draft with 4-D deferments. And since it had nothing to do with Israel . . .

"F—— Hoffman, Free Seale!" she read, blushing at the obscenity, not recognizing either name. "Black is Beautiful."

13

It was strange, she mused briefly, colored people wanting to be called black. That had always been considered such a rude term for Negroes. Not that she had ever personally known a colored person—there weren't any in Orchard Park—or had reason or opportunity to call them anything. But she knew that the change in terms didn't matter much. Among the people she knew, colored people would continue to be called "the *schvartzes*," just as everyone who was not Jewish would always be referred to as "the goyim."

As she walked along, she did not feel uneasy at these reminders of the vast gentile world that strained all around her; nor did it even underline for her the dreamy fragility of the self-contained world out of which she had suddenly stepped. For she did not really perceive anything outside the grid of streets and avenues containing her friends and relatives, her kosher food stores, synagogues and schools. Her mind simply didn't register rude graffiti, stores selling ham, gentiles of any color, or Jews who acted like gentiles. There was no malice in her rejection. It was simply good housekeeping: if there was no place for something, if you had no use for it, why bring it into your well-ordered house?

Although Rivkie's apartment was only a few blocks away from her own, it was in an area only newly inhabited by the religious Jews of Orchard Park. Each time housing became expensive or scarce, young religious couples would set up little pioneer outposts in fringe areas where Poles, Italians, and now even Puerto Ricans and blacks still held sway. Rivkie's apartment was in an older building that had only recently been colonized. Like humans sent to a distant, hostile planet, the young Orthodox couples created a self-contained little world, a world totally cut off from its surroundings.

As usual, Rivkie looked perfect. She hadn't gained an ounce from her pregnancy and was back into the size six designer petites she managed to buy for next to nothing in Orchard Park outlets stocking one-of-a-kind samples, reduced because they were practically unsalable except to starving models unburdened by hips or thighs.

Her lips were bright pink. Her cheeks glowed.

"You're a lifesaver. I'm telling you, another minute in this house and I'm a crazy person." She kissed Tamar hastily. "Look what I did to you!" she said, rubbing the bright pink mark off her sister's cheek. "Your skin's a little dry, you know. And I think I see a few crow's-feet just near the upper lids. Do you use night cream? You should take care of your skin, Tamar. Try this new Helena Rubinstein cleanser. . . . It'll dry up the blackheads without stripping the moisture." She neatly touched the corners of her own lips to check if the lipstick application had been mussed. She looked Tamar over critically. "My neighbor tried this new diet. Powder and water in the blender three times a day. Like a milk shake, she says. And she lost twenty pounds. Love your blouse. New?"

Tamar felt her forehead bead with perspiration. A conversation with Rivkie was like a minor traffic accident, something that left her feeling bruised and sprawled without dignity in a public place. It had been going on ever since they were little girls.

"The blouse is a Christian Dior. Mismarked. I found it on the racks in Lord and Taylor. Instead of fifty-two dollars, they had to let me have it for five dollars and twenty cents," she offered up hopefully, trying to redeem herself.

Rivkie's eyebrows paid tribute to her, rising in a comrade's salute. "It's gorgeous! Just watch out for the buttons. They're so hard to replace."

"It's got four spares in a little bag, attached."

"Four? Christian Dior . . ." She shook her head slowly, impressed, recognizing a real coup. There was nothing more to say. "I'm *shvitzing* in here. Are you *shvitzing?*" Rivkie abruptly changed the subject. "It's like the snake house in the zoo in here! Hot. Wet. Here, I'm opening the window. We need a little circulation." She unlocked the window leading to the fire escape and pushed it up. "I'll be back in two hours at the most. . . ." she headed swiftly toward the door.

"Two hours!" Tamar cried after her. "But I can't, Rivkie! You said one. . . ."

"It just depends . . . if . . . well, I'll try," Rivkie called over her shoulder. And then she was gone.

15

In an hour the mikvah would be reasonably full. In two it would be packed. She walked restlessly around the room. Well, what could you do about it? Nothing. Nothing at all. She walked over to the baby, fast asleep in his carriage in the living room, and tucked the delicate hand-knitted blanket more securely around his tiny shoulders. As she touched him something flamed through her, an ache, a shout of longing for growth, for fecundity, for tiny, perfect, needy creatures to be mothered.

Little sweet boy, little baby! she thought, her finger grazing the pure silk of his cheek, careful not to scratch him. If only he was awake. If only Moishe was around. . . . Just spending some time holding their soft, young bodies would have erased all her bad feelings. . . .

What was she going to do now? she fidgeted. Like all the houses of young religious couples in Orchard Park, Rivkie's had no television set and only a few magazines. Walls were dominated by bookcases filled with religious books—the Talmud, the Mishna, the biblical commentaries as well as the whole set of Pentateuch and the major and minor prophets. Tamar glanced up at them. She didn't feel in the mood for the Pentateuch or the major or minor prophets. So she walked into her sister's bedroom, turned on the bedside radio, and sat down on the large rocking chair.

The new wig felt suddenly heavy and confining in the warm damp room. She took it off and laid it carefully on the table. A sudden urge to mow her hand through her hair, freeing it, went through her. But she resisted it, letting out a deep, burdened breath. She rummaged through the night table for one of Rivkie's *tichels* and tied it carefully around her head.

"Please reward me for my strict adherence to your laws. Give me my heart's desire," she prayed casually, tucking in the wisps with a determined, righteous finger. G-d was always with her, day and night, a good friend whose hand she held all her waking hours. Her conversation with Him was constant and natural—a breath in, a breath out—needing no outer trappings of synagogue and prayer book.

Curling up on the comfortable chair, she took her sister's

crochet needle and thread and worked on the blanket Rivkie was making for a friend. Even as she worked, she knew her sister would probably tear out all the stitches, which would no doubt fall below her high standards. She didn't care. The lovely blue and green threads slipped easily over her fingers, dulling her restless thoughts like a drug. Such pretty colors, she thought. I must make my own baby such a blanket. Someday, she thought drowsily.

And then she heard the footsteps.

Her first reaction was one of pleasure. Rivkie had seen her distress and had come back early to apologize. Or maybe the lesson had been canceled. She put down the crocheting and walked into the living room.

"Rivkie?"

He was a black man of medium height and average build, wearing a pair of unclean brown pants and a checked shirt. "What are you doing in here?" she said reasonably, almost politely, her body tense but controlled, believing in honest mistakes, in polite strangers stumbling inadvertently into lives meant to be detached forever from their own.

Later, her calm, her doubt, would all seem so ludicrous, so much that she would deny it even to herself, ashamed that she had not instantly perceived the winding downward spiral into the stuff of nightmare.

The flash of the knife would always be the beginning of the memory for her.

"Shut your mouth and do exactly what I say. I'll kill you and . . ." The knife slashed the air, pausing above the baby's head.

She froze, her heart, her mind, suspended, as if quick-frozen by some sudden snowy avalanche.

His small, dark eyes looked her over appraisingly. "Now turn around."

She did exactly as he told her. The strange freezing horror radiated down her limbs, like the numbness of an anesthetic that slowly encroaches into more and more territory. It was a numbness of horror akin to calm, and she felt almost grateful as she looked at the wall, grateful for this tiny space of time, this one moment when she didn't have to look at him or his knife, when she could concentrate. "*Shema Yisroel,*" she whispered, the proclamation of G-d's oneness that is a Jew's last rites. She heard the wooden slide of drawers, the rustle of materials, the tap of undefined metals.

The moments stretched out and she was still not dead.

"G-d," she prayed, concentrating all her heart and soul and faith into what she was about to ask, understanding limits, choosing her request wisely: "Just don't let him kill the baby. Just don't let me die. Anything but that. Let us live. Please, dear G-d!"

"Now go into the bedroom."

No!! G-d, no! She couldn't move. And then she thought of the knife and the small baby, her sister's child, the child whose fragile skin even the scrape of a fingernail could harm. She took a deep breath and walked into the bedroom.

She found herself facing the dresser mirror. He was standing behind her. He had thin lips, strangely shaped, sunken cheeks pockmarked by bad acne, and thinning hair. He had put on tinted glasses with dark rims.

He fingered her head covering. "You Jewish?" he asked. A simple, neutral question.

Why did he have to ask me that? she thought with sudden rage. Why did he have to make this personal? She nodded.

He ripped the *tichel* from her head.

A deep well of humiliation and rage and hatred ripped through the soft center of her body as the carefully pinned hair tumbled down her back. And suddenly she felt she was no longer just a female, a chance stranger found home alone. And he was no longer just a marauding thief who had stumbled across her. She was a helpless Jewess. And he was a goy, a Roman centurion, a cossack, a Nazi. He was a *schvartze*. A *schvartze* rapist. The living incarnation of every religious Jewish woman's worst nightmare.

He took a paper bag out of his pocket and pulled it down over her head. It smelled of murky uncleanness, of grease and the sweat of palms.

She felt him push her back, and she lost her balance and fell onto her sister's bed, the bridal bed bought with her parents' money as a wedding gift. She could see unclear amber shadows as the paper pressed her long lashes back into her eyes. Sharp, cold metal touched her throat, and then she heard the long swift rip as he sliced through her clothes. She felt the warm damp air touch her skin where he had slit open her lovely new blouse, her Sabbath skirt, her underthings.

He's going to rape me, she thought, only now fully believing it, fully understanding it. He is going to force himself inside me, inside my most personal and private space. Her mind raced frantically. She thought of advice she'd once read in a woman's magazine.

"Don't do this," she pleaded. "I have cancer, I'm going to die. You might catch it if you do this. It'll make you sick. . . ."

She could hear his breathing growing thicker and faster as he pushed her clothes to her sides, exposing her body completely.

She felt the icy cold sharpness of metal circle her nipples. And then the brutal warmth of cupping hands take its place.

Now!!

She lashed out at him, but her nailless fingers made little impression.

"Now you stop that fooling, hear? Or I'll smash your face in and break your arms and make sure you don't ever have to worry about no birth control," he whispered with chilling calm, in a way that a woman who did not know him, a woman who was pinned beneath him helplessly in amber shadows, would have no reason to doubt.

She stopped struggling. Never to have children, she thought, almost willing now for it to begin, so that it would begin and then be over. Never, she thought, never to have children.

He was speaking to her, she realized. Terrible things, terrible, disgusting words. Wave after wave of feeling went through her. She felt a strange energy, a desire, both new and potentially useful, to destroy. So much, so much she wanted to smash, to avenge. But it was stopped up, like a dammed river. Stopped up. . . . She screamed silently as the private pain like no other ripped through her most secret, private self, trampling everything she held sacred, everything she had ever been or ever wanted to be. Desecrating her very core of self, her separate, private oneness of being, that G-d-given self without which we are no longer human. That core was invaded, humiliated, destroyed. She felt his hand over her mouth, suffocating her.

When would it be over? Be over, be over. . . , she chanted to herself. Just be over. And then: Die, die, die, she told herself in a rising crescendo of silent disintegration, her whole core of being flowing out like afterbirth. She had no core, no private self. Anymore.

Ugly, she thought, willing herself not to feel, not to understand the things he did to her simply to humiliate her, for no one surely could get pleasure from such ugliness. Cold, strange, penetrating her sacred singleness, going where no one had a right, *no one!!* Her mind screamed with impotent rage. No one, she repeated, already feeling too tired to imagine a shout. She felt the hot tears, like blood, stream down her face.

She had not known there was such ugliness in the world. That one human soul should brutalize another simply for its own amusement. Even animals had no such malice as they tore each other apart. Their instinct was a pure one: survival. But the human predators? Their motives and dark pleasure had nothing to do with survival.

Survival. Her mind drifted to her mother's tales of concentration camps: "A man is as strong as iron, and as weak as a fly." To survive. To live.

He pulled the bag off her face. And the smell of him—dusky and unfamiliar—the breath of him, intrusive and unfamiliar, settling on her eyes and mouth, invading her nostrils, like nothing else, nothing else.

And then, he kissed her on the mouth.

Her whole being rose up to vomit it out, her whole soul. This was worse somehow than the rape, which in comparison had been a battering, a hammer's blow far away and unseen. This was an act of love transformed into a disgusting violation. This she had seen, and tasted and smelled and felt. She would never forget those lips on hers. Her whole being heaved in utter revulsion.

This she would never, ever forget.

"Now close your eyes and count to ten and I'll be gone."

She was beyond feeling hope. Beyond feeling. She closed her eyes and heard him fumbling through the dresser drawers and then his footsteps growing fainter and then silence.

Was he still there? Was he going to kill her anyway? she wondered, wondering, too, why it was she didn't care.

❖2❖

For several moments (several years? A few lifetimes?), she lay perfectly still, listening, as if waiting for some kind of command, some indication of what she was to do next. She heard the wind rustle the curtains, and for some reason it reminded her of a rat scurrying through dry, old newspapers. The idea of it made her want to scream and scream and scream until all the neighbors came pounding at the door. . . .

The neighbors. Her mind suddenly reared up, as if out of a dream. She looked at herself. She was half-naked, filthy. . . . She sat up, then stood. She felt disgustingly wet and sticky as the viscous liquid drained down her thighs. She wanted to wash herself off. That mattered more than anything. To wash. To be clean again. But police, she thought dimly. Doctors. Evidence . . .

She gathered the sheet around her and walked into the living room. The window by the fire escape was still open, showing no trace of the man who had come and gone. She slammed it shut and leaned against it, trembling, staring at the door, feeling the blocked screams rising with almost irresistible force.

She swallowed hard. The neighbors. Her own kind of people. They would gather her in their arms. They would call Josh, her sister, the police . . . She leaned heavily against the window frame, her whole body aching for those kind, protective arms.

But then she thought: Everyone will know. Every time I come to visit my sister, they will all look at me and think of me this way: violated, repulsive, and somehow blameworthy.

I won't ever again be a young, respectable married woman, part of a young couple, like all the other young couples. The warm conviviality, the social cocoon, would simply burst trying to contain what it had seen. The moment I open that door, I'll become the worst possible thing in the world. The worst possible thing in *my* world. Different.

In the growing shadows, she touched her tender stomach, envisioning a black-and-blue mark. She touched her breast and face. They were cold but seemed unharmed. She sat down on the couch and rocked, hugging her body like some dear object lost, then suddenly found, but dirtied somehow, and not half so lovely or precious as she remembered it.

What should she do now?

She felt that tightness in her chest, that smothering loss of breath as if some savage wind had flown up her nostrils and down her throat. Her head felt cramped, as if a dozen small hammers were banging above her eyebrows, pressing down, making her lids twitch. Gingerly, she traced her face. There were the bones of her forehead, her eye sockets, her temples, hard and clear, as if she were a corpse, fleshless and unprotected.

My whole life. . . , she thought vaguely, not understanding the end of the thought, then suddenly understanding. My whole life, there was a shine to living. A shine, a glow of beauty that covered the world where G-d sat regally protecting the weak, punishing the wicked, watching over His faithful, like the apple of His eye. Never again would it have that lovely innocent shine. My whole life . . . Never, never again.

She wanted to cry. And then she did cry. I'm sorry, so sorry! she cried helplessly until another thought dawned on her. The baby! Shlomie! How could it be that she had forgotten all about him? She walked to the carriage. It was silent, unmoving. A feeling of indescribable horror went through her as she lifted the coverlet.

But he was all right, she saw, feeling his little body warm against her chest. He stretched and twitched in protest, uttering little mewing sounds. Still, she undressed him, her hands and eyes roaming from his tiny, transparent toenails to the soft fontanel, scanning him like an x-ray. He was all right! Thank G-d! She dressed him and put him down. She saw his shoulders heave peacefully as she pulled the covers over him. For a long time she stared at him numbly, the horror of what could have been chasing her relief.

She had to call the police, she thought vaguely. That was what people did, wasn't it?

The police?

She thought of the big, good-natured cops of her childhood and felt a small comfort, imagining their solid presence. They would call Josh, and he would come to the police station. . . . And then she would have to tell them everything that had happened. She would have to describe it. The paper bag. The kiss. To Josh. To strangers . . . Maybe they would ask her why she had done everything he asked and made no attempt to fight him off. They would blame her for the window being open, for being weak and foolish. And perhaps they might think somehow she had done something . . . something to provoke it.

What did I do? she asked herself. Why did this happen to me? Why was I punished like this? her thoughts wandered. They would say she had led the man on. . . .

And even if they didn't, even if they were all wonderful and helpful and understanding, still, a doctor would make her lie on a table and spread her legs; he would probe her battered insides. . . . The thought was sickening and unendurable. Then they would make her look through books of pictures of criminals, strange ugly men. And what if she found the man? And what if they brought him to the station? She would have to be in the same room with him again, would have to see that face, those lips . . .

And then the most terrifying thought of all occurred to her. Someone would be sure to see her go into the police station. And then the word would spread. Rebbetzin Finegold had been raped. The pious rabbi's wife had been defiled. Every time they looked at her, she would read it in their eyes: the terrible knowledge, the pity, the unspeakable questions as the filthy images flitted unwillingly across their brains. How had it been done? What had been done? Sitting in the synagogue as her husband rose to speak before the congregation, she would feel the eyes bore into the back of her piously covered head.

She ran to the bathroom and knelt in front of the toilet, heaving and heaving.

It was unthinkable.

No police. Just home. To Josh. Just home to her well-lit, safe home, to the kind arms of her husband, who would support and comfort her. . . .

Her mouth went suddenly dry. But would he? She had slept with another man. She was a married woman. A rabbi's wife. She had been defiled by another man. Would Josh have to divorce her? What was the *halacha?* Her throat ached. Whatever it was, Josh would follow it to the letter. There would be no hesitation, no reprieve.

She walked over to the baby, watching his peaceful sleep. "The only witness," she murmured to herself. Then she walked into the bedroom and began to pick up her ruined clothes. Tiny pearl buttons scattered everywhere. She got down on her hands and knees and searched frantically for each one, clutching them in her palm.

Rivkie would notice the buttons, she thought, reaching out for them through the dust balls. Then she stopped, shocked, suddenly facing her decision, realizing with dim understanding that she had reached one. She would search for the buttons one by one, leaving none behind. She would gather up her torn clothes and hide them. And she would tell no one what had happened.

She would cover it all up.

Forever.

No one. No one had to know. Not Josh. Not Rivkie. Not her mother. Not the neighbors. Not the police. Not rabbis. There did not have to be any questions, and inquiries. No one had to ask. And she would not have to answer. If only . . . if only she kept quiet. How could they know, she reasoned, looking at the sleeping baby, if she did not tell them? And suddenly a calm certainty began its silent flow through her, like the smooth lapping of a summer lake against its banks. A strange relief coursed through her.

I can wash it all off, she thought. The filthy viscous liquid, the taste of his lips, the memory. Wipe the slate clean. Make time disappear, events vaporize. Why should anyone have to know? Like Zissel, she thought. Like little Zissel safe in the house under her aunt Malka's protective wing. What's not nice, you don't show. No one to know, no one to ridicule. Safe.

The idea beckoned her seductively, clutching her like a lover's hand, leading her where her heart wanted to go, despite the doubts and guilt. She felt her heartbeat slow, her very physical motions grow efficient and unwilled, as if she were some factory robot programmed to do tiny, perfect gestures without discretion or judgment.

My whole life . . .

It was suddenly very clear what she was going to do now.

She went into the shower and put on the water full force. It went on and on and on, in a hard, pelting stream. She couldn't imagine it ever ending. Only when the water grew cold did she consider turning it off. She dried herself with small, reluctant pats. Myself? Could it be? She looked into the foggy bathroom mirror. Were those my eyes? The very color seemed drained. Instead of silver, dross. They were all dilated pupil, almost black, with only a slight gray rim. A look of tragic shock rose from them. How to hide that? she thought. How to hide my soul?

Rivkie. Not yet. Not yet. Don't let her come back and look into those eyes now. . . . Later she would figure something out, some way. Eye drops, or makeup, or dark glasses. Until the look went away. She felt suddenly panic-stricken. She went through her sister's closet, looking for clothes and underwear. Everything was too tight! She felt a scream rise from the back of her throat. But there was a loose early-pregnancy dress. She reached out and grabbed it like a life buoy. Get dressed, she told herself calmly, as if talking to a small, hysterical child. There, you look fine. She pulled the new wig over her head, combing it, re-adjusting it . . . The elegant new wig.

She looked over her sister's apartment, the ransacked dresser drawers, the open cupboards. Should she clean it up? Had he stolen anything? She considered her options. Slowly, she unlocked the window and pushed it open. Then she wheeled the baby into the hall and locked the door of her sister's apartment behind her.

She knocked on the neighbor's door. She heard the safety lock sliding open and saw two big brown eyes looking out at her. The kindest eyes. Like looking at myself, she thought. Once. So gentle and innocent. A young bride. Part of a young religious couple. Like she had been, once. And for a moment, the urge to lay her head down upon that clean, soft shoulder and mourn was almost overpowering.

She could envision herself telling those eyes. She could envision sympathy there, shock, concern, horror, unconditional compassion. She could not conceive of anything unjust or unkind there: blame or disgust. No, there would not be that, she realized. But something else, something infinitely worse: A shying away. A distancing. A wariness. The inability to keep a secret. The whole community would know sooner or later. She would become, forever, "The One Who Was Raped." No. They wouldn't blame her, but neither would they really want to befriend her, to share in her taint. Neither would they want their children to play with her children. And when the time came to pick out husbands and wives for their sons and daughters, neither would they want her children, the children of "The One Who Was Raped," as sons- or daughters-in-law.

She could understand that. She would feel the same.

She lowered her eyes. "I have to leave now, and Rivkie's late. Could you watch the baby?"

"Of course," was the immediate reply, the kind eyes searching, clouding, disturbed. "Are you sick?"

"No, no, fine. . . ." She looked at her feet. "Just rushing." It wasn't enough, she realized, to justify imposing like this. She had no choice but to use the most pressing excuse she could think of, hoping that the woman would blame herself for provoking such an unwarranted intimacy. Lowering her voice, she whispered: "The mikvah."

"Oh!" the neighbor stammered, blushing. "I didn't mean to pry. The days are so long now. It gets so crowded. . . ."

Tamar looked at the painfully red, discomfited face. And all this because she had had the indelicacy to mention the mikvah! She tried to imagine how that face would look if she told her what had just happened right next door. How Josh's face would look. It was a good deed to hide it from them, she realized. To hide the ugly details. A good deed to cover it all up, to let the suffering and pain end with one victim, one sacrificial lamb.

She wheeled in the baby carriage, smoothing the coverlet over the baby's back. Then she taped a note to Rivkie's door to let her know where Shlomie was.

The streets of Orchard Park, the streets of her childhood, the safest, most comfortable place in the universe. So why did it look so suddenly, chillingly dark? Where had all those narrow, shadow-draped alleyways come from? And whose footsteps were those behind her, pounding in her brain each time she turned the corner, so that by the time she neared the mikvah entrance, she was flying toward it in a terrified run?

She rang the bell, her finger lingering a trifle too long and too hard. She saw the peephole cloud, the door open. The moist warm air settled comfortingly on her chilled, sweating skin.

"We heard you," the mikvah lady complained, with a raised eyebrow.

"Sorry, finger . . . slipped."

The waiting room was packed. All of the women seemed to look at her with one pair of damning, suspicious eyes, eyes that could see beneath her clean, borrowed clothes, beyond the long shower. Eyes that, if allowed to stare long enough, would somehow divine everything.

"Please, I don't feel very well tonight. I was attacked by a dog on the way here," she told the mikvah lady. "I fell. I think I may be bruised. Could I just go in without the line, just this once?"

"A dog! *Gotteinu!* Were you bitten? Maybe we'll call a doctor!" There was immediate motherly concern. For a moment she loved the staunch, matronly figure in her orthopedic shoes and unstylish brown *tichel.* "So come in *maideleh,* come. I'll give you the private suite," the woman said, leading her past the grumbling of the impatient seated women toward the back.

Always before, the luxuriating bath, the careful scrubbing, the thick fragrant shampoo followed by the baptizing purification of the ritual bath itself had been intoxicating. Always before, she had left the mikvah feeling utterly clean and pure. A holy vessel ready to receive the precious gift of a holy new life.

Now, the hot water still tingling on her skin, which was soft and fragrant and burnished to a fine sheen like a bronze statue well buffed, she felt nothing had changed. The dirt, the sticky, viscous liquid still clung. She scrubbed herself raw.

"Are you all right, *maideleh?*" The mikvah lady came in unannounced. "An hour already. The women, they complain. . . ."

"Yes, I was just about to call you."

She emerged from the tub, wrapping herself in a towel. Never before had the mandatory inspection of her body by the mikvah lady before immersion been so hateful to her. She wanted to hide, to cover up. And yet there was no choice. It was the *halacha*.

The woman unwrapped the towel, looking her over matter-of-factly, as only a pious, matronly rabbi's wife who sees fifty female bodies a night could look over a female body. She examined Tamar's shoulders, back and breasts for stray hairs or scabs, anything that might prevent the mikvah water from touching every part of the body, invalidating the immersion. She examined Tamar's toenails and fingernails to make sure they'd been properly trimmed. She slid her hand beneath Tamar's heels and soles, feeling for rough loose skin that needed to be removed.

Tamar closed her eyes, enduring the agony of the scrutiny, trying not to scream. It was almost the last straw.

"Your whole chest is scratched, *maideleh*." The woman shook her head.

Tamar looked down at the long, circular scratch marks below her throat and around her nipples, remembering the hard steel.

"I ran. I fell. . . ," she stammered.

The woman eyed her strangely. "Are you sure you're all right, child?"

"Yes. Fine. Fine. Just . . . I'd like to get home."

"Yes, of course you do, poor *maideleh. Kum, kumaher* into the mikvah," the woman crooned comfortingly. And just for a moment there was some softness, some forgiving kindness in her voice that reminded Tamar of her childhood.

Mameh, Mameh. Not the sick, frail old lady who needed support to get to her weekly chemotherapy sessions. Her *mameh.* Laughing and strong and young, able to solve any problem, soothe any hurt.

Mameh.

Tamar grasped the metal railing and walked down the steps into the small deep pool until the water came up to her chest. It felt warm and clean. Bending her knees, she plunged her head under the water seven times.

"Kosher, kosher, kosher, kosher, kosher, kosher, kosher!" the mikvah lady intoned as Tamar emerged. Seven times. Could the words make it true? Tamar thought. Would she ever be a pure wife again, deserving of love?

"A kosher *maidel*!" The woman smiled, examining Tamar's white body as she handed her a towel. Her eyebrows puckered. Such scratch marks from a fall? What kind of fall could do that? she wondered. "Are you sure you're all right, *maideleh*? Do you want me to call your husband to pick you up here?" she pressed.

"*G-d in heaven! Leave me alone!*" Tamar exploded.

She watched the woman's back arch, stiff with the unde-served insult.

She would never be able to come back to this mikvah again.

"Tamar?"

The bedroom was black, all the shades drawn, the lights extinguished.

"I'm here," she told her husband. "Here in bed. I have been to the mikvah." Even though he knew, she had to tell him, to say the words. That was the law, part of the ritual.

She felt his arms come around her, and she leaned into his

warmth, her heart breaking. She rubbed her cheek against him and smelled his clean, familiar, husbandly smell, her lips seeking out his clean, familiar, loving face.

She clutched at him with a small sob as he performed the marital mitzvah of procreation, glad for his arms around her, his body covering and cleansing hers with his acceptance.

They had never been so close. They had never been so far apart.

❖3❖

She got up the next morning with a feeling of heaviness, as if an iron pole was pressing from the roof of her mouth down the back of her throat to the edge of her stomach. Her sides seemed like rude strangers squeezing up against her, and her eyes pressed up against her lids sending aching pains shooting down her cheeks to the tip of her nose. Her teeth throbbed, a flashing, stabbing pain that wandered from tooth to tooth.

All day, she lay on the couch, immobile, her mind filled with frightening images of evil, images in which she found herself holding knives and guns; in which she found herself shooting, stabbing, kicking, pouring burning oil, slashing, smashing . . .

Would she become evil? Like a dark rain, would the constant bad thoughts, the hatred, penetrate her soul and suffuse it? The idea frightened her. The idea of going out of the house frightened her. The idea of being alone in the house frightened her. She checked all the doors, all the windows, again and again. She refused to let in the nice young delivery boy and insisted he leave the groceries on the doorstep, slipping him the money underneath the door. It took her a long time to open the door to take in the food, but finally, worrying that the cats would get it, she did.

It was a strange and hopeful thing, her worry about the cats, her concern for the waste of good food. It was like a short visit with her normal self, proof that self still existed. But once she had put away the groceries, that self seemed to go away again.

She sat on the edge of her old blue velvet sofa, sinking into its softness. She rocked and rocked, hugging her damaged body as if trying to prevent it from shattering like glass in the wind, sending slivers drifting away into nothingness. The tears rolling down her cheeks were comforting in their real warmth, another sign of normal function.

The phone rang. It was Rivkie.

"You'll never guess what *mazel.* Someone broke into the house right after you left! I guess I should keep the windows locked! Went through all the drawers and took a few dollars and my silver bracelet and some other cheap stuff. But of course he didn't find my good jewelry. I'm not stupid. I hide my jewels in a place no one could find. The safest place!" she gloated. "Wasn't that a *mazel* you left early? I'll tell you the truth, I was not too happy to see on that note that you went. But then when I saw the house, I knew it was all *beshert*, that *Hashem* was just watching over you, you should get out early. So I'm calling to tell you I'm not mad you left early, even though you promised to stay, and you never said anything about leaving. . . . I'm really not even a little mad anymore. But isn't that something? Must've happened not a minute after you went! . . . Tamar?"

"I have a headache, Rivkie. I'm going to lie down."

After that, she let the phone ring, the mail lay unopened until daylight began its slow retreat. As the light dimmed, she forced herself to begin dinner. But as she took out her butcher's knife to trim the tips of the chicken wings, her fingers flexed in a gesture of horror. The knife fell. She heard it clatter behind her as she fled to her bedroom. She slammed the door, then crawled into bed, pulling the covers over her head.

Josh came in late from the yeshiva, searching for her, softly calling her name. She reached up for him urgently, pulling him down, needing to feel his clean, wholesome body cherish her unclean, battered one, her defiled and destroyed self. In his arms, she could forget for a moment.

He was surprised and shyly pleased at her ardor and happy to return it. He was a man whose mind ruled his passions, who lived by rules. And when the rules told him it was permissible, even praiseworthy, to make love to his wife, he brought to his passion the total commitment he brought to every other aspect of his life. He was a man free of guilt and full of pure intentions. He loved his wife.

It was like a balm to her wounds, his loving warmth. Pressed along his body, made one with him, she seemed to draw from him some of his serene purity. Sex was no longer something she did for a mitzvah, something she did for him. It was not an extra, a frill removed from the necessities of life. It had become an oxygen mask. It told her she was still alive. It told her she was still loved.

Yet later that night she only pretended sleep, waiting for him to start his gentle snoring before climbing out of bed. She left the room quietly, sitting again on the couch, rocking and rocking, hugging herself against the enemy, protecting herself against the silent annihilation taking place inside her soul.

He felt her absence and wandered into the living room, sitting down beside her. "What is it?"

She looked into his eyes, so filled with softness and concern. Could she tell him? Could she take the chance of seeing the softness fade, transformed into the hard, unrelenting glare of judgment? Would the *halacha* command him to be kind to her, or to divorce her? She didn't know! But one thing was certain: whatever it demanded, however noble or painful or tragic, that was exactly what he would do. If only I knew! she thought, trembling.

He put his arm around her shoulders. "Are you cold, my love?"

His warm arm. Why should she take such a chance? Why should she cause him the pain of knowing, the pain of horrendous choice? Better, she thought, to sacrifice myself. To know alone. To suffer alone.

"Just a stomachache. I took a Tums. Please, darling, you have to get up so early. Go to sleep, Josh. I'll be in in a minute."

"Are you sure? Maybe you should see a doctor in the morning, Tamar?"

"We'll see."

"No, it's important. It's written: 'And you shall take exceeding care of yourselves.' This is the law, Tamar."

34

Another law, she thought wearily, but without resentment. His face was too full of anxious concern for resentment. "Don't worry. If I don't feel better, I'll go see a doctor. Now go to bed, Josh. Go to bed, my love."

He kissed her and turned toward the bedroom. She watched his back with hot, unreasonable disappointment, crushed at having achieved her goal.

"Are you any better this morning, my dear?" he asked her the next morning, sitting on the edge of the bed.

She had not slept all night. "It's just a bad cold," she murmured, and then, inexplicably, she added: "And I have my period."

He jumped up guiltily. "How can that be? Just the other night you went. . . ?"

"Not really a period, just spotting. I'm sorry," she lied. For reasons she couldn't understand, she suddenly didn't want him to touch her.

His face fell. Spotting, those tiny drops of blood that some-times inexplicably appeared between periods, wreaked havoc on married religious life. It meant another two weeks' separa-tion, just as you'd gotten back together again. But that was the Law.

"Well, you should see a doctor, darling."

"Yes, maybe, a doctor," she murmured. He was so kind, so concerned! She wanted to throw herself into his arms and weep. She wanted to tell him everything, to explain all her lies, to be loved and forgiven unconditionally.

"No! Not 'Yes, maybe.' A doctor. Today, Tamar." His voice went suddenly strident and harsh. "This is *not acceptable*. You must take care of yourself. This is the Law." He took a deep breath. "Can I bring you a cup of tea, something to eat?" His voice softened, yet his eyes, Tamar noted, were still hard.

She shook her head, close to tears.

"If not, I'll leave for yeshiva. It's getting late."

Yeshiva, she thought. Where he would sit and learn the Law. All day, all day. The sacred Law, which only men were allowed to study. The Law that governed their lives and that a Jew ignored at his peril. And if the Law said: "Divorce your wife," he would, wouldn't he?

For what was human emotion, human longing, in light of G-d's infallible word? "And you shall take your son, your only one, your beloved, and offer him as a sacrifice." And Abraham had not hesitated, had not questioned. And only G-d's word had stopped his hand from killing his own child, his one beloved. . . .

She pulled the covers over her head.

Only later, when she was sure he had gone, did she get out of bed. She did not bother to pour the ritual waters over her fingertips to rid them of the unclean residue of sleep. She had not slept. Besides, she was totally unclean. A filthy, unclean, disgusting, worthless. . . . she thought, beaten down by each word, beaten down and oppressed by the very thought of herself.

She walked into the living room, looking up at the bookcase filled with the Talmud, the Pentateuch, the major and minor prophets, the Mishna, and hundreds of commentaries. Where to begin? She opened the Bible she had studied day in and day out, ever since she was a little girl, the sacred text she could recite practically by heart. She knew exactly where to look: Deuteronomy 22:22. "If a man be found lying with a married woman, then both of them shall die. . . ."

She sucked in her breath. But this was not the case. It was rape, not seduction. She read on: "If a man lies with a betrothed maiden in the city, then you shall bring them both out to the gate of that city and stone them with stones that they die; the maiden when it is proved she did not cry out in an inhabited place and the man when it is proved that he has humbled his neighbor's wife. . . ."

Because she did not cry out.

She pressed her fist into her mouth, biting hard on her knuckles to keep from screaming. No, she reasoned with herself, shaking her head. The words proved nothing. They were not the Law, she'd learned. The written Torah, the five books of Moses, were like a shorthand. The true explanations and clarifications of the Bible had been whispered to Moses by G-d on Mount Sinai, and Moses had told Aharon and the elders, and they had told the people.

For example, although it was written "An eye for an eye and

a tooth for a tooth," the Oral tradition explained that this did not mean take out your neighbor's eye if he took out yours; it meant that you must pay him damages for the loss of the eye. The unbroken Oral tradition had lasted hundreds of years, until people began to forget and the rabbis had decided to write it down. And thus the oral tradition had become the voluminous Talmud. Only there were all the cryptic utterances of the Bible expounded and applied. Only there was the *halacha* to be found.

She took a heavy volume off the shelf. Its sheer weight amazed her. She opened it. The page, divided into text surrounded by columns and columns of printed commentaries, made her head swim. Her whole life, everything she did and thought and felt and aspired to was shaped and governed by these words. Yet although she could read Hebrew fluently, their meaning was totally inaccessible to her. It might as well have been written in cuneiform or Chinese.

"He who teaches his daughter the Torah, teaches her impurity," expounded Rabbi Eliezer ben Horkanos in the Talmud, the famous opinion that encouraged Jewish leaders, communities and families to keep Jewish women unschooled and in ignorance for centuries. The Bais Yaakov movement to provide girls with some kind of religious and secular education had only begun in 1917, her mother's generation! And even there education was severely restricted. Girls were permitted to learn the five books of Moses, the prophets, even Mishnah—a codification of Talmudic laws—her teachers at Ohel Sara had explained. Just not the Talmud. Women's minds were too flighty, their intelligence wasn't made for Talmud study as was a man's, they were told. And when, rarely, a particularly rebellious or intelligent girl protested, she was placated with "But a woman's role in life is different from a man's. She cannot offer a lifelong devotion to Talmud study, the only adequate commitment necessary to reach some understanding. After all, someone must care for the home, the children. . . . After all, someone has to!"

Talmud study had been absolutely off limits to her. Her teachers, her rabbis, her parents, the community, Jewish history, had made sure of that. And she had never questioned it. Besides, she had seen her father learning Talmud. It seemed so dry, so analytical, so difficult. She and all the other girls she knew had always been thrilled they didn't have to learn Talmud. But now, realizing she did not have the tools she needed to delve into its intricacies, to find the answers on which her life depended, she wondered if her former joy had not been simply that of the slave relieved of the burden of his own life by the slave master.

She put away the Talmud and took down Maimonides' Mishna Torah. She knew how to learn Mishna. It was so beautifully simple after the Talmud. Often, she had seen Josh pore over the Mishna to discover the final *halacha*.

She took down the *Tractate of Women*, guessing what she needed to know would be in there. She flipped through the pages until something caught her eye: "Who is seduced and who is raped? One who is taken with her consent, and one who is forced. Unless witnesses testify otherwise, one who is taken in the wilderness is considered raped, because even if she cried out, there was no one to hear her. And one who is taken in the city is considered seduced, because if she had cried out, someone would have heard her. If a woman does not cry out and has no witnesses to testify that the man had a sword and said 'Cry out, and I will kill you!' she is considered to have lain with him willingly."

And a married woman who is seduced, who lies with another man willingly, is an adulteress, forever forbidden to her husband. This she did not have to look up. This she knew. And an adulteress deserves death. At the very least, the husband must divorce her.

It was so unfair! She had not been seduced. She had been raped. There had been a knife. G-d knew this!

But she had no witnesses.

She slammed the book shut and pressed it against her chest, the last tenuous threads holding her heart together finally dissolving.

Perhaps she had misunderstood, she thought wildly. Perhaps she should call a *rav*, ask him the *halacha*. . . . But she knew the moment she asked a rabbi a *shaileh,* a *halachic* question, she would have to do exactly as he told her, no matter how painful. Misunderstanding the law was much less serious a sin than knowingly doing the wrong thing.

And what if his answer was the one she had just discovered?

Do I really want to know?

A chill of horror passed through her as she considered the blasphemous thought. "Do not do what is just in your own eyes!" How many times had the Children of Israel been warned? How many? It was heresy. It was . . . almost idolatry. To put yourself beyond the Law? A cold sweat broke out on her forehead.

She got into bed, and her eyelids, weighty and burdensome, closed over her aching eyes.

She awoke in a blaze of light. "What. . . ?"

"Darling . . ."

"You've been sleeping for two days, Tamar. You had us . . ."

"You were burning up with fever!"

"Tamar, tell us what's wrong!"

Her mother was sitting on the bed, stroking her hand. Josh was standing nearby, his expression a mixture of exasperation and genuine concern, his fingers nervously fiddling with his black skullcap. Her sister, Rivkie, stood at the foot of the bed, baby Shlomie in her arms, little Moishe tugging at her skirts. Jenny stood close by, her high, intelligent forehead white and troubled beneath the girlish dark bangs, her green eyes full of compassion.

She looked at them in confusion, her heart yearning for them, almost forgetting she didn't deserve to be one of them anymore, almost forgetting she was a defiled, filthy, shameful thing that had no place in this clean, beautiful religious family. She kneaded the sheet, looking at them wretchedly.

The faces of those she loved looked back at her with such care and love and compassion. The dark glass shattered. She buried her head on her mother's shoulder and wept, her shoulders heaving. Mrs. Gottlieb looked questioningly at Rivkie; her once pleasant, amused face made stoic with pain uncharacteristically frightened. Rivkie shrugged in surprise, and Josh moved swiftly closer to his wife. Tamar looked at him in alarm, remembering she had not seen a doctor as he'd demanded.

But he was not angry. "Tamar, what is it?" he pleaded, genuinely worried.

"I was . . . I am. . . ," she began, her voice almost inaudible.

Her mother's warm, familiar arms held her close, and the small child in her wept and wept and grew stronger through the unconditional love. But it was not her mother's arms she needed. She needed her husband's adult love, his compassion. His unconditional acceptance. She lifted her head. She could see him straining toward her, wanting to comfort her. But because he thought she had seen a spot of blood, he would not touch her. It was the Law.

And suddenly she felt inexplicably better. She loved him. She admired his honesty, his steadfast loyalty to his beliefs, his decent struggle with his human emotions when they clashed with those beliefs. Why should she harm him by telling him the truth? Why should she place him in some heartbreaking dilemma, giving him some terrible choice to make? Why should his life be defiled? She would protect him by taking it all on herself. She had been raped, but she had not cried out. She had been raped, but she had no witnesses.

She did not want to be divorced.

She would take that burden, the burden of her secret defilement, all on herself, out of love for all those around her. Her family. The way her mother had swallowed in silence the horror of her past in Hitler's camps. Her mother too had never described what had happened to her in the camps. It was the past. It had not been her fault. She had raised her family with joy.

She would be strong, the way her mother had been strong, surviving the defilement of brutal men. Had it been her mother's fault? She'd been an innocent bystander. It could have been anyone in that place, at that time. The idea blossomed. An innocent bystander. It could have been anyone. My mother did not do anything wrong. I did not do anything wrong.

She took a deep breath. "When I was walking to the mikvah, I was attacked by a strange dog."

"A dog?" her mother repeated in disgust.

"Tamar, why didn't you tell me!" Josh said, shocked. Then he considered. "Was it before you went to the mikvah or afterward?"

"Before," she answered him, her eyes hardly flickering.

"Ah, it's all right, then. If it had been after, some would consider the immersion invalid. You would have had to go back, to immerse again." He stroked his beard, and she could see his almost palpable relief in knowing that he had not lain with her when there was some doubt as to her purity. . . .

"Have you seen a doctor?" Rivkie remarked authoritatively. "Are you sure the dog didn't have rabies? Or some kind of infection? You know you can get an infection from an unclean bite."

Only Jenny said nothing, simply reaching over and taking her hand, squeezing it encouragingly. The two women looked at each other, a tiny flash of questioning, a responding flash of refusal passing between them, in the intuitive, profound way there is between women who have been friends for a very long time. Jenny wasn't fooled. Tamar avoided her eyes.

"I was afraid to go. I thought they'd give me rabies shots in the stomach. And I don't think I was actually bitten. At least that's . . ." Her mind raced on inventively.

"Tamar, so foolish." Her mother stroked her head. "You just need a good antibiotic, a good rest. I'll stay with you."

"It's all right, *Mameh*, I'll take a few days off from the yeshiva," Josh offered, very worried.

Tamar looked at her husband, a spark of love warming her heart. Days off from the yeshiva! It was, she knew, a supreme sacrifice. One she would not let him make. "I'm all right, really." She shook her head, holding on to Jenny's hand, squeezing it like a woman in labor squeezes the hand of the midwife, magically transferring some of the pain.

❖4❖

There followed a gradual return to life. It was not that the nightmares disappeared, or that the iron pipe melted, but just that she awoke at two A.M., having slept three or four hours, and was able to return to sleep at four until the light of morning broke. Slowly, instead of the sharp, unbearable pain of a life ripped asunder, she began to feel the soft itch and ache of a scar wound beginning to heal.

And then, about a month later, she began to feel strange again. Her stomach bloated, and she felt the unmistakable signs of her monthly flow. To her surprise, nothing happened. She waited a week, wondering if she could have been injured in some way, or if just the emotional trauma had put off her cycle. She remembered hearing tales of women during the war whose periods had stopped altogether.

And then one day, as she was going down to the grocery, she felt an unmistakable small movement inside her womb. She stopped and put her hand over it, as if to hold on to its reality. But it vanished too swiftly for it to have been anything more than her imagination, she concluded.

A tiny movement, like the swish of a fishtail moving silently through the water, she thought. And the thought refused to leave her.

She waited for the reassuring rush of blood that would tell her that her body had been cleansed, restored to normalcy. She, who had so much wanted a child, now prayed this month, of all months, for that cleansing flow.

Five weeks. Six weeks. Seven. Eight.

Her clothes would no longer button. And now, early in the morning, the nausea that had begun weeks before and that she had dismissed as a mild flu slapped her down like a tidal wave. She, who even as a child had never once thrown up, found herself in the bathroom on her knees, retching green bile.

She called Jenny.

"Mazel tov!" Jenny said.

For a moment, she forgot. A pure wash of happiness streamed through her. It lasted only seconds. And then the horror struck her full force. It was like a looming nightmare when you are a sick child and your comfortable, familiar room becomes a dark jetty of sharp rocks and the tidal waves rush toward you, unstoppable from the distance, assuring you that you will die. That nothing can stop your death, your horrible death.

Not this month, O G-d! Not this month!

There was silence on the line, and then Jenny's calm, intelligent voice, the voice of her best friend: "What's wrong, Tamar?"

"Nothing!" she shouted, then took hold of herself. "Nothing," she repeated in a strangled voice.

"I'm coming right over."

"No! Don't!" To hide what needed to stay hidden. She couldn't. Not from Jenny. "I think I need to see a doctor first."

"Are you afraid? Is that it? I thought you wanted a baby more than . . ."

Not afraid. Afraid is to lock the door. Afraid is to hide. What is it called when the horror is inside you? When it is there or not there? When it can be either the greatest good or the darkest curse?

"I know it seems scary, a little stranger moving into your body, sitting on your stomach and liver . . ." Jenny laughed sympathetically. "Do you want me to go to the doctor with you?"

Come with me Jenny, please! Make me tell you everything, the way I did when we were children. And you were always so strong. You, who had so little—no father, a distant mother— were always so self-reliant. My parents were kind and soft and caring. Except for *Tateh* dying, there has never been any

43

toughness in my life. Would it make a difference now if there had been? And what would you do, Jenny, if there was a child growing inside you that was either planted there by the honorable man you loved or by a goy and a rapist?

A black rapist.

Why did that matter, his color? Was she a racist? If it had been a blond German who had come in through the window, would it have been any different?

Yes, she thought. It would have been a different kind of horror, a different kind of violation. Maybe worse, she thought. But there was no point pretending it didn't matter that he was black. It mattered.

Yes, she thought. Shem, Ham, and Japhet. The three sons of Noah, from whom were descended mankind's three separate races. Shem had fathered the Semites, race of the spirit; Ham, the dark races of passion and physical instinct; and Japhet, the descendants of Greece and Rome, the race of intellect and aesthetics. She had learned it all in Ohel Sara. She was of Shem, he of Ham.

It mattered.

Whose child? She felt the room go dark and seemed to lose consciousness a moment.

"Tamar. . . ?" Jenny's voice, far away, sputtered through the phone.

Tamar opened her eyes and cursed the unforgiving clarity of morning light. The world was bathed in that strange ugliness, like an amateurish photograph of an aging woman taken in the harsh sunlight . . . a strange, hostile clarity. She might have to do things, terrible things involving blood and death, things she did not want her best friend to know about or talk her out of. It was one thing to go to the synagogue, to bake lovely cakes for the Sabbath—but quite another when religion asked you to do something that you believed would damage you forever. She did not want Jenny's preaching. She did not want a rabbi's opinion. She did not want her husband's straight and narrow goodness and adherence. This was her life, her body. She wanted to do her own will, not G-d's.

She was shocked at her bitter determination. Disappointed

and thrilled beyond words. Her love of G-d, of the Torah, was it so shallow, then? Such a thin veneer? And was she really able to cast off this way, alone and determined, with no lifeboat? Was she really more like Hadassah than Jenny? A feeling of unpleasant excitement flashed through her.

"Tamar?"

"I will . . . I think . . . my own doctor would be better. I'd just feel more comfortable. You'll be the first to know, though." Her hands caressed her bloated stomach. It might still just be water. It might still be a delayed period. . . . Please, G-d! Not this month, please don't answer my prayers this way. . . not this way. . . .

She put on her new wig and clean underwear and called a taxi, unable to bear the thought of being on public transportation where strangers might rub up against her or look into her eyes. Besides, she wanted to minimize the time when she would be far from a bathroom if she needed to throw up.

The waiting room was painted in gentle nursery pastels that calmed her brittle nerves like a lullaby. How she had longed to be in an obstetrician's waiting room feeling nauseated! And now . . .

"Mrs. Kahanov?"

She did not look up until the voice repeated the name impatiently. Only then did she remember it was the name she'd made up and given the receptionist over the phone.

She lay down on the examining table, closing her eyes against the burning light, her hands gripping the sheet as the cold metal speculum slid inside her. Her feet strained against the stirrups. The horror of opening yourself so wide, of revealing the hidden, the private . . . His gloved fingers probed her gently, professionally. She was so grateful to hear those blessed words: "You can get dressed now."

She sat across from him, her legs crossed, her skirt lowered.

"How old are you, Mrs. . . . ."

"Kahanov," she lied, but not easily. She was not used to

lying. Not yet, she told herself grimly, thinking of a future where—depending on what he was about to say—lie might be piled upon lie, a growing mound without end. She had gotten his name from the phone book. A gynecologist at a big, anonymous hospital clinic. "I'm twenty-one."

"And have you been using any kind of birth control?"

"No. It's against our beliefs. . . . That is, we wanted children."

"Wanted?" he questioned

"Want," she stammered in confusion.

"Well, then let me congratulate you!"

It's true, true! The nightmare leaping into the light, staying there! Everything suddenly went black.

She awoke, lying on the examining table covered with a blanket.

The doctor smiled down at her. "You aren't the first woman to take it this way."

"It?"

"A pregnancy."

The nightmare.

"Doctor, I can't be pregnant. I mustn't be. . . ."

"Musn't? Can't?" He raised a gray eyebrow quizzically. "Young married religious girls are always thrilled about their first. Is there something you'd like to tell me?"

Doctors were like priests, weren't they? You could tell them anything, and they couldn't reveal it?

"Doctor, I'm not sure who the father is."

He looked very surprised, but said nothing.

"Two months ago, I was raped. On the same night, I also made love to my husband."

He was very still, very noncommittal. "Did you report it to the police?"

"No one knows! They mustn't!"

"Well, I think, religious beliefs aside, the safest thing would be to have an abortion. . . . It isn't dangerous done under proper conditions, you know. It wouldn't stop you from having more children. . . ."

Kill it, he was saying. Kill the baby. Religious beliefs aside . . . She had considered as much herself. But now, in a place filled with all the precise instruments of sharp cold steel necessary to abort this fragile new life, to commit this sensible murder, the idea became utterly abhorrent.

"But what if it's my husband's child! Doctor, what if it is a perfectly healthy baby, the child of my husband? Can't you tell me if it is, Doctor? Can't you?"

"There isn't any way to tell until it's born."

She closed her eyes tightly.

> *But I will say of the L-rd,*
> *Who is my refuge, my fortress,*
> *my G-d in whom I trust,*
> *That He will deliver me from the snare that is laid,*
> *from the the deadly pestilence*
> *He will cover me with His pinions and I will take*
> *refuge beneath His wings: His truth is barbed shield*
> *and an armor.*
> *You need not fear the terror of night, nor the arrow*
> *that flies by day*

"But are you sure there isn't some way to tell, Doctor?" she pleaded with him.

He shook his head. "And the longer you wait, the more dangerous it will become. Talk it over with your husband and call me."

He opened the door and called for his next patient.

She walked out into the clean, pastel waiting room. She paid the bill and pocketed the clean, white receipt. Then she walked out into the street and waited for a bus, hoping that it would take a long time to arrive. She was in no rush to go home.

"Jenny. It's true."

There was soft, uncertain breathing at the other end of the phone. "Are you all right? You don't sound all right. Can't you tell me, Tam?"

47

"There's nothing to tell. Of course I'm happy. I'm . . . thri. . ." She couldn't finish the word. The lie.

"G-d bless you. Trust in Him. He'll help you."

"Yes," she answered, her heart cold and as hard as marble.

Long after she'd hung up, she sat by the phone, waiting for something she couldn't describe, her fingers clenched together fistlike, squeezing her knuckles white. Her eyes wandered to the small flowers on the wallpaper. Buds about to open, pink and fragrant, full of promise. But they would never open, would they? Her fingers eased open, palms up, questioning.

And suddenly she realized there was only one person in the world she wanted to talk to. The only person to whom she could tell everything, and from whom she would receive the most self-serving of advice. But how could she get in touch with her? No one had her number, except Jenny, perhaps, who would think it awfully odd for her to ask. . . . Unless.

"Jenny. Me again. I need Hadassah's phone number."

"Can I ask why?"

Tamar, who had planned to lie, to tell tales of meeting Hadassah's mother at the mikvah, of having messages to share with her, suddenly felt tired. "Please don't."

Jenny gave her the number. She wrote it down silently.

"Tam, you know I love you, don't you?"

Hot tears stung her eyes. "I know."

"I'm here, Tam. Remember that."

"I'll remember," she said hoarsely.

She put down the phone, staring at it. Then she picked it up again and dialed.

⊷5⊷

"I think you should go with cinnabar walls," said the decorator, a slim, youngish man in a trendy silk shirt with emphatic suspenders. "Cinnabar says serenity, quality, opulence."

Hadassah Mandlebright ran her red, shiny fingernails through her mane of burnished gold hair as if pausing a moment for control. "And I say cinnabar is rust, the color of old pipes. I say it's the dress your mother bought you that you never wanted to wear. I say I hate cinnabar."

"Well, of course, it's your home," the decorator conceded grudgingly.

"It's Peter Gibson's home, and I'm just his mistress," she said matter-of-factly, tucking her long legs beneath her, her toes wiggling comfortably against the white damask silk of the down-filled sofa.

She looked like an odalisque by Ingres suffused in a pale golden light, indolent and almost threateningly female, the kind of woman men love and other women can't stand. Still, even another woman would have had to admit that Hadassah Mandlebright knew how to take care of herself. She was wearing a silk lounging outfit of pale gold that set off the golden highlights in her tawny eyes. She wore no makeup, and her lightly tanned skin was sun kissed and rosy, like a young child's after a lovely day at the beach. She looked fresh and young and unfairly beautiful.

She looked at the young man, her pretty lips pursed in

annoyance: "Still, I guess I have some say. A little more, at least, than the hired help."

She couldn't stand homosexuals. Was it because she was a woman who measured her worth by what she saw in young men's eyes, and handsome young homosexuals were so ego wounding? Or was it simply the last moral holdover from her Ohel Sara days? She wondered.

There was a silent pause.

"Well," the decorator said with acidulous courtesy, "what colors would you prefer, sweetheart?"

She stared at him, her naturally heavy-lidded eyes suddenly widening with malice. "Sweetheart?" she repeated incredulously.

He rolled his eyes ceilingward, clasping his clean white fingers together in front of him. "I'm sorry. Miss, Mrs. . . ?"

"Mizz will do fine. Ms. Desirée Bright," she said, her eyes relaxing again into that misleading languid sleepiness that those who knew her well and didn't like her identified with a cobra's curled up on a rock in the sun. "Use Hawaiian colors," she ordered him. "I want this transformed into some lush tropical island. I want to forget where I am. . . . So please save the rusty pipe reds, subway dust grays, or any industrial muck waste black greens you had in mind for your boyfriends," she snapped, getting up abruptly and walking to the large glass windows facing the Manhattan skyline.

It was like a jumbled drawer of old stainless-steel knives and forks, she thought, hating the gray pollution masquerading as air, the distant patch of pale blue that substituted for sky, and the anemic rays of an unseen sun.

Why, oh why, had she ever agreed to come back?

She closed her eyes and pinched her lovely young forehead together with two perfectly manicured fingertips. The purple-hued valley of Kalalau. The cliffs of lush green pandanus overhanging Hanalei. The heart-shaped taro leaves growing wild beneath the gnarled kukui trees along the tumbling streams of Na Pali. The creamy white sands and turquoise waters of Kalapaki Beach.

What was that little twerp droning on about now? she

wondered, his voice a grating annoyance. "Look, now that I've told you what I want, why don't you just use all of that so-called talent of yours and leave me alone?"

Why did Peter have to inflict this on her too? she fumed. Wasn't it enough that he'd installed her as his official mistress of the month in his official mistress apartment? He knew none of this garbage interested her. "I'll tell him to do it himself," she said out loud, knowing she didn't have the guts. You didn't tell Peter Gibson off. The spoiled brat in her secretly loved that most about him. He was like a substitute father, but one who let you do all the things you really wanted to.

She walked off into the bedroom and flung aside the great mirrored doors leading to the closet, wondering why its multifaceted reflections always felt like a slap in the face. It had once been Peter's library and study. When she'd agreed to move in, he'd had all the books removed, replacing them with clothes racks, shoe trees and lots and lots of mirrors. "I wanted you to feel at home," he'd said with that cryptic smile, and in a tone that someone else—someone who didn't know him as well as she did—might very easily have mistaken for contempt. He was going to be home in a few hours, and she still hadn't decided what she was wearing tonight, let alone made an attempt at getting dressed.

She knew it didn't make any difference. Whatever she put on, he would only look at the spaces in between. Whatever she put on, she would have to slip it off and then back on again at least once before they left the house for the party. She hugged herself, slipping her hands up her arms to touch her soft shoulders and the firm slope of her collarbone. Had he once been this way with Yvonne, too? she wondered. Back then . . . She shrugged off the thought. Old discarded wives. What did they have to do with her? She was young. And very, very lovely. Her skin was flawless, her hair shiny dark gold, her body full of free-running sap, like a tree in spring going crazy with blossoms.

Yet, in some strange, annoying way, the whole dressing and undressing thing reminded her of her mother. She remembered the childhood ritual of being inspected before she left the house, having to dress and undress until it was absolutely clear that not an inch of flesh that didn't rightfully belong to her face and hands would be visible. Nothing less would do for the great Rabbi of Kovnitz's only daughter.

She reached in and pulled out a tight tropical blue jersey with sequins and large pink flowers. The neckline, heart-shaped and plunging, the skirt a clinging bit of colored jersey, left nothing to the imagination. She held it against herself halfheartedly, then finally put it back, flipping impatiently through the rack with that practiced wrist movement developed by someone with lots of clothes on lots of quilted hangers.

She wasn't quite sure what she was looking for. Something to please Peter? She took out the low-cut backless black dress that hugged her behind and revealed large tracts of thigh. She held it up against her and felt that familiar twinge of anxiety. You couldn't call it guilt, really—it was too unfocused, too bravely ignored.

Every once in a while, she found herself seeing things through the eyes of her father's Hasidim—especially their wives, the matrons of Forty-eighth Street and Thirteenth Avenue, Orchard Park, Brooklyn. In fact, in a way which truly embarrassed her, she sometimes felt her own vision was not that different. She slipped off her clothes and pulled the black dress over her head and down as far as it would go, which was not very far. *Pritza, zonah!* her mind screamed at her. Tramp, whore. The blond, Polish girls in their short shorts riding through Orchard Park in their wide-finned De Soto convertibles with dark greasy-haired boyfriends, cigarettes dangling from too red lips. *Shiksas* ignored or ridiculed and spat upon.

Pritza. Zonah. They'd already sat shiva for her, piling ashes on their heads and wailing for seven days, pretending she was dead. Her nostrils flared in an odd gesture of anxious defiance as she smoothed the tight black jersey over her breasts and behind.

She looked at her long, tan legs, the taut skin of her slim thighs—bare except for an expensive body lotion—her naked throat, and deep cleavage, remembering the high-buttoned collars and opaque stockings with seams, the long-sleeved blouses and midcalf skirts she had worn even in summer, until the very moment she had left her father's house, her husband's house, behind her for good.

What did the memory make her feel? she pondered. Misgivings? No, never! she protested, unsure of the truth. Relief? It would be good to think that, and it would please Peter enormously if he knew. But, truthfully, she didn't have the sense of ease that would give substance to such an assertion. All there was, really, was a blankness, a void of feeling, as if that whole part of her life was encased in a sealed vacuum bag that prevented any smell or taste or living image to emerge and confront her indifference. Her memories were like the dead cremated beyond form, she thought. They'd lost all semblance to truth, evoking only mild wonderment and a slight suspicion and distaste. They'd lost their power to move her.

It was better not to think about the past at all. Like a walk on a newly tarred roof, it was sticky and unpleasant and potentially dangerous, filling your lungs with a bad dose of pollution and ruining things with indelible stains. And once you started walking, you never got to the end, you just stayed there bogged down in the middle.

She lifted the dress over her head and threw it on the floor, lying back on the silk sheets, her arm flung across her eyes. The Past. The streets of Brooklyn. The Hasidim singing at her father's table, their sidecurls bobbing, their mouths, dark pink against their black beards, swaying and singing until the room rocked with untainted joy.

Untainted joy. Tainted joy. Very, very tainted joy. Yehoshua, Cliff, Peter. Brooklyn, Maui, Manhattan.

It was that decorator, she decided. It was cinnabar, she thought furiously. Why else would she have started thinking any of these things? She would not think of them again, she swore, picking up the ringing phone.

"Hadassah?"

No one ever called her that anymore. "Who is this?"

"It's Tamar."

"Tamar?" She shook her head incredulously. The Past. "How did you find me?" she said with no pretense at cordiality. They had not exactly parted on good terms on that dark, dangerous Brooklyn street the summer they were fifteen. In fact, she had promised then and there never to speak to Tamar Gottlieb again as long as she lived.

There was a pause. What was that sound? Water running? A soap opera? A sob? "Well, how are you, Tamar?"

"Hadassah, can I come to talk to you?"

For Pete's sake! "Well, sure, I'd love to one of these days, but just, you see, right now, everything is sort of crazy. . . ."

They hadn't been friends for so long. And even when they were, when they'd gone to the same school and practically lived next door to each other, there had always been that antagonism. . . . And now, after all this time . . . What did she want?

"Did my parents ask you to call me?" she asked sharply.

"No—nothing like that. It's me. Please, Hadassah. I'm in terrible trouble, and I don't know what to do."

"Go to your local Orthodox rabbi. Or better yet, go to my father, the great Kovnitzer Rebbe. He knows everything. I thought you knew that," she said, lighting a cigarette and taking a deep, nervous drag.

"Please, Hadassah. I know a lot has happened. But I need to talk to someone who won't judge or preach. Hadassah . . . I've been raped. He was black. I'm pregnant. I don't know what to . . ."

The smoke caught in her lungs, choking her. She gasped for air.

"Hadassah?"

"I'm here," she replied, stunned, appalled, and feeling somehow vindicated. "I can meet you at four, but no later."

The Past.

⚹6⚹

Orchard Park, Brooklyn, 1955

In the late 1940s, New York's Hasidim and the Orthodox middle-class children of devout immigrants trickled, then flooded across the Brooklyn Bridge, relinquishing the keys of Williamsburg, Bedford Stuyvesant and Lower Manhattan to the black and Hispanic families who had come after them. Joined by streams of young Orthodox families from East New York, Crown Heights, and Brownsville, they joined forces to found a new outpost in the wilderness where they could build a private little world governed entirely by their own religious beliefs and practices. The result was Orchard Park.

To outsiders, the neighborhood often seemed like a fortress. But for those who knew which buildings housed friendly private Sabbath prayer services, warm soup kitchens, welfare centers, and women's study groups, there was no safer or more hospitable place in the world.

If America were to be compared to the planet Earth, then Orchard Park, Brooklyn was the moon, a benign presence circling at a safe distance. The survivors of death camps who assembled there were not like earlier immigrants who had come to better their lives. They had run away to America because they couldn't go back to where they belonged. And though their bodies were in America, their hearts were in Europe and their souls in the little, struggling independent State of Israel.

It was a second life for most of them—new wives and husbands and children to replace the irreplaceable dead—new lives most of them really didn't want. They fought hard to bring the old life back. They fought hard to keep America out.

And so they listened to the news on WEVD in Yiddish read by Shlomie Ben Yisroel, who spoke of America as: *Fer Einick Da Shtates Fon Amerika,* and of Europe as: *Der Alter Heim* (the old home). At home they read the news in Yiddish in the *Daily Forward.* In Yiddish, the Korean War seemed far away, as did Ike and Mamie. And no one dreamed of buying the newfangled barbecue grills or Schwinn bikes they viewed contemptuously in the homes of American relatives.

And so in Orchard Park in December, one would find no Santa Clauses, but row upon row of lighted Chanukah menorahs. In April, no store would boast marshmallow Easter chicks, but rather boxes of hand-rolled Passover matzoth stamped with rabbinic approval. And when the rest of the country was languishing in holidayless March, Orchard Park was gearing up for the carnival, drinking feast, and general merriment that is Purim.

It was Tuesday, seven in the morning, holiday eve. The laughter and squeals of excitement spilled over from the kitchens and living rooms of Orchard Park into the streets.

"If you don't hurry, Tamar, Rivkie, you'll be ready in time for Passover and not Purim," Ruth Gottlieb said, attempting severity but, as usual, achieving indulgence. She just had that kind of face, sweet and round and full of humor, with only her gray eyes betraying an incongruous darkness. Even when she was really angry—a very rare occurrence—there always seemed to be an irrepressible giggle lurking just beneath the surface, as if she were overcome by the whimsy in any situation, however bad. It was a characteristic that thoroughly confused her children, who as a result were very merry and quite undisciplined.

Ruth watched her two little daughters buried in heaps of pretty scarves, unraveling sequinned gowns and piles of sparkling costume jewelry. "Girls, you've got school in an hour—you have to make up your minds already!" she begged, exasperated and yet awfully pleased they were having such fun. Their only reply was an increase in the wild giggling that filled the comfortably furnished, fairly new three-bedroom home.

It was a home clearly in the hands of a *baleboosteh,* an accolade that described Ruth Gottlieb as nothing else ever could. She was nothing if not a *baleboosteh,* a worthy successor to countless generations of Jewish women whose lives had been spent keeping the surface of life as scrubbingly clean, thriftily comfortable, and respectably ostentatious as possible. And so she bought soup meat—flanken, not steak—but cooked it well and served it appetizingly on pretty dishes. Her clothes were never fashionable but new and absolutely clean and well ironed. And in furniture and lighting fixtures, she never lagged behind her neighbors. Her furnishings were always the most expensive items offered in Jewish-run stores on the Lower East Side.

Indeed, in this area there were often periodic wild splurges that left her indulgent husband drained and that filled her heart with great joy. A case in point was the large chandelier that hung over the dining room table, almost, but not quite, ludicrously large for the dimensions of the room. It pleased her to always leave the shades up and the drapes drawn open in front of it, leaving it comfortably visible to those passing in the street below.

"Now what have we here, *mamalehs?*" Aaron Gottlieb said with mock horror, a broad, kind smile creasing his placid face. It was a face a little more careworn than those of the other men in their late thirties in the synagogue where he prayed. Ever since coming to America after the war, he had gone from job to job, trying to find a respectable way to support his growing family. First he had tried his hand at teaching and had enjoyed it. But teaching Talmud in the yeshiva hadn't paid enough for flanken, let alone large crystal chandeliers. So he had enrolled at Brooklyn College night school, earning a degree in accounting, and finally becoming a CPA. Now, tempted by a fellow shul member, he had with great trepidation gone into business importing perfumes from Europe. He had also considered watches from the Far East but, after consulting with his wife, had decided perfume would be better. After all, who in the prosperous, modern world of the 1950s would want a watch (or anything else?) that was "made in Japan"?

He was a yeshiva boy at heart. A family man who loved to be home perusing his beloved religious books. The suit of a businessman hung limply from his shoulders. And his hands, folded placidly over his modest black briefcase, had nails that were harshly bitten down, the cuticles savagely ripped and slightly bloody.

He crouched on the floor next to his little girls. He hated to leave for work.

"*Tatee*, guess who I am, just guess?" eight-year-old Rivkie begged him.

He looked at the gauzy veils of old scarves that hugged her slender waist; at her round little arms weighted down with the bedazzling sparkle of cheap glass sapphires that picked up the color of her shining eyes; at her mysterious half smile; and at the paste tiara that crowned her bouncy auburn curls. She was the prettiest little thing imaginable.

"Well, I think I'll guess a nurse."

"Oh, *Tatee*, a nurse!" she screamed in hilarity, as he had hoped she would, her rosy face and eyes incredulous with pleasure. "A nurse wears white, white!" She danced around the room.

"Well, then . . ." He shrugged as if completely baffled. "If you're not a nurse, then . . ." He felt his trousers tugged urgently.

"Guess who am I!" six-year-old Tamar demanded, as usual imitating her older sister, her mentor and last authority in all things.

Tamar was a head shorter and about ten pounds heavier than Rivkie. Her round cheeks, blessed with a constant rosy blush that made her always seem in the midst of some maidenly embarrassment, created a false impression of shyness where none existed. Sadly, "cat's eye" glass frames hid her best feature, enormous gray eyes with amazingly thick lashes, eyes as exquisite as they were hopelessly nearsighted. She was wearing a heavily hemmed old evening gown, and the tulle ballooned out around her waistless figure to amazing proportions. Her cheeks had been relentlessly rouged, and great joy had been taken with a tube of dark red lipstick. Her hair, usually neatly braided by her mother, now fell wildly around her shoulders in a profusion of blond curls. She reminded him of an overweight little witch.

She looked up at him hopefully. "Guess!"

"This," he said very seriously, swallowing hard, "this can only be one person. One person. Esther, the beautiful Queen of Persia? Am I right?"

"Oh, *Tatee!*" She swung herself into his arms and he lifted her cuddly round body, crushing all its little-girl sweetness to him, breathing it in. He buried his forehead in her fragrant hair, closing his eyes for a moment, letting the creases of his face relax.

"You can't be Esther also!" Rivkie stamped her foot. "We can't both be Esther!"

"Oh, so that's who you are!" Aaron Gottlieb exclaimed in a tone of absolute amazement, putting Tamar down and lifting Rivkie up. "Why, of course!" He slapped his forehead. "Just look at the crown!" he exclaimed loudly, trying to head off the waterfall of tears he saw coming with the inevitability of floodwater rushing toward a cliff edge. "A beautiful queen you are. The most beautiful!" He glanced nervously at his younger daughter.

"The most beautiful!" Tamar agreed readily, hiding her hurt and disappointment at being demoted to the second most beautiful Queen of Persia, heroine of the Purim saga. Her body still tingled from her father's warm embrace. There had been nothing second best about that. Besides, it wasn't nice to be jealous. It wasn't nice to throw tantrums or to cry or act spoiled. Everything was so much nicer when you didn't. And your father looked at you proudly, and your sister was smiling and satisfied. Besides, there was nothing surprising about Rivkie looking more beautiful than she. She always did. That was simply normal, like rain or the sun shining.

There wasn't a jealous bone in her body, sweet little thing, her father thought proudly, taking both his little daughters' hands in his own: "The most beautiful women in all the world," he said very seriously as both girls collapsed into paroxysms of hysterical giggles over being called women.

"What's Zissel going to be for Purim, *Mameh?*" Tamar asked.

She saw her mother bite her lower lip as she always did when her niece Zissel was involved. "Oh, Zissel's too young for a costume!"

"But Aunt Malka will bring her to shul this year, won't she, to hear the Megillah?" It was the highlight of the holiday, the recitation of the Purim story, during which children were not only allowed, but encouraged to make a tremendous racket each time the villain Hamen's name was mentioned.

She saw her parents glance at each other significantly.

"We'll talk about it later. Hurry, you're late, darling."

It was suddenly very quiet in the room.

❖❖

Around the corner, in a sumptuous ten-room apartment above the magnificent synagogue of Hasidei Kovnitz, a little girl stood on a high footstool in the dining room. She was six years old, very slim, with silky honey-brown hair and eyes the color of golden topaz. She had a very pretty face: high cheekbones, a slender nose, and a rosebud mouth. She stood very still as the seamstress sewed the finishing touches on the magnificent russet velvet costume. Only a very acute observer would have noticed the fidgety restlessness of her fingers, which tore rather savagely at the expensive beaded embroidery.

"Is it long enough?" the child's mother asked the seamstress.

The woman didn't answer, having known Rebbetzin Surie Mandlebright long enough to understand that the length of hems or sleeves was not a question of style, but of religious observance—an area in which the pious seamstress felt herself hopelessly outclassed in the company of the wife of the Kovnitzer Rebbe, world leader of Kovnitz Jewry.

So she said nothing, engrossed in admiring her handiwork so much that she almost forgot the little girl inside it whose forehead was beginning to bead with perspiration and fatigue. The gown was very heavy.

"Just turn a little this way, Hadassah," the seamstress ordered her once more, finding a tiny imperfection in the length of the sleeve.

The child hesitated, her fist clenched.

"Why, Hadassah, what is it, darling?" Rebbetzin Mandlebright said sweetly, feigning motherly concern to hide her grow-. ing dread. There wasn't going to be another tantrum was there, not this morning, when her husband's study was already packed with dozens of prominent Hasidim come to bring him gifts and receive his blessings in honor of the holiday? There just could *not* be another shouting match with Hadassah this morning! Already she felt her head beginning to ache.

"It looks like doody," the child fumed.

"Hadassah!" her mother gasped, humiliated in front of the crestfallen seamstress.

"It's not what I told her!" She stamped her small foot in its russet velvet party shoe. "I said blue. I said make it blue for Vashti, not Esther. It looks like doody," the child repeated nastily, mightily pleased with the word's effect, "and it itches!" she whined, tearing at the lovely stand-up lace collar that grazed the bottom of her chin.

"Well, maybe we could fix the itching, *kleinkeit*," her mother said with deadly good cheer, her nostrils flaring. "Six-year-olds." She shrugged, forcing a smile, inviting the shocked seamstress into the conspiracy of womanly indulgence toward difficult children.

The woman didn't accept the invitation. "Vashti!" she sniffed, shocked. "Vashti was the evil queen! And a shiksa. The one the king beheaded before he married our beautiful Jewish queen Esther, who saved the Jewish people from the wicked Haman," she instructed the child, who knew the story perfectly well. "Why would you want to be Vash—"

"Because nobody tells Vashti what to do! Her husband, the king, tells her to come and show off in front of the men, and she doesn't." She stamped her little foot again. "Esther's just a goody-goody. . . ."

"Oh!" Rebbetzin Mandlebright laughed sharply, interrupting the child—whose every word would no doubt be broadcast throughout the entire Hasidic community of Kovnitz before noon, like everything else that happened in their home. Hasidim studied not only their leader's words, but every minute detail of his life and his family's, sifting for concrete examples of G-dliness that they could apply to their own lives. Long ago the rebbetzin had learned the sad truth: they lived in a ten-room, richly furnished, gold-plated fishbowl.

"Who knows how these little ones get such ideas into their heads?" The rebbetzin laughed gaily, her eyes grim. "You wanted to be funny, darling, didn't you? And it would be very funny for the Rebbe of Kovnitz's own little girl to be Vashti instead of Esther, now, wouldn't it? And you'd make everyone laugh and be happy, which is what people are supposed to do on Purim, isn't that true, darling?" She nodded encouragingly, her eyes going steely.

She had no idea why the child suddenly wanted to be Vashti. Or was it sudden? Had she mentioned something about it a while back? Who could remember! She was always asking for the most unacceptable things, always whining and complaining. . . . She just didn't pay attention anymore to the child's spoiled rantings. She just tried to get through one day at a time, giving in when she could to gain peace.

The child looked at her mother blankly. Making everybody happy had never occurred to her. What had occurred to her was that everyone else in the first grade at Ohel Sara School for Religious Girls would be Esther, and why should she, the great Rebbe of Kovnitz's daughter, be like everyone else?

Certainly nothing else about her life was similar. Kovnitz Hasidim took her to school in a white Chrysler Imperial and picked her up in a Lincoln Continental. They brought her sweets and toys and gave her pretty dolls and fine wooden doll furniture.

The only thing no one ever did for her was take her seriously.

"I hate it! I wanted blue! Take it off me now! Right now, I said!" the child screamed.

"Of course you may not take it off," her mother said firmly, busy encircling her, checking the outfit at every angle for any immodest exposure of skin or too tight outlining of childish curves.

"I won't wear it! I hate it! I want blue," she whined shrilly.

"She looks splendid, doesn't she, Ilsa?" mused her mother. "Come now, Hadassah, let's show *Aba*. He'll be so pleased."

Color suddenly flooded the child's pale, unhappy face. She

stepped quickly off the stepstool, taking her mother's hand and walking eagerly down the hall toward her father's study. It was a rare treat to see her father in the daytime. Not only to see him, but to be seen, to be the center of attention! Usually he was head deep in visitors who flocked to the house all hours of the day and night. And while her brothers Jonah, Shmuel, and David were always at their father's side, she, like a pretty ornament, was displayed only on special occasions. She had learned not to mourn their infrequency, but to relish every moment. Forgetting all about her discomfort, she lifted her head and walked proudly into the room.

Leather-bound books rose in ten-foot-high mahogany bookcases on either side of a long, polished table of rare veneers. The black-coated Hasidim rose and pressed themselves to the walls to allow the rebbetzin and Hadassah to pass.

The great Rebbe of Kovnitz pushed back from the table. He was a man of singularly impressive physical dimensions: broad shoulders, a large imposing head, a thick dark beard. But more than that, he radiated an aura of almost frightening charisma, so powerful that those privileged to be sitting closest to him instinctively pulled back a little as if from something dangerously hot. Ceremoniously, he took off his glasses and peered carefully at his daughter.

Everyone held their breath.

Then he slapped the table and laughed: "A *shayne, shayne maideleh!*" He lifted her up, placing her on his broad lap, stroking her hair lovingly. Delighted smiles creased each face, to see their beloved leader so human, so moved by the ordinary joys of life. It was comforting to them to see how much he—who hovered so near the heavens—resembled themselves so bound to earth. They smiled at the little girl, destined for a royal marriage that would unite Kovnitz to some other Hasidic dynasty. A little *tzdakis*, a little *baleboosteh*. A princess and future queen. And deep inside, each of them also harbored the distant but glorious hope that one of their sons—through sheer brilliance in the halls of Talmud study—might somehow win the priceless hand of the Rebbe's only daughter.

Hadassah snuggled into her father's arms and peered out at

the admiring glances, warmed by the glow of approval that covered her like a royal velvet robe. As the youngest and only girl, she was simultaneously spoiled and badly neglected, something it would take her years to fully perceive. It made her bad mannered, haughty, and miserably lonely.

"And what are you this Purim, *shayne maideleh?*" her father asked her.

Hadassah felt her mother's pleading glance. She looked past her father's deep, dark beard, his thick, black forbidding brows, into the depths of his dark unpredictable eyes. "Esther," she said as sweetly as she knew how, her lovely cheeks dimpling and blushing.

"And a beautiful Jewish queen she is!" someone cried out.

"A *shayne, shayne maideleh!*" The voices rang out, until the Rebbe pounded the table to put an end to such immodest praise, such unseemly glorification of female beauty, no matter how young. But because it was Purim, the merriest of holidays, he lightened his disapproval with just a glint of a smile in his eyes and began to sing:

> *Shoshanas Yaakov, Tahala ve'Samecha*
> *Berotam Ya achad techalet Mordechai*

Everyone immediately joined in, their faces relaxing as their bodies swayed, their fists musically pounding the table, their feet tattooing the floor.

Hadassah leaned back into her father's arms and watched. She saw nothing of the deep happiness that filled their hearts, the spiritual pleasure that made their voices rise. She saw only their earlocks swaying, their beards flapping. She covered her mouth, laughing.

"Jenny, what do you mean you can't go to school without a costume? . . . Davy! Shut that radio off! I can't hear myself. . . . Now, honey, just put on this little skirt, and I'll find you a clean blouse. I know I have one somewhere," Ida Douglas said distractedly as she walked through the small, dingy apartment over cheap stores on the wrong side of Newrose Avenue, just outside the boundaries of Orchard Park. It was a neighborhood inhabited by older Italians who hadn't the means to follow their countrymen to the green spaces of Long Island; by Polish Catholics; and by families newly arrived from Puerto Rico.

The little girl gnawed her inner cheek nervously. "Everyone's gotta have a costume. . . . It's a holiday."

"You mean like Halloween?" the mother mumbled, hairpins in her mouth, her arms aching as they struggled to pin her long, thick hair into something businesslike. The alarm clock hadn't gone off. Again. Was it broken or just the fuses out again? she wondered, beginning her day with the usual sense of defeat.

"No . . . well . . . something . . . but not the same," the child attempted to explain, although she wasn't quite clear herself, never having experienced the holiday before. "Not witches or scary things. . . ."

"Honey, please don't bother Mommy this morning! If I show up late for work once more . . . Well, you know. Now that Daddy's gone Mommy has to make all the money for food and rent."

"And I have to be the big helper, 'cause I'm the oldest. . . ."

"Right!" the mother agreed, smiling broadly until she saw the tears trickling slowly down her daughter's small, sweet face.

She had Jack's Gypsy coloring, Ida thought, dark with a rich undertone of peach, and his straight, almost oriental black hair. Her eyes were the purest green, like those big apples you used for making pies. A beautiful little girl. She felt her heart contract. The big helper. She might be the eldest, but she was still only six and a half years old.

"But I told you about the costume last week. I told you about Purim . . . remember! I can't go without a costume," the little girl sobbed.

The mother sagged down on the couch, her eyes avoiding her daughter's. "You sure about that, honey? I'm sure I would've remembered if you'd a said something. Maybe then I could've managed, something. . . ." she said without great conviction, her eyes on her fingers as they stabbed the oozing stuffing back into the torn upholstery.

"I did tell you, Mommy! About the king and queen and the wicked Haman. I told you about the gift packages and the Haman's ears—cookies with prune filling," the child protested.

Another one of those holidays I never heard of until Jenny started going to that school, Ida thought. Once again she wondered what had possessed her. Ohel Sara School for Religious Girls. It didn't even sound American! She had only wanted to see her with other nice, proper little Jewish girls, instead of all those wild Italian and Polish juvenile delinquents in public school; only wanted her to get better teachers for English and math. Besides, Jack's mother had always been religious, and the school had taken her in on scholarship. . . .

But all these holidays, all these rules and unexpected expenses and demands . . . Jack would have gotten the costume ready. He would have brought something home in a big, shiny cellophane box. . . .

She thought of her dead husband a moment with that small, stabbing pain that should have been getting blunter by now, according to the unasked-for wisdom of friends and relatives, none of whom had ever been widowed at thirty-five. A year had gone by. It had only gotten worse.

What was she supposed to do now about a costume, twenty minutes before she had to catch the express train to Borough Hall? She tore a savage handful of stuffing out of the couch, squeezing it tightly in her fist, then throwing it against the wall. "It isn't fair!" she sobbed, jumping up and pacing the room. "I want someone to take care of me! Someone to take care of the fuses, to hand the rent to the landlord, to bring home cellophane boxes!"

The child stared at her, her eyes filling once again.

"Oh, I didn't mean to frighten you, Jen. Don't cry anymore, honey. You know I can't stand it when you cry!" She wiped her eyes and then the child's. "Wait . . . just . . . I've got . . . maybe . . . I'll get it. *Don't cry!* Just a . . ."

Jenny watched her mother drag a kitchen chair into the bedroom and over to the closet. She saw the chair wobble and then tilt as her mother stretched up to reach the highest shelf. She ran, holding out her hands, waiting to catch her mother when she crashed.

Her mother stepped down, unaware of the child's terror. She was staring at the white box she held in her palms like a delicate piece of porcelain.

"Still, after all those years," her mother murmured, breathing deeply. "Lilacs." She opened it, taking out the white satin dress folded neatly in tissue paper. It was slightly yellow with age, but with a delicate sheen. She held it up against her chest in front of the dresser's fly-specked mirror.

" 'I'll be loving you always. . . ,' " she sang to herself, taking one small waltz step and then another. " 'Always, always . . .' " She closed her eyes.

Davy joined his sister in the doorway, his soft brown eyes wide. They stood there together, watching their mother dance.

"Here, Jenny, here's a costume for you. Come try it on," the mother said with a gaiety the little girl found frightening.

She shook her head. "No, Mommy!"

"Come on, Jenny darling," the mother repeated, her voice rising a little hysterically.

Jenny walked to her mother, nuzzling into her small bosom. She touched the white material. It was soft and lovely.

"Come, sweetie, try it on. Don't you like it, darling? Will it make a good costume?"

"It's beautiful, Mommy."

"It's too big, though, and there's no time to hem it." She fumbled, pulling out a large pair of scissors. Her eyes were hard and bright.

The child looked at the shining blades with horror. "No, Mommy! No!" She caught her mother's hand. "I forgot. It's not today, Mommy. It's next week. I just forgot."

"Next week?" Ida hesitated, the scissors hovering in midair. Finally she put it down.

Jenny breathed.

"That gives us lots of time. We'll manage something by then, won't we, Jennifer? Now please hurry and get to school. And make sure Davy goes into Mrs. Cohen's. You know, that time I left him out on the steps he wandered halfway down the block looking for me, until . . ." She lost her train of thought, looking again at the dress, the scissors.

"It's such a pretty dress, Mommy. Don't cut it!"

"No. Why should I? There's no need to, not now. Next week, well . . . by then, oh, we'll manage some . . ." She caught the little girl under the chin and searched her eyes. "You're all right, aren't you, honey? I mean, you're okay, aren't you?"

The child reached up and tucked her mother's hair neatly into the chignon. "Yes, Mommy. I'll get dressed now. You want me to dress Davy, too?"

"Oh, would you, darling? It would be such a help. Jenny, everything is all right now, isn't it? You're happy, aren't you, darling?"

"Yes, Mommy. Very happy," she said, her throat knotting and her eyes full as she buttoned a dark flannel shirt on her four-year-old brother.

Holding her brother with one hand and pinching her nostrils closed with the other, she hurried down the dark, narrow stairway filled with the smells of knockwurst and boiling cabbage. She did not allow herself to breathe normally until well past Romano's Italian grocery with its curing hams and big Parmesan cheeses.

Sometimes she'd close her eyes and try to remember the way the lawns had smelled in Jersey right after her father had cut the grass, or the smell of juicy green apples from the tree outside their living room window right after you bit into them. It had only been six months, but already the images, the sounds and smells, seemed like old photographs, fading and distant. Even her father's face was no longer always clear in her mind. Oh, sometimes she could see him as if he were there, standing right in front of her. But then as she tried to hold the image, to focus, it got loose and jumbled, like bad TV reception.

That was the worst thing. The jumbling. Not remembering. It was like losing him all over again. But she had no control over it. It was, she thought, like the waves at the beach. They came in so strong and real and beautiful, and then somehow they lost their power and dribbled into foam which melted and disappeared even as you watched.

"I'm cold," Davy complained.

She pulled the earflaps down on his leather hat and put his icy hand into her pocket.

"I don't wanna go," the child whimpered.

She thought of the classroom full of snobby little girls in their lovely costumes. Her hand tightened around his. "I know, Davy. I know."

❖7❖

The March winds that are supposed to come in like a lion and go out like a lamb blasted the trees of Orchard Park, bending them into question marks. Outside, little yeshiva girls crowded the streets as they hurried to school, their gloved hands clutching their heads to keep the crowns of tinsel from sailing off. There were no yeshiva boys in the street. Their classes began half an hour earlier and ended an hour later. This was no coincidence. The neighborhood's rabbis and teachers had colluded to put the boys safely behind closed doors before the girls came out. Besides, the extra time was needed to drill the boys in Talmud, the sacred Oral Law of the Torah forbidden to females.

"You're walking too fast!" Tamar complained, her pudgy feet beginning to go numb in the tight party shoes whose thin soles did nothing to insulate them from the freezing pavement.

"It was stupid to wear those silly shoes! And take off some of that stupid red lipstick!" Rivkie ordered her, all pretense of kindness dropped once out of their parents' earshot. "And don't twirl around in that dress, it makes you look like a little elephant. . . ."

Tamar, her hands thoroughly occupied in guarding her headdress from the marauding wind and her skirt from the filthy wet pavement, could not even wipe away the quick tears that froze on her cheeks until the wind whipped them away. "I don't!" she planned to cry out, but the wind filled her throat and choked her, carrying off her words. She closed her mouth and hurried to catch up with her sister, which she was never quite able to do.

Rivkie was always just a little ahead of her. It was not that her legs were so much longer, but rather that she walked forward deliberately with no pauses to look at shop displays or pretty curtains flapping in windows or gasoline rainbows on sidewalks. She was not burdened by imagination or the idle dreams that slow a person down or detour them from getting through the simple, ordinary goals of life. And she never stopped to look back or to wait for anyone else to catch up.

Tamar was constantly distracted. The authoritative honk of a new car, the tramp of feet, the glitter of crystal in pavement, were all enough to excite her wonderment and curiosity, which she satisfied with the expensive investment of time in dreamy reflection. Often, she got lost. Often Rivkie got punished for losing her.

"It's freezing! Hurry up, you dummy!" her sister called over her shoulder with her usual kindness and patience.

Tamar struggled with the shoes, her frozen feet, her chapped wet face, the ballooning dress.

Jenny walked Davy up the stairs of the old brownstone and knocked on Mrs. Cohen's door. She felt Davy's hand tighten around hers as the crack of light widened in the hallway and Mrs. Cohen's no-nonsense voice welcomed him in. The apartment was chilly and smelled like something old carefully waxed and polished, but not quite clean.

Jenny urged her brother over the threshold with a yank on his arm. He swayed a little, but his feet gripped the floor. He wouldn't budge.

Jenny bent down to him, surprised. "What's the matter, Davy? Does she hit you?" she whispered.

He shook his head no.

"Well then, you've got to go. Mommy says. It's just like school. Everybody's got to go to school," she coaxed him, her sympathetic voice loosening his feet just long enough for her to drag him over the threshold. But when she tried to leave, his fingers just tightened around her skirt until, finally, she had no choice but to pry them loose almost cruelly.

71

She ran down the steps. But once outside, her footsteps slowed, exhausted as only a small child can feel handling adult problems. She felt so sorry for her brother: shy, affectionate, easily frightened little Davy. Why should he have to spend his day with strangers? She felt the rage and pity tighten her jaw and chest muscles. She had every child's intuitive hatred for injustice tremendously heightened by the bereaved child's experience with death, the ultimate injustice. Although she was not particularly vehement or headstrong, unfairness drove her to extremes.

The feeling lodged in her heart as she slowly crossed the street, defying the wind and the lateness of the hour, ignoring the bone-chilling shadow of the overhead el, which had sucked away whatever weak and useless sunlight there was. She was in no hurry to get to school.

As she neared the familiar quaint brick building, she was shot full of a whole new set of emotions that made her stomach go queasy. She was the new girl in the class, the one who lived outside the neighborhood. The one who had no father. And no new clothes. And who didn't know Hebrew very well. . . . So many things to be ashamed of. So many disabilities to hide and overcome. And now she would be the only girl in the class—if not the whole school!—who would not be wearing a Purim costume. Her stomach turned over.

"Yehudit!" she heard someone calling in the distance. It was her Hebrew name, the name the school had given her because Jenny was too American, too goyish. Most of the other girls had been given two names by their parents: a *real* one, for parents and teachers and synagogue and friends, and an American one, for hospital records, passports, and naturalization papers. So Shaindel was Shirley. Baila was Brenda. Zissel was Zelda. There seemed almost a terror of discovery, a desire to hide the strong Orthodoxy, the differentness, from the authorities.

"Yehudit!"

Who was calling her? Her eyes blinked and squinted against the wind. It was Tamar (somehow she didn't remember her English name, since no one used it. Was it Tammy?), one of the few kind children she'd met in that class. Tamar was not really her friend, though. Friends, after all, you invited to your home, and you went to theirs. She'd never been invited to Tamar's, and if she had been, she'd have made up some excuse to beg off. She was terrified of owing a return invitation. No one must ever know where or how she lived. They must never know about the couch full of holes, the panties hanging over the chipped bathtub, or the ash of incinerator smoke that coated the grimy windows. They must never know about her mother, who worked all day like a man, who wore no white apron and baked no cookies and had no dinner on the table. They must never know about the bed in which her mother slept alone and the shameful cold earth that held her father.

Still, Tamar's friendliness warmed her cold heart. She hurried toward her. "Tamar! You look so . . . so . . ." She gulped as she neared her, taking in the thick makeup, the extravagant flounce of blue tulle, the mountain of jewels. It was all a bit too much, even for a child's taste. "It's so . . . beautiful!" she finished kindly, for want of a better word.

"Do you really like it?"

"I really, really, really, really, really, really . . . do!" she assured her, deciding to love the flamboyance without reservation, seeing in it a just compensation for her own total lack. Together they were perfect. Tamar linked her arm happily through Jenny's.

They giggled.

"But you should see my sister. She *really* looks beautiful!" Tamar told her, thrilled but uneasy with the compliment, her cheeks still burning from the icy tears.

"I think you look fantabulous!" Jenny said generously, using the ultimate accolade known to little girls in the 1950s. She had no interest in the distant older sister, who'd already disappeared inside the building, anyhow.

"You also look fantab—fantab—lous," Tamar answered, struggling valiantly with the four syllables, two too many. She gave her friend a sudden searching stare. "But what's your costu. . . ?"

"I'm an Ohel Sara girl, dressed for school!" Jenny tried gaily.

"Well, that's . . . that's a . . ." Tamar floundered, searching for something encouraging to say. "That's a very fun idea, to come regular! I bet no one else will have such a fun idea!"

Jenny smiled at her, painfully.

Just then a car shiny with chrome and with tail fins that practically spanned the street pulled up at the curb. A Hasid got out and opened the door, his chapped hand holding down his black *shtreimel* against the wind. Picking up her skirts daintily, Hadassah Mandlebright stepped out onto the pavement.

The girls on the sidewalk surged forward, coalescing into an admiring throng. Their eyes shone with the light of envy, awe, and admiration one sees in the eyes of fans. She nodded to a lucky few, waved to privileged others, ignored the great mass, which included Tamar and Jenny, who soon found themselves pushed back as the girls surrounded Hadassah and ushered her up the stairs like ladies-in-waiting to some little queen.

"*Oooh*, what a fantabulous dress!"

"Ahh, it's got real beads!"

The voices gushed and gushed and rose with girlish relish, filling the corridors.

Tamar and Jenny followed the entourage up the stairs with slow, thoughtful steps.

"Did you see the velvet and the beads?" Tamar whispered with frank admiration.

"No, not really good," Jenny said carelessly, her stomach turning over in desire, the memory of the gorgeous beaded velvet dancing in her head like a fairytale.

The classroom was large and well heated, with a cheerful collection of decorations depicting the lives of biblical heroes and illustrating maxims from Proverbs. Screams and giggles and shouts of hilarity filled it as the little girls took off their heavy winter coats, gloves, and hats to reveal the costumes underneath. They hugged each other and touched the tinsel and paste and ribbons and scarves with innocent delight.

Jenny sat down in her seat quickly, taking out her books.

"You look so gorgeous, Hadassah!" a group of girls began, inundating her with an effusion of praise that had it been water would have soon drowned her.

A faint smile of acknowledgment played around Hadassah's tight lips, but her eyes ignored them all.

"It's the prettiest color!" Freda Einkorn gushed. She was the daughter of a diamond merchant, a Kovnitz Hasid. She considered herself Hadassah's best friend, although she had stingy evidence to prove it. She was constantly, nervously wooing her.

Hadassah's lips compressed and her nose wrinkled as she turned malevolent eyes on Freda.

"I mean, you are the prettiest girl here," Freda stammered, unnerved. "I mean, look at Tamar!" she tried, knowing Hadassah loved to talk behind other girls' backs. "What is she supposed to be?" Her eyes rolled upward mockingly.

"Why don't you ask her?" Hadassah said. It was more like a command.

"Tamar, what are you supposed to be?" Freda asked, nudging Hadassah and making a big show of trying and failing to keep her lips straight.

Tamar stood a little straighter, spreading her blue skirts to their full advantage. "Queen Esther," she said, delighted to have been asked, missing all the unpleasant nuances that would have rung warning bells and set off red flares for a more wary child.

"Well"—Freda rolled her eyes, looking at Hadassah for approval, believing she'd found it—"that's the first time I ever saw an ugly Queen Esther!"

Tamar's rosy face went pale.

There was dead silence broken only by a few nervous giggles.

"You take that back!" Jenny said suddenly, rising behind the protective shield of her desk.

"Why, what's it to you, butinsky?" Freda bristled.

"You doody-head! Take it back, I said!"

Freda took a step back. She was hopelessly in the wrong and knew it, which makes even a small child nastier than they really are. "Why, you're not dressed up at all! I mean, look at her!" she suddenly addressed the class, her eyes sweeping the room anxiously to unearth allies. "Just an ugly old blouse and skirt. . . ." She looked at Hadassah a bit desperately for approval. But Hadassah's eyes had a faraway look of boredom.

"I came as an Ohel Sara girl on her way to class," Jenny said weakly, her defiant eyes beginning to cloud in humiliation at this public interrogation.

"That's no good. That's just nothing at all!" Freda hooted unpleasantly, taking a step forward.

A mysterious light came into Hadassah's eyes. "You're wrong, Freda. It's a swell idea," she pronounced. "It's the swellest idea I ever heard," she said to the total annihilation of Freda Einkorn. She walked over to Jenny.

"I think Tamar looks beautiful!" Hadassah said charmingly, her perfect white teeth gleaming in her lovely face. "And I think your costume is the best idea I ever heard. Please, please, trade with me? Just for a day?"

Speechless, Jenny just stared at her.

"Tell Tamar how beautiful she looks, Freda. Go ahead, tell her. Have a little *chesed*. You know you're not allowed to talk *loshen hara*," Hadassah called over her shoulder, never taking her charming smile off her charming face as she continued to look at Jenny. "Tell her. I can't hear you," she said a little louder.

"I guess," Freda agreed sullenly.

"Will you? Trade me? Even steven? Yours for mine?" Hadassah begged Jenny. "Pretty please?" Her charming smile went a notch higher, into mesmerizing.

Jenny, with all the caution of a small starving animal who knows its vulnerabilities in venturing forth for food, hesitated. "I don't know," she finally answered, examining the other girl's eyes for signs of mockery or worse—charity. She found neither. "If you want."

Hadassah caught her hand and led her urgently to the bathroom. They took two separate stalls. "Push me your clothes underneath, and I'll push you mine."

When they returned, the class stared, amazed.

Later, Mrs. Kornbluth, their teacher, told the other teachers the entire story. "A little *tzdakis*, a true saint. Such an act of *chesed*—kindness—to give that poor child her own beautiful Purim costume." Of course, the story got back to the *admor* of Kovnitz before lunch, and made the rounds of all the Hasidim before the day was out. It was repeated with pride and awe and deep spiritual satisfaction. The apple doesn't fall far, they told each other in triumph.

Surie Mandlebright looked at her little daughter in the poorly ironed blouse with unraveling buttonholes and the stained blue woolen skirt, her lips bunching with fury and her smooth fingers knotting into a fist she thought best to hide in the pocket of her elegant holiday dress.

Hadassah stared back. It was a look of triumph.

❈ 8 ❈

The next morning, Tamar sat at the kitchen table. Her cousin Zissel was playing on the floor with a puzzle, and her aunt Malka was busy helping her mother roll out the cookie dough for more prune-filled Hamen's ears cookies.

"Tamar asked me if you're bringing Zissel to shul this year," her mother whispered to her aunt. The low tone immediately attracted Tamar's full attention.

Malka shook her head. "What for? She won't hear anything. She won't understand. And if she wants to ask me something, she'll start using her hands, making those funny sounds. . . ."

"But the girls, they want her to come, to see the costumes. . . ."

"No, I don't want. I don't want the stares, the talking behind the back. You know what I mean. I've got to think of Daniel. He's also my child. I don't want everybody to know our business. You know what happens. They don't let the kids come over, they get scared. . . . It's better this way, Ruth, believe me. What's not nice, we don't have to show. . . ."

Tamar heard her mother sigh. "But Malka, you can't keep her locked up forever! What about school next year?"

"I've asked around. There's only one place: the Manhattan School for the Deaf. Such a *goyische* place." Malka's voice lowered, full of shame. "I thought I'd, maybe, keep her home another year."

"It's not right to do to the child . . ."

"Don't tell me what's right to do for my child! I know what's right for my child! I stay home with her, not you. I'm the prisoner, not you!" Her voice took on a bitterness that made Tamar look away, frightened.

The two women glanced at her and then at each other.

"Malka, G-d knows I'm not blaming. . . . It's just Zissel, what's best for her . . ."

"But what else can I do?" Malka continued in a fierce, pleading whisper. "You know they'll send a special bus to pick her up. It'll stop right in front of the house, where all the neighbors can see. . . . I'd die of shame."

Tamar found herself waiting anxiously for her mother's reply. But she heard only a long, resigned sigh, which surprised and frightened her even more. She looked at her cousin Zissel, the long red hair, the pink cheeks. She was so pretty! And smart. Why, that puzzle had three hundred pieces, and she was nearly done! She was used to Zissel's unmodulated voice, her elaborate hand movements, which seemed like some clever game of charades. Always before, it had seemed just a different kind of normal, Zissel-normal. . . . For the first time she realized that it might be something to be ashamed of.

"Maybe you could ask the bus to pick her up a few blocks away," Ruth suggested in a whisper.

They were ashamed of Zissel. Because she wasn't perfect. And if something wasn't perfect, it was best if you kept it locked up behind closed doors, so no one would see. Even her kind mother believed that.

She felt her stomach lurch in fear as she watched her mother's dark head, her shapely, efficient arms bent to their task, rolling the pliant cookie dough. *Mameh* was perfect, she thought. Slim, with large blue eyes and auburn hair. Why couldn't she look like her mother? she mourned.

"You eat nothing, Tamar. Are you sick?" her mother asked, placing a damp, floury hand across her forehead. "You're not hot." Ruth rubbed the flour mark off the child's forehead. "You're not wearing your costume!" she suddenly noticed.

"*Mameh*. . . ," Tamar began, not knowing where to begin. "*Mameh*, am I . . . ugly?"

"Ugly?" Ruth's face was incredulous. "*Gotteinu!* Malka, Aaron, you hear this? What is she talking about? Come, eat a cookie, drink a little milk with it. Don't forget to make the *broocha*."

"*Mameh* . . ." She tried again, looking desperately for

confirmation in her mother's loving eyes. But all she saw was herself reflected there, small and forlorn, with long curly hair and big glasses. She swallowed hard. What was the point of asking? She had gotten the answer yesterday, in school. The only ugly Queen Esther . . . She, too, would have to hide. She too would never go outside, never go back to school again. She would stay home, like Zissel.

"What was that?" Aaron Gottlieb said, sauntering with leisurely ease into the kitchen. He had taken the day off in order to hear the reading of the *Megillah* in the synagogue, to give out the gift baskets and to participate in the Purim *seudah*, the large eating and wine-drinking feast that made the holiday such a merry one.

Her mother said something in Yiddish too fast and low for Tamar to catch. She saw her father looking down at her.

"What, Tamar, no veils, no evening gown? Where did that beautiful Queen Esther disappear to? You didn't happen to see her, did you?"

A tear trickled down her cheek.

"*Oy vey is mere!* On Purim, *mamaleh, mamaleh,* what could be so bad? What?" He picked her up and she flung her arms around his shoulders with greedy affection, burying her head beneath his chin.

"Rivkie, what's the matter with your sister? Did she say anything to you?" Ruth asked.

Rivkie, already in costume, flipped one of the hot cookies from hand to hand. "No," she said, finally eating it. "What's wrong with her?"

"She said something about looking ugly. . . ."

Rivkie's bites slowed down and she chewed meditatively. "I only told her to take off some of that lipstick . . ." she said cautiously. "But she didn't start crying about it then."

"Come," Aaron Gottlieb said, walking into the living room with Tamar's head still burrowing into his shoulder. He stood in front of the large mirror over the couch. "Now look at yourself." She shook her head. "Come on, one little peek, all right?"

She cautiously lifted one eyelid, already feeling something pleasant was about to happen. Just being off the floor made her feel taller and more beautiful. The prisms of the chandelier caught the light and flung it over her, like fairy dust.

"Now both eyes," her father coaxed, looking over her flushed face, her tender, vulnerable mouth, the eyes almost fierce with distress. "See what pretty hair, so long and curly. Why, in Europe, if a little girl had curly hair like this, all the other little girls were so jealous they made their *Mamehs* sit for hours dipping their hair in sugar water to make them curls!"

Her eyes were wide with interest but skeptical.

"Oh, yes." He nodded solemnly. "Now look at those eyes." He took her glasses off. "Look how large and beautiful they are, like silver. And those pretty red cheeks . . ."

She looked at herself. Could she trust his vision? Could she trust him? She wasn't sure. But somehow the look on his face seemed to shine over her, like the flattering light in a photographer's studio.

"Now will you please put your costume back on?"

She hesitated.

"Well, it would please me so much to escort such a lovely queen around Orchard Park to give out the *shalach monos*. Won't you please, little queen?" He winked at her. It was a special wink, a code between them that left everyone else out. It meant "Come, we'll have fun, just the two of us!" She could never resist that wink.

She was about to ask, "What about Zissel?" when she thought better of it. She knew the answer. She accepted it. Besides, she was too relieved and grateful at her own rescue from the cliff's edge to risk reaching out for Zissel's hand, which might pull her over.

"Is Rivkie coming with us?"

"I think Rivkie is going to be busy making up more *shalach monos* baskets with your mother and Aunt Malka." He winked again.

That settled it. A two-wink outing with her father. Without Rivkie. Not to be resisted. Ever. Her arms tightened around his neck, and she planted a big, wet kiss on his cheek. How she loved him! And if he thought she was beautiful, who else mattered?

She put the veils and dress on again. But this time she smoothed down the tulle cautiously and carefully tied her hair back. The lipstick no longer even tempted her.

"Ready?" Her father beamed.

"Ready!" She bounded into his arms, her face reflecting his. "Just, I want to say good-bye to Zissel."

She crouched down, touching Zissel on the shoulder. The child turned around and smiled.

"Happy Purim, Zissel!"

"Ah-pee Pooh-rim!" Zissel answered as usual. But it sounded different to Tamar now, strange and loud and funny. It sounded shameful.

❈

"*Tateh?*"

"Uhm?"

"Can we bring a basket to a new friend?"

"Who?"

"Jenny Douglas, from my class."

"Jenny?" He shrugged, surprised at the very American name. "Where does she live?"

"Fifteen-fifteen Newrose Avenue," she read off a slip of paper where she had written it the day before.

"It's a long walk, *mamaleh*. Why specially this girl and not somebody closer?"

"Because . . . she's . . . my friend."

"But you have lots of friends!"

She shook her head: "Please *Tateh!*"

"I suppose." He smoothed down Tamar's curly hair, and the child caught his hand and kissed it.

They gave out the heaviest basket first, the one laden with choice wines and expensive chocolate bonbons. The Kovnitzer Rebbe's basket.

The Gottlieb family were not Kovnitzer Hasidim. But like many other Jews, particularly those who'd survived the war in Europe through a thousand haphazard decisions, they had a certain longing for the clear, dilemma-free lives of the

Hasidim, who could ask their rebbe any difficult life decision and be relieved of the burden of personal choice. After all, they reasoned, following a few new customs, listening to words of wisdom from a great learned man like the Rebbe . . . How could it hurt?

And while they would not have trusted the Rebbe with the selection of a surgeon or advice on a particular medical procedure—as would bona fide Hasidim of Kovnitz—they were nevertheless happy to have his advice about what business to go into or how to overcome sudden setbacks through charitable donations. . . . Like wearing a rabbit's foot and a star of David, they were simply hedging their bets. Their relationship to the Rebbe gave them a set of training wheels as they rode the wobbly bicycle that was their new life in America.

Tamar knocked on the door, hoping Hadassah wouldn't be there. She didn't want to face anyone from her class in this costume again. Rebbetzin Mandlebright opened the door. Tamar handed her the basket.

"A *frelicht* Purim." She smiled, accepting the basket and handing Tamar a dime, the custom.

"A *frelicht* Purim, Rebbetzin," she answered politely.

"What a pretty Queen Esther! Hadassah wanted a blue dress too. She really did. She's upstairs. Do you want to say hello?"

She did not want to say hello to Hadassah Mandlebright. Or good-bye. Or anything. Hadassah's role in yesterday's disaster, her sudden, belated defense after her initial participation, was uncomfortably undigested in her mind.

"My *tateh* is waiting. . . ," she said, backing away as quickly as she could.

Out of nowhere, Hadassah suddenly appeared at her mother's side. "Hi! What are you doing?" She seemed bored.

The rebbetzin patted Tamar on the head and left the two girls alone.

"I'm giving out *shalach monos* with my father."

"Is that him?" Hadassah pointed over Tamar's shoulder to where Aaron Gottlieb stood waiting patiently on the pavement. He smiled and waved.

"Yes," she said proudly. "That's him."

"And he is taking you all over Orchard Park, just you and him?" Hadassah asked wistfully. "He has time?"

"My *tateh* doesn't work today." She was proud of that, too, and exhilarated by the inexplicable envy in Hadassah's eyes. "But your *tateh* is home all the time!"

"So, big deal. I never see him. He never takes me anywhere. All those people in the house. They make so much noise. It's so boring." Hadassah looked at her wistfully.

"I'm going to Jenny's next. I mean Yehudit. Come with us?" Tamar said impulsively, feeling suddenly very sorry for Hadassah Mandlebright.

Hadassah's dull eyes brightened. "I'll have to ask. Wait a minute."

"But we're walking, my *tateh* and me," Tamar suddenly hedged, beginning to regret, just a tiny bit, that she would have to share her father. Besides, she had never in her life seen Hadassah walk anyplace except on the Sabbath and certain holidays when the *halacha* forbade driving.

"I don't mind. Wait, I'll ask my *mameh*."

The white Chrysler Imperial let Tamar, her father and Hadassah out in front of Romano's Italian Grocery on Newrose Avenue. The driver, an affable Hasid with a long red beard and eyes as bright as new copper pennies (from the Purim liquor at the Rebbe's table, already half gone), said he would wait in the car to take them back.

"This can't be. . . ," Tamar said, scrambling out to the sidewalk, looking at the run-down stores.

"Come girls," Aaron Gottlieb said quietly. "Let's do a mitzvah."

"Who is it?" Jenny called. Her mother was at work. She wasn't allowed to open the door for anyone.

"It's me, Tamar. And Hadassah. And my *tateh*, and we've come to bring you *shalach monos*," Tamar said excitedly, feeling somehow brave and adventurous. And full of pleasure at doing a mitzvah.

"I'm not . . . dressed," Jenny said, a great panic-stricken ache slicing through her stomach at the idea of girls from her class knowing where and how she lived.

"Is your father home, child?" Aaron said in his quiet way.

There was a short silence. "No. He's dead."

The two girls looked at each other, horrified and impressed.

"And your mother, is she there?"

"My mother's at work and I'm not allowed to open the door to anyone."

"It's all right, child. We can leave it on the doorstep," Aaron Gottlieb said, the shame in the child's voice awakening within him ghostly memories of unwanted knocks on the door, of powerlessness and undeserved disgrace.

The two little girls, well fed, well dressed, with doting parents, had no such ghosts.

"Jenny, it's us. Open the door!" Hadassah banged imperiously.

"Yes, you don't have to be afraid," Tamar chimed in. "It's just us."

"Sha, girls, we go now," Aaron Gottlieb said firmly, taking both of them by the hand.

Slowly the door opened.

"A *frelicht* Purim, Yehudit!" Tamar and Hadassah sang in chorus, handing her two baskets of sweets.

She took them in wonderment.

The two little girls walked in easily, looking around. Tamar took in everything with simple curiosity and without judgment, feeling strangely comfortable amid the worn and simple furnishings, while Hadassah made a mental list of everything that needed to be fixed or replaced.

"Where's your room?" Tamar asked with a big smile.

"My bed, my little brother's bed . . ." Jenny guided them.

"Ooh, little brothers," Tamar said, wrinkling her nose with distaste.

"He's not so bad. He's the father when we play house, and sometimes we play dates and I even get him to take me dancing," Jenny confided.

"Does he wear a hat? Does he take your arm like for real?" Hadassah questioned breathlessly, her mind suddenly flooded with the pleasurable possibilities of enslaving a helpless male sibling.

Jenny nodded. "And sometimes we make believe his tricycle is a taxi, and he picks me up and takes me to the ballroom in it!"

The girls sighed in satisfaction over such a lovely idea as a house where you could ride a tricycle from room to room.

"Open the baskets. My *mameh* makes the best hamantaschen. Just taste one. Go on!" Tamar pleaded, getting a little hungry. She was always a little hungry.

Jenny tore open the basket and took out the cookies. The sweet prune filling, still warm, ran down her fingers. She licked it off, smiling.

With just a tiny bit more effort, Aaron Gottlieb thought, watching her, the corners of her mouth really will touch her ears. His eyes misted, thinking of this little orphan girl—for in the Bible a child without a father was always called an orphan—alone in this dingy house with no hint of the holiday festivities taking place all over the neighborhood. G-d bless Tamar's generous little soul, he thought, moved by the simple evidence that a child of his had absorbed so naturally and so well the values he held dearest. That she was capable at such a young age of running after a good deed, the way she had pursued this one.

"And what about the *seudah?* Are you invited, or is your *mameh* making one?" Tamar asked.

"*Seudah?*" Jenny said doubtfully.

"You know, the big party with all the food and soda. . . ."

"And the big people drinking and drinking and going nuts. . . ." Hadassah stuck her tongue out sideways and crossed her eyes, her fingers making fast little circles by her temples.

Aaron Gottlieb looked at her oddly, amused and appalled to hear such a description of *seudas Purim* at the great Rebbe's illustrious table by such a reliable and intimate a source as his daughter. But he didn't find it difficult to believe. If Hasidim were joyful and fond of drinking, singing and dancing on ordinary days, then on Purim, when ordinary Jews behaved that way, Hasidim could certainly be imagined without prejudice to fit Hadassah's blunt but probably accurate description.

Jenny looked at her shoes.

"Perhaps you'd like to join us, at our house?" Aaron said with quick compassion.

"Oh, *Tateh!* Could she?!" Tamar hugged him and beamed at Jenny.

Jenny shook her head. "I have to pick up my brother at three. . . ."

"You could bring him, too!" Tamar hugged her. "Please come!"

"I don't know where you live!"

"You could also come to my house," Hadassah said suddenly. "The car could come to get you and your little brother. Pretty please! Tamar won't mind, would you, Tamar? You have a sister. All I have are big brothers. It's so boring. . . ."

"I don't. . . ," Aaron began. This was all getting very complicated. But there was a reason for it, he trusted. G-d never let anything happen by accident. Maybe it was all *beshert*, divine providence, after all, that the little princess and the little pauper should give each other joy this Purim. And maybe Tamar wasn't an overweight little witch after all, but simply a *zaftig* fairy godmother. "Why don't you and Hadassah call your mothers and ask permission? How does that sound?"

"But whose house?" Tamar piped up. "Ours or Hadassah's?"

"I think I'll let Jenny decide that."

Jenny, who had expected to spend the holiday alone doing homework and counting the cars passing beneath the el, looked joyfully at the two anxious faces vying desperately for her company. Tamar had this hopeful smile on her face she hated to disappoint. But there was something mysteriously lonely about the beautiful Hadassah that touched her.

"Could Tamar come over to your house, too, Hadassah, after her own *seudah?* Then we could all play together," Jenny suggested.

Aaron looked at her, impressed at the Solomonic compromise and utterly relieved the choice wasn't going to be thrown into his lap. Hadassah nodded eagerly. "Then it's all settled." He rubbed his hands together with satisfaction. "Fine. All settled. So go downstairs to the car, girls," he said, shooing them. When they were out of sight he hastily put some bills into an envelope and sealed it.

"Here, take. For your mother," he told Jenny.

"Is this also part of Purim?" she asked with a fatherless child's delicate, quivering suspicious pride.

"Yes, of course. Of course. All part of the holiday," he assured her, tucking the envelope into her small hand.

It was no lie. Gifts for the poor. That too was Purim.

✣9✣

On every polished surface of the Mandlebrights' elegant home, elaborate straw and gold foil baskets rested temptingly, a cornucopia of abundant sweets, cakes, and fine wines.

"Take anything you want from the baskets," Hadassah told Jenny and Tamar magnanimously.

"Does your *mameh* let?" asked Tamar, who knew how these things worked.

"What will we do with them? Pesach is just around the corner, and it's all *hametz* anyway and will have to be thrown out," she said maturely, in a perfect imitation of the rebbetzin of Kovnitz.

This sounded reasonable to both girls. Tamar dug in first and came up with a box of strictly kosher Barton's chocolate-covered candies. Her first one was a sticky confection of caramel, chocolate, and pecans, which held her teeth together like cement. It was the most scrumptious thing she had ever tasted. She hunted greedily for more, filling her hands and the pockets of her new dress with them.

"Taste it. It's fantabulous," she told the others. "You're so lucky, Hadassah." Tamar sighed, her jaws aching in blissful agony from all that candy chewing.

Hadassah gave her an odd smile of acknowledgment and contempt. "This," she said with queenly authority, "is no fun at all!"

Tamar, busy digging through the next basket, looked up at her in amazement. "No fun? This is no fun?"

"Don't *you* think it's noisy and boring?" Hadassah asked, as anxious and apologetic as only children who are very lonely can be when showing their home to potential new playmates.

"It's like a fairy story," Jenny said quietly with frank admiration. "Just like something you read about."

Hadassah cocked her head and considered.

"Well, so you wanna see it all?" she asked with secret pleasure, surprised and mollified.

Jenny, Davy, and Tamar followed her through the rooms like Dorothy down the yellow brick road: wide-eyed and smiling. Jenny felt her feet sinking into the deep, soft pile of the green velvet carpeting, like nothing she had ever felt before. Other things, like paintings or furniture, a poor child can experience in places like museums and department stores. But that kind of carpeting . . . It was impossible to imagine such a thing unless your feet touched it in the home of someone who could afford it.

The house was filled with people. Men in satiny black *bekeshers* and fur-trimmed *shtreimels*, women in elegant long-sleeved designer discounts from local shops and new hats or wigs fresh from the *shaytlmacher*. Children roamed the house wearing costumes that ranged from store-bought Halloween clowns and cowboys to exquisite hand-sewn linen high priest's robes, complete with fake jeweled breastplates.

Jenny stood in front of the great china closet. She held Davy's hand, her eyes mesmerized by the sparkling riches dancing before her eyes. There were great silver seder plates engraved with Hebrew letters and dozens of beautifully wrought silver wine cups almost encrusted with elaborate designs, a dazzling silver Chanukah menorah the size of a small tricycle, gold spice boxes in the shape of castles and flowers and small boats, and silver Sabbath candlesticks so thick she felt sure even a grown man would need both hands to lift each one. But her favorite piece was a little silver matchbox-cover to hold the matches used to light the Sabbath candles. The idea of it thrilled her. Even an ordinary box of matches could become something holy, she thought, enchanted.

"Just old junk." Hadassah tugged at her. "Come upstairs to my room." She ran up the steps, opened her door and threw herself facedown on her bed.

Tamar and Jenny raced after her but stopped, standing still

at the threshold, just staring. The bed was a confection of pink-and-white lace, canopied and immaculate. Long shelves the full length of the wall held dolls with delicately painted porcelain heads dressed in ruffly old-fashioned long dresses and hats, the kind of dolls any little girl would sell her soul for. White wicker bookcases held row after row of books, perfectly arranged according to size.

"Oh, can I hold one?" Tamar pleaded, her eyes covetous and delighted as they devoured the dolls.

"Who cares?" Hadassah said nonchalantly. "Sure."

It was the books that mesmerized Jenny. "What stories are they?"

"Don't know. *Mameh* reads them to me. How the rebbetzin went to Israel and kept all the mitzvos. How the rebbe's daughter stayed in Russia and kept all the mitzvos. How the rebbe lived in Brooklyn and kept all the mitz—"

"Don't they have any fairies in them?" Jenny interrupted her, disappointed.

"Not fairies. Maybe a *malach*. I don't know. I don't like to read much," she admitted.

"*Malachs* are angels. That's good too. Do they have wings and golden yellow hair?"

"Wings, maybe, but I don't remember any hair," Hadassah said, sucking meditatively on a lock of hair.

"Oh," Jenny sighed, crestfallen. A book without fairies with golden hair wasn't worth much.

Still, to own a whole shelf of books, any books! She fingered them longingly. She hated the constant tension of library due dates, the threat of expensive fines, which would end her precious weekly visits. The idea of owning your own shelf of books was simply magical.

"I love fairies," she sighed. "Books with castles and enchanted forests. But I guess if I lived here"—she looked longingly around the room—"I guess I wouldn't read so much either."

Hadassah pondered that uncertainly.

"Why would you want to live anyplace else but your own house?" Tamar asked, puzzled.

"Nothing ever happens at your own house!" Hadassah flounced down petulantly, carelessly creasing her beautiful bedspread, pulling all the lace-covered pillows into her lap.

"Lots of things happen!" Tamar protested.

"Like what?"

"Like . . . like . . . like Ed Sullivan!"

"Who's he?" Hadassah asked.

"You don't watch Ed Sullivan on TV?"

"We don't have a TV."

"We don't either," admitted Jenny. "But my ma says she might get one on time and pay out for it. . . ."

"We'll never get one, my father says. He says it's *toeva*," Haddassah informed them.

"What's that mean?" Jenny asked.

"It means disgusting, like bowing down to idols. Anything really fun is *toeva*," Hadassah said morosely.

"My father says the TV is silly, *narishkeit*, but it makes him laugh," Tamar contributed.

"Your father watches TV?" Hadassah asked incredulously. The very thought of a father doing something so frivolous and relaxing was beyond her experience. She never saw her father do anything she remotely considered fun, oddly discounting his participation in the daily joyous singing and dancing of his Hasidim. That, she considered, was simply part of his job.

"Sure. Sid Caesar. *The Sixty-four-Thousand-Dollar Question. I Love Lucy . . .*"

"But what else? What else isn't boring?" Hadassah persisted.

"My sister, Rivkie. Playing house and jumping rope, and playing queen and servant . . ." Tamar went on, oblivious of Hadassah's eyes narrowing into envious little slits.

"You're so lucky. I wish I had a sister. I wish I did," Jenny said.

"Well, Rivkie isn't . . ." Tamar's face reddened with the effort of telling unpleasant truths. "She doesn't always play. She goes out a lot. And sometimes she hits me. . . ."

"Do you hit her back?" Hadassah asked, her eyes losing their malevolent shine.

Tamar, who had tried to hit Rivkie back a number of times

and had come out much the worse for it and now usually hid or ran to her mother, began feeling inadequate and defensive. "Just sometimes," she said slowly.

"I wouldn't let anybody boss me." Hadassah bristled, suddenly wishing she had an older sister who would try. Her brothers were in the yeshiva most of the day, and when she did see them they were adoring or, at worst, mildly teasing. They would never have dreamed of laying a hand on her. This, at the moment, seemed to her a terrible injustice, part of what made life so boring.

"Ah, there you are," Hadassah's mother exclaimed, opening the door with a sudden impatient push that sent it flying toward the wall. She caught the handle just before it banged against the delicate rose-patterned wallpaper. "Your father is already at the table." She tapped her elegant patent-leather shoe against the thick carpeting, tugging at her beautifully coiffed and stiffly sprayed blond wig.

The lazy ease with which Hadassah uncoiled herself from her bed pillows surprised both girls, who had reacted to the imperious words by jumping to attention, Tamar quickly putting the doll back on the shelf and Jenny shoving the book into its correct slot in the bookcase. Even Davy had stopped chewing his candy and was watching warily. They suddenly felt like trespassers.

"Do I have to? I'm not hungry," Hadassah whined, a tone of voice the others had not heard her use before. It seemed like a performance to them, and they watched with fearful interest and secret admiration.

"Yes, *maideleh*, but maybe your . . ." Her mother hesitated, noting there were three extra children to be dealt with, when she had been expecting only one. "Your *guests* are ready to eat." Who were these children? she wondered, and why wasn't the house full of Hadassah's usual friends, children of prominent Kovnitz Hasidim?

"Oh, I ate already," said Tamar, reading the rebbetzin like a neon sign. She had this unsettling ability—shared by many children—to hear what people meant rather than what they said. It was a talent that had led to more than one embarrassing incident with uncles, aunts, and older cousins. "Really, we finished our *seudah* at our house. I just came to play."

"Well, still, you're most welcome to join us anyway," the rebbetzin said, her pale face going slightly pink and her nostrils flaring with chagrin. She felt ashamed. After all, it wasn't their fault that the house was in an uproar, and sticky fingers and candies and mushed cookies were going to be wedged inside sofa pillows and ground into the new carpeting. And all this with Passover cleaning just around the corner, when every cookie crumb became an enemy to be routed at all costs!

Why did Purim have to come just before Passover? Really, it was most unfair, most unfair, her tired mind repeated irrationally. Couldn't Haman have picked a different date to annihilate all the Jews? Really. Another reason to shout down his name during the reciting of the Purim saga.... "So your family's eaten already." She nodded once, as if saluting the achievement. "We're always a little late over here." She sighed, looking suddenly as if she would like nothing better than to join Hadassah facedown on the bed for a few hours. "Please come, children, I suppose there is room for everyone," she said, trying to make amends. "Come, come . . ." She shooed them down the stairs, following behind slowly, her hand testing the mahogany banister for stickiness. She found it, in abundance.

The dining room was already packed.

There was so much noise! So much food! So many bottles of wine! And the singing, the hands tattooing the table, the feet pounding the floors, and then the utter silence preceding the Rebbe's *vort*—his words of wisdom—said in slow Yiddish, punctuated by occasional slaps on the table.

Jenny didn't understand a word of it. But what would stay with her always was simply the look on the faces of the Hasidim: rapt, almost painfully concentrated and at the edge of ecstasy. She had never seen anything even remotely similar, except, perhaps, in those Norman Rockwell drawings of children's faces on Christmas morning.

Tamar, her stomach filled with her own lavish *seudah* and all those delectable Barton's candies, sat there politely, intending to simply watch. But then the rebbetzin put a plate of warm, sweet noodle kugel in front of her. Just the smell of the hot raisins and apples and cinnamon made her mouth water.

She loved noodle kugel. Just a taste, she told herself, and wound up eating the whole thing. And then the fish with almonds, which she would have let pass if the rebbetzin hadn't been staring right at her. So she ate it to be polite. And then the main dish: roast beef with new potatoes and sweet potato *tsimmes* swimming in brown sugar and pineapples. . . . She ate and ate and ate until she started to feel her eyes blur and her head swim as if in a bad dream.

She felt the nauseated groan of her stomach as it churned in angry protest at the overcrowding and abuse. She needed a bathroom, but the room was so crowded, it would have meant pushing her way through all those men to get out the door. And then they'd all look at her. The idea of it, of being the center of disapproving glances, was unbearable to her. So she sat very still, like someone holding an egg sunny-side up trying to keep the yolk from running. Very still, she told herself, until the room clears out a little. She could do it. She wouldn't throw up all over the table. She wouldn't pee in her pants. She calmed herself. She would simply sit there and not move a muscle. She would simply sit there and suffer quietly, allowing everyone to continue having a good time.

The singing and rejoicing went on and on and on.

Jenny sat watching, mesmerized and wholly delighted. She had never experienced such joy before. Oh, there were happy memories of birthdays and Sundays in the park. But this shouting-out exuberant gladness; this wholehearted adult merriment devoid of any frightening underpinnings, like the mean, drunken laughter of men in bars—this was entirely new. She drank it in like the most delicious of new drinks.

In the swaying joy of the moment, the irrational pure pleasure of voices raised in song, the natural distance between adult and child, man and woman melted away. It was so sweet, so sweet, she thought, to be part of something bigger than yourself, to be joined together with a whole that accepted you and let you mingle your voice with theirs, your clapping hands with theirs.

All her pent-up sorrow and isolation welled up inside her small chest and flew out of her heart in the songs, like a great shout of joyous pain, it flew from her, rising and hovering and disappearing like polluting smoke dashed against the sky by the clean wind.

She closed her eyes and clapped and clapped and clapped, her voice humming the melodies that rang like a chime in her deepest consciousness of being, enlivening her, scrubbing away her mourning, her loneliness. And when she opened her eyes, she felt herself staring into the dark, compassionate eyes of G-d himself, who seemed to view her with pleasure.

"*Baruchim Habayim, maideleh*," G-d told her, and without anyone translating she knew it meant "Welcome, child. May you be blessed for coming."

She stared, speechlessly, until Hadassah nudged her and giggled. "You can close your mouth, Jen. My father doesn't bite."

The face of the Rebbe of Kovnitz shone down on her with a strange power.

Was it simply the power of fatherliness over one aching for a father? Or was it gratitude for simple acceptance, from one who felt she belonged nowhere? Or maybe it was just the rare experience of unadulterated kindness she was feeling, kindness without motive?

Hadassah's father. She blushed and looked down at her plate.

"You are one of my Hadassaleh's new friends?"

She nodded, too overwhelmed by the attention to speak. But the voice was so kind, not the thundering voice of G-d, but simply a kind man's.

"You were very kind to give Hadassah your Purim costume. I understand she didn't like hers very much."

"No, *Tateh*," Hadassah protested, chagrined. "I gave her mine because she didn't have one!"

Jenny watched Hadassah staring at her father, who returned the look with a piercing honesty that seared away all pretension, leaving behind a nugget of pure truth. Hadassah's voice faltered, and her eyes dropped. Jenny could see her lips tremble.

"Hadassah!" Tamar suddenly cried out, tugging at her sleeve.

Hadassah pulled free, annoyed at the interruption. "What?"

"I've got to go to the . . ." Tamar gulped hard, clapping her hand over her mouth.

Reluctantly Hadassah turned her attention from her father to Tamar, who was turning a delicate shade of green. "Come on, I'll take you down to the bathroom!" She laughed, dragging her through the milling crowd to the ceramic-tiled heaven on earth nearby.

The singing went on and on.

The light slowly faded from the windows, replaced by the brilliant illumination of street lamps.

"*Maariv!*" one of the men said suddenly, slapping a book down on a table. As if a whistle had been blown, the men turned and hurried out of the house to the synagogue downstairs to join in evening prayers.

"It's dark. I have to go home I guess," Jenny said reluctantly.

"Me too. I had a very nice time," Tamar added politely, her stomach still churning, but much relieved.

"Do you have to?" Hadassah said, disappointed. "Well, I'll tell my *mameh* and *tateh*. They'll get the car for you."

She disappeared and then returned with a strange look on her face. "My *tateh* says you should come in."

Jenny held Davy's hand tightly with an odd feeling of excitement as she followed Tamar and Hadassah into the small room off the study.

"Come in *tirelehs*, come, come in," he said gently.

"Rebbe, the minyan is ready," a black-bearded Hasid said diffidently, his eyes lowered.

The Rebbe of Kovnitz waved his hand impatiently. "Tell them to say a few *tehillim*, their Rebbe is involved in something too important to be disturbed."

The Hasid looked at the children with questioning intensity, then walked slowly out the door.

"Come here children," the Rebbe said, motioning them forward. "Did you have fun? On Purim you're supposed to have so much fun you don't know the difference between Haman and Mordechai."

The girls looked at each other and giggled. Haman was the villain and Mordechai the great hero and savior of the Purim saga.

"Ah, I made you laugh. This is good!" He turned to Tamar. "And what is your name?"

"Tamar Gottlieb," she said, hoping she wouldn't have to dash out to the bathroom again until this was all over.

"And why didn't you wear your costume, *maideleh?*"

"Because my mother said Purim or no Purim, no child of hers was going to go to the house of the great Rebbe of Kovnitz in flimsy veils and tinsel," she answered honestly.

The Rebbe swallowed hard, his serious eyes bright with amusement. "I see." He turned to Jenny. "And you are new in the class at Ohel Sara, my daughter tells me. What is your name, child?"

"Jenny," she said, then bit her lip, remembering she had a different name, a name he would probably like better. "I mean, Yehudit."

"Did you know that a person's name means something? G-d chooses a name for every person, even before he or she is born. A person is fortunate when the name his parents' choose is the same as G-d has chosen and the same as a person chooses for himself. Herself," he added, his dark eyes lively. "One day you will decide, Jenny or Yehudit. Where do your fathers *daven,* at which synagogue?"

"My father goes to the Sephardic minyan," Tamar said.

Jenny looked on uncomfortably, her stomach tightening. She hated telling anyone her father was dead. It was sad, but mostly it was embarrassing to her, like admitting some defect of character or material well-being. She felt somehow to blame. And she hated being pitied.

"My father's gone away. Passed away," she corrected herself in an agony of embarrassment.

The Rebbe looked at her reassuringly, pressing her small hand into his large warm one. "A child is never without a father," he said softly. "You have a father in heaven, the Father of us all. You may talk to Him, and He will watch over you. No one in the world is more important to our Father in heaven than an orphan. They are His special children. Will you try to remember that, child? Whatever you need, you ask Him and He will make sure you get it."

"But a father in heaven doesn't talk back, and he has no arms," she blurted out, her face going all red, her hand tightening around her brother's.

He was thoughtful. "Children need words, don't they? You can always come here when you need words. That I can give you. As for arms, these too are yours, anytime you want," he said, drawing her close to him with a fatherly hug.

Hadassah watched her father, jealous and proud and aching with a need she could not name.

❖10❖

As usual, it was Jenny who made the discovery that changed their lives the year they were nine years old. For it was Jenny who took out Anne Frank's diary from the public library and brought it to school for the others to read.

"Read it. It'll make you cry," Jenny assured them, the highest praise.

Hadassah read it next with breathless concentration behind her parents' back. There was way too much boy-girl business in the diary for her mother, Hadassah realized right away. It wasn't acceptable reading for her little girl.

The book was a revelation to her. Anne was such a rebel, such a lively, imaginative clever girl. Even in that jail cell of a house, cut off from the world, she created her own secret life, full of intrigues and jokes and interesting stories. How was it Anne's life in the attic had been so interesting, when her own life was always such a crashing bore? The end was so sad. She couldn't believe it. She had never read any book with a sad ending before, except for the book of Deuteronomy, where Moses died and wasn't allowed to enter the Promised Land. And Anne had been so brave, so good.

Why hadn't G-d saved her? Why? she wondered. It wasn't fair! He was supposed to be all-merciful! He was supposed to be so kind and good, such a tzadik! Why hadn't He just arranged for an earthquake to swallow up all the bad Germans, the way the earth swallowed up Korech and his men in the desert when they rebelled against Him?

The ideas triggered an avalanche of questions that disturbed and fascinated her, filling her with the secret pleasure of rebellion. She would have loved to ask her father, to challenge him. But since she wasn't supposed to be reading the book, she had to content herself with the far less satisfactory imaginary debate that went on in her head. A debate, it must be said, she always won to her satisfaction, no matter the blasphemous nature of her arguments.

Tamar got the book next. Ruth eyed it doubtfully, discussing it with Aaron when he got home from work.

"Should we let her?" Ruth asked him. He shrugged.

They were both survivors. But they'd decided early on in their marriage that they hadn't survived in order to pass the horror on to their children by talking about it. One of the main tenets of their parenting had been to shelter their children from the ugliness and brutality of the past, to see that the work of the Germans did not live on to destroy the gentle, sweet dreams of yet another generation of Jewish children. And so, they did not speak of the past, of gassed grandparents, murdered aunts and uncles and cousins. As far as their children were concerned, their parents' lives began the year they moved to America.

"Do you know what it's about, Tamar?" Ruth asked her.

"About a little Jewish girl, just like me."

Were her survivor friends right, Ruth wondered once again, that the only way to prevent another Holocaust was to educate the next generation, to make them strong and wary? To shove their faces in the ashes of the crematorium, to make them sick by showing them the inventions of sick, perverted minds? She looked at the delicate pink blush on her daughter's young cheeks, her shining, untroubled eyes. Let the Germans show their children the crematoriums. Let German and Polish and Hungarian and Ukrainian children learn all about Zyklon B and the gas chambers and the medical experiments until they were ready to pass out. Why should her children have to know?

"You can't find a nicer book, *maideleh?*"

"All my friends are reading it, *Mameh*. They all like it. Please!" the child begged.

"So read," she said, sighing deeply.

Tamar read it straight through. Strangely, she did not

identify with Anne Frank. The more she read, the more that little girl's life seemed like the life of a Zulu or a Martian. What had Orchard Park to do with a strange European city where brutal sirens wailed in the night? Where Jewish families celebrated St. Nicholas Day? Where someone wanted to kill you because you were a Jew? Except for a few Italian children who were very friendly and playful, she didn't know a single person who wasn't a Jew.

The idea that anyone could think bad things about people like her mother and father, her teachers, the rabbis in the synagogues, was incomprehensible to her. No, it had nothing to do with her, nothing at all, she decided. In some unfathomable way, her mind did not connect Anne's fate to her parents. Vaguely, she knew they too had been in something called "concentration camps," which were terrible places. But her parents never talked about it. Her parents were alive, healthy, beautiful, loving. Everyone her parents' age she knew were survivors. In a strange way, to have been in the camps seemed normal rather than heartbreakingly shocking.

Why hadn't Anne and her sister and mother survived the camps, the way her mother had? she wondered. And the conclusion she came to was St. Nicholas Day. If Anne had been more religious, had kept more of His laws, then she, too, would have survived. She was simply being punished, which was very sad. Why couldn't everybody just keep every *halacha*, and then no one would ever have bad things happen to them? She just couldn't understand people. It seemed so clear, so easy.

A few days after finishing the book, she went to her mother. "*Mameh* . . ."

"Umm?" She was hanging out the laundry. Her mouth was full of clothespins.

"*Mameh*, do you hate the Germans?"

Her mother turned to her, the pins falling out of her mouth. She bent down to retrieve them and stayed there, crouched near the floor, a little longer than necessary. When she finally rose to her feet, Tamar saw her mouth was tight and the light dulled in her merry eyes. "I don't think about them." She paused, biting her lips. "And G-d will pay the Germans back."

Tamar had been about to ask exactly what it had been like in the camps, but something about her mother made it impossible. She did not want to hurt her mother by dragging her through bad memories. She felt suddenly very protective of *Mameh*.

"Was it very hard for you?" Tamar whispered, and then was sorry she'd even asked that.

"Hard," Ruth repeated, her eyes blank and distant. And for a long time, she said nothing.

Tamar waited expectantly.

Finally, her mother looked at her and said: "Tamar, darling, why don't you go to the library and get a *nice* book to read? Zissel's reading *Rebecca of Sunnybrook Farm*. That's a good book for a girl your age." She filled her mouth with pins again, turning back to the laundry.

Tamar lingered silently, unsatisfied, until another idea occurred to her. "*Mameh*, could you buy me a diary?"

"*Vus is dus, kleinkeit?*" her mother asked.

"A diary. You know, with dates, and you write in it every day what happens to you."

Ruth looked at her daughter. "The teacher told you to do this?" For Ruth, anything to do with books or reading or writing had something to do with school. She couldn't imagine it in any other context. But in that context, it was sacred.

"Well, not exactly," Tamar said, hating to lie, but pressing her advantage. "But she said it would be good if we spent part of the summer reviewing our vocabulary. And if you buy me a diary, I can practice using the words in sentences," she argued brightly.

The diary was red imitation leather with gold, cursive lettering across the front.

"*Dear Diary*," Tamar wrote, feeling rather foolish using such personal terms. After all, it was just a bunch of blank paper. But she thought of Anne's opening remarks. After all, something might happen to her, something dramatic and world-shattering and they would dig up this diary and it would become millions of copies in thousands of bookstores. . . .

"*I asked Mother . . .*"

That sounded high class, American, she thought, which would be wise just in case of publication.

to get you for me because I like to have a diary to confide in. I will tell you things no other mortal but I and you know about. I will trust you with my secrets. I will confide in you with my troubles, and I will also keep in you a record of my daily happenings.

Very nice. But what troubles did she have? After all, in Orchard Park no one was threatening her life, except Rivkie, and only when she touched her napkin collection. And even Rivkie didn't really mean it. Tamar closed the diary a little chagrined, deciding to wait for a day of suitably dramatic events before beginning her confession.

A week later, it came.

Dear Diary,

Today I am sick in bed with swollen glands. I'm so sorry to miss school.

This wasn't true. She was actually thrilled to miss school, but she felt that if it was published, she wanted the adults who read it to think well of her.

Maybe it wasn't as dramatic as Anne's trials, but it was moving in the right direction.

Dear Diary,

Today I went to school, and we had a party in Hebrew. We had it because we finished the book of Barashis and started Shemot.

She looked that over and crossed it out, replacing the transliteration of Genesis and Exodus with laboriously written Hebrew letters. She hated using English letters to spell out Hebrew words, seeing in it a dangerously confusing overlapping.

The pattern of her life, like the schedule of her days, was

strictly compartmentalized. There was the Jewish part and the American part. In the morning, she was taught Bible lessons, stories of the Hebrew prophets, ritual laws for preparing kosher food, and certain rules of Hebrew grammar. Her teachers were bewigged and head-scarved rebbetzins, who wore long, dark dresses and thick, seamed stockings. But after lunch, the rebbetzins disappeared, replaced by pretty young English teachers in red lipstick and high heels and attractive, mysterious middle-aged math teachers from the local public schools, who were the only men allowed into the school except for the principal, a rabbi, and the janitor, a friendly Puerto Rican.

Her identity was equally divided.

She was an American, nurtured by *Father Knows Best*, Ed Sullivan, Hula Hoops, commercials for new Ipana toothpaste, and the Good Humor ice-cream truck. Yet her real life, and that of her family and all those she knew, had nothing to do with America, or New York City or State. It was *halacha*, and tradition, and custom, and cherished family practices handed down from father to son, mother to daughter. Her Saturdays were Shabbos, festivals of candles and wine and sweet challah bread, a holy day spent in the synagogue and prayer and in delightful *oneg Shabbos* groups full of storytelling, tag games, and cookie eating.

What did that have to do with Bud mowing the lawn on Saturday morning, taking long bike rides? With Elinor Donahue's sleeveless dresses, her ham and eggs for breakfast? With Santa Claus and the Easter bunny? They were simply the manifestations of a distant foreign planet, which like some astronomical oddity at regular intervals crashed into her own, needing to be observed and dealt with.

And yet that planet, like the sun, had *everything* to do with her life. As much as her outward appearance and her activities were governed by a loving and faithful adherence to the special ways of her family and community, her values and dreams were undeniably American. Happiness was not something you felt. It was something you bought. The Jewish concept of "Who is happy? He who is satisfied with his portion in life" crumbled almost totally before the bulldozing philosophy of American advertising executives of the 1950s: "Who is happy? Whoever has the latest model."

For all the trappings of impermeability, all the carefully constructed dams and intricate stone breakwaters put up by parents to preserve the cherished values of the past, the streets of Orchard Park were flooded by the immense power of the American dream, which swept away effortlessly the minds and hearts of the American-born children who lived there. Their parents never even suspected.

✖11✖

Orchard Park, 1960

It was Saturday afternoon, a lovely spring day. The streets were hot with human movement, with dainty little girls in neat braids and satin hair bows, with howling little boys in *payot* and blue knickers. Matronly grandmothers in dark head scarves, bewigged middle-aged daughters, and slim, long-haired granddaughters linked arms and promenaded down the wide, tree-lined avenues. Their footfalls fell in perfect unison.

The occasional gentile wandering through felt oddly threatened by the strange holiday atmosphere, though a more broad-minded outsider might have been more appreciative, discerning a gentler bygone era, a street scene by Renoir come to life. The little girls would have stared at such an appreciative stranger with frank disapproval, noting the absence of a skullcap or wig, clothing not exactly like that of their parents. The little girls, like smoke detectors, whiffed immediately the scent of anyone who was not "one of us." They would not have made such outsiders feel welcome.

There was no room for tourists in Orchard Park. No room for diversity of opinion, practice, belief. Even the houses, long rows of attached buildings, seemed knitted together, erasing all separations. Homes, lives, human beings, bonded together seamlessly.

Three girls skipped down the street. They were nearly twelve, with lovely shining hair in delicate shades of black, blond, and honey brown. They took frisky strides, like colts, on long legs promising shapeliness.

"They control everything," one announced to the others, her

voice earnest and indignant. "Everything. They make you wear uniforms to school. They tell you how long your Shabbos dresses have to be . . . what to eat, what to say, what to think. . . . But there's one thing they can't control."

The other two girls looked at her breathlessly, waiting for some revelation.

"They can't tell you what socks to wear!"

"*Oh!* That is so not true!" Jenny shook her head. "You're wrong about that, Hadassah. They can tell you about socks, just like everything else."

"No they can't. As long as you cover your legs up to your knees, they can't say anything. You can wear any color, any style."

"So why doesn't Ohel Sara let us wear red tights, then?" Tamar asked, perplexed. She had lost so much weight in the last year that the idea of emphasizing her now slim legs was very tempting.

"They can't stop you! You can just tell them it's not the *halacha.*"

"*You* can tell them, Hadassah, but *I* can't." Jenny shook her head.

"You can get away with anything because of your father," Tamar chided.

"This has nothing to do with my father." Hadassah bristled. "This has to do with what's right. And as long as your feet are covered they have no control."

The three girls, their arms linked, walked briskly, studying their legs.

They wore summery dresses of bright floral prints, white tights, and hair barrettes. Their faces were earnest and lovely in the dappling shadows of the heavy trees that met over the roads like a bower.

"Don't look, don't look, *don't loook!! I will kill you if you look!*" Tamar hissed at Hadassah and Jenny.

"But he's looking at us!" Jenny protested, glancing across the street at the crowd of young Ruach Chaim yeshiva boys sauntering slowly up the avenue on their way to Sabbath afternoon Talmud lessons.

"Don't be such a creep, Tamar. Boys don't bite!" Hadassah said contemptuously, giving the fellow a sly once-over. "Uch, look at all those pimples!"

"Ah—" Jenny sucked in her breath. "He's going to cross the street, look!"

The girls glanced up at the young man in question. He was two or three years their senior, wearing a black suit and fedora. He was wavy haired and clear visioned but—alas!—destined for acne scars of monumental proportions. He did indeed seem to be changing directions, waiting on the corner for the light to change.

"Oh, I'll just die if he talks to us! What will we do?! What if somebody sees and tells our parents or one of our teachers!" Tamar said in a whispered shriek.

"Let's just go . . . run!" Jenny suggested.

With an abrupt about-face, they turned and took off at a pace that caused the staid matrons of Orchard Park to wrinkle their noses, bunch their mouths and shake their heads in disapproval.

Turning the corner, they sat down on the steps of Temple Emanuel, trying to catch their breath, to control their hysterical panicked giggling.

"What if he catches up?" Tamar asked anxiously.

"We could always go inside," Jenny suggested.

They looked up at the imposing doors of the Reform synagogue. Built in the early twenties to serve German Jewish immigrants who wanted above all else not to offend the gentiles, to put the word *respectable* in front of the word *Jew*, it was now a shameful oddity with a dwindling congregation in Orchard Park, where Hasidim proudly wore their dark coats and long *payot* and spoke to each other in Yiddish, totally contemptuous of outside opinions.

The girls had heard of, but had never dared see for themselves, the synagogue where men and women sat next to each other in the pews instead of decently separated by partitions; where an organ played music, desecrating the Sabbath; and where a beardless rabbi wore priestly robes and spoke in unaccented English.

"We couldn't hide in *there!*" Tamar protested, scandalized. "What if someone saw us?"

"So what?" Hadassah countered.

"What if your father found out?" Tamar asked. "Aren't you scared?"

"He won't," she answered confidently. "And I can always say I didn't know it was off limits, that I'm sorry." Her face fell easily into an oft used, well-practiced "I'm-a-good-girl-and-it-wasn't-my-fault" mode, lower teeth biting upper lip, eyes crinkling prettily with worry.

The other two stared at her, impressed.

"I don't know how you can lie to your father," Tamar said in amazement. " 'Honor your father and mother so you'll live a long life.' That's what the Torah says."

She hugged her knees. At the moment, she wanted to live a very long life. The world was such a beautiful place, full of such interesting things to see and do, new people to meet on every corner, the trees all budding, the flowers sweet! G-d had arranged everything in the world so pleasantly for those who followed his commandments. She wanted to live forever! Forever. Always in His protective shadow.

She settled her skirts modestly around her until they practically covered her ankles. She liked the pretty new dress, even though it was homemade and the material was an inexpensive cotton that didn't stand out half as far as Hadassah's taffeta or Jenny's blue sateen. At an abrupt point years past, Jenny had suddenly started wearing the loveliest clothes. She wondered again how her poor widowed mother managed it.

She tried not to be jealous. For some time now, her own mother had been scouring cheaper and cheaper stores for bargains to clothe her and Rivkie. For reasons her parents never discussed, money had long ceased to be that comfortable, taken-for-granted commodity that graced their lives with small luxuries.

But as she rested her chin on her kneetops, taking pleasure from the firmness of her own young bones, her joy stirred again. Nothing bothered her for long. She was in love with being alive. She felt well and happy in the knowledge that she was on the edge of womanhood, time sweeping her down like a white river rapid toward some fearsomely sweet embankment. Only the other day she had taken her dolls out to play and had held them at arm's length, puzzled that they had suddenly, without warning, turned into heavy, lifeless plastic. With a sense of frightening finality, she'd tossed them back onto her closet floor.

I'm such a pretty girl, she thought secretly, the knowledge of those soft breasts, growing like sweet new fruits beneath her childish dresses suddenly filling her with deep pride and pleasure. I like myself, I really do, she thought.

" 'Honor your father and mother'! There's a verse for everything!" Hadassah complained, stretching out her legs and examining her new white shoes, bought for Passover a month before. They had the tiniest heels, but enough to make all the other girls long with envy for the day their own parents would allow them to pass over the line from flats to heels, a passage as pivotal as any Bar Mitzvah.

Their own coming of age—that is, the legal age when the Torah and the community would hold them responsible for their own sins—was months away. They expected it to come and go with little fuss. A girl's Bas Mitzvah was a year earlier than a boy's and was routinely ignored. The boys, in contrast, got to stand before the entire congregation and read the Torah portion, to feel candies and mazel tovs rain down upon their heads, to dance to real bands and reap a cornucopia of gifts in noisy, crowded, expensive affairs held in catering halls.

This discrepancy was barely noticed by most religious Jewish girls, American feminism being years away from pointing it out to them. Their wedding would be their true coming-of-age celebration, as well as the first and last time they would be in the public eye.

"I don't see what you're making such a big *tsimmes* about," Hadassah pointed out. "After all, we're not going in to pray, just to hide, or maybe to look around. I mean, it's not like going into a church or worshiping idols, or anything."

"I don't think we should," Tamar said, shaking her head vehemently.

But just as the words came out of her mouth, a familiar acne-covered face turned the corner, his eyes seeking them out.

"Would you rather people see us talking to a boy? Come on!" Hadassah giggled, running up the steps and into the synagogue. Jenny and a reluctant Tamar followed close behind.

It was almost deserted, and except for the scuffing of their own measured footsteps, absolutely silent.

"Let's go into the shul part," Hadassah suggested.

"All right," Jenny agreed.

"Really, I don't think my *tateh* would like. . . ," Tamar protested weakly.

"Tamar, don't be such a baby!" Hadassah scolded her.

Not wanting to go home by herself when "a boy" was out there somewhere, Tamar reluctantly followed them.

The synagogue, with its enormous stained-glass windows and upholstered benches of polished oak, was a striking contrast to the *shteibels* Tamar prayed in—crowded, makeshift prayer groups set up in the living rooms and dens of local homes.

The girls stared at the muted colors of the filtered light, the lovely golden sheen of the oaken pews. They walked up the aisle toward the beautiful ark that held the Torah scrolls.

"Could you imagine sitting here and davening?" Jenny asked. "I mean, it's so quiet, and you could see everything . . . ."

"I wouldn't want to see what they do in a place like this!" Tamar said, piously resisting the temptation to be impressed by its beauty. "Just look at this siddur!" she gasped, scandalized, holding up a prayer book. "It's all in English! And all the prayers are changed. It sounds so *goyische*. I wonder if they've changed their Torahs, too?!"

"I'm sure the Torahs are the same. Nobody would dare do that! I'd love to open the ark and kiss one!" Jenny exclaimed.

"Why would you want to do that?" Hadassah gasped,

flabbergasted. "Besides, girls aren't allowed to touch the ark or the Torahs." Her voice took on an uncharacteristic tone of haughty piety.

"You're so funny, Hadassah! One minute you're leading us up the steps and telling us how you'll lie to your father, and the next you're preaching to us like some *tzdakis*," Jenny said puzzled, but without malice.

Hadassah went scarlet. "I'm not a *tzdakis!* I just don't know why you'd want to . . . I mean, I live right on top of my father's synagogue. I could do it any time. But why would I?"

"Why not?" Jenny challenged her. "Aren't girls worthy enough to touch the ark, to kiss the Torah, the way the men do? Why do we always have to be closed off from it, to be kept so far away? Where's it written?" she demanded.

They stared at her speechlessly. Jenny was always taking them by surprise, questioning things they both took for granted.

For Tamar, who accepted her religion and enjoyed it the way a French child accepts wine instead of milk with his meals, this attitude made no sense. Religion was like breathing, she thought. It was not something to question. It was something to get used to, to accept blindly. Seeing how things were done in her family and community was enough. There was no point in asking the why of any of their practices. If she did, there would always be some long, involved explanation that would bore her to tears. You either did what you were supposed to or you secretly, guiltily, didn't.

"I don't know where it's written, but everybody knows a girl can't go near the ark or touch the Torah."

"You don't mean touch," Tamar corrected her. "My mother always kisses her pinkie, then sticks it through the partition to touch the Torah when it passes by. . . ."

"Okay. But I mean to hold it, like with both hands, like a man, or to go up to the ark and stand there. . . ."

"I always did when I was little," Tamar remembered.

"Well, that's when you were a baby, so it doesn't count," Hadassah hedged, uncomfortable in her sudden role as religious mentor. She was much happier being the bad girl and having the others lecture her. But somehow the idea of going up to the ark and touching the Torah appalled her in a way she couldn't explain.

"It was so nice! I used to sit on my father's lap during the whole davening . . . until I was five or six." Tamar remembered wistfully, recalling those lovely days of being only touching distance away from the Torah scrolls, of hearing the voice of the hazan so easily and seeing her father's face so clearly. Now, banished to the women's section, however she craned her neck and drew aside the curtains, she could only catch a pale glimpse of those glories for which she had once had a front row seat.

"Well, if you can't tell me where it says you can't, then I'm going to do it," Jenny informed them, taking long, deliberate steps down the aisle toward the ark.

"You shouldn't! What if Hadassah's right? G-d might punish you!" Tamar wrung her hands. But Hadassah only watched, a strange look of fear and puzzlement on her face.

Jenny walked to the end, climbing the steep carpeted steps until she reached the platform that held the imposing, gilt-framed ark. She pulled back the gold-embroidered velvèt curtain, sliding open the wooden doors. Inside, it shone like a precious treasure hoard, light bursting from the silver-and-gold ornaments, burning against the scarlet-and-green velvet scroll covers. The faint light of the eternal lamp that swung gently above cast strange shadows along the inner walls. She clasped the nearest scroll, hugging it to her. It felt warm and good, almost human in her arms. Again and again she kissed it.

Hadassah watched, feeling a sudden ache as a flood of poignant memories washed over her: following her father up to the *bimah* as he lifted the Torah before the congregation; burying her facc in his tallis, feeling the tickle of the fringes over her cheeks. She couldn't have been more than a tiny child of three or four. By the time she was in kindergarten, she had already been banished to the women's section. And the more she grew toward womanhood, the more he continued to distance himself from her, as if growth itself were somehow tainting.

"It's so beautiful! Why don't you both come closer?"

Hadassah shook her head vehemently.

Tamar, on the other hand, found herself stumbling slowly down the long aisle, propelled by something she couldn't explain. She climbed the steps in a dream, her heart pounding as she neared the holy ark she had seen only from a distance for so many years. As she climbed the steps, her face grew hot.

She stared inside the open ark. It was like nothing she had ever seen or even imagined. It was not just the ornamentation. It was the idea of approaching the holiest of holies, the spot on earth closest to G-d. This idea made her tremble.

"Go on. Hold one!" Jenny smiled encouragingly.

She felt her body freeze. She was just a girl. What right did she have to put her arms around such a holy object? But then she remembered Simchat Torah, the holiday when all the Torah scrolls were taken out of the ark by the men and boys and danced around the synagogue. Jonathan Markowitz, a boy two years younger than she who picked his nose and wiped it on the wall, had been handed a Torah to hold. He had not felt unworthy. He had clasped it to his chest.

She reached out timidly, touching the velvet scroll cover, tracing the thick gold embroidery. Then she moved closer, breathing in the slightly acidic smell of the leather scrolls, the warm, musty scent of the rich fabrics. She put both hands around the scroll and leaned her cheek against it, closing her eyes and feeling a strange quiet contentment wrap itself around her heart.

"Somebody's coming!" Hadassah called out in a panic.

Quickly, they closed the ark, running out into the spring sunshine.

"You two are really nuts!" Hadassah glared, unreasonably upset. "I mean, of all the crazy, dumb things to do . . ."

Tamar and Jenny walked slowly behind her, lost in thought, feeling weak and strangely elated, as if they'd spent a whole day in fasting and prayer.

"I'm home," Jenny called out. She could hear the TV blaring and her mother banging pots in the kitchen and singing. The change from the sublime to the ordinary almost broke her heart.

"Have a nice time with your little friends, honey?"

"Yes, Ma. Ma?"

"Come into the kitchen. I'll make you something to eat."

She sat on the kitchen stool, watching her mother turn on the gas and light the stove. "Ma," she began hesitantly. "You know, you really . . . it's wrong. You shouldn't be lighting a fire on the Sabbath. It's a terrible sin. I mean, people used to get stoned to death for lighting a fire on the Sabbath."

Her mother looked at her, taking a long drag on her cigarette. "Don't you start in with me, young lady! Don't you start with all that fanatic stuff! I'll take you out of that crazy school faster than a jet plane!"

"Ma!"

"Look, you know the only reason I sent you there to begin with was so you'd have better teachers, nice little Jewish girlfriends. But don't you start acting crazy on me!"

"But it's not crazy. You just don't understand."

"So explain it to me. I'm listening."

"Well, the Bible says that six days you should work and the seventh you should rest."

"Well, I'm not working. I'm relaxing. I'm enjoying myself. And if I cook up a meal or go to the beach, that's not work. Let me *tell* you, honey—work is typing those damn briefs. Work is filing those mountains of carbon copies that stink to high heaven in those horrible gray metal filing cabinets. That's work."

"But it's not that. Ma, do you believe in G-d?"

Her mother lowered the light under the frying pan and cracked the eggs with thoughtful care. "I don't really know. Maybe. Okay, yes. Let's say yes."

"So do you believe He made the world?"

"Okay, for argument's sake, let's say yes."

"And everything He made was good, right?"

"I suppose." Her mother smiled, thinking of a few things

she could live without, like roaches and mice and dust, and her fat, disgusting boss Mr. Arnell.

"Well then, He made the Sabbath day. He says not to light fires or cook, or . . . well there's a whole bunch of things," she said, flustered, finding it impossible to repeat the very complicated explanation for all the minute do's and don'ts of the Sabbath day she had learned in Ohel Sara. Jenny really didn't know how the don'ts translated into such a special day. She only knew that once you started doing things, ordinary things, like cooking or watching TV, the plug was pulled and the Sabbath feeling drained away, leaving behind an ordinary hot Saturday morning, full of cartoons and cigarette smoke.

"I know it sounds silly. But you're supposed to do what He tells you to do. You're not supposed to make deals and think up your own ideas. He's giving you this great gift, a day off to be with Him. And if you don't keep it, then it's like throwing it back in His face."

Her mother stared at her.

"Ma, my friends and their parents have so much fun, and it's so beautiful. They light candles and drink wine and dress up. It's so, so quiet and clean and nice. I like it better than anything. Couldn't you try?"

"So how do they eat if they don't cook? And what do they do all day? Sit home?"

"They cook the day before and make so much they never have to worry about what to eat. All the best foods—lots of cakes and roast chicken and potato and noodle puddings and big desserts. And they stay home but not all day. They go to the synagogue in the morning, and then eat lunch—the whole family together—singing, telling stories. And then they go to classes or rest or read. And the kids play games and drink soda and have fun. Beaches are so noisy and crowded, and the subways and buses are so dusty. . . ."

"You're happy?" her mother asked her, puzzled and strangely touched. Most kids were so silly. She was proud her daughter even thought about such things. But also defensive. It made her nervous.

"I like it, Ma. Come with me to synagogue once, please?"

"I don't know. It's my day off. I don't know any of those people. . . ."

"You know Hadassah's father!"

"I don't know him. I only met him once, that time . . . you remember." It was an uncomfortable subject.

"Well, Tamar's parents are nice. You'd like them. Come with me once. You'll see. It's fun."

"Hmm. We'll see," her mother answered, calmly scrambling the eggs.

They tried it the following week. And never again. Once was enough for Ida Douglas.

❖12❖

It started with Elvis. Ed Sullivan tried valiantly to focus his cameras on Elvis's face, but the girls in the live studio audience focused on his hips, and girls all over America (and their mothers, who were not as disapproving as they seemed) hated Ed Sullivan. And although the adults pursed their lips and shook their heads, secretly they too were glad, bored with the sunshiny, miniature-marshmallow-and-Jell-O upbeat fifties, which had come to seem like a long, wearingly optimistic commercial for new refrigerators.

They were happy to see the era begin to crumble, glad to have someone like Elvis to bring it down. The era of fathers in white shirts and respectable hats with suit jackets slung over their tired shoulders as they made their way home to little suburban tract houses on commuter trains; the era of mothers in aprons who were dull and pleasant and smelled of cookie dough and Ajax; the era of dress codes in public high schools, where boys wore ties and girls skirts and blouses. The era began to fade as subtly and silently as photographs in a picture album.

In 1960 the American people said good-bye to their balding, gray-haired general and his dowdy wife and turned over the keys of the nation to a relative youngster. Handsome, charming and dark haired, with a stylish First Lady and a beautiful child, John F. Kennedy fertilized expectations that bloomed—depending on your point of view—like wildflowers or like dangerous weeds, all over the staid, carefully cultivated Republican lawns.

The residents of Orchard Park also felt some of that wild

119

spring growth, but reserved judgment, viewing Kennedy the way their tradition had advised them to judge any man claiming to be the Messiah: Wait and see. If he was the Messiah, he would bring about the world's final redemption. If he didn't, then he wasn't. It was really very simple.

So they waited to see if Kennedy would be good for the Jews or bad for the Jews. Would he be for merit, against quotas in jobs and education? Would he keep Christ out of public classrooms and government ceremonies? Would he preserve the social order, laws, and bylaws, by which Jews felt themselves protected from the hostile goy? But most of all, would he support the little sapling state of Israel, planted in the desert, surrounded by woodcutters?

And then Kennedy was killed.

Aaron Gottlieb hung heavily on the subway strap of the overheated, rush-hour IRT express train. He felt the sweat pouring down his forehead from beneath his respectable black felt hat and wondered whether he would manage to keep his balance if he let go to wipe his brow. The train lurched, the wheels screeching against the old metal rails, filling the air with the smell of burning rubber and filthy hot metal.

Better not, he thought. Better wait. Maybe someone would get off and he'd be able to sit down, and then he'd use both hands to take out a handkerchief and lift the hat brim to wipe his face and neck properly. But as station after station whizzed past and the stops in between brought a crush of new passengers who squeezed him between them in a way that hardly seemed possible, he began to lose hope that the near future held anything better. Hardly able to move, he began to regret not having taken the chance earlier of locking his briefcase between his legs and using one free hand to tend to his need.

What was going to happen? he thought hopelessly, the sweat gathering in his eyebrows and dripping down the sides of his face. Kennedy was dead. He still could not believe it. Gunmen, murderers. In America. In America. Blood again, on the young widow's pretty suit. Blood on the streets. In

America. He shook his head. Thought, different people. A different place. But that is the way it started in Germany, too. The Jews so comfortable, so assimilated. And then the murders. The political murders. He felt his heart racing ahead in fear. This is the way it begins. Kennedy, then Oswald, then Ruby. On television, they showed it. Murders on American television. In America. He felt his heart begin to beat, heavy against his ribs. Loud and lumbering, like heavy feet running down a staircase.

He looked down at his watch to see how much longer the ride would last. Then his mind wandered and he looked around at the people near him, searching out their watches. If only he had gone with the watches instead of with perfume. He sniffed the rancid air filled with the sweating vapors of too many tired bodies. Perfume was a luxury.

He thought of the black and red numbers on the papers in his black briefcase. How much longer could he go on? Orders were down to almost nothing.

A mistake, a real mistake. America. The Goldena Medina.

He felt his knees begin to buckle and with a great effort, he stiffened them. He thought of the wallpaper in the kitchen, all stained and peeling. Ruth kept patching things up, pasting down the frayed edges, scrubbing off the dark spots. But it was just a matter of time until they went from respectable middle class to shabby poverty. They were skirting the edge already.

He could live with that, but Ruth . . . the girls. . . .

He closed his eyes, suddenly transported to another train on a track thousands of miles and a lifetime away.

It was the summer after the war had ended, staggering to a strange, disorganized close that had left millions stunned, wandering in the direction of homes that no longer existed. The railroad train rumbled on its old tracks, its aisles and seats a human carpet of agonizingly thin refugees flooding from Poland back to Czechoslovakia. She was sitting near the window, her chin in her hand, her auburn hair thick around her painfully thin face, her long-sleeved blouse rolled up to her elbows, revealing the blue tattoo of numbers on her arm.

He glanced at her for a second, struck by the modesty of her outfit among the women in sleeveless summer shifts. He watched the horrid blue dance of the numbers. A religious girl, he thought, aching. What she must have gone through.

He was on his way home, or what was left of it. Word had reached him through that network of friends and relatives that his wife and two small children had been taken early in the German occupation along with the rest of the Jews of Usti. The end of the story had come in a rush from a distant relative. How his wife had held their baby daughter in her arms on the platform in Auschwitz, and how their three-year-old son had held on to his mother's skirt crying and how she had bent down to dry his tears and had nearly fallen over.

Menashe Goldman, a cousin from a different town who'd been picked up months before, had been on the platform to help herd the Jews into trucks that would take them to the gas chambers. He'd recognized Genya Gottlieb and helped her lift her son onto the truck and she had thanked him.

"We weren't allowed to talk to the newcomers. Germans would shoot you on the spot if they caught you. But I told her anyway. I told her . . . begged her . . . to leave the children and to go back to the selection. She was still young."

Even now, so many years later, he could still hear the man's voice crack with emotion as he spoke. "But she didn't seem to hear me. There was nothing I could do. . . ." The tortured voice of the man, long dead, rose up inside the subway car like a ghostly echo. Wife and children, lost forever in a moment of telling. The man had wept, and Aaron had comforted him.

So there was nothing left to go back to. Just the wood and metal and fabrics that were his belongings and which he somehow wanted to see again. Also, he could not think of anyplace else to go. And in the back of his mind he thought: Maybe. . . , just maybe Goldman was wrong. Maybe some miracle. Maybe someone would have heard something, would know something. A further telling in which maybe Genya had left the children after all and had worked her way through the war in some factory complex in Auschwitz.

He knew the idea was preposterous. There was no way

Genya would have left the children. But still, a small shred of hope. (Was that what it was called, to wish your two children had been left by their mother to be murdered among strangers? he thought. What other word would you use? And what else can a person do but hope for life, however partial, however tainted?)

And so he'd taken the first train.

He looked up at the subway billboard, at the smiling, bleached-blond secretary who was this month's Miss Subways. A pretty girl, he thought, his bones aching.

He got off the train in Usti with only a handful of others. The rest of the passengers were traveling on to larger cities and towns where there were refugee agencies and soup kitchens. Here there was only a small relief agency room staffed with medical supplies and food, a few beds and toilets.

His hometown. He saw again the grove of poplars near the soccer field and heard the shouts of the students of the gymnasium echo through the green fields. Young boys together, Jew and gentile together. They were the boys he'd grown up with. Alex, the baker's redheaded boy, and fun-loving Karel, the ironmonger's intelligent eldest, his best friend. They all went to the cinema together and dreamed of wearing a white straw hat like Fred Astaire and dancing with some lovely young lady in a filmy ball gown.

They'd all been drafted together into the Czech army. But when the Nazis took over, they'd been separated, the Jews going into units that provided slave labor to the advancing Hungarian troops, the gentiles remaining with their unit. The Hungarians had put them into open cattle cars in subfreezing weather with no food or drink for two days. Cold like that. Never even imagine such a thing. Like sitting in an ice bath naked for a week. Oddly enough, it was a German soldier who'd saved him, just some private who happened to be on the same train platform. "Please, we are soldiers too. We are cold. Could you get us some hot coffee?" How had he had the courage to ask such a thing from a German soldier standing on a train platform? A soldier with a gun? And why had the soldier returned with a whole thermos of boiling hot coffee when he must have known they were Jews?

They were gentlemen, some of those German soldiers, much more than the Hungarians or the Ukrainians. . . . Strange.

He must have been cold too, that German soldier straggling back from Stalingrad.

The smell came back to him of dark pine trees, unpruned apple and pear orchards, budding wildly in the spring air. He left the train platform and walked on foot toward the town.

There was the tree beneath which he and Genya had first held hands. Soft buds, pink and green and yellow. Soft young hands, yielding and yet alive with resistance, with personal need. She'd rumpled his hair and made him laugh.

Genya, of the dark blond hair and flashing dark eyes. Genya, the warm, young body in the white wedding gown, circling him seven times beneath the wedding canopy held up at four corners by her four brothers. Genya, Genya.

He walked quickly toward the village and up the dirt path toward the small house with the familiar cast-iron door handle in the shape of a tail Karel had given him with a wink the day before his wedding. He'd had such trouble attaching it. Finally Karel had simply soldered it on. He touched the melted part of the metal where the soldering iron had done its work. The door handle had survived. Even the plants (Genya's roses, her potato patch) bloomed, no worse for the years between in which the whole world had reveled in an orgy of red, bloody slaughter. . . . The door handle was fine. The earth, unvaryingly fertile.

He knocked on the door. An unfamiliar woman answered, opening it slowly. When he told her who he was, she let the door go and threw her apron over her head with a sob, running out the back door.

The living room was filled with strange bare wooden pieces he did not recognize. Except for the hand-stitched pillow on the couch and a few vases and pictures, he recognized nothing as belonging to him. He picked up the pillow and traced the fine, small stitches in red and green thread in the pattern of a single rose. He remembered the small, childish white hands holding the tiny needle, the way the hands would fall on the full, pregnant belly to rest, the belly that had held his first-born son, Benjamin.

Strangers crowded around the door, and the woman in the apron returned with her husband and others. Their suspicious, frightened eyes darted toward the pillow in his hands. Only one of them he recognized: Vladek Kushner, whose family had always lived down the street and whose younger brother had been one grade below him at the gymnasium.

"Aaron!" Vladek said, extending his hand sorrowfully.

Had he been one of those who had stood at their doors laughing and clapping as the Germans rounded up Genya, Benjamin, and little Rivka? His wife and his children? Oh, yes, that is what they did, those friends and neighbors. Stood by their doors and laughed. Enough people had survived to remember and to tell. He looked at Vladek's hand, wondering. But then, he'd taken it. It was not in his nature to refuse friendship.

"Tell them it is my house, Vladek."

There was silence. "These are cousins from Slovania. They mean no harm."

"They are living in my house, the home of my wife and children . . ."

"The house was empty!" the woman protested. "We found nothing here. It was filthy, neglected. We took care of it." Her voice rose.

And who emptied it? he thought, but did not say, because he did not want to hear excuses and see the faces turn hard. Because he felt a sudden deep hatred of which he was not particularly proud. So instead he said in his soft, gentle way, "You needn't worry. I have not come back to live here. I simply want my things."

"We found nothing. . . . The house was empty of everything when we came. I swear!" the woman screamed and pleaded.

Aaron walked through the house, filling his arms with his belongings and then walked out the front door and dumped them on the ground in a great pile. And each time he went back, a few more people had gathered around to watch.

"You see that house down there, that's Malek's house. He

took your bedroom set," an older woman told him with malicious pleasure. "What are you going to do about it?"

"And the Husaks took the china closet and the wardrobe," someone else called out to him. And all of a sudden everyone was surrounding him, telling him the details of the pillaging, the carrion eating.

"Does anyone have a wagon? Just for the afternoon, to load all my things? I will give you a good price," Aaron suddenly asked.

"I will bring you one," offered a man he didn't recognize.

They arranged to meet in the evening in front of the tavern.

Like a general with orders, he went mechanically and methodically from house to house, loading the tables and chairs, the cabinets and hope chests, the mirrors and silver candlesticks, ignoring the protests of the outraged housewives who had come to think of these things as their own, staring coldly into the averted and guilty eyes of the men, some of whom he knew.

They had been his friends and neighbors.

By the time he climbed up into the wagon, it was early evening. He sat behind the reins for a long time, uncertain about what to do next, until lengthening shadows flung themselves greedily over the wagon, distorting all his familiar belongings into strange, sinister shapes.

He sat there a long time, watching the moon rise over the village of his boyhood, the same moon he had seen on his way home from the cinema, the same moon that had cast its lovely, silver glow over him and a young woman as they'd held hands beneath the old, fragrant trees.

But it was not the same. *Nothing.* . . . The word stuck in his mind, refusing to be part of a sentence. Nothing, he thought, a great wave of exhaustion, disgust and despair draining him of all his life forces. So tired. Could you be so tired and still be alive? He knew you could, because he had walked to Siberia with rags on his feet, sleeping as he walked. He had lived through that. He was suddenly sorry he had not simply lain down in the snow like so many others. He had lived for one thought: Genya, the children. To see them again.

But now . . . nothing.

But because he'd promised to return the wagon and the man was waiting for it, he slapped the reins and got the horses moving. The man was standing outside.

"Where do you want to unload?" he asked, but before he could answer, a voice called out his name. He turned.

At first, he didn't see anything familiar about the old man, but then he suddenly recognized him.

"Manik?"

"Yes."

He was the barber. How many times had he sat on that old chair smelling of peppermint and cigar smoke, those large, kind hands turning his head this way and that? Once, when he was a little boy, he remembered crying and being given a large piece of rock candy.

And suddenly everything fell into place. "Here, Manik. Take everything." He hugged him and handed him the reins, then he turned his back and walked toward the train station, taking only the small bag he'd come with.

He went into the transit station and took a piece of bread and a bowl of soup. She was sitting nearby, the young woman with the thick auburn hair and the modest blouse.

"You look tired," she said hesitantly, like a woman who is not accustomed to speaking to strangers.

"You are not from here. Why did you get off the train?" he asked her.

"I . . ." She blushed. "I had some stomach trouble and needed to be near a bathroom."

The blush, the idea that such delicacy had survived, made him want to weep.

She ran her fingers nervously over the collar of her blouse. He could see that it had been scrubbed and bleached and starched and ironed. She had taken time to do it. It had been important to her. If she could do that, after all she'd been through . . . If she could still care about that . . .

It was at that moment he fell in love with her and decided to live. To build a new home that would be filled with lovely new things: closets full of beautiful, new clothes, new furniture, and new children.

They were married ten months later with two other couples in one of those quick, mass weddings so common among grieving survivors after the war. The ceremony had taken place in some Czechoslovakian town along the train route neither one had ever heard of. They began again, a new apartment, a small factory making buttons. Rivkie's birth. A small new life to fill the emptiness in those closed chambers of his heart he couldn't bear to open.

Then the communists had taken over, grabbing him one day on his way to work, forcing him to help build a new munitions factory. The very same night, he wrote to relatives in Brooklyn to sponsor them for American immigration quotas. They'd put their names on the list, and two years later their number had come up.

He gave the key of his thriving little business to one of his workers and walked away, never looking back. Another start. A new language. A new country. A new struggle to earn a living.

Aaron Gottlieb opened his eyes. Newrose Avenue. His stop. He felt the cool outdoor air touch his wet face, drying his sweat-filled clothes as he stepped onto the outdoor platform. He shifted his briefcase from arm to arm. It was suddenly so heavy, he wasn't sure he could carry it all the way home. He suddenly felt he had no strength left.

Dinner was on the table when he walked in.

"Go, darling. Take a shower. We'll wait for you," Ruth urged him, taking his jacket and briefcase.

He held her briefly around the waist, feeling the familiar, pliant give of her flesh beneath his hand. She smelled so clean. He suddenly didn't want to touch her, as if his unhappiness were something unclean and contaminating.

The shower revived his body but not his spirit, which lay upon him like a heavy winter blanket on a hot summer night.

After dinner Rivkie disappeared. When she came back, she was wearing a beautiful new suit.

"*Tateh,*" she said hesitantly with a big smile, "what do you think?"

He looked up from his paper at his pretty teenage daughter in the rose-colored suit. She looked lovely. And the suit looked very expensive.

"You went shopping?" He looked at Ruth, who bit her lower lip.

"I didn't mean to." Rivkie smiled. "I was just in the city and found myself in Abraham and Straus, and they had this reduced rack. . . . Oh, *Tateh,* it's pure wool, a real Pendleton, and it's three-piece—two skirts and a jacket, so it's really like two outfits for the price of one. . . ."

"How much did it cost, *maideleh?*" he asked calmly, his heart sinking.

"Now, Aaron," Ruth placated him, "she needs clothes, and she has been good about not shopping so much lately. . . ."

"How much?" Aaron Gottlieb asked patiently, closing his eyes.

"It was reduced from seventy-five dollars!" Rivkie said with clear-eyed triumph, though her voice was still a little anxious.

"Rivkie!"

"It cost fifty dollars," she whispered, fiddling with the buttons, averting her eyes.

"*Fifty dollars!*" Dresses cost $15.99—$20.00 was already expensive. But *fifty dollars!?* It was an enormous amount of money. Beads of perspiration sprang up like a crown of thorns around his head.

"I know it sounds like a lot of money, *Tateh,* but just feel the quality," Rivkie said in a sweet, wheedling voice, moving quickly and taking his hand to rub against the fine new fabric. "Aren't you always telling us that it pays to buy good quality, that in the long run it saves money? I mean, I'll get so much use out of this, and Tamar will have it next."

The fact that Tamar was already two sizes larger than Rivkie did not seem to figure in these calculations. And since

Aaron Gottlieb had no idea about women's sizes, he didn't ask.

"What did you pay with?" he asked softly.

"Well, I gave her some money for clothes I'd been saving," Ruth answered reluctantly.

"But that was for you! To buy yourself something, wasn't it? Weren't you saving that for yourself? To buy yourself something new, Ruth?" He felt a lump in his throat.

"Me?" She laughed a little ruefully. "What do I need new *schmattes* for? Rivkie needs clothes. She's a *kallah moide*."

"She's only sixteen, Ruth. She's not getting married tomorrow."

"Oh, but you know the busy tongues, you know what it is. She doesn't dress nice, already there's talk, there's trouble. Already the phone doesn't ring so fast with *shidduchim*. It's not too early to worry, Aaron, believe me."

He believed her. He wiped his brow with the back of his hand. The salty perspiration stung his torn cuticles.

"Come, *mamaleh*, turn around, show us again how beautiful," Ruth urged her daughter.

Rivkie obliged willingly.

That night Aaron Gottlieb had a strange dream. "Here is a letter," Ruth told him in his dream, handing him a large white envelope. "Deliver it or the children will die. I will die." She was wearing a tattered pair of his old army pants, an old shirt with a strangely white, starched collar. He found himself walking down a long corridor with no exits. He felt a sense of urgency that made him walk at a pace far too fast for him, so that he had a feeling of exhaustion and resentment. He wasn't sure where he was walking to, and suddenly he was. He was supposed to find something. He was alone, but the thing he was supposed to find, it was not for himself. Ruth was waiting for it, and the girls. He began to push himself, but the faster he walked, the longer the corridor became, with no end in sight.

Then all at once he spied a door, and a sense of relief coursed through him. If he could just reach the door, he would be able to get what it was they were waiting for, and he could rest.

The door loomed closer and closer. He reached out to touch the handle, and the moment he touched it, he remembered the letter Ruth had given him. But it was not there anymore, and he didn't know where in the corridor he had dropped it. Now they would all die, and it would be his fault.

He wept, large gulping sobs that woke his wife. She shook him gently, than harshly, with a frightened urgency.

"Aaron, what is it? A bad dream, darling? . . . Darling! What!?"

But he couldn't stop. He wept and wept and wept.

Tamar and Rivkie came running in. They stood at the door of their parents' bedroom, appalled.

"*Go back to sleep girls!*" Ruth screamed at them.

"*Mameh*, what's the matter with *Tateh?*" Tamar ran to her, putting her arms around her mother's slim shoulders. "*Mameh, Mameh*. It's Tamar. What's wrong?"

"A bad dream, that's all," Ruth murmured, her eyes stunned.

"Call a doctor, *Mameh*," Rivkie pleaded.

"*No!* No one must see him like this! He wouldn't want that. Please girls, if you want to help, go to sleep. I will take care of your father. Go now. Go!" she commanded them.

The sisters looked at each other, and then at their weeping father and frightened mother. They didn't want to leave. But out of long ingrained habit of doing their parents' bidding even when it went against their own ideas and desires (they were good Ohel Sara girls), they did what they were told.

"I will take care of you, my darling," Ruth said, moving close to him beneath the warm blankets. Wordlessly she put her arms around him as if he were a frightened child. "Sha, sha, sha," she crooned, rocking him in her arms.

Still, he could not stop weeping.

"Not so loud, my darling. Sha. The neighbors will hear."

❈13❈

Orchard Park, 1964

"Three little maids from seminary," Jenny sang. "We don't smoke and we don't chew and we don't talk to boys who do!"

"We don't drink and we don't smoke and we don't go with boys who're broke," Tamar called out, collapsing with giggles on Jenny's bed.

"Wait, wait, listen to this one," Hadassah commanded them. "We don't make out and we don't dance, and we like men who wear tight pants!"

"I'm not going to sing that!" Tamar said piously.

"That's over the line, Hadass, come on. . . . " Jenny shook her head. Hadassah looked at her and then at Tamar, and they all collapsed in hysterics.

It was a warm Sunday in July. Already the heat was rising from the Brooklyn pavement like some invisible sea creature, its warm, thick tentacles winding around them, taking their breath away. Sunday afternoons at Jenny's. They'd made a ritual of it that summer they were fifteen, before their sophomore year in high school. Behind those closed doors they could do anything they wanted with no parental supervision, since Jenny's mother didn't count as a parent as far as Hadassah and Tamar were concerned. Used to the relentless iron chisel of parental sculpting, they viewed the easygoing, mutual respect between Jenny and her mother with wistful fascination and envy. Often, Ida Douglas was gone altogether, taking Jenny's younger brother to visit relatives or the planetarium or down to the beach in the Rockaways. So that

132

summer Jenny spent Shabbos at Hadassah's or Tamar's, and they came to her the next day.

Sundays at Jenny's. They'd put on their first curlers, tried their first eyelash-curling mascara. They'd practiced painting each other's faces with enough cheap makeup from Woolworth's to hide the wrinkles of a dowager, let alone the pretty, clear complexions of young teenage girls.

The image would come back to Tamar later, so strong and sweet. Jenny, her hair in little pink bundles all over her head, and Hadassah on her back, her toenails wriggling in the air as the red nail polish dried, while she, Tamar, changed the records on the record player. *"Wake upa, little Suzy, wake up."*

And the guitars moving in, strong and as virilely insistent as the picture of the heavenly Everly Brothers on the single record cover jacket bought for twenty-eight cents (four singles for a dollar) in bins at Woolworth's.

And then Neil Sedaka's sweet high tenor: *"Breakin' up is hard to oooo oooo do. . . . "*

Jenny was the first one to hear of the mop-headed English boys.

"What's that supposed to mean, Beatles?" Hadassah argued with her. "As far as I'm concerned, Elvis is still king."

She was the only one who really liked Elvis anymore, which Jenny and Tamar couldn't understand, since both of them had always found Elvis too much of a *shegetz* to get excited over. With his long, greasy hair and black leather jacket, he was just too much like those Italian kids in Newrose diners who beat up Ruach Chaim yeshiva boys on their way home from school. But of course, since Hadassah couldn't keep her Elvis records at home, she always wanted to play them again and again on Sundays.

Paul McCartney, however, in his neat, if longish, haircut and suits and ties, was nice enough to fantasize over, even though he wore no skullcap, a definite problem. Jenny tried to convince Hadassah, but Hadassah just laughed and wiggled her toes. "Elvis," she'd tell them, "is the King." And then she'd jump up on the bed, wiggling her hips in a wonderful, banned-for-television imitation.

Tamar and Jenny rolled on the floor, and the unpleasant old Polish man downstairs banged on the ceiling with his broom handle.

"Nobody dances like that anymore, Hadassah! They do this thing called the twist and something else called the frug and the swim. . . . You keep your feet in one place and kind of move your hips like . . ." Jenny gave them a demonstration.

"They don't do it that way on *American Bandstand!*" protested Hadassah, who eagerly studied the dancers when the show played on televisions displayed in the storefronts of appliance stores on Fourteenth Avenue.

"Dick Clark is out, Murry the K is in. He's this disc jockey . . ." Jenny went into a long explanation, trying to bring the other two up-to-date on what was happening in the World Outside Orchard Park.

Jenny's house was the refuge, the place to join the planet for a little while, to get off the dizzying satellite that was Orchard Park, where the only singing group recognized was a group of nice yeshiva boys called the Yeshiva Boys (how'd they ever think of such a wild name? Hadassah wanted to know), who sang verses from the Bible and commentaries of very fine spiritual value with rousing Hasidic melodies they made up themselves. All the girls in Orchard Park were secretly in love with the members of the Yeshiva Boys. All except Hadassah.

"They look like such goody-goodies. Like they go to bed at ten and let their momma tuck them in," she said, taking a sophisticated drag on a pencil and blowing the imaginary smoke up to the ceiling with half-lidded, sleepy eyes.

"I don't know. They look pretty neat to me," Tamar protested.

"Nobody says 'neat' anymore," Jenny informed her.

"What do you mean? Are you sure?" Hadassah asked curiously. Like a desert plant thirsting for any drop of moisture to keep going, Hadassah thirsted for information. Without regular access to newspapers or television or movies, her slang, her knowledge of the latest teenage fads were hopelessly outdated and she knew it. By the time an expression or fad filtered down to Orchard Park, the rest of the country had long discarded it. "So what should she say?"

" 'Cool' or 'hip,' " Jenny suggested.

" 'Cool'? But what does that mean?" Hadassah wanted to know.

"It means the latest thing that's going on," Jenny explained.

Hadassah hoarded the information jealously. She didn't dare challenge Jenny, who was not only—as far as she knew—the only girl in Orchard Park allowed to take the train to Manhattan all by herself, but also enrolled in Greenwich Village art classes. Hadassah was hardly allowed to go to the corner by herself. Even visiting Jenny was an anomaly, something her mother adamantly opposed. It was, oddly, her father's strange insistence that had allowed the visits to continue. "Poor orphans are the true home of the Torah. Whoever shuns them, shuns the Creator himself," he'd tell her mother, pushing the rebbetzin into paroxysms of silent aggravation.

"Well, the Yeshiva Boys look pretty cool to me. Especially Benjamin."

"Oh, Ben-ja-min," the other two girls sighed, clutching their chests in mock devotion.

"Why, what's wrong with him?" Tamar said, aggrieved.

"Why, nothing is wrong if you like nice yeshiva boys with dark raincoats and black-rimmed glasses and super short hair . . ." Hadassah mocked.

"I do!" Tamar said innocently, the sarcasm, as usual, lost on her.

"How can you?! They're so boring!" Hadassah exclaimed, abandoning subtlety. "They look exactly the same. I can't even tell one from the other."

"I think Benjamin looks very nice. Very pale. Like he sits inside and studies all day."

"Give me a tan and long hair!" Jenny sang out.

"And sideburns, not *payess!*" Hadassah screamed. "You can do anything, but get *off* of my blue suede shoes," she sang at passing cars, hanging out of Jenny's window.

"Did you hear what happened to Esther?" Tamar asked.

"Mrs. Kravitz caught her talking to a boy, so what?" Hadassah said listlessly. Anything to do with rabbis and rebbetzins and Ohel Sara bored her.

"My mother knows her mother. Her mother's shaved off all of Esther's hair."

Jenny and Hadassah stared at Tamar in horror.

"You're making it up!" Hadassah accused.

"No, I'm not. You just see tomorrow. I bet she won't come to school at all."

"I want to tell you something else. Mrs. Kravitz told Esther if she does it again, she'll be expelled. And . . ." She hesitated.

"Come on!" the girls screamed.

"I don't know. It sounds so terrible to say it."

"*Say it!*" they both screamed. The irritated Pole banged on the ceiling.

"Mrs. Kravitz told Esther: 'Why would a man want to buy an opened bottle of soda?' "

The girls sat quietly, letting the meaning of the phrase break over them like a wave. They began to scream in delight and anguish. "She didn't!"

"Okay, don't believe me. But that's what Esther said."

"That is so disgusting!" Hadassah giggled, glancing at Jenny, who also started giggling.

"I just don't see what's funny about it," Tamar complained. "You just don't take things seriously enough. It's our lives . . ."

"Oh, Tamar, what are you worried about? Your husband will get a new bottle. . . ."

Jenny took the pillow and threw it at Hadassah, and then Tamar hesitantly picked one up and did the same, a big grin covering her face.

"You're messing me up!" Hadassah complained.

"You're so messed up already, what difference does it make?" Jenny tickled her until Hadassah pinned her hands to her sides.

They breathed heavily, exhausted from the laughter, gulping big drafts of air.

"This is so babyish, pillow fights! Let's do something cool," Hadassah begged.

"There is a great new exhibit at the Met . . . and there are all these crazy things happening in the Village. Street artists and weird clothes stores. Come with me next Sunday?" Jenny urged them.

"But how would we get there?" Tamar shrugged.

"What do you mean? By subway. It's easy."

"I'd have to lie," Hadassah said, considering.

"But why? What's the big deal about going on a subway?" Jenny asked, exasperated.

Hadassah and Tamar gave each other grudgingly intimate glances. This was the area in which Jenny was the outsider. A respectable religious teenage girl did not go to "the city" by herself and certainly did not traipse around *goyische* halls of entertainment like museums, which were full of indecently dressed portraits of *shiksas*, as well as totally undressed marble statues of Roman *shkotzim*.

Moreover, Orchard Park was a safe island. Something could happen to a girl who swam to the mainland. After all, hadn't they all learned in *chumash* class what had happened to Dina, the daughter of the patriarch Jacob in the city of Shechem? She went out, the Bible says. She was a young girl and she was curious, the biblical commentator Rashi explained. And the prince of the city looked on her beauty and dragged her off and raped her (as nature intended and not as nature intended, the commentaries clarified, although these commentaries were skipped over at Ohel Sara, where the plain text was difficult enough to deal with). The "You see! You see!" was embedded between every line.

"My parents would never let me," Tamar said without regret. She felt a certain smug pride in her restrictions. Her parents were always there, an enormously important part of her life. Their judgment was always infallible. Besides, she felt very pro- tective toward them, especially with her father's failing health.

"You're so unbelievably lucky, Jenny, that you can do whatever you want! I can't sneeze without the whole world knowing about it and telling me how to blow my nose! I don't really mind lying," Hadassah said, considering. "It serves them all right. It's so stupid to be treated like a baby when I'll probably be matched up and married off in another two years. . . . "

"Doesn't that ever bother you?" Jenny asked. "I mean, having your whole life just mapped out like that for you?"

Hadassah looked surprised. "Why should it? What else is there for me to do?" she said calmly.

"What do you mean? I mean, I'm just . . . I've just got a million things I want to do. I just don't know where to start."

"Like what?" Tamar asked, thinking Hadassah incredibly fortunate, wishing she could be sure the matchmakers would be banging down her door in two years.

"Like, deciding which college to go to. Of course if my grades are good enough, I'll try Barnard or Sarah Lawrence. But that means getting a merit scholarship. Those places cost a fortune! And I'd have to board. If not, I can always apply to Brooklyn College, or City. . . ."

"After all this time at Ohel Sara, I'm surprised you haven't changed your mind about going to college," Hadassah shrugged.

"What do you mean, changed my mind? I have to go! If you don't go to college, then you can't really be anything or do anything. Just a secretary like my mother. I don't know, I'm thinking about being a journalist, or maybe a marine biologist, or a curator at an art museum."

"Sure, I guess you could do any of that if you don't care about *chilul Shabbos, gelui aroyos,* and *tarbus hagoyim,*" Hadassah said in the haughty tone reserved for occasions when being the Kovnitzer's Rebbe's daughter was a convenient way to defend herself from feelings of ignorance and inadequacy.

Jenny, stung, turned pale.

"Hey, that's not nice," Tamar broke in. "I mean, Jenny wouldn't ever work on Shabbos, or do anything wrong with a boy, or. . . ," she floundered. *Tarbus hagoyim,* the great crime of accepting—worse, enjoying—gentile culture. She thought of Jenny's trips to Greenwich Village, the novels of Ayn Rand on the shelves, the Beatles records. . . . Jenny was certainly guilty of that. "But Hadassah, you also like *tarbus hagoyim!* You like Elvis!"

Jenny leaned back against the wall and looked steadily at Hadassah. "I'm not like you, Hadassah. I don't have this wonderful bunch of people carrying me around like I'm crystal, taking me places, buying me things. I've got to think ahead about making a living." She looked away wistfully. "But sometimes, you know, I envy you and Tamar. I wish someone would be strict and careful and lay down the law with me. I wish someone would worry and care. . . . My mom always says I'm so reliable, she never worries."

"And sometimes I wish the whole bunch of them—my whole wonderful, caring, worrying *mishpachah*—would just disappear! Not die or anything bad like that," Hadassah added quickly, "but just go to a place where they'd always be happy and have what they want—far away from me! And I would be able to get out of Brooklyn and do what I want. . . ."

"But what *do* you want to do, Hadassah?" Tamar asked, bewildered by the sudden, strange turns in the conversation, which were happening too fast for her to follow. Life was so simple. Your parents and family were the most important people in your life until you got married. If it took you a while to find somebody, you marked time by going to a religious teachers' seminary or a religious business course to learn shorthand and typing. You worked as long as you had to until the right man came along. And when you got married, you had as many children as you could. You loved G-d. You kept His commandments. And one day, if you were really, really lucky, you bought a house in Orchard Park, one with a big, nicely kept garden. You followed your parents' good lives. . . . She couldn't even imagine doing—or wanting to do—anything else.

"What difference does it make what I want? I can't ever do anything *I* want," Hadassah said tragically.

She sounded almost serious, Tamar thought, shocked, like she isn't joking around at all.

"But let's pretend," Jenny prodded her.

Hadassah stretched out, resting her elbows on the floor, holding her chin up in both palms. "I'd like to be by myself. I'd like to fly in airplanes, and eat in restaurants and shop, all by myself."

"But what would you like to *be*, Hadassah?" Jenny persisted.

Hadassah rolled over on her back, resting her long white fingers on her stomach. She closed her eyes, and her lovely dark lashes swept her rosy cheeks. She looks like Snow White in the glass coffin, Tamar thought. Poisoned, waiting for the Prince to awaken her to life again.

There was no possible way for Hadassah Mandlebright to answer such a question. There were no role models for women in Orchard Park. No religious Jewish women doctors, or lawyers, or accountants, or businesswomen. Only Jewish wives and mothers who helped their husbands out in the store, or with the books, or with the congregation, the way Hadassah's mother helped her father. To aspire, even to imagine, a separate existence independent of the man you would marry was impossible.

"I'd like to be the queen of Sheba and walk through the desert in long flowing robes," Hadassah said, giggling.

"And I'd like to be Marilyn Monroe," Tamar joined in.

Jenny shook her head and laughed. "And I'd like to be Lois Lane."

"But you couldn't go flying with Superman on Shabbos! And you couldn't eat any food on Krypton unless it had a *hechsher* from the rabbi of Krypton," Tamar giggled.

"Oh, the rabbi of Krypton isn't religious enough. I wouldn't eat any food he supervised," Hadassah said severely. "You'd have to have your meat skyrocketed in from Orchard Park."

"That's no problem, since Krypton exploded millennia ago and Superman can't take me home to his parents. So he'll have to live in Orchard Park. You see, Hadass, Tamar," Jenny said wickedly, "it's not impossible to be Lois Lane and stay religious."

"Except my parents wouldn't let me visit you because Superman isn't Jewish and they'd tell your mother to sit shiva for you and pretend you were dead," Hadassah added.

"Oh, I'd get him to take off the cape and tights and convert. We'd buy him a black hat and an outfit something like Batman's . . . you know, all black!"

They rolled on the floor. The Pole had a fit.

"I can't imagine not going to college," Jenny shook her head, wiping the tears of laughter from her eyes. "I mean, we'll graduate in another two years. Is that all we're ever going to know?"

"But you could continue learning Torah in the teachers'

seminary. All those things you'd learn in college . . . what do you need them for? It's just *narishkeit*. You can learn everything you need to know just from studying the Torah. Everything else just confuses you. It's better to keep your mind clean of such things. To leave room for the really important things," Tamar said sincerely.

"Like cleaning pinfeathers off chickens and how much sugar to put into the gefilte fish," Hadassah drawled lazily.

"No, like how much charity you have to give and how hard you have to concentrate on your prayers," Tamar defended herself, insulted.

"But I think that you can learn a lot of good things from Shakespeare, too," Jenny said thoughtfully. "I mean, remember last year in English when we learned *Othello?* Doesn't that show you what jealousy leads to, and the evils of gossip? I mean, isn't it better to learn and learn and learn and take out the good, useful things wherever you find them?"

"I think it's a big waste of time to go through all that funny English just to find out that gossip is a bad thing!" Tamar said.

"All that funny English!" Hadassah giggled and looked at Jenny, who burst out laughing.

"I don't see what's so funny," Tamar complained, piqued. It was as if the two of them had this secret code language, much the way parents did. Often she felt like the stupid child when the three of them got together.

"It's just that Shakespeare has written some of the most beautiful sentences in the English language, Tamar," Jenny apologized, trying to stop her giggling. But it was no use. She looked at Hadassah, and the two of them howled.

"Read *Romeo and Juliet*, Tamar," Hadassah finally said. "It's worth plowing through the 'funny English,' believe me!"

"See, Hadassah, that's what I don't understand," Jenny said, flopping down beside her, resting her elbow affectionately against her shoulder. "You read, constantly. Everything you can get your hands on. Why, I think you've gone through every art book, every art history book, every single D. H. Lawrence, Conrad, Forster, and Virginia Woolf in the library! Don't you want to continue? Why are you so afraid? Your father is a very kind, intelligent man. He'd understand. I'm sure if you just talked to him . . . It's not like you to be such a coward!"

Hadassah jumped up abruptly, flicking off Jenny's hand. She paced the room. "You know, Jenny, for a very intelligent girl, you are sometimes so stupid! Don't you understand that college is out of the question as far as my parents are concerned? And don't think Ohel Sara is going to help you fill out *your* college application either! Do you think they're going to give you your transcripts or the letters of recommendation you need to get in anywhere?"

Jenny's face went white. "What do you mean?"

"Ohel Sara's claim to fame is that none of its graduates would be caught dead in any secular, G-dless place like a university. Any Ohel Sara graduate who winds up in college is a failure, a bad advertisement. They are going to do everything they can to talk you out of it. And if that doesn't work, they will screw up your records so you can't get in."

There was complete silence. "How do you know this?" Jenny said, horrified.

"I have cousins, relatives, friends. I'm from that world, remember? You're kidding yourself. As for a merit scholarship, do you think they're even going to let us take the exam? And my father is one of them, the top one. I've never understood your relationship with him. . . . "

Jenny looked at her, stricken. "You're just exaggerating! Ohel Sara is going to give me my transcripts and letters of rec, or I'll . . . You'll see."

"No, Jen. *You'll* see. But what do you need this for? You're so lucky. You could just go to public high school right now and save yourself all this crap. Why don't you?" Hadassah asked with a mixture of real curiosity and simple provocativeness. Despite years of friendship, Jenny had never really opened up to her completely. There had been this strange relationship between Jenny and her father for years, ever since that first Purim. But she had never really gotten to the bottom of it. She alternated between satisfaction that her father thought so highly of one of her friends and simple jealousy.

"But I don't want to go to public school! You should see

my brother. He's just this simple kid, with nothing on his mind but basketball, football, baseball, cars, and girls. . . . I want more. I want what you both have: the magic of the holidays, the candles, the white tablecloths and challah breads. I have this other part of me, a *neshamah*, a soul. I want to feed it, too."

"Talking about food," Tamar pointed out.

"Nobody was talking about food, Tamar," Hadassah said, rolling her eyes skyward.

"But still, I'm hungry."

"You're always hungry!"

"Let's get some pizza at that new Israeli place on Thirteenth Avenue."

"Moishe's?"

"I can't go," Hadassah said flatly.

"Why not? It's perfectly kosher. Even the cheese is *cholov Yisroel*. There's a rabbi that actually watches them milk the cows so nobody adds pig's milk," Tamar chattered on.

"It's not that. I know it's kosher. I can't because my father says that it's a place where boys go and so it's unseemly for girls to go there too."

"But we're just buying pizza and leaving," Jenny said. "That's really overboard!"

"Now do you understand about college? He won't let me buy pizza if there's a yeshiva boy behind the counter. How is he going to let me learn French literature with a classroom full of handsome Christian boys from Manhattan?"

A thoughtful silence ensued.

"So don't go in. We'll buy you a pizza and bring it out," Tamar suggested practically.

"See, there's always a solution to everything." Jenny laughed, but her eyes were serious.

"Jenny, trust me. You just don't know the half of it," Hadassah informed her.

"We'll see," Jenny replied.

"What will we see?" Tamar wanted to know.

Hadassah flashed Jenny an imperceptible smile. "Let's go see the Met and the Village. Next Sunday! And we won't tell anyone. We'll just go!" Hadassah exclaimed with sudden enthusiasm.

"I can't lie." Tamar shook her head. "Not to my parents."

"Well, then don't tell them exactly where you're going. Just say you're going with the great rebbe of Kovnitz's daughter. That should satisfy them," Hadassah said ironically. "Only make sure they don't check it out with my parents, or my gefilte fish is really cooked!"

"They won't," Tamar said confidently. Her parents would never have presumed to call the great rebbe of Kovnitz on such a trifling matter.

❧14❧

The following Sunday afternoon, Tamar and Jenny stood waiting at the subway station.

"I wonder if Hadassah's coming," Tamar said, biting her nails, glancing nervously at the dark subway entrance bathed in the dirty shadows of seedy diners and discount stores. She kept telling herself she was happy and excited, yet her stomach had this heavy "I don't really want to do this" feeling. She chalked it up to a combination of not eating breakfast and a fear of rocketing up into the dangerous, far-off planet that was Manhattan.

She had heard there were crazy people who talked to themselves, black teenagers with knives who ripped gold chains off women's necks, and Puerto Ricans who made rude remarks to young, respectable ladies. Her hand went to her throat, and she tucked the thin gold chain with its Star of David inside her high-collared white blouse. She would just die if anyone did anything like that to her!

"Hadassah will be here, don't worry," Jenny said calmly, wondering if she would; wondering if they all wouldn't just be better off going home. She was unhappy about the deception. Yet, she had so much confidence that they weren't actually doing anything wrong, that she didn't feel guilty. Besides, her first loyalty had to be to friendship. Still, if Hadassah didn't show up . . .

In the distance a flash of bright, tawny hair waved like a banner. "Breakfast took forever," Hadassah said breathlessly.

"It's the first day of the new month, and they had to say all the prayers for *Rosh Hodesh*, and until they finished *hallel* . . ."

Tamar was staring at her feet. "Where'd you get those?!"

"They're go-go boots. Aren't they dreamy? I got them last week and hid them in my closet. I put my other shoes in my bag. I thought if I'm going to 'the city,' I should look right." She smiled, delighted and content as she looked over the white, knee-high leather that hugged her calves.

"But boots, in the summer? You'll boil." Tamar shook her head.

"They look awfully sexy," Jenny said doubtfully.

"I know. Aren't they great?" Hadassah leaned over, smoothing down the leather over her slim legs.

"What did you tell your parents?" Tamar fretted.

"Do we have to talk about this?! Okay, I told them Jenny wasn't feeling well, and I was going to pay a sick call and get a mitzvah. Which isn't exactly a lie, is it?" she said, winking at Jenny.

"I'm not feeling at all well about lying, that's the truth!"

"You sound like Mrs. Kravitz! Are you going to ruin this? Are you? Because if you are . . . Wait! There's a train coming in!"

They clattered up the rusty metal stairs, whizzing through the old turnstiles and onto the platform. They landed in the car just before the doors closed.

It was a Sunday train. Empty and dull and a little sinister.

"Let's go to the first car," Hadassah giggled, elated. They followed her through the swaying joints of the clanking cars, their hands flat palmed against the dirty metal to keep from falling. They crowded together just outside the driver's box. Through the dirty, ash-flecked window, they felt the city rush fiercely down on them in vast, brick buildings, shining stretches of water, smoke-belching factories, and frightening abandoned lots. And then suddenly, it was black.

The swift transition from the city's bright, complex face to its dark, mysterious bowels, was thrilling. Like astronauts launched beyond the known world, they curbed their fear, allowing themselves the mad pleasure of hurtling beneath the water toward the unknown and possibly glorious destiny that was Manhattan Island.

"It's like going back in time to chaos, *tohu ve vohu,* when the earth and water were all mixed up and there was no sun or moon," Tamar said, almost close to tears.

"I wonder what all those red and green flashing lights are for?" Hadassah asked.

"I can't believe you two! For Pete's sake, it's just the subway! We haven't even gotten to the city yet and look what fun you're having. Talk about easy to please!" Jenny laughed. "But it's a long ride. We should sit down."

"Oh, I don't know, I sort of like standing and the view," Hadassah murmured, fascinated by the rushing darkness.

"View?!" Jenny laughed.

"It is sort of like the funhouse in Playland," Tamar agreed.

"That's not what I meant, Tamar! Oh, never mind, you'd never understand." Hadassah's eyes glowed with excitement.

But soon they were all tired, weary of the monotones, the effort to keep their balance.

"So, where to first?" Hadassah asked Jenny as they settled themselves on the grimy red plastic seats, sticky soft with summer heat.

"The first stop is the Metropolitan Museum of Art."

After two train changes, and what seemed like forever, they got out, gulping the city air, which seemed fresh and clean after the stale subway ride. On Eighty-second Street and Fifth Avenue, the three yeshiva girls just stopped and stared for a few moments at the museum's glorious neoclassical facade.

"It's gorgeous," Tamar pronounced.

But Hadassah said nothing, just staring as if she were in the middle of a very good meal and had not yet finished eating.

"Oh, the outside's nothing. Wait 'til you see the inside!" Jenny laughed. They ran up the steps and into the cavernous entry hall.

"Where should we start, Jen?"

"I always skip the ground floor and go up one flight. I start with the American collection, then skip all those guns and things and go to the European paintings and sculptures and then the Greek and Roman art."

"Are those the naked men?" Tamar asked anxiously.

"I don't believe you! Lord, they're not naked, they're works of art!" Hadassah exclaimed with utter contempt.

"I don't care what you call it, I'm not going to look at any naked men," Tamar said firmly.

"The human body is a beautiful thing, Tamar. It's G-d's creation," Jenny said seriously. "We're not embarrassed about seeing other living creatures naked, why should we be embarrassed about humans?"

"I don't know. I can't explain it. . . ."

"She'll come," Hadassah prophesied.

They wandered through the pictures of George Washington standing and sitting, of pretty landscapes, of fur traders on canoes. . . .

"Whenever I see or learn about anything American, I think, like, what has this got to do with me?" Jenny said thoughtfully.

"What do you mean? You're an American. We all are!" Hadassah protested.

"But, Hadassah, you know in our book on American history where it says how our forefathers did this and that—you know, *Mayflower*, Civil War, Dutch in New York, that stuff—I always think: My forefathers were in Russia or Poland. And before that, they were in Jerusalem, and before that in Canaan. They wore white robes and had flocks of sheep. What does Washington crossing the Delaware have to do with me? It's somebody else's history."

"I know what you mean. That's why I don't think all this trouble with Negroes and Southerners has anything to do with me. I mean, we never had any slaves. But when I see those Southern sheriffs on TV, it does kind of make me sick. I keep thinking about the faces of the Germans looking at Jews. I bet they had the same faces," Hadassah said.

"Goyim." Tamar shrugged. "It's just an accident which goyim we happen to be living with. It's not really important, is it, their history, their culture? It's just goyim!"

"Sometimes you just blow my mind!" Hadassah said, rubbing off a spot of dust from her boot. "What's that supposed to mean, 'just goyim'? We are all part of the planet, aren't we? We're part of humankind. We're also goyim!"

"*What!*" Tamar said indignantly.

The guard turned around and looked at them severely.

"You're going to get us thrown out before we reach the naked statues, Tamar!" Hadassah hissed at her.

"What I think Hadassah means, Tamar, is that the word *goy* means nation. So the Jews are also a nation. We have a country. Israel."

"But we're Jews, not Israelis. You know how funny the Israelis are, at least the ones in our class. They bring those weird sandwiches to eat two hours before lunch, and they wear those open-toed shoes even in the winter. . . ." Tamar pointed out.

"But Israel . . . that's where David lived, and King Solomon. It's where Abraham and Sarah, Isaac and Jacob, and Joseph are buried. . . . It means something," Jenny said slowly. "I suppose any place else Jews wind up can never be as meaningful. Any place else is sort of just an accident in a way. . . ."

"I don't believe this! Any place else is not just an accident!" Hadassah exclaimed passionately. "Any place else is where you got locked up and gassed and tortured! They don't do things like that in America. America took in my father and mother. America is the best country in the world, and I love it! Besides, it's so dangerous in Israel. I mean, you can't even pray at the Western Wall. Jordan's got it."

"But it won't be like that forever. We'll get it back. This is just the beginning of the redemption. I wish I could go there," Jenny said wistfully.

"My friend was telling me that Israeli toilet paper is just like cardboard." Hadassah wrinkled her nose in distaste. "I couldn't live like that! . . . Oh, look at this one."

They stopped before the painting of a woman in a black evening gown.

"*Madame X* by John Singer Sargent," Tamar read.

"Look at how white her shoulders are!"

"What a snooty face!" Tamar giggled.

" 'Born Judith Avegno in New Orleans, she married a French banker and became one of Paris's notorious beauties during the 1880s,' " Tamar read from the card. "I wonder what that means, 'a notorious beauty'?"

"It probably means she had many lovers," Jenny enlightened her.

"But she was married!" Tamar's face got red. "You lose your whole World-to-Come if you're married and you sleep with another man. It's like the worst possible sin. Like murder. How could anybody . . ."

"Well, Tamar, I guess she missed out on an Ohel Sara education, so she didn't know all that," Hadassah said under her breath, staring at the portrait, mesmerized by the tilt of the head, the lift of the chin, the supercilious heavy-lidded eyes. Instinctively she lifted her head and narrowed her eyes. *Hell with you,* the picture screamed. *Take me or leave me, but leave me alone! I really don't give a flying hoot either way!*

She loved it.

"Come on, Hadassah!" the girls called back to her.

She looked up, startled. They were already halfway down the hall. She gave the portrait a smile and then hurried to catch up.

"Oh, this is awful," Tamar said, her head aching from the medieval depiction of Jesus, Mary, the saints, and the martyrs.

Hadassah shrugged. "All religions are silly, when you think about it. I mean, all those cows and sheep being sacrificed in the Temple in Jerusalem. Could you just imagine what that must have smelled like? Like Mr. Weinblatt's kosher meat and poultry! Not very inspiring!"

"How can you say that, Hadassah! Don't you remember that we learned G-d made a miracle so that there was never any bad smell or flies in the temple!"

"I guess I wasn't paying attention that day, Tamar," Hadassah said dryly. "But I think if we are going to talk about miracles, we shouldn't talk about flies and dead cows. I just think miracles should be saved for worthier occasions."

"Sometimes you're so . . . so . . ."

"So *apikoros-y*?" Hadassah helped her.

"You say it so lightly." Tamar was shocked. If anyone had accused her of being a heretic, she would have turned white.

"You know, it's like living over the store, that shul we have downstairs. I guess it takes away some of the awe."

"If I see one more picture of a naked man with nails through his hands . . ." Jenny shook her head. "Why do they focus on that? I mean, wasn't it his life, his teachings, that they think were holy? Why focus on death and suffering?" She shrugged.

"But I guess they have to. That's what made him important. He died for their sins. So now all they have to do is believe in him and tell the priest all their sins, and they get forgiven," Hadassah informed her.

"That's not fair! What a deal!" Tamar said. "You mean they don't have to do *teshuvah?* They don't have to correct what they've done, or be punished for it?"

"Wouldn't that be great?" Hadassah smiled. "We could all go to Schrafft's and eat ham sandwiches and ice-cream sodas and then go around the corner to the nearest shul and confess to the rabbi, and it would be fine! Or I could go to the movies on Shabbas and then just admit it, and it would be fine," Hadassah went on, lost in the interesting possibilities.

They hurried farther on, not bothering to stop at most of the Flemish and Dutch paintings. But Jenny insisted they spend some time looking at the Rembrandts.

"I don't like the colors. They're so dull," Hadassah complained.

"Just study the light," Jenny urged her.

"The Toilet of Bathsheba," Tamar giggled. "The Toilet?"

"Grow up," Hadassah moaned.

"And she's so ugly! Look at that fat stomach! And is that supposed to be David watching her?"

"Look at the way she's caught all that light. She lights up the whole painting. She glows. It's beautiful," Jenny said.

"Well, I think I understand," Tamar tried. But the truth was, it was not at all how she'd imagined Bathsheba. She looked awfully fat for any man to risk his World-to-Come for, as David had risked his by having Bathsheba's soldier husband sent to the front and killed so that he could marry her himself.

"My feet are starting to hurt," Tamar pointed out.

"I hate to admit it, but mine are too. These boots aren't the most comfortable things I've ever worn," Hadassah joined in.

"Come to the French paintings. You'll like those better," Jenny suggested.

They turned to leave, when something caught Tamar's eye: it was Rembrandt's *Portrait of Gérard de Lairesse*. Tamar moved closer and closer to it, blinking, not believing her eyes. He was hideous, the ugliest human being she had ever seen! His nose looked as if someone had mashed it in with a boot heel; his lips were swollen; and there was something apelike about the eyes, which looked out brashly with a kind of brazen contempt.

It held her with a horrible fascination.

"Eweeee! Why would anyone want to paint such a *chazir?* And why would such a *chazir* want to have his portrait painted? I mean, if it was me and I looked like that, I'd just hide forever and do all my shopping by phone and Sears catalog," Tamar said, shuddering, feeling the goose bumps rise along her arms.

"What's not nice we don't show, right, Tamar?" Hadassah mocked in perfect imitation of an Orchard Park yenta.

Tamar blushed. It was exactly the way her mother would have said it.

"But Rembrandt didn't feel that way," Jenny pointed out. "Look how carefully he's worked the details: all the light in the curly blond hair, the satiny gleam of the white lace collar and cuffs, the beautiful sheen of that black coat. Look at how he's done the fingers—he's made them so long, so sensitive, and intelligent."

"So why couldn't he have just made his face nicer, too!"

"I read in the catalog that Lairesse's mother had syphilis. He was born that way. His looks weren't his fault. And Rembrandt isn't ignoring them, he's looking beyond them, to what the man's made of himself. He's looking at him with compassion."

"I'd hate to be a misfit and have people do things for me because they felt sorry. I'd rather just hide away and be by myself than be a *rachmones*," Tamar said.

"Tamar, you're not getting it! It's not pity. Rembrandt really saw things he respected and liked in Lairesse. Rembrandt looked him straight in the face and didn't blink."

Tamar looked at the portrait again, lost in thought.

"My feet!" Hadassah implored. "Let's look at some pretty things, please!"

"Come on. When you get to the impressionists, you'll forget about your feet," Jenny promised.

They did.

When Hadassah saw Gauguin's *Ia Orana Maria,* something inside her leapt up like a small child given a gift box with a red bow. Drinking in the bright, tropical colors, the bare-breasted dark woman, the foliage painted with lush, dreamlike abandon, she felt transfixed.

"I read someplace Gauguin was this wealthy banker who just left his wife and kids and took off for this tropical island, just painting his heart out," Jenny said, moving in beside her.

"Take me with you, Paul!" Hadassah said suddenly, out loud.

"I knew you'd like these!" Jenny laughed.

"I love them!" Hadassah embraced herself, closing her eyes.

"I do, too! But you know what? I still think Rembrandt's Gérard de Lairesse is worth all of the Monets and Manets and Gauguins put together," Jenny said.

"What?! That horrible. . . !" Tamar gasped.

"A very wise rebbe once told me that it's easy to accept the good things, the beauty of the Creation. But it takes a very special kind of wisdom to accept G-d-given ugliness, to accept Gérard de Lairesse. I mean, the crippled, the blind, the retarded, the deformed . . . they're also His will."

"They're not His will! They're punishments for being bad." Tamar shook her head. "Wasn't that disease his mother had something you catch from being . . . bad? You know! If you keep all His commandments, nothing bad like that will ever happen to you or your kids."

"That's silly. Of course it will," Hadassah said. "Besides, Lairesse's mother probably caught it from Lairesse's father! It wasn't her fault! Look at Job! He didn't do anything wrong, Tamar, and he lost all his money, his children died, he had a terrible disease . . . and on top of it, he had friends who kept telling him he was probably being punished for his sins and a shrew of a wife who kept nagging him to curse G-d and drop dead. . . ."

"And all Gérard de Lairesse did was to be born," Jenny added quietly.

Tamar was silent, thinking of her mother and concentration camps, of thousands of small children gassed to death in the Holocaust. What could they have possibly done to deserve that? She felt confused and a little anxious, the way she always did when people revealed the holes in the fabric of her understanding of faith, G-d, and providence.

"Well, you've both been very good girls. As a reward, I will now take you to see the naked statues." Jenny smiled.

"You go on ahead, I'm going to look for a bathroom," Tamar said.

"I can't believe you're really serious! You're just chickening out! Come on, Tamar, admit it. Isn't this what you've been waiting for?" Hadassah teased her.

"I really . . . just . . . go ahead. I'm . . ."

"Okay, but you'll be sorry! We're going now," Hadassah warned her.

"It's fine. Don't let Hadassah bully you. We'll come back for you," Jenny comforted.

Tamar walked back until she reached the Rembrandts. She stood in front of the portrait of Gérard de Lairesse and stared. He was ludicrous, hideous, sickeningly ugly. He was G-d's will. And the artist had not judged him, seeing in him neither a monster nor a curiosity, but a human being. And he was forcing her to do the same, she realized with a start.

"There she is! We thought you'd gotten lost," Hadassah called.

"You should have come with us. They weren't so terrible." Jenny smiled.

"Yeah, most of them are broken and have fig leaves." Hadassah sighed, disappointed.

"But why did you come back here? . . . I thought you hated the picture?" Jenny asked.

"My feet are really killing me now. These boots! Come on, Tamar!"

As if awakening from a dream, Tamar's eyes slowly focused. "Were they any good, the statues?"

"We just told you!"

"You did? What did you say?"

"Never mind, let's just go! I'm starving!"

They made their way outside, caught the Fifth Avenue bus, and got off at Central Park. They bought cool cans of Coca-Cola, which they all agreed was kosher even though it didn't have a rabbi's written stamp of approval. They took out homemade sandwiches and fruits.

"It's so unfair, not being able to eat out," Hadassah mourned, biting into her soggy tunafish. "It's like standing with your face pressed up against the window to some wonderful party that everyone is invited to but you. I hate it!"

"I don't know. It doesn't bother me so much. I wouldn't want to eat that stuff anyway. It probably tastes terrible!" Tamar said.

"You're not supposed to say that! Remember we learned you're supposed to say: Oh, how I'd love to eat bacon and a cheeseburger, but what can I do? G-d doesn't want mc to. So for Him I have to give it up," Jenny corrected her. "Besides, in my youth, I tasted all those things, and they taste great! But I envy you, Tamar. It's so easy for you to be religious. I wish it was easier for me. I just feel like I'm fighting every single minute! I . . . I have such doubts all the time. I mean, my mother is this totally nonreligious person, but she's . . . well . . . she's a good person. She does things in her own way, and she means well. But every time she cooks something on Shabbos, or crumbles bacon on top of a salad, it makes me ashamed and sad. Sometimes, it even makcs me feel like I hate her a little! So what kind of a good person can I be if I feel that way about my own mother?"

Hadassah daintily took the last mouthful of her sandwich and dabbed the corners of her pretty mouth. "Want to hear what I think? I think you're damned if you do and damned if you don't. You know Shayndee Libner? She once told me she wants to be a doctor. She's really interested in medicine and everything. Her uncle is this big doctor. But she said if she went to medical school, it would break her parents' heart. And if she doesn't go, it will break her heart. So whatever she does, she's damned, damned, damned."

"So what do you think she'll do?" Jenny asked.

"She says she's just going to give it up because if she doesn't go, then only one person will be unhappy, her. But if she does go, she'll make her whole family miserable. Majority wins!"

"But it's not an election! It's her whole life! You can't just take a vote on that!" Jenny exclaimed.

"I think she's right not to go," Tamar said. "Being religious is a sacrifice. Look at us! Aren't we sacrificing all the time? Not eating ice cream in Schrafft's, not going to the beach on Shabbos . . . But it's for a good purpose. After all, we're not here to be happy. We're here to do His will."

"But didn't we also learn that G-d created man as a kindness? That we're supposed to be happy, to enjoy every good thing in this world we're allowed to? Otherwise we're just ingrates," Jenny pointed out.

"How come you always remember good stuff like that, and I never do?" Tamar complained.

"Maybe because I'm always hoping to hear it, and when I do I don't forget." Jenny laughed.

"Talking about enjoying ourselves, let's go to the Village and see all the street artists," Hadassah suggested, her eyes restless.

"Or we could watch the skaters in Rockefeller Center," Jenny said.

"I don't know. It's getting kind of late. Maybe we should start home."

"*It's two o'clock in the afternoon, Tamar!*" Hadassah yelled at her. "I'm not going back to Orchard Park any faster than I have to. Skaters are boring. I say the Village."

"Are we agreed?" Jenny asked.

Tamar bit her nails. She had told her parents she'd be with Hadassah. They wouldn't worry unless it got dark and she wasn't home. If it got dark, they'd worry.

She didn't want to worry her parents.

She envisioned her father, his pale delicate skin, the dull

surprise in his eyes, like the faces of convalescing soldiers in wheelchairs in old photographs of World War I. *Tateh,* she thought painfully. A relative had given him a job packing boxes for a novelties jobber. His footsteps were careful and measured as he walked to the bathroom every morning; sad and defeated as he walked back into his bedroom every night.

Her mother was working full-time at a linen factory near the house, sewing blanket covers and curtains. Often, she would stay late and use the machines to sew clothes for herself and for her daughters. Pretty clothes, carefully made from the latest Vogue patterns. But she and Rivkie were under strict orders not to tell anyone that the clothes were homemade. They were also strictly forbidden to reveal that their mother worked or that they had sold the bedroom set and the little spinet piano. . . . But most of all, no one was ever, ever to know that their father had been hospitalized.

Even they hadn't known. They'd just come home from school one day and found him gone. A vacation, their mother explained. Where? When is he coming back? Soon, *mamalehs,* soon.

She'd found out the truth by accident, three weeks later. "How is your father doing? Is he out of the hospital yet?" their kind Hungarian landlord had asked her one day, and she'd stared at him blankly, like an idiot.

They'd moved soon afterward to a cramped two-bedroom rental on the third floor of an old apartment building on Seventeenth Avenue and Fiftieth Street. Her mother had paid the moving man extra to hang the crystal chandelier in front of the living room window facing the street.

"Well, I'm not traveling home on the subway myself. But we've *gotta* be back before dark. My parents . . ."

"You're such a good child, Tamar. Such a dutiful daughter. What *nachas* for your dear parents," Hadassah said venomously.

"Cut it out, Hadassah! There's nothing wrong with not wanting to hurt your parents. I think you should worry a little more about that yourself," Jenny warned her.

"Me! I should worry about my parents?!! I'm going to spend my entire life doing exactly what my parents want me to do!

I'm the precious bird in the gilded cage. I flap my wings, but I'll never have enough room to use them, to really fly."

"You're here, aren't you? Not exactly where your parents would want you to be? How would you feel if they found out?"

"They won't."

"But what if . . ."

Hadassah was silent.

"Exactly. So don't make fun of Tamar. She's just honest enough to admit she cares very much about her parents. We all do. We're good Jewish girls, remember?"

"Oh, all right. Sorry, Tamar." Hadassah smiled with irresistible charm. "Please come to the Village. I promise to leave whenever you want to after that."

"All right," Tamar agreed, pacified.

Girls in brightly flowered ankle-length skirts or tight, short leather ones that barely covered their behinds sauntered lazily down the tree-lined streets. Big, teased bouffant hairdos exploded off heads, and wild manes of long, shaggy hair trailed down slim backs. Thin guys strutted with open-necked ruffled Byron shirts, suede leather vests, and pointy-toed boots. And everything had this bright, wild, unregulated, unwashed, and uncombed kind of look. The absolutely, dead opposite to Orchard Park look.

They wandered, wide-eyed tourists. Babes in *goy*land.

"Look at that girl's eyes! They look tasseled!"

"False eyelashes," Jenny the tour guide informed them.

"How does she keep them on?" Hadassah asked.

"With glue!"

"And then how do you get them off?" Tamar wondered.

Jenny shrugged.

"Those pants look like they're painted on."

"Stretch pants."

They did stop at some sidewalk art displays, but the offerings seemed so pale in comparison with the still undigested glories of the Met that they couldn't take them seriously. Besides, the real works of fantasy and imagination were the people themselves. So they stopped pretending to be interested in the art and just bobbed along with the joyfully disrespectable, happy-looking, and somehow childishly harmless-looking people all around them.

Hadassah stopped at a small store with Indian shawls spread around the floor and came out with a little bag.

"What'd you buy?"

She spilled the contents into her hand. Colorful glass and metal beads, exotic feathers on a leather thread. She put it around her neck. "How do I look?"

"Like Purim." Jenny laughed. "But so does everybody else here."

"But when will you ever wear it?" Tamar asked, perplexed at the waste of good money.

"Why, on our next trip to the city! I can't believe I have to go back to Orchard Park. I never want to leave! It's so much fun here! Not one person is wearing the same thing as anybody else. It just makes me feel like I can—I don't know—just dance in the middle of the sidewalk," she said, skipping down the block.

"You're *meshugah*." Jenny laughed, skipping after her.

"Everybody will look! How can you?!" Tamar whispered furiously, hurring to catch up.

"Look around you, Tamar. Nobody's even noticed!"

It was true. Someone was playing bongo drums, and a few people were dancing. On the other side of the street, a young man was holding on to his stomach and moaning, lurching down the sidewalk. No one's attention could be gotten so easily, let alone exclusively, on Greenwich Avenue.

Hadassah laughed out loud. "See, isn't it wonderful? No one pays any attention at all!"

"I don't know. It kind of scares me," Tamar said, her eyes following the man's uneven spurts of violent, painful progress down the street. "It's close to four. I think we should go."

"Wet blanket! Next time, let's not take her, Jen, what do you say?" Hadassah said malevolently.

"She's right. I also want to go. I wouldn't want to wander around here in the dark."

"Why not? I bet there are a million fun things to do at

night—Look at that: 'Trude Heller's Discoteque, Twist and Bossa Nova'!"

"You wouldn't catch me here by myself at night. Anything and everything goes! You know that man we saw across the street? Drugs."

"What do you mean? Like aspirins and penicillin?" Tamar asked in all innocence.

"No, these other things you can't buy in the drugstore. It's supposed to make you feel good. High, they call it. They smoke this stuff called pot and get these crazy visions, and then some inject themselves with needles. . . . It's called dope."

"They do this for fun?" Tamar shook her head. "Dope is right."

"What does it do? The dope," Hadassah probed.

"I don't know. But this girl in my art class who tried it says it's the most wonderful feeling in the world. Like . . ." She blushed.

"Nu?"

"Like sex."

"I never heard that was so wonderful. I thought it hurt but you did it anyway because it's a mitzvah and you—"

"Tamar!" Hadassah wailed, overcome. "Open your eyes! If it was so horrible, why would all those girls on the other side of Newrose Avenue be doing it all the time even though they're not married and they don't want to have babies? For the mitzvah? . . ."

"Tamar's right. We have to go. Come on, Hadassah. If you're a good girl, you can come with me again soon."

"Not soon enough," she said, mesmerized, looking over the passing girls with envy and fascination, longing for it to be next Sunday at Jenny's so she could try out all that black eyeliner. . . .

The late afternoon train was, if anything, even emptier than the morning's.

Their feet began to ache, and no one suggested standing up and looking out the window.

"Let's get the map out and plan our next trip," Hadassah suggested, spreading it over their three laps.

"I was thinking maybe we'd go over to the Guggenheim, or the Museum of Modern Art. Just seeing the outside of the Guggenheim is worth the trip," Jenny suggested.

"What does it look like?"

"Like an upside-down laycr cake or the inside of a washing machine is as close as I can get." Jenny laughed. "Actually, it doesn't look like anything a sane person could imagine awake. It's wonderful! And then I thought we'd travel up to Fort Tryon Park and see the Cloisters—this Benedictine monastery they shipped from Italy. It's really another world!"

"Another world . . .," Hadassah said dreamily.

"I don't know. That sounds so far way. What if we got lost or something?" Tamar worried.

"You can ask directions. Most people are really nice . . .," Jenny began.

A shadow fell over the map. They looked up, startled. Three boys in their late teens lounged over them, blocking out the light. They wore black leather jackets, and their hair was long and greased back into kind of a long ducktail.

"'Scuse me. Any you girls got a cigarette?"

Jenny pressed her lips together and shook her head slightly, staring warningly at Hadassah, who seemed about to say something. She folded the map and put it away and sat absolutely still, looking down at her hands. Tamar began to tremble.

"I mean, youse ain't offended or anything, us asking? Whaddya think, Sal, they seem *offended* to you?"

"No," said a taller, worse-complexioned version of the first boy. "Not offended. But they're not very friendly."

"Yeah, I seen friendlier ones, you might say."

"Like your boots, doll," the shorter boy said to Hadassah, who didn't turn her head but stared resolutely out the window.

"Whaddya say, Sal? You like the boobs . . . oops . . . boots?" He guffawed, suddenly slipping onto the seat next to Hadassah and pressing his thigh against hers. "Whaddya say, Sal, you like those shoes?"

"Nice shoes," Sal drawled. "But I like her friend's better," he said, gesturing toward Tamar. "They'd all look a whole lot better with a lot less clothes. Ain't you ladies heard of summer?"

"Hey!" the third one finally spoke up. He was the shortest of the three, but broad-shouldered, like somebody who'd been a ninety-pound weakling and had taken those comic book ads seriously and built up his biceps. There was something touchy and arrogant about him that made him the scariest one of all. "That ain't no way to talk, Marty. Talk nice. So whaddya say, girls? We wuz onnar way to Coney Island. Whaddya say you join us and we go together, have a little . . . fun?"

Tamar started to cry, and Jenny seemed about to join her.

Hadassah got up and took Jenny and Tamar by the hand. "This is our stop. We get off here."

The boys started hooting and laughing, forming a half circle by the subway door.

The doors opened and Hadassah slammed through, pulling the other two behind her. They ran down the deserted platform, the sounds of hooting laughter ringing in their ears. They tried to perceive if the laughter was getting closer to them or fading but couldn't tell without turning around, which they didn't want to risk. They just kept running up the exit staircase into the street so quickly, they didn't even notice the name of the station.

"Where are we?"

"I don't know, Jenny. Tamar, don't cry. Here, nothing happened. They're gone."

The light was fading as they wandered down the unfamiliar streets boarded up for Sunday. It was dead quiet and almost deserted.

They kept walking, trying instinctively to put as much distance as possible between themselves and the subway station.

"Do you think they got off the train and are looking for us?" Hadassah said, her voice a strange vibrato. She was scared but excited, too. Nothing as interesting as this had ever happened to her.

"I don't know," Jenny said, trembling. "I was just paralyzed. If you hadn't grabbed me, Hadassah . . ."

Tamar said nothing. She was walking with her head down.

It took Jenny and Hadassah a few minutes to realize she was hysterical, the tears pouring down her cheeks.

"Hey, Tamar. It's okay. We'll be fine now, thanks to Hadassah." Jenny put her arm around her.

"Here, wipe your face. You're ruining your lovely complexion with all that salty water," Hadassah said, dabbing her eyes. "I'll protect you, Tamar. Don't worry."

Tamar looked up, so surprised Hadassah was actually being nice to her for a change that she stopped crying for a minute. But then she started again.

"Tamar, what is it? Nothing happened. We're fine," Jenny repeated, exchanging wondering glances with Hadassah.

"Look, Tamar, I know you're scared. But we are in a bit of trouble and everyone has to help or we're not going to do too well. I need your help," Jenny said firmly.

The sobbing stopped. "What are we going to do?"

"We can wander around here and try to figure out where we are, and then try to get home on a subway or a bus."

"I'm not going back down there!" Tamar cried.

"Okay. But I don't have any idea about where the buses are, and I don't think we have money for a taxi, even if I knew how to hire one here, which I don't."

They saw a group of men coming down the street. They were weaving unevenly, supporting each other. They carried paper bags with uncapped bottles in them.

"Run!" Hadassah commanded them, crossing the street.

They ran.

"What are we going to do!"

"There's only one thing to do. Call our parents," Tamar said.

"You can't do that, Tamar! If my parents find out, you know what will happen to me!" Hadassah cried.

"I don't care. It's dark, and my parents are going to worry."

"So what? We'll figure something out. Please, Tamar, don't do it. Love your neighbor like yourself. If you were in my shoes, you wouldn't want somebody to do this to you. . . ."

"I don't want to get you into trouble, Hadassah. Really. But my parents . . . My mother's got enough worries! We shouldn't have lied to our parents. This is our punishment. G-d always punishes me right away for anything I do wrong." Tamar shook her head, mournfully resigned. "I'm calling my parents and telling them everything."

"If you do that, I'll never speak to you again as long as I live!" Hadassah said with cold fury.

Tamar hesitated for a moment. "I'm calling my parents." She went to the phone booth.

"The little bitch!" Hadassah fumed.

"Look, I hate to admit it, Hadassah, but it's really the only thing we can do."

"We could get out of this without calling if we tried a little harder."

"I'm scared, Hadassah. I know more about these kinds of neighborhoods than you do. My mother brings home the *Daily News*. I don't want to be in the 'beautiful young girl raped and murdered' section."

Tamar came back. Hadassah didn't look at her.

"Did you call?"

"It's broken." She hugged herself. "What are we going to do now?!"

"I think I see a neon sign flashing down the block. Maybe it's a luncheonette or something and they'll let us use their phone," Jenny suggested.

Hadassah glared. "I still think we should try—"

"I'm going," Tamar interrupted her, walking briskly ahead.

It was not a luncheonette. It was a bar.

Tamar stared at it, horrified. "We can't go in there! What if somebody finds out? I'd just die!"

"We can and we will," Jenny informed her, taking her arm and pushing open the door. Hadassah followed behind them sullenly.

They had a phone. Tamar used it.

Twenty minutes later a dark Lincoln Continental driven by a burly Kovnitzer Hasid picked them up and drove them home.

❖15❖

Orchard Park, Brooklyn, 1970

"Please, Hadassah."

Then the coughing. That choking, smoker's cough. The sound of a sharp intake of breath, the gasping for air.

"Hadassah?"

"I'm here," she said faintly with such noncommittal, passionless calm that Tamar's heart sank. "I can meet you at four, but no later."

Four, but no later, Tamar thought, long after she'd agreed to come and hung up. A sudden stab of hatred, of regret for having called, washed through her. She's putting me on her schedule, like a dentist's appointment.

She was tempted to forget the whole thing. After all this time, why rest such a heavy burden on the thin, shifting ice floes of childhood memories? And even as a child, she'd never really understood Hadassah, never really admired the liveliness and courage Jenny so loved in her. The most she'd ever felt was a childish compassion, because, even as a small child, she'd perceived the dark brass stain on the golden life of Hadassah Mandlebright, something tarnished and sinister beneath all that seeming perfection and glitter.

So why did it have to be Hadassah now?

It was something she couldn't even explain to herself, one of those crying-out gut feelings that seemed to cut you like a dull kitchen knife, pressing and pressing with an urgency that didn't give you time to analyze, but simply to act.

But why, her mind kept up its constant questioning, why her? Because.

165

Because why? the childish rejoinder continued.

Because she won't preach, she won't idealize. She'll be cold and practical and selfish, the way she's been about pursuing her own life, her own needs. She won't ask me to sacrifice, she won't plead with me to have faith, she'll simply sit back with those shrewd catty eyes of hers and listen. And what she tells me to do will be the most self-serving and practical of solutions.

There was a sudden silence in her head, the silence of a dinner party of polite strangers after one of them has thrown up all over the table.

She was shocked at this revelation.

She, who had always felt herself morally superior to Hadassah, who had stepped back into the outer circle and joined hands in the community *hora* around Hadassah's downfall with . . . if not exactly joy, then secret satisfaction. She, who had let that downfall strengthen her the way it had strengthened the others, the "good" girls and women who had never forgiven Hadassah her privileges or her family honors, who were thrilled to say: See, family isn't everything; beauty isn't everything. See how true the words are that our husbands and fathers sing to us Friday nights: *Sheker ha chen ve hevel ha yofee*—Charm is false and beauty is worthless—a woman who fears G-d, she should be praised! . . .

What fun they'd all had! Like burning a witch, Tamar remembered with a gulp of remorse. Yet there it was. And she'd been an active part of it. Still, she needed Hadassah now. She couldn't think of another living soul she needed more.

She thought of *Mameh*, aging and worn, her eyesight dimming. She thought of her *Tateh*, a tear falling down her cheek. Would she have been able to tell him, that kind, broken man who had spent the last years of his life dragging himself through the motions? Thank G-d, at least she'd been spared that decision. She thought of her husband: his hard, unbending, sheltered righteousness that hid so much fragility. The loving warmth that could so suddenly grow cold . . .

And then she thought of Rivkie. It had happened in Rivkie's apartment. The rapist had been meant for her. But as usual,

Rivkie had done the smart thing without even knowing it and stupid, incompetent Tamar the wrong thing. She remembered the gloating phone call the day after. It would be easy to destroy Rivkie, to let her know how close she'd come to the abyss. But then she thought of her little nephews. Somehow she didn't really want to hurt Rivkie.

She took a deep, courageous breath. She didn't want to hurt anyone. Why give them nightmares and fill their lives with ugliness and fear and degradation? Would it sew back on even one pearl button? Would it alter the lethal chemistry of that poisonous kiss? Would it change even the smallest detail?

She could tell Hadassah because Hadassah wouldn't care. "Four, but no later. . . ." She suddenly smiled to herself. Hadassah was exactly the right person to help her reach a decision. My decision, she thought. My tragedy. Everything to lose. Everything to gain.

She looked at her watch. Not later than four. That meant using the subway. She felt the cold sweat bead the back of her neck. Even before the rape, she'd tried never to use the subways unless it was early morning or evening rush hour when the sheer number of people made her feel safe. And even then she was careful to keep her back to the wall so that no one could get behind her and push her onto the tracks, a frequent occurrence according to the *Daily News*.

To get to Hadassah's by four, she would have to take nearly empty subway cars and risk having them fill up at three-thirty with rampaging public school kids, young animals of all sizes and shapes and colors, who would have everyone cowering in their seats, praying to get out alive.

So what? she told herself fatalistically, feeling like someone with a terminal illness. What difference would it make now?

Yet on the other hand, she was more terrified than she had ever been.

It was not the rational fear of New Yorkers who know bad things happen down there in that filthy underworld of rusting metal and rancid dust. It was not even a fear based on memory: those juvenile delinquents with their ridiculous margarined hair and silly movie tough-guy pickup lines seemed laughable in retrospect. No, it was more like roaches, mice, and rats, she decided.

The first time you saw a roach, they seemed so disgustingly menacing and powerful. And that feeling lasted until you saw a mouse and realized how easy it was to catch and crush a roach and how big and fast mice were in comparison. So you feared and loathed mice until one day you saw a rat, and then mice seemed almost Disney-cute. She had seen and felt and been bitten by the biggest rat of all. The City Beast. Nothing smaller could scare her now. But that did not mean she was not afraid.

On the contrary. You could live without fear in the city only if you secretly believed that the City Beast was a mythical creature, like a unicorn, the product of old women's timidness, children's exaggerated fears and newspaper sensationalism. But once you saw the Beast yourself, once you felt its savage power and all doubt was erased forever, life in the city became almost unbearable.

The existence of such brutal humans was something she had never before understood or considered. The idea of their existence, their living out their daily lives so near her, was absolutely petrifying. And whether she was in the dark of an alleyway, on a subway car, or in her own bedroom, that knowledge made her life a constant agony.

She tied back her hair and tucked it into her simplest, most inexpensive hat. This was her first ritual for subway travel. She had started doing it after witnessing a big Puerto Rican girl gratuitously spit on someone's head and then run out of the train just as it left the station. The victim—a pretty young girl in a bright orange suit, whose only crime had been wearing too nice an outfit, with shoes and a purse to match—had taken a piece of paper from her purse and tried to scoop off the glob. Her hand had trembled and her face had gone blank and white with humiliation. She'd hurried off to another car, escaping the looks of horrified sympathy.

\ The random violence of the city. It had nothing at all to do with one personally. There was no way to protect yourself. You were prey in the jungle. A simple, minor decision to go down one street and not another, to see a play, or a movie, or to baby-sit your own nephew in your sister's home, could put you in the predator's path.

Worst of all, it was completely meaningless. At least if you got brutalized by terrorists, it was premeditated, founded on some cause, some high ideal that had to do with G-d and country. But to be savaged to satisfy some sick stranger's idea of a good time? To lose your life because someone needed a necklace or designer sunglasses?

For a moment, she considered forgetting the whole thing. She could just lie down and take a long nap with the shades drawn, all safe, all locked in with bars on all the windows, and triple locks on the door, and an alarm system in the front. . . . Why not? The thought was almost irresistible in its seductiveness. She shook her two hands as if shaking off the paralyzing fear were something that could be accomplished physically. No! She couldn't afford to sleep anymore! There was a life growing inside her. A little blessing or the worst curse. A gift or the greatest punishment a woman could ever have. And whatever it was, it was thriving on her passivity. It wanted her to sleep.

To destroy the possibility of the curse, she would have to uproot the blessing as well, annihilating the child she had so prayed for, her husband's child. I won't think about it now, she thought. I'll be like Scarlett O'Hara. I'll think about it tomorrow. After I've spoken to Hadassah.

I wonder what she'll look like, Tamar thought, trying to distract herself. She tried to imagine Hadassah no longer religious, bereft of the imperial aura of her exalted family. Would she be wearing something fashionably goyish and embarrassingly immodest? Would *he* be there, and would he be tall and blond without head covering and wearing a cross?

A little prick of shameful pleasure touched her heart at the idea of the Rebbe's daughter wallowing in wickedness. But it was just for a moment, just until she remembered the baseness of her own humiliation, the sickening degradedness of her own body, her own life. She fought the almost irresistible urge to get undressed and shower, a compulsion that was hitting her ten or fifteen times a day lately.

She fought it, she fought the nausea, she fought the fear of the lonely subway cars, the deserted stations, snapping her purse shut and adjusting her hat in front of the little mirror on the refrigerator door. Originally she'd put a mirror there because a friend claimed it helped with dieting. Now she stared deeply into the gray depths of her own eyes, suddenly finding someone she didn't want to meet there; someone she would have gladly crossed the street to avoid.

Those eyes had been there. They'd witnessed everything.

Maybe someone will kill me on the subway. Yes, that would be best, she thought. Then I would never have to look into those eyes again.

She looked away, frightened at the depth of her self-loathing. G-d heard you. And she hadn't really meant it! What good would it do, after all, to be dead? Your soul lived on, with all its memories, all it had done to be ashamed of, to be thankful for. It would only end the painful activity of living, the way deep sleep ended the painful clarity of day. But it would not end the existence of her eternal soul. The torture would simply go on in another form, as the day continued in the dreams of night.

Then, suddenly, out of nowhere, a series of images hit her: A tiny, perfect head of silky dark hair. Tiny, white flailing fists of perfect little fingers. The heaviness of the head resting on the crook of her arm as she gently transferred the weight to Josh. Her husband's dancing blue eyes as he looked down.

My child, my child. My perfect little baby. The festive circumcision ceremony. Her mother's wet, happy eyes as the child is named for *Tateh*. The precious little boy, precious *kaddishul*. Love and hope and happiness . . .

She felt giddy, as if she'd swooped down the highest loop in a roller coaster and was heading back up.

No, she did not want to die. Not yet.

She closed the door behind her and walked quickly to the subway station.

"Well, well, Tamar," Hadassah said, opening the door, her tone an unnatural octave higher with forced enthusiasm. "Long time."

They stared at each other, trying to find something in each other's eyes to hold on to and care about.

"The last time I saw you was at your wedding," Tamar said nervously. "You probably don't remember."

She didn't.

"Oh, yes, the famous wedding." Hadassah flinched. "Ten thousand people packed into the ballroom of the Waldorf-Astoria. The Waldorf's kitchen taken over and koshered by ten rabbis and Cohen's Glatt Kosher Caterers. A lavish, costly, golden affair. A wild, joyful, foot-stamping, schnapps-drinking marathon. The closest thing to a day in Hasidic heaven anyone is likely to experience on this poor and limited earth. The closest thing to a royal coronation Orchard Park is likely to see," she said, nervously mimicking the exaggerated tones of an overwrought disc jockey.

"You looked like a princess," Tamar said sincerely, wondering at Hadassah's sarcasm. It had been all of those things and more. And Hadassah, whom she'd glimpsed only from a distance, had looked even younger than her seventeen years, like one of her own elaborately overdressed alabaster dolls, all painted-on smiles and glassy, visionless eyes.

"Yes, well, let's talk about something else, shall we?" Hadassah said impatiently, a bright hard smile freezing over her features.

Tamar, who'd been about to say: "I was surprised you even invited me," caught herself up short.

For years she had wondered at receiving the highly coveted invitation. There had been no contact between them since that Sunday at the Met. Two years. The rebbe and rebbetzin of Kovnitz had forbidden it. Hadassah had been yanked out of Ohel Sara and put into Bais Yaakov of Williamsburg—the strictest girls' yeshiva in the city. Sundays at Jenny's had ended forever.

Mameh and *Tateh* had been so deeply hurt, unable to comprehend why the Rebbe did not want their precious Tamar to play with Hadassah anymore. Tamar squeezed the bridge of her nose with taut fingertips. She could forgive Hadassah many things, but not that. What had she told her parents? Certainly not that Tamar had been the most reluctant participant, the one who made sure they left on time, the one who made the phone call that brought them all safely home?

Whom had Hadassah sacrificed in order to save her own neck?

"Can I use your bathroom?" Tamar suddenly asked, her knees wobbling, a sudden nausea taking her breath away.

"Of course. It's there, on your left," Hadassah said quickly, feeling a growing alarm. Tamar looked absolutely green.

"Thank you," Tamar whispered, hurrying.

She splashed cold water on her face and rinsed out her mouth, deciding against using the mint mouthwash because she didn't know if it was kosher or not. She had an urge to open the medicine cabinet, to check for all kinds of illicit, nonkosher things, but she restrained herself.

"You okay now?" Hadassah asked, her eyes flickering with unwilling concern.

Tamar nodded. "It's the train ride. I'm usually just nauseous first thing in the morning."

"So . . . you're really pregnant?"

Tamar nodded, trying to keep her face blank, unwilling to give Hadassah the pleasure of seeing her misery. She wondered again if this was going to work. "I'm sorry to bother you after all this time, but I just didn't know who else to tell," she began stiffly. "I'm so afraid of hurting everyone, you know, so embarrassed, humiliated."

"What's not nice we don't show," Hadassah murmured, but without mockery, sadly. "But you can tell Hadassah, right? She's such an outcast lowlife, it doesn't matter what she knows. Is that it?" she said, amused.

"I suppose," Tamar said wearily. The witch. She *would* figure it all out in two seconds. She wondered if this whole thing wasn't the second biggest mistake of her life. She got up shakily. "Maybe I should go."

"No, no. I'm just being a bitch as usual. It comes very naturally to me, I find. That's what I always was and Ohel Sara and my parents' rules just put this nice little party dress over it. . . . Would you like a drink?"

"Yes. I mean, no, thank you."

"I know, you can't even drink water in my house. The cups are unsanctified by a dip in the mikvah, the orange juice without rabbinical supervision. . . . But look, a paper cup filled with Coke from an unopened bottle and just a touch of rum! Even my father would drink that."

"I don't think I should. . . ." Tamar hesitated, wondering if there had been some wicked intent in the phrase *unopened bottle*. She sighed, deciding to ignore it, to be less touchy. She never drank liquor except for a sip from a tiny paper cup in the synagogue on Shabbos afternoon after *kiddush*.

Hadassah pushed the rum Coke into her hands. She gulped it down gratefully. "Thank you very much."

Hadassah slid onto the white damask couch pillows, tucking in her feet daintily beneath her. "You look like hell," she said affably, her eyes narrowing.

"I know," Tamar said. "And you look . . ."

"Say it. Like a bimbo shiksa that the little Ruach Chaim boys would throw leaves at if she walked down the wrong street in Orchard Park."

Tamar, who had been thinking along those lines, blushed. "Your clothes look very nice on you," she said honestly.

"Why, thank you dear," Hadassah drawled, genuinely surprised, her eyes wary, searching for some body language, some veiled imprecation of her tight jeans and sleeveless leotard, an outfit chosen specifically for this visit in the hope that it would send little Rebbetzin Tamar Finegold running back to Orchard Park, disinvolving her from boring melodramas.

But Tamar didn't look as if she were capable of moving, let alone running. She seemed quite doggedly settled and comfortable, Hadassah groaned inwardly, annoyed by the dumb animal look of pleading and pain in her eyes. Guilt trips. She *hated* guilt trips.

So where do we begin so we can get this over with? Hadassah thought. How does one help an ultra-Orthodox former classmate, with whom one has not been on speaking terms for at least five years, with the most important decision of her life? "Soo, how's your trip down? Found me okay?" She smiled brightly.

Tamar began to weep.

Hadassah got up and walked slowly over to her. "Do you want to talk . . . about . . . it?"

"*No! G-d, no!* Please, I can't. Never!!" She shook her head vehemently. "It was so . . . " She shuddered. "No, I didn't come for that. To talk about that. Please don't ask me!"

"I'm sorry. I didn't mean to upset you. Here, take a tissue."

"Thank you," she said, wiping her eyes and blowing her nose firmly.

"Tamar, I'd like to help you. But what is it you want from me? Advice, encouragement, comfort?"

"I want you to tell me what you would do if it was you. And why," she said slowly, with a great effort at control.

"But why me? I mean, why not Jen, for example? She's like you. Religious. Besides, you were always closer to her."

"I spoke to Jen this morning. She was so happy for me. She knows how long I've been praying for this to happen. . . ."

"Praying? For *this?!*"

"To be pregnant. For a child. She doesn't know about the rape."

"You didn't even tell Jen?" She sat down, pressing her steepled fingers nervously against her mouth. "Why? No, don't tell me. Because she's one of you now, isn't that right? Even though she's in college, she's moved into Orchard Park, so that disqualifies her."

"Something like that," Tamar admitted slowly.

"Look, you can do anything you want. But if you want to know what I think, I think you should let me call Jenny. She should be here with us."

"*No!* G-d, I feel sick—" She ran to the bathroom.

Hadassah dug her sharply manicured nails into her scalp. Why had she agreed to this?! Why hadn't she stayed in Hawaii? How long was this going to take, anyway? She wouldn't want Peter walking in on it. She walked into her bedroom and closed the door. She dialed rapidly.

"Jen? It's me. You're never going to believe this. . . ."

She told her everything. "Well, say something! . . . I don't know. How would anybody be? She's throwing up in my bathroom. And she wants me to tell her to have an abortion, to give her permission. . . . No, I'm not really sure. . . . Well, that's what . . . No, I can't handle it! You get down here and fast! . . . Well, I don't care . . . just do it. You know how she gets. . . ."

"Hadassah?" she heard faintly from the other side of the door.

"Gotta go. . . . What's the fastest time you can possibly make it, Jen? . . . Fine, I'll keep her here. Hurry." She hung up. "Feeling better, Tamar?"

"I think I better go. I think maybe this isn't—"

"No, no, no. Don't go, we have so much to . . . uhm . . . catch up with . . . old times," she mumbled unconvincingly.

"You've never forgiven me, have you, for phoning my parents that night? I see that now. It's been such a long time, and I did get invited to your wedding. . . . I'd forgotten. But we were friends once, weren't we? When we were little and during those Sundays at Jennys. . . . And you saved me from Freda that Purim she called me the only ugly Queen Esther. . . ."

"Sure we were friends. There were some good times . . . like I remember. . . ," Hadassah began, but then got bored with it. "Admit it. You always thought I was the big snob, the spoiled rich, rotten, *apikores*. And when my family decided to bury me, you put in your self-righteous shovelful, too, didn't you?"

Tamar stared at her, stricken.

"Hey, it's okay. You were just behaving normally. I wouldn't have expected anything else. And you know what? I don't really care enough to be mad. So why don't you tell me how it is I can help you? What is it you want from me, Tamar?"

"I want. . . ," she began, when suddenly her mind went blank. She was so desperately tired, so glad to be off the subway and in a safe apartment house with a doorman, behind locked doors with windows fifteen stories up, and to have company, even if it was a reluctant Hadassah. "I'm so . . . exhausted. I was frightened on the subway the whole way I was coming to you. . . ." Her eyelids drooped.

"Why didn't you take a car service?!"

"If I spent that kind of money, Josh would have to find out. I'd have to explain. . . ."

"You mean, you haven't . . . Your own *husband* doesn't even. . ." She poured herself a straight vodka on the rocks and drank it down in two large gulps. "You haven't told anyone but me?"

Tamar nodded, "And a doctor. He said I should have an abortion." Her eyes began to close.

"Come. Lie down. Take a little nap. We can talk later."

"No, very important!" Tamar shook her head and tried to get up, but halfway she fell back softly into the couch pillows.

"Come on now," Hadassah whispered, placing a pillow beneath her head and taking off her shoes. She tiptoed into the bedroom and brought out a light summer quilt.

Plump little Tamar. The only ugly Queen Esther in Ohel Sara. Soft and pure and white. With all the stamina of whipped cream cheese. Pious and self-righteous and stupidly innocent. Terrified to death of what people would say and think. A first-quality, A-1 perfect product of Orchard Park and Ohel Sara. Of all people to have been forced to . . . live through such a . . . such a . . . horror! Hadassah shuddered, not wanting to even imagine what it must have been like for her. She felt her eyes sting. The son of a bitch had really picked the perfect victim. She shook her head and tucked the blanket in gently around her.

There was no question of what she herself would do in similar circumstances, she thought. She'd get rid of it. Even if it was her husband's child. No way you could take a chance like that. Crazy even to think of it. . . . Imagine, a little black baby born in Orchard Park to the rabbi and rebbetzin, pillars of the community. All hell would break loose! Her husband would probably divorce her. The community would just have kittens.

Tamar Finegold hadn't a clue what it was like when a place like Orchard Park had kittens. But Hadassah Mandlebright did.

You became a nonperson. All your childhood friends crossed the street. (Yes, Tamar. I saw you do it to me, too. Don't think I didn't.) The butcher, the take-out food guy, the woman who sold linens, all your former teachers, staring straight through you. You would be ostracized and asked to leave the synagogue where you'd prayed all your life. And if they let you stay, no one would come up to you with friendly questions after the service. You'd be left alone, the matronly whispers shutting off the moment you appeared. You would be willed dead by the collective prayers of the multitudes. You would be cremated by silence, your living ashes scattered by the cold, unfriendly winds created by a thousand wagging tongues.

She sat brooding, watching the light fade. It was five-thirty. Reluctantly, she picked up the phone.

"Peter, I can't make it tonight. Some old friend popped by in a bad state. Of course female." A pause, her tongue explored her cheek. Slowly: "Yes, . . . I'm . . . sure. I know you were looking forward . . . Listen, don't raise your voice! *Don't raise your goddamn voice, I said!* You don't own me. Nobody tells me what to do. I said I can't make it. I'll call you later. Good-bye."

Men. The great Rebbe of Kovnitz had many clones.

The buzzer.

"Jenny."

They held each other at arm's length. "You look beautiful, except for the long sleeves and the long skirt." Hadassah smiled, suddenly strangely embarrassed to be wearing her tightest jeans and skimpiest top. Through it all, Jenny had never crossed the street. Their relationship had continued.

"Hey, this outfit is the deluxe model," Jenny protested, laughing. "Designed by Mrs. Weinblatt herself and sold in her own shop on Thirteenth Avenue. I paid fifty-five bucks for it, so let up. You look like Miss Hollywood movie star. Glamorous. Whew!" Jenny shook her head, then her face suddenly went very sober. "How is she?"

Hadassah waved toward the couch. "Look for yourself."

Jenny's eyes welled. "I can't believe it! Poor Tamar! Did she tell you . . . anything? Describe it?"

Hadassah shook her head. "She got hysterical at the *thought* of having to describe it. I don't think you should probe, I'll tell you that."

"The best thing would be for her to let it all out, to tell everything, to scream, not keep it bottled up! So what *are* we going to do? How are we going to help her?"

Hadassah shrugged. "You know better than me! Get her to talk about something else, I guess. Beat around the bush. Try to find out what she really came here for. It won't be easy. You know Tamar: What's not nice we don't show, we also don't think and don't say and don't feel. . . ."

"We'll have to create the atmosphere. Make it just like one of those Sundays at my house where we never shut up and just told each other everything. Just talk and talk," Jenny said.

"And not interrupt and not preach." Hadassah looked at her meaningfully.

"Why are you looking at me? Do I ever do that?"

Hadassah grinned. "No. You just have this way of imparting all these invaluable words of wisdom all the time. . . ."

Jenny looked at her sheepishly. "Most of the time I'm quoting someone else. I'm just sharing the wealth, I guess."

Hadassah smiled. "Well, Jen dear, tonight's the night to keep a little more of it for yourself. Let's face it, if Tamar had wanted a lecture on the 'right' thing to do, she wouldn't have come to *me*."

"I hear you. So what now? I guess I should call her husband and tell him she's staying over at my house. He's going to ask questions. . . ."

"You'll think of something. Want me to call for some take-out?"

"Good idea. Call Katzberg's for deli. They deliver. They even have Dr. Brown's Cel-Ray soda. Remember that?"

"That horrible green soda that tastes like vegetables?"

"Nectar of the gods!" Jenny laughed, catching Hadassah's arm. "It's good of you to get involved."

"You know me. A real *tzdakis*," she said soberly.

❖16❖

"Hi, Tamar."

Tamar opened her sleepy eyes wider, wondering if she was dreaming. When she saw it really was Jenny, she sat up abruptly, her nails digging into the sofa pillows. She turned her eyes malevolently on Hadassah. *"You had no right!"* she shouted, and then, drained, she almost whispered: "I shouldn't have trusted you."

"I don't believe this." Hadassah shook her head.

"But why, Tamar? She was thinking of you. Of what was best," Jenny pleaded. She sat down next to her, putting her arm around her shoulder. "Tamar, this is a time when you need the people who love you around you. It's wrong to shut them out."

Tamar rested her face on Jenny's shoulder and wept, wetting Jenny's dress, her bra straps, straight through to the skin. Then she sat up, pale and still and slightly shell-shocked, wiping her face with a tissue Hadassah shoved into her hand.

"You may not know why you came to me and not Jenny, but I do," Hadassah said calmly. "Not for advice about the baby—you're not really upset about that. If it was blue, you'd keep it and love it. I know you. You're just terrified to death about your precious reputation, about being disgraced. You just wanted to see what a person looks like after Orchard Park bad-mouths you into the ground, spits on you, and then buries you alive. Heck, they'd have burned me at the stake if the Code of Jewish Law said it was okay! So look, Tamar! See? I've survived. I'm even happy. My advice to you is, screw 'em, Tamar. Do what you want and screw 'em all."

179

Tamar looked up at her, a nervous smile suddenly breaking out on her tearstained face. "You could do that. You're different from me. You always were."

"Not that different. I just made different choices."

"But how could you choose to do the things you did?" Tamar asked in wonderment. "How could you get a divorce after such a short time? . . . How could you ruin your reputation and leave your parents heartbroken like that?"

"Would knowing that help you make your choice?" Hadassah demanded.

Tamar considered. "Yes. Yes, I think it would."

"Well, fine." Hadassah shrugged. "I'll tell you.

"I always knew my life was going to be different from yours or Jen's; that I'd get married very young to someone my parents picked out for me. But, you know what? That didn't really bother me because I always just fantasized it would be somebody superwonderful. After all, they kept saying how special I was, so I just assumed the guy they picked would be some great—I don't know—brilliant, handsome, well-connected, rich . . . The works. I was ready to be a good daughter. I didn't know any better, now did I? I didn't really know there was any *choice* involved here.

"Yehoshua Chaim came with a big introduction—what am I talking about—a big sales pitch! Madison Avenue has nothing on my mother. To hear her talk, this guy was the next Messiah, king of the Jews. Brilliant, an *illui*. And pious—he wouldn't even drink water on Passover because someone might have thrown bread into the New York City reservoir. And handsome . . . Funny, I don't remember what she said about that. Oh, yes, I do. She said he was very 'nice looking, a kind face.' But he was in England, you see, the son of the Mannheimer rebbe. Heir to the great Hasidic dynasty of Mannheim.

"They showed me his picture. It was blurry and he was next to his father, who must have been sitting because he made Yehoshua look tall. How was I to know? So the drum beating began. Solucky, solucky solucky, such*mazel* such*mazel* such-*mazel*, the drums beat out, until finally they actually invited him to Brooklyn for the engagement ceremony."

"I still can't understand how you agreed to get engaged to a man you'd never met," Jenny sighed.

"Good point! You know why? Because I started believing the drums, and also I kept getting all these phone calls telling me what a handsome boy, what a wonderful family . . . Why do you agree to spend forty dollars on a theater ticket to a play you've never seen? The critics! Well, the critics were ecstatic. And I figured that if I didn't like him, I would just tell them it was all a big mistake and he'd get on the next plane and that would be that.

"I didn't like him. But he didn't get on the next plane, and that wasn't that. In short, he was short. He was very English. He reminded me of that butler on one of those comedy shows. He even spoke Yiddish with an English accent! Physically, he didn't do a thing for me, but I figured, Hey, what do I know? I had never been out on a date. And all the boys I did find physically appealing were either *shkotzim* or yeshiva bums or rock stars. So I thought I better forget about sexiness. I thought there was something wrong with me. So I tried to like this guy. He had one thing going for him which I found irresistible: he was absolutely crazy about me. . . . This doesn't sound very convincing, does it?"

Jenny laughed. "No."

"Not even to me. So let's see. How can I explain why I married a not very appealing stranger? It was June. My friends were getting married. I wanted to plan a big wedding. I even had the dress picked out and my colors—rose and yellow. And he was the son of the Mannheimer rebbe. You know the trouble they have finding wives and husbands for Queen Elizabeth's kids, and those royals from Monaco? Well, Hasidic dynasties have the same problem, a dwindling of royal candidates to choose from.

"And my father wasn't well. And he and my mother wanted this very, very much. And despite everything everyone in Orchard Park now thinks about me, I was at one time a very dutiful, pious daughter. Tamar may not believe me, but I know you will, Jen."

"I believe you," Tamar interjected quietly. "Really."

Hadassah looked at her, her expression softening subtly. "Good. Chapter Two: 'My Marriage to Yehoshua.'"

"Girls, what can I tell you? You were at the wedding. Did you ever see so many flowers, so much food, so many women in diamonds? Did you ever see a wedding with three bands— one for the men, one for the women, and one just to entertain when we walked down the aisle? And did you ever see such a lovely bride? And such a short, sweating groom? But let's not talk about the groom. Not just yet.

"The son of the Mannheimer rebbe was a great tzadik. He learned all day, every day, until midnight. At midnight he would come tiptoeing into the bedroom, and I would feel this, well . . . *push*. Like I was being mauled by some not very polite stranger on a bus line. It was like, pitch dark in the room. He could have been a spirit for all I knew . . . I couldn't see anything. And then all this urgent fumbling, like this is distasteful, but we've got to do it because it's a mitzvah, and fully clothed, well, almost, he'd somehow manage it. And I'd feel like I'd been slimed over, you know, *used*. Dirtied.

"This went on for about two months. For two weeks every month I was a *niddah*, and he wouldn't touch me at all, or even let me pass him a plate or fill his cup with something to drink. And you know, I'd started working, teaching in Bais Yaakov. I'd get up at six every morning, and he'd still be in bed asleep. And I'd clean up the kitchen, because he always took a snack when he came in at night and never washed out anything, just left it. And I'd get home and pick up all his laundry. And that was it.

"Well, of course, girls, I don't have to tell you how much that kind of life appealed to me. You know how I dreamed about being a housewife and a teacher in Bais Yaakov! But I still thought I could deal with teaching, I could deal with Orchard Park. I just couldn't deal with him! So I told my mother the truth: that I was beginning to hate the little man's guts. So my mother, in a panic, runs and blabs to my father. And my father calls me in and I sort of . . . well, you know I have never really been able to talk to my father. He just zaps me with those eyes of his and I feel my blood congeal, like I've died and I'm being judged by *Hashem* himself, being interviewed for entry into heaven. So we talk. I told him some stuff . . . sort of. So then I go out and he calls in my husband. 'She isn't feeling appreciated,' he tells him—of course I was standing right outside the door and heard everything. 'You have to show you care about her, that all her *mesiras nefesh* and hard work are worthwhile. That you understand how hard she works. Buy her things, little gifts, and give them to her to make her feel loved and appreciated.'

"So, listen to this. A few days later I get up and he sort of sits up in bed and tells me this: 'In the hall closet are some presents. Take one every time you're not feeling appreciated.' "

"Lord!" Jenny laughed, covering her face with both hands.

"I love it!" Tamar said, forgetting herself, letting a giggle escape.

"Okay, stop laughing now. Yes, it's true. You know where that's from, that thickheadedness? It's yeshiva-itis. A common disease. They learn the Law, all the exact dry legalities. Do this, do that. It's all abstract. They forget that what they're doing has some basis in the real world, that they're doing it because it's just or kind. And if there isn't an exact law which tells them exactly what to do, then they're lost.

"So this is what happened. The day he said that to me, something snapped. I just started to laugh. I laughed so hard, I thought I would throw up and pee in my pants. I just couldn't stop! And every time I looked up and saw him standing there in his neat little pajamas and neat little beard and this creased forehead, saying with that Yiddish-accented Oxford English, 'You're being very rude. Really, very rude, Hadassah,' I cracked up again and got hysterical. It was just so . . . *ridiculous!*

"Finally, I just walked out. I didn't even call the school to say I wouldn't be in or I was sick or something. Didn't bother. I just took the train into Manhattan and spent the morning in the Metropolitan Museum. I sort of wandered back to the Gauguins and spent some time with them. And then I started taking buses, asking for transfers. I wound up on Madison Avenue and kept walking, down to Park and then onto Fifth, crossing over to Central Park. It was late April, an early spring day that started out like winter and warmed up fast. All my clothes suddenly felt so heavy. I remember reaching down and pulling up my sweater over my head, and I remember having this funny feeling, like 'Is anybody watching me? I'm embarrassed to be undressing' and at the same time 'Is anybody watching me? I hope he thinks I'm beautiful.'

"I got on the bus, and there were these two men in front of me. One had neatly combed graying hair and a very cultured voice, and he was speaking in these very sincere low tones, saying something like 'My daughter is producing it, it's her production.' He was talking to the guy next to him, who was dressed in an old blue raincoat with a frazzled ski cap on his head. A ski cap! It was seventy degrees outside and he was wearing a ski cap! And I kept thinking, Why would a man in a nice suit who has a daughter who's a producer be talking to someone wearing a ski cap on a Fifth Avenue bus? And I tried to imagine all kinds of scenarios, like some kind of rare medical condition for the ski cap guy. And then I thought: He's probably some rich powerful eccentric, like the publisher of *Time* magazine or the owner of the Waldorf or something. And I thought: This is New York City. You can do any damn thing you want here. Anything! Even wear a ski cap in the heat!

"And that's when I decided to do it. To go all the way.

"I went to the Plaza Hotel and checked in with my American Express card. I ordered up room service and had this tall glass of orange juice—I was still being very careful not to touch anything that wasn't kosher—and I put on the TV. It was the week Martin Luther King was assassinated, and there were pictures of the riots. There was an advertisement for the musical *Hair* and another one for *2001: A Space Odyssey*. I thought about buying tickets for both, and then I sort of decided I'd better call my parents. I was talking to them, telling them I wanted a divorce and my own apartment, and to enroll in New York University, and they were talking back, not really hysterical, but firm, you know, tough. And I kept looking out the window, thinking about the play and the movie and the ski cap guy and how I could do anything I wanted, and I finally said, 'I'm hanging up. I'm fine. I'll call you tomorrow. We'll talk more.'

"How long were you there?" Jenny asked.

"About a week. I wouldn't tell them where I was. I had a great time in the city. I saw *Hair* and sang 'Age of Aquarius' everywhere I went. I remember looking at the tulips in front of the Plaza, all those little red and yellow caps, lined up like little soldiers, already in overbloom and beginning to fade. That sort of scared me, because you always think about the bloom but never about the overbloom, the time when it's all over, and how fast that happens. And I knew I was in bloom. I was pretty gorgeous. I got bumped into and smiled at and asked the time fifty times a day by all these purple-jowled businessmen in the Plaza. It made me laugh. I'd just flash my wedding ring at them and they'd go away quietly.

"At the end of the week, I called my parents again and they told me Yehoshua had canceled all my credit cards. They said they wouldn't help me with anything, and if I didn't want to wind up in jail for not paying my bills, I better come home."

"I can't believe your parents would threaten you like that!" Jenny said, horrified.

Hadassah shrugged. "Believe it. Luckily, I still had some money in this engagement account that was in my name. I took out a bunch and paid the hotel bill in cash. Then I called my parents and told them if they wouldn't help me, I'd do it on my own.

"The first thing I did was check out of the Plaza and go down to Abraham and Straus's employment office. They offered me a job on the spot as a saleswoman in some teen boutique. I guess they liked the way I looked. Without help, there was no way I could afford NYU tuition or Manhattan rents, so that same day I found out about Brooklyn College's summer program. It was just before open admissions turned the place into a zoo. The campus was still green and fairly well kept. After that, I just wandered around looking for signs in windows that said FOR RENT. I saw one on Ocean Avenue. In fact, I actually saw the super hanging the sign out. It was a studio—one big room, a tiny kitchen behind louver doors and a bathroom with a dressing alcove. The building even had a doorman, a Jewish guy who worked as a cantor on the weekends.

"Of course the super said he had a long list of people interested, but I smiled and kind of . . . well . . . you know, was very nice about it and told him I'd be living there alone. . . .

"He rented it to me and even helped me buy some furniture very cheap from some of the other neighbors who were redecorating. I guess they liked the way I looked, too.

"I worked at A and S during the day, and when summer session started, I went to classes in the evening. Music 101, History of Art 101, English 101—all the 101's. Brooklyn College was perfect. It even had a Student Union Building—SUBO to the natives—with a cafeteria full of Glatt kosher dispensing machines. Kosher corned beef on rye. Kosher hot dogs, knishes.

"I wasn't in touch with my parents at all. And then I started seeing these Hasidim popping up everywhere. At first I thought it was my imagination. But there is nothing more conspicuous than a Hasid in a teen boutique. They don't exactly fade into the woodwork. One even knocked on my door and told me to call my father. I told him if he didn't leave me alone, I'd call the cops.

"And then one day, I was sitting in SUBO peacefully eating my Glatt kosher something, when this woman sits down next to me. Very Orchard Park. Stiffly sprayed wig, seamed stockings, expensive designer suit . . . the one who tells all the little kids to shut up in shul during the service. Well, she starts in on me! 'A religious girl, such an important family. Your parents are ill, such disgrace, such shame, your poor heartbroken husband . . .'

"Well, girls, that was, as they say, the very last pickle in the barrel. Which reminds me of this saying: Life is like a pickle—you start out fresh and green and end up wrinkled and sour. Anyway, that was it. I realized a little brainpower was called for here, a little cold-blooded strategy.

"So I called my parents. My mother cried. My father spoke very softly and painfully and seriously—I'd never heard him speak like that before. He asked me what I wanted. I told him I wanted a divorce, a property settlement.

"Divorce!! *Oy-oy-oy!* That word, that word! Don't even say the word! The *shandah*, the disgrace, the . . .

"Welllll, what can I tellya? There were a few more phone calls, another visit from the seamed-stocking emissary. Finally, we came to an understanding. I'd come back home and my father would get rid of Yehoshua—that is, he'd get me a *get*. He'd arrange for a generous settlement and monthly alimony.

"So I went back home.

"Who said you can't go home again? That sloppy fat Southerner, right? Tom something with the messy, brilliant, rambling thousand-page books? He was right, old Tom. It was like being slowly sautéed. The stares. The averted eyes. Old friends crossing the street. Remember that, Tamar?"

"I'm sorry," Tamar said in a small voice.

"Now, now, don't go all red on me. No hard feelings. You were just conforming, doing the acceptable, respectable thing, right?

"Yehoshua went back to whence he had cometh. I'm sure he's had at least two children by now with some very pious, very short, very accommodating new bride. . . .

"So, my bank account was full. I had my religious divorce and my civil one. I left my parents a short note—basically, Thanks for the help, but you don't own me—and then I split.

"But this time, I did it smart. No more Brooklyn. It was too easy to find me. I went straight to Manhattan, enrolled in fall session at NYU, and dormed.

"It was the *best!* One big party. This sweetish kind of smoke filled the halls. I think someone even figured out a way to put marijuana on their toothpaste. Every other day there was another demonstration, sit-ins in the dean's office. What fun! The guys walked around shirtless, with all this long, wavy hair. Tall blonds, very Troy Donahue, except with brains and commitment. Everything was questioned. It was wonderful. No rules, make them up as you go along. No bras. Bounce and be happy. No dress codes . . . beads, feathers, microminis in psychedelic pinks and oranges, Indian saris, Nehru jackets, hair going from stick straight to wild curls.

"I loved it. It was everything I was looking for. Complete freedom. Try anything. Think anything. Turn the world upside down and shake it out. No conformance. No convention. Do it. Try it.

"I met this guy. His name was Cliff. He was about six feet four and blond with these fantastic blue eyes. He looked so slim and . . . well, perfect. All my roommates were into group gropes, you know, communal things, sharing beds, casual onetime flings. Black men were very in. Every black man enrolled in NYU had about fifty girlfriends each.

"I wasn't into any of that. But Cliff and I would have these long discussions about how religion is just mind control, how it causes wars and hatred, and how the world would be better off if there was no god, but just people believing in each other, helping each other.

"I don't know if I really bought any of it, it's really amateurish compared to my father. But it sort of fit into what I wanted to do anyway, so I let myself relax. I ate a crab. No big deal, it tastes just like chicken. I ate sweet-and-sour pork—that was delicious, girls. Perfecto mundo. I tried ham, but the color repulsed me. Cheeseburgers were the best, though, especially if washed down with a large milk shake. . . ."

Tamar gasped.

"Spare us, please," Jenny murmured.

"I smoked pot, but it just gave me a headache and stuffed up my nose. No . . . well . . . to be perfectly honest . . . it did a little more than that. It sort of loosens you up, you know? Makes you relax.

"And then I discovered sex for fun. Girls, let me tell you, it's not the same as the 'Be fruitful and multiply and fill the earth' sex I had with Yehoshua the butler. It bears no resemblance. This guy was so gorgeous, just watching him was . . . Well."

"Let's draw the shower curtain at this point, shall we, Hadassah? Friendship has its limits, *n'est-ce pas?*" Jenny shook her head, amused and mildly shocked.

"Please," Tamar agreed, horrified.

"Okay then . . . My parents were still trying to find me. Every once in a while you would call, Jenny, and tell me this and that. But you never told them where I was, did you? You could have, easily, and earned yourself two thousand kosher brownie points with my father. But you didn't. I tip my wigless head to you. It was a gutsy thing to do."

Jenny nodded back. "It never even occurred to me, Hadassah."

"Really? I'm surprised and gratified. Where was I? . . . Yes. Cliff. Cliff was tired of school. He said we should start living out all our ideas about love and building a new world. There was this commune he knew about in Hawaii, on the island of Maui. He knew some people, who knew some people."

"And it didn't bother you at all that he wasn't Jewish?" Tamar asked, trying not to sound shocked and judgmental. She failed.

"I don't make separations between people based on race, religion, or national origin," Hadassah responded a little haughtily, then suddenly smiled. "If the guy is blond and tall, he's my race and my religion. Besides, it didn't last very long. Cliff, it turned out, was a jerk who was interested in exploring new worlds as long as the planet he landed on believed in ten girls every night to every guy, ten *different* girls, mind you, and surfing and lying on the beach during the day. I mean, the commune was great for the guys, but for the girls, it was 'wash, cook, clean up, and get pawed' city. It was being wify, except without the hubby who worked all day and protected you from your lecherous neighbors in suburbia. I had some bad . . . Well, it doesn't matter now. I learned how to take care of myself.

"But Hawaii was everything I dreamed of. It was that painting at the Met, Gauguin's *Ia Orana Maria*, come to life. The plants, they are just so big! Lush. It's all that volcanic ash. Very fertile. The colors, so bright—like some kid with a Crayola box going crazy: oranges, reds, greens, nothing muted or washed out or halfway. And the people, dark, a little Chinese, partly Asian, a touch of Indian here and there. All mixed up and nobody looking twice or giving a damn. I was happy in Hawaii. . . ."

"So why did you leave?" Tamar asked.

"Isn't that enough of me for one night?" she said a bit impatiently, then sighed. "Okay. I left because of the man in the picture on the coffee table. But that's another story. . . . You were going to ask me about the man in the picture, weren't you, Tamar? Peter Gibson. This is his apartment too. One of

189

his apartments, I should say. He's got a wife in the other one, and Lord knows maybe a few more like me someplace else in the city. I'm his mistress. His concubine. Like Zilpah or Bilha, the wives of Jacob no one remembers, although they had most of the kids. . . . I'm not ashamed of it. No, I'm not ashamed of anything I've ever done in my life, except maybe all those years I spent in Orchard Park letting myself be stepped on by a bunch of hypocrites who think they own the keys to heaven. . . . And if I have any advice to give you, Tamar, it's don't do anything for them! Don't sacrifice. Don't make any choice because of those uptight, narrow little eyes and brains. Hold up your head. Be proud. . . ."

She paused, running her hands through her hair. "And now I've got a question. It's for you, Jen. How could you move into Orchard Park? How could you let yourself become one of them?"

❊17❊

Jenny ran her fingers through her long, dark hair. "But this isn't about me. It's about Tamar."

"It's something I've always wondered about myself," Tamar said suddenly. "Your choices have always confused me! You became more and more observant, but then you left Ohel Sara. You enrolled in college, but at the same time came back to learn at the most religious women's seminary in Orchard Park. Why? What happened to you?"

"If you both really want to know, I'll tell you. What happened to me was the great Rebbe of Kovnitz."

"My father? My father changed your life?" Hadassah said, shocked.

"When I met your father that Purim, he was like . . . he was more than just a person. He was like a transforming act of nature, like a change of season. That first time I was at your house, he seemed . . . now you're *both* going to laugh—I know it! He was Santa Claus to me! What can I do? That was my frame of reference, coming from my family."

"Actually, that's hysterical," Hadassah said, smiling, her eyes grim.

"I never told you this, Hadassah, but the day after Purim, I came back to see him. Just walked in. I knew you wouldn't be there because it was your piano lesson time. And your father put everything aside and just listened to me. He made me feel as if I were sitting on Santa Claus's lap, asking me what I wanted and what I needed. . . . But it was more than that. He wanted to know in the deepest sense about my life . . . how I

191

felt. He was really interested. He listened to everything I said, just nodding, not asking questions or anything. And I know I must have been very careful not to tell any family secrets. I didn't want pity. I hated it! But when I was all done, he asked me . . . he asked me if me and my brother had enough to eat.

"I was just . . . floored! This was my biggest secret. It was something I hadn't even admitted to myself yet. My mother worked, and sometimes, many times, there was no food in the house. I always told myself it was because she didn't have time to shop or cook. But of course it was more than that. She just didn't have enough money. There was never enough food. I remember feeling so shocked, because the moment I heard him say it I knew that it was true. I was so amazed that he'd figured that out! That he knew more about me than I did myself! I didn't bother to deny it. And the most amazing thing was, I wasn't insulted, which I definitely would have been had anyone else asked me that, like a teacher or one of you. Why was that? . . .

"Well, a few days later I opened the front door, and I found five containers of milk just sitting there! Little glass bottles, chilled and wet. Fresh looking. I took them in and opened one. All the cream was on the top, and I just licked it off. To this day I remember how it tasted: scrumptious! Pure luxury.

"You know, that milk kept coming for years. Then baskets of fruits and vegetables started arriving twice a week. And on Fridays, a whole Shabbat meal—roast chickens still warm, kugels, salads, challahs, wine, cake . . . Just left silently at our doorstep. And before the holidays, boxes with new clothes would come, for me and my brother. I saw you wondering at all my nice clothes, Tamar. But I couldn't ever tell either of you."

"I can see why," Tamar murmured, amazed.

Hadassah pursed her lips tensely.

"At first my mother was very huffy—really 'I'm no charity case!' about it. And when I mentioned that I thought your father might have something to do with it, Hadassah, she went storming down to tell him off. But when she came back, she seemed calm and, well, sort of relieved. She said your father explained to her that the Hebrew word for charity was *tzdakah*, which comes from the word *tzedek*, meaning justice. He said that people didn't really own anything, since everything they had was given to them by G-d on a temporary basis. He explained that according to *halacha*, a person had to give ten percent of their earnings to those who needed it because this part of their earnings wasn't really theirs, but was lent to them specifically to give away. So when a person who had money shared it with a person who needed money, it wasn't an act of pity, but simply an act of justice: he was giving away what didn't belong to him. To my mother, a diehard socialist, this made perfect sense. She thanked him and left.

"I know you're both listening to what I'm saying, but do either of you have even an inkling, a small clue, as to what all this meant to me? Probably not. It's hard for anyone who has spent her childhood with a father and a mother to understand what it feels like to be fatherless. It's like being left adrift in the middle of the ocean. You can't plan anything; nothing will sit still. You just drift and float, and you can never be sure you won't lose your other parent too and drown completely. And you think an awful lot about dying, about the soul separating from the body. Heaven. Hell. G-d. Earth. You are one messed-up, miserable little person.

"When your father looked at me that first time, Hadassah, I felt as though someone had dragged me to shore and put solid ground under my feet. From then on, whenever I had a problem, or didn't understand something, I always went to him."

"How come I never saw you?" Hadassah challenged.

"You didn't see me because I went through the synagogue entrance straight into that little office of his on the first floor. That was his idea, so I shouldn't have to explain anything to you."

"His idea?! And he had time for you?" Hadassah whispered, amazed.

"Whenever I came, day or night, he was always surrounded by people, always busy beyond belief. I never realized until years later how strange it was that he never turned me away or even kept me waiting. Whenever I'd show up, he'd just tell everyone that there was an emergency and they'd clear out. And then he'd send for me and close the door. He always seemed so calm, as though he had all the time in the world and was happy to spend it with me. He made me feel . . . important. I always thought you were the luckiest girl in the world to have him for a father."

Hadassah flinched involuntarily, her mouth going suddenly bitter around the edges. "The *tzdakah* part doesn't surprise me. But that he gave you all that time . . ."

"And you he turned away?"

"No . . . yes . . . well, not really. I just stopped asking after a while. I guess I just got tired of fighting my way through the Hasidim. . . . And at a certain point, I didn't really want his advice anymore. . . ."

"You're a lot like him, you know."

"Come again?!"

"You're tough. You believe what you believe. And in your own way, you're searching for beauty and truth."

"I am nothing at all like him, or like any of them," Hadassah said curtly, shifting uncomfortably on her seat.

"Anyway, I once asked your father why he was being so kind to me when I wasn't even a relative or anything. He said I was wrong, that if you went back far enough, everyone was related because they came from Adam and Eve. He said not only was everyone in the world related, but we were all interconnected, and that just one person doing one good or evil deed could tip the scales toward joy and heavenly reward or toward war and disease. We were all responsible for one another.

"And that was when I understood the real beauty of faith: Believing in a G-d who was one, made it possible to believe that human beings, the universe, the birds and animals, trees, flowers, mountains, sunsets . . . everything was part of this 'oneness,' all of it good, all of it interconnected and meaningful. I wanted to be part of that. Remember that time I hugged the Torah?"

"I bet you never discussed *that* with my father," Hadassah said, snickering.

"As a matter of fact, I did. I told him what you said, about it being wrong for girls to hold the Torah. He said you were mistaken. He said the only reason women didn't go up to the ark and hold the Torah during services was because then all the men would look at thcm, and thcir thoughts would be turned away from G-d because men are so weak when it comes to women. He said he thought it was a truly beautiful thing, and he was sorry you didn't join us."

"I didn't need to hug any Torahs." Hadassah shook her head. "*It* was hugging me. To death. I was being suffocated by old parchment. . . ."

"I always thought you were so lucky to have been born into such a beautiful set of traditions. But now I understand the other side of it. I suppose I was lucky in a way. My mother not being religious and all, it gave me so much freedom of choice. My mother brought all kinds of other things into my life you two didn't have in yours: art, music, movies, plays, literature. I had total freedom of choice to take whatever I wanted from religion, from Western culture. I didn't see that there had to be an either-or situation. Why I couldn't just take the best from both worlds? So in the middle of ninth grade, in all innocence, I went into the office at Ohel Sara and told the secretary that I needed PSAT scores for college. She looked at me as if I'd announced I was pregnant! 'Don't let Rabbi Erlicht hear you,' she whispered. 'This is not allowed. Not allowed.'"

"I tried to warn you. . . ." Hadassah sighed.

"I remember. I was flabbergasted! My American core, that idea that a person is a free agent, allowed to pursue life, liberty, and happiness, was outraged."

"Did you ever tell me any of this?" Tamar asked. "I don't remember it."

"I never told you, Tamar. I thought you might be on their side, or maybe not want to be friends anymore if I told you I was going to switch to public school."

"So why didn't you switch?" Hadassah asked.

"I was registered in public school and everything, but somehow I wound up talking it over with your father first. His reaction was very interesting. On the one hand, I can't say he ever approved of the idea of college. But on the other, he didn't try to talk me out of it. Instead he advised me to switch to a more liberal yeshiva like the Hebrew Institute of Flatbush. He said I would get into a better college than if I went to a public school." She grinned. "It was the most persuasive argument he could have used."

"HIF was an expensive yeshiva prep school with a basketball team and cheerleaders. . . . The tuition cost a fortune. But your father said that if it was a question of my going to public school or going to HIF, he'd make sure I had what I needed to go to HIF."

"I would have loved to go to HIF! The boys had sports cars and the girls wore minis. . . . My father would *never* have *dreamed* of sending *me* there," Hadassah murmured resentfully. "Did you like it?"

"Uh-huh. Loved it! College prep courses, special SAT classes. Hebrew literature taught by good-looking Israelis. . . . But— don't laugh!—I sort of missed all that Ohel Sara thundering about *tarbus hagoyim*, short skirts, and talking to boys. At least you knew where you were at Ohel Sara, what was expected of you. But at HIF, it was almost the opposite. It was: Let's try to show how normal, how American, we can be and still be Orthodox. I can understand your father in a way. . . .

"In my senior year, I was accepted to this special freshman program at City University's graduate center, right off Fifth Avenue, across the street from the Forty-second Street library. Stanley Milgram was teaching psychology, Leo Steinberg art, Irving Howe English literature. . . . The names didn't mean that much to me then, but later I understood how famous each was in his field and how unheard of it was to have them lecturing freshmen. City college freshmen, at that. I was so excited about starting college. But just before I graduated high school, your father asked to speak to me."

"Here it comes." Hadassah sighed. "He tried to talk you out of it, right?"

"I don't know what you'd call it. But I'll never forget what he said: '*Maideleh*,' he told me, 'you are walking into a battle with an enemy much more powerful than our people faced with Roman centurions or Spanish inquisitors. Rome and Spain said: Become one of us or die. But America just shrugs and says: Look how much fun we're having, sure you don't want to join the party?' He shook his head slowly and closed his eyes. 'Even the Jews of Orchard Park who think they are in a safe little valley, living such traditional, religious lives, their children too are listening to the distant party music coming over the mountains. . . .' "

She glanced at Hadassah, who caught her eye and shrugged, swinging her foot listlessly. "He said: 'The children are going beyond the mountain, to universities with American names and green leaves on the walls. They'll get jobs with big American corporations. Their bosses will ask them to come to play golf on Shabbos. At first they'll find an excuse. They'll go to shul instead. And then the boss will ask again, and they won't have an excuse and they'll do it and feel guilty. And then they'll convince themselves it's not so terrible after all, a little game. That they are still good Jews despite a few minor sins. And finally they'll stop feeling bad and guilty and start feeling abused and defensive. And in the end, they won't feel anything at all. They'll just be good Americans. And they'll marry other good Americans and light Chanukah candles and give to the UJA. And their kids, who might or might not be Jewish depending on intermarriage, will just forget about the candles and give presents, and forget about the UJA, and give to the United Appeal. Millions and millions of them will just disappear. The synagogues will be big and empty. Community centers and day schools will close down. Like those piles and piles of shoes in concentration camps, there won't be anyone left to fill them.' "

Hadassah slowly wound a lock of silky hair around her forefinger into a tightening coil.

"What did you tell him?" Tamar asked, appalled at the image the words evoked.

"I said: 'It won't happen to me, Rebbe, I'm not going to disappear.' He nodded. But he was as sad as I have ever seen him. And then he said: 'I can't stop you. I can't stop anyone. Go to the university. And then move to Israel, to Jerusalem.

This is where our future is. There is no future for us here in America. No way to keep the children from going to the party, from disappearing over the mountain. If you go to Israel, whatever happens, at least you won't disappear. You'll be part of the Jewish people, part of Jewish history.' "

There was a thoughtful silence.

("I looked at him. He seemed older than I'd ever seen him. And for the first time, what he said didn't sound wise, but simply old-fogyish and incomprehensible. I couldn't think of anything to say. I was on my way to college. I couldn't wait to get to the other side of the mountain. . . . And for the first few months in college, it made even less sense.

"College was great. I learned so much that was worthwhile. Literature full of moral dilemmas, moral choices: Tolstoy's "Alesha the Pot," Dostoyevski's *Crime and Punishment*, Turgenev's "The District Doctor." . . . I could go on and on. And then I'd get to Shakespeare, and that would take a few weeks. Tales of modesty, humility, hubris, self-sacrifice . . . I saw it as a wonderful complement to what I'd learned in the Bible.

"Then there was Professor Milgram, who taught us about his experiments in testing people's submission to authority. How many would give others electric shocks if they thought the 'doctor' was taking responsibility. It taught me about the human mind, how it molded character. And then, of course, there was history, the whole cycle of Western civilization. We were being introduced to beautiful music I'd never heard before, paintings and sculptures I'd never seen. My life felt so enriched. I couldn't understand why your father was so apprehensive.

"It was also the first time I'd experienced so many different kinds of people. They were a smart, sophisticated group, from good New York public high schools. I felt like an ignorant child among them. But then, toward the middle of the term, students kept disappearing. I kept asking: Why isn't Jean or Joan here today? And someone would whisper to me: 'Hepatitis.' I couldn't figure out why everyone was coming down with hepatitis. So I very naively asked: What is this, some kind of epidemic? And then someone enlightened me. You got hepatitis from shooting up with dirty needles. I was floored! Such pretty, smart girls!

"Another very bright girl who sat next to me in psychology started telling me how her boyfriend had moved in with her. She explained how living together made more sense than going out on dates because all the guys ever wanted on dates was to push you down on the car seat *splat!* and you'd have to fight, fight, fight to get them off you. Her boyfriend wasn't working because he had a few felony convictions because of radical student politics. But she said she didn't mind doing all the cleaning and cooking and shopping and working to pay the rent because she just 'oohfed' him. That was the expression she used. 'I just *oohf* him,' she'd say, hugging herself and giving a big, dreamy smack with her lips. And wasn't that better, she asked me, than living with her parents and fighting off guys in cars? But toward the middle of the term she started complaining to me that he was slapping her around and didn't want to have sex anymore.

"I wondered where all the 'oohf' had gone.

"Another girl in my English class, a lovely blonde, very gentle and sweet, told me her boss—this overweight, middle-aged, married *yutz* store owner—had pressed her up against the door after closing time and told her he'd set her up in an apartment of her own. That he'd take care of her.

"I smiled, because I was waiting for her to tell me how she'd kicked in his . . . bloated misperceptions. But then she said she was thinking about it. Rents were high. She was finding it hard to work and keep up with her schoolwork and papers. That it wouldn't be so bad.

"That really shocked me. It was too sad, too awful. I realized all the things we were learning—psychology, English, history, music—left a person adrift. They didn't give you any direction on what to do with your life, how to live each day meaningfully.

"But I kept thinking, There has to be more. I looked for it in the theater, in the opera, in the ballet, in plays and movies. I listened for it in concerts, and searched for it in museums. I felt lost, as if I were playing some never-ending children's game that kept sending me back to the beginning when the end seemed near. And I began to see that there wasn't really going to be any counterpart, anything that wrung my heart like Yom Kippur or filled it with contentment like Shabbos. Or anything like hugging the Torah that day in Temple Emanuel—that feeling of being one with the universe, with goodness. I wasn't going to find it in witty dialogue, screaming sopranos, or the stylized movement of people in pink tights.

"I began to accept that what passed for seriousness, for spirituality, was only this odd posturing, these empty slogans about changing the world, not trusting anyone over thirty, and bringing down the Establishment. But what, I kept asking—I think I really wanted to be convinced!—what will we change? And what happens when *we* get to be thirty? And what are you going to replace the Establishment with?

"I never heard any answers."

"You should have asked Cliff. He had plenty," Hadassah said dryly.

"I mean answers that made sense, that rang true. Most people, especially my women friends, felt the same way I did. But they got intimidated and sort of pushed the questions to the back of their minds. They'd start parroting stuff like 'There'll be time enough once the Establishment is brought down to deal with that question.' Or 'We'll build a new society together.'

"But they never convinced me. All those 'don't ask any questions' intimidation and mind control techniques had already been used on me in Ohel Sara. They didn't work. I knew dogmatic garbage clothed in piety when I heard it. Believe me, Mrs. Kravitz was much better at it than Johnny SDS radical with the unwashed feet.

"And so I decided that a college education was one thing, and answers to my life were something else. I didn't drop out of college, but I went back to Orchard Park, where some of my first answers had come from. I enrolled in the highest-level, most serious women's seminary program I could find and started learning Torah, Mishnah, Jewish history, and the prophets again. But this time as an adult, with teachers I wasn't afraid to question. I went to college during the day and went to seminary at night. . . .

"It's so strange, Hadassah, isn't it? We both went to college and came out with such different conclusions? So, choices, Tamar. Do you understand mine any better now? Will they help you with yours?"

☆18☆

"I shouldn't have come. I don't think either of you can help me," Tamar said.

"What?" Hadassah exclaimed, her half-closed lids flinging open in surprise.

"Nothing we've said?" Jenny murmured, stricken.

"What did you think I could learn? You're both so completely different from me . . . always have been. Hadassah was always the princess in her enchanted castle, high above the rest of us ordinary folks. The great Kovnitz Rebbe's daughter . . . And now she thinks she has the right to do anything she wants . . . that she's beyond any rules.

"And you, Jen . . . you were also never really part of my world, tied down by obligations. Did you listen to your own story? 'I had total freedom of choice,' 'I was a free agent.' And now you're going to college in the morning and to an ultra-*frum* women's seminary at night, looking for answers in both places. And if something you learn makes sense to you, you'll do it. And if it doesn't, you simply won't. Things don't work that way in our world, Jenny! There are no choices. At least, I never found I had any. If you love G-d, if you have faith, then you have to do everything the rabbis tell you, no questions asked! The worst decisions I ever made, the ones that got me into the most trouble and deeply hurt my parents, happened because I tagged along with you, letting you talk me into thinking I had a right to defy things!"

"Tamar, that can't be true!" Jenny exclaimed.

But Hadassah just looked at her steadily, her expression

entertaining just a flicker of change, a slight paling, then a deepening of color. "Care to explain?"

"Didn't I tell you both we shouldn't be lying to our parents that day we went to Manhattan? Didn't I try to get you two to leave early for home? And then you go and tell your father it was my fault, Hadassah. Why else would he have forbidden you to see me anymore? . . . Do you have any idea how that broke my parents' heart? The great Rebbe of Kovnitz banning their precious little Tamar from seeing their Hadassah? Thinking badly of her? And my father wasn't well to begin with! And my mother was sick with worry, working day and night. All they had left was their religion, their standing in the community. And your father gave them this *zetz* just when they needed it!"

"First of all, I never lied to my father about that trip to Manhattan," Hadassah said quietly, pouring herself a large vodka and orange juice. "I told him, in fact, that the whole thing was my idea. He forbade me to contact the two of you after that because he thought *I'd* be a bad influence on *you.*"

There was an eerie quiet. The three women listened to the whir of the air conditioner, the soft flap of drapes against the windowsill, the muffled honking of distant traffic.

"Oh, he knew Jenny and I were in touch, but that didn't bother him so much. I guess he thought Jenny could hold her own against his willfully dangerous daughter. But you, Tamar, you were corruptible and thus needed to be protected. Anyway, I hate to remind you, it was *you* who insisted on calling your parents that night. Your parents got a *zetz* only because they misunderstood my father's intentions. Besides, compared to the *zetz* I got, what happened to your parents was nothing . . . Believe me!"

"What do you mean?" Tamar demanded.

"Jenny knows some of it, but I never told anyone everything—I was too embarrassed. Until the day I got married, I wasn't allowed to leave the house by myself, except for school. One of my father's Hasidim drove me there and picked me up. I wasn't allowed to talk on the phone without my mother being in the room. My room was searched for reading materials, records, inappropriate articles of clothing. Everything they didn't approve of was taken away and burned. And the worst part . . . they cut off my hair . . ." Her voice caught.

Jenny's eyes filled. "You told me you got tired of taking care of it," she whispered, stunned. "Your beautiful hair!" She shook her head, wiping her eyes. "He tried every way he knew how to keep you from disappearing over the mountain, and wound up pushing you there instead. It's so sad. It's my fault, really. If it hadn't been for me, neither of you would have gotten into trouble. I had no idea what I was getting us into. Can you forgive me? Forgive each other?"

"For that. But I can't forgive Hadassah for calling you now behind my back!" Tamar said bitterly.

"But why? Why didn't you want me to know?"

"Because I knew what you'd tell me, Jenny. What you always tell me: to love G-d, to have faith! As if I don't! As if I need reminders! All the things you've just discovered, I knew when I was five years old! We had a deal, G-d and I. He was supposed to take care of me—" Her voice broke. She buried her face in her hands.

"Tamar," Jenny implored.

"Let her cry, little hypocrite. . . ."

"Hadassah, really . . ."

"No, I'm just sick of all this garbage! Let her hear the truth! You always kept telling us the right thing to do, huh, Tamar? But you also came to Manhattan with us, didn't you? You lied to your precious *Mameh* and *Tateh* exactly the same as I did. You know what? I've never considered you more religious than I am. You're just a better actress, that's all. If you're so religious—why don't you go to a rabbi now and ask him the precious law, ask him what the *halacha* says about rape and abortion, et cetera, et cetera? But no, instead you sneak off to me, hoping that I'll encourage you to get an abortion. . . . Why is that, Tamar? It couldn't be, could it, so that later on you could say you didn't know the *halacha* and Hadassah, the wicked apikorsa of Orchard Park, talked you into doing this awful thing?"

"That's a disgusting . . . I never even thought . . . or planned

. . . Believe me, where I'm coming from, seeing Hadassah Mandlebright is not something to be proud of . . . to mention to people!"

"Then why did you call me, Tamar?" she said with deadly calm.

"Because you are the most selfish person I know! I wanted you to tell me what a person with no conscience, not an ounce of self-sacrifice or concern for her family would do in my situation. I wanted to know what someone who is the opposite of me would do! And you told me, didn't you? 'Screw 'em all!' Isn't that what you said? I should have known! But who knows, maybe you're right. All my life I've tried so hard to be a good person, and where has it gotten me? Maybe it all was an act, but I was the best, the *goodest* girl you ever met." She wiped her eyes.

"My parents survived Hitler, so I had to be a good girl for them, protecting them from any more harm or pain or worry. I let Rivkie push me around and never made trouble. And I really tried to fight all those feelings our teachers taught us weren't nice for a good religious girl to have. I tried never to be jealous; never to talk behind anyone's back; never to refuse to lend my things, even if the people who asked me never lent me theirs. . . ."

"And you're trying to be a good girl now, too, aren't you?" Jenny said thoughtfully. "You want to do the right thing for Josh and your family and even for this baby. You aren't thinking of yourself even now."

"You're right, Jen. I don't care about myself. I never have!" Tamar said with sudden passionate despair. "I wish I could just die—disappear. That would be best. Josh would remarry. . . some nice girl who'd give him many children. My mother would have her faith to sustain her. Rivkie would find another baby-sitter doormat. . . . It would solve everything—"

"You don't really mean that," Jenny interrupted her.

"Yes she does," Hadassah mocked. "Poor little self-sacrificing me. Let me put myself on the altar, like Isaac. A real *tzdakis*. . . ."

"I hate you!" Tamar shouted.

"Who cares? But you know what? Since you came here for

my wise advice, I'll tell you what you should do: You've chosen your life. Now live it! Do what a pious matron in Orchard Park would do in your situation. Have faith. Have the baby. Surely G-d, your good pal, your close friend, wouldn't let it turn out black. . . . After all, He's the one who controls these things, isn't He? So what are you worried about?"

"Hadassah, shut up!" Jenny said with sudden fury. "Tamar, listen to me. We aren't Catholics who put the unborn child's life before the mother's! If this baby threatens your life physically or emotionally, it's considered a *rodef*, someone who's trying to kill you. Your life comes first."

"But what if it isn't a *rodef*? What if it isn't the rapist's child? What if it's Josh's child?"

"Josh? Your husband? But how could that— Tamar! You didn't?! Not the same week!"

"The same night," she whispered.

"How could you!"

"It was my mikvah night. You're supposed to make love on your mikvah night. But it was more than that. I thought if I made love to Josh, that would wash it all away, all the ugliness and pain and degradation. His body would wash away the other man's, his kisses would cleanse me. . . ."

There was complete silence.

"You idiot!" Hadassah shrugged.

"Hadassah, stop it!" Jenny pleaded. "Tamar, what's done is done. Don't decide this by yourself. Don't have it on your conscience. You and Josh should talk. . . ."

"It isn't fair," Tamar said almost inaudibly, ignoring them both, her eyes looking off into some dark, distant corner of the room. "We had a deal. The window shouldn't have been open. I shouldn't have agreed to baby-sit. The rapist should have been run over by a car on his way. . . ."

"There is no deal, Tamar." Jenny shook her head.

"*Yes!* There *is* a deal!" she screamed, a primal, awful sound that stunned them, a sound like an animal's caught in a torturing trap. "There is! G-d is supposed to interfere—to watch out for His obedient children. . . ."

Jenny put her arms around her, hugging her tight, swaying

with her back and forth as she sobbed. Hadassah leaned back, her face pale, her fingers trembling.

"Why? Why me? And my parents, all those horrible things in the Holocaust, why them?"

"Why anyone?" Jenny said softly. "G-d can't stop evil things from happening. He can't stop rapists and murderers and dirty old men. . . . Because if those people can't choose to do bad things, then none of us can choose to do good. We'd all be like little machines, wind-up toys, puppets. What value would our lives have? What value any good thing we choose to do? But you must have called on Him when it was happening? Are you sure He didn't hear you?"

G-d, just don't let him kill the baby. Just don't let me die. Anything but that. Let us live. Please, dear G-d!

Tamar looked up, surprised, her tears gone. "I did call on Him, and He gave me everything I prayed for," she whispered with strange wonderment, startled by the sudden insight. "And I want a child so badly, so badly! I've prayed so hard and so long, and now I'm pregnant. . . ." A tremor rolled downward through her body, making her shake. "G-d, I don't know what to do!" she said suddenly, hugging herself, all her anger suddenly, piteously, draining away, like a bottle left gently on its side.

"Here, drink this," Hadassah said, handing her a drink and pouring another for herself. She looked down into Tamar's tearful eyes and felt a stab of compassion and a curious sense of bitterness.

"What's in it?" Tamar mumbled, looking at the orange liquid.

"Trust me on this one small thing, dear. I don't know much about anything else. But in this one area, I'm sure I'm right." She sighed. "Just drink it."

"She's right. Drink it, Tamar. And then just tell us what you think it is you want. What would make you happy," Jenny urged.

Tamar drained the glass and felt the liquid course down her throat, heating up her veins, dulling some of the sharp pain in her soul. She felt her eyelids grow heavy and her chest grow warm and light. She thought that she now understood drunks. Sometimes life couldn't be borne unanesthetized.

"All I want is to know where I went wrong." She shook her head despondently. "That's the worst part of the . . . the . . . whole . . . Afterward, picking over my entire life, searching for what I'd done that had earned me such a punishment. It's like sifting through some stinking garbage can, looking for something you've accidentally thrown out that you desperately need back.

"Over and over I've gone through my life. I thought maybe it was because I wore that hat instead of covering all my hair with a wig that time. . . . Or maybe it was because I had these bad thoughts about the mikvah that night, wishing I didn't have to stand there naked and be inspected. Or maybe because I once put cold chicken to warm on the hot plate Shabbos morning even though I knew it was against the *halacha* to let it get so hot the fat would melt. Josh told me I had desecrated the Sabbath and made me throw it out. . . . I still don't know . . . can't figure . . . But I was never very smart, both of you know that.

"I could never keep up. Rivkie is perfect. She always comes out on top in every situation. And Hadassah is so beautiful and from such an important family, and Jenny is so smart and self-sufficient. . . . And what am I? Remember what Freda Einkorn called me? 'The only ugly Queen Esther.' You have no idea how many years it's taken me to get over that! I don't know if I ever will. I felt so lovely and glamorous in all those veils and all that lipstick. But that's me. I always think I'm doing the right thing, that I'm *b'seder*, but it's not true, never . . . never true . . . right . . . not right," she slurred, the vodka gradually loosening her control. "Exact opposite. Nothing I do, think, feel . . ."

She closed her eyes for a moment as a weariness washed through her. "Can't understand cruelty . . . cruel people. Makes me feel like . . . choking. Parents' fault. They are . . . were . . . still can't believe *Tateh's*—my *tateh's*—dead." She wiped her eyes harshly. Jenny patted her arm.

"I'll be all . . . Just . . . wait a minute. . . . Kind. My parents

. . . always so kind. And both of you. My friends. Kind. To spend this time with me. . . . Hadassah has other things . . . better things . . . And you, Jen . . . I tried not to . . . didn't want you to have this pain. Wanted to keep it all hid, not to hurt anybody, embarrass anybody. Not to make anybody sad. Just like . . ." She took another long sip and sat quietly, contentedly, her eyes closed. They watched her sleep.

Her eyes opened drowsily and she smiled at them sadly. "*Mameh* and *Tateh*. They always smiled. They never talked about the camps, the war. . . . Only last year I found these photographs in *Mameh's* drawer. A picture of a handsome young man and a pretty woman holding a beautiful little boy in her arms; a photograph of a small, charming woman with a little girl and a baby boy in her arms. . . . 'Who are they?' I asked *Mameh*. 'Me,' she said, 'and my first husband and my firstborn, my little Duvid. And the other is your father's first wife, his two children.'

"My half brother Duvid starved to death in my mother's arms on the train to Auschwitz. My father's children were gassed with their mother. I had two half brothers and a half sister who were murdered, and I never knew! My own parents' children, and I never knew! And because I never knew, I had a happy childhood, you understand? My parents protected me.

"Hadassah makes fun of 'what's not nice we don't show.' But I understand it. All you have sometimes is appearances. Self-respect. *Mameh* told me that in a factory in Auschwitz she used to make white collars out of bits of material and iron them against the factory radiators. She would sell these collars to the other prisoners for bread. And you know what? Even in Auschwitz starving people were willing to give away their precious bread for a clean, ironed white collar. . . .

"When Rivkie got engaged, there was no money, but nobody was allowed to know it. My parents took out these huge loans for the wedding and for her trousseau. *Mameh* said we had no choice. And the in-laws kept asking *Tateh* for more and more. . . . You know—lamb chops instead of chicken for the wedding.

And to pay the couple's rent for a year. And to buy them living room furniture. It just went on and on.

"It was a beautiful wedding. And six months later my *tateh* . . . they called us from his job. He had to be rushed to the hospital. But when we got there . . . I think he must have died at his desk at work, and his boss just didn't want to tell us. He wanted the doctors to tell us. Anyhow, this is how I comfort myself for getting there too late.

"I loved him." She wiped her eyes and stared at the backs of her hands. "My mother had to take charity from relatives for the funeral. Afterward I lay in my bed without getting undressed for two days. I just lay there on top of the cover, trying to figure it out, to understand. Death, suffering . . ." She felt Jenny's hand squeezing her shoulder comfortingly. "You both knew him. It wasn't just because he was my father."

"He was one of the finest men I ever met," Hadassah whispered. "I always envied you your parents, Tamar. Especially your father."

"You? Envied me?"

"Remember that first Purim when you came to give us *shalach monos?* I couldn't believe a father could take off a whole day from work just to be with his family, just to be with one daughter. . . . I never had that."

Tamar looked at her, her eyes suddenly softening. "He didn't even get to see me married. But he would have loved my husband and been so very proud." She took a deep breath. "After *Tateh* died, most of the matchmakers stopped calling. It got around about our finances. Rivkie's in-laws talked. You know. My mother couldn't really offer anything financially.

"Then my aunt called and said she knew a wonderful boy who was a great *talmid chachom* not interested in money.

" 'What could it hurt to try?' *Mameh* said. And I said: 'It could hurt. A lot it could hurt.' But in the end I agreed. What choice did I have? I spent the whole afternoon bathing and perfuming myself, curling my hair, and putting on my best Shabbos clothes. I remember standing in my room listening to him come in and talk to my mother. I'll never forget how my fingers tingled when I opened my door and went out to meet him. The moment I saw him, my knees got weak and my heart began beating so . . . He was the handsomest man I'd ever seen. Dark blond hair and blue eyes. There was something strong but sensitive about his face and hands. Sensitive and fine. And when we spoke, he bent his head to me, looking down so that I wouldn't be embarrassed and could talk without blushing my head off. He had a soft voice, yet he could be very passionate too when he spoke about the things that mattered most to him. And what mattered most was learning. He had this fire, this flame, inside him. Nothing would stop him, he said. He didn't want to be bothered with running after all the silly material things other people spent their lives acquiring. That was the exact way he'd said it: spent their lives acquiring.

"I'd never heard anyone speak that way. It seemed so educated and old-fashioned and gentlemanly. I told him I wanted to spend my life as the wife of a *talmid chachom*. That I would consider it a great honor to sacrifice in the name of Torah. That the real things that were important to me were spiritual things. I don't know how much of it I meant. Some of it, I guess. I had nothing else to offer him, did I, but my piety?

"He nodded and nodded, and seemed to get happier and happier. 'And where do you think we should look for an apartment?' Josh finally asked me.

"And somehow, when he said 'we' like that, I understood I'd passed a certain line. The word kept sounding in my head as I listened to him speak. 'We' I kept thinking. This man and myself. And when he spoke about the hardships of being the wife of a Torah scholar, I thought: Yes. We could do this. I would wear rags and eat stale challah for you, for the honor of being yours, the wife of a great Torah scholar.

"You have no idea how people treat me now. As his wife, I sit in the best seat in the *shteibel*, and all the older women smile at me and get up and shake my hand after davening. They come to me and say: 'Please, Rebbetzin, could you ask your husband to make a little time for me? I have an important *shaileh* to ask him.' And 'Good Shabbos, Rebbetzin.' And 'For you, only forty-nine cents a pound, Rebbetzin. I hope the rabbi enjoys the roast this Shabbos. I'll have your order delivered right away.'

"I'm not Tamar Gottlieb anymore. I'm Rebbetzin Finegold." She turned to the other two with a desperate kind of sadness in her eyes. "Do you get it now? Do you understand? That's all I am. I'm a 'we.' It's the best I can ever be. If this thing gets out . . . the disgrace, the blot . . . if Josh should ever leave me . . ." She drained the last drops from her glass. "I'd rather be dead."

"Well, in that case, why risk having a black baby?" Hadassah said matter-of-factly. "Wouldn't the easiest way out be to have an abortion? It isn't illegal anymore. You can easily hide it from Josh. Just tell him you've got your period. By the time you need to go to the mikvah, you'll be all healed. . . ."

"But if she aborts this baby, she can't hide it from herself or from G-d." Jenny shook her head thoughtfully. "What if it's a perfectly healthy, legitimate child? Josh's child?" She turned to Tamar. "Do you really want that on your conscience your whole life? Would that really be the easiest choice to live with?"

"I thought you weren't going to preach! No wonder she didn't want me to call you!" Hadassah smiled. "Not helpful. Bad girl, Jen."

"I'm not telling you what to do, Tamar! If the baby's a threat, abortion is an alternative. Just don't be naive about the consequences. It's not like having your tonsils out. . . ."

"It's so hard!" Tamar wept.

"If you can't talk to Josh, go to a *rav*, Tamar. Someone you respect. Let him help you decide."

"*No!* I can't take the chance! If I ask a *rav*, he'll look up the *halacha*, and then I'll have to do exactly what he tells me or ignore it and know I'm living in sin. I'd rather not know. Rather not take the chance."

Hadassah walked over to the window and stared out at the skyline. "It's almost dawn."

"I think I'd better be going now." Tamar wiped her eyes and got up. Her knees suddenly buckled.

"Whoa!" Jenny caught her. "Steady. Can you imagine what'll happen in your ninth month if you can't keep your balance now?" She laughed, patting Tamar's stomach.

Then suddenly the cheerfulness faded. They looked at each other soberly. Would there be a ninth month for this baby?

"I have to ask both of you to promise you'll never tell anyone what I've told you tonight."

"Who'd be interested that's still talking to me? Okay, okay, I promise. But I missed something here. What's the decision?" Hadassah asked.

"I think Tamar's decided to make her own decision," Jenny said quietly. "Am I right, Tamar?"

"Yes. There really isn't any easy solution. Even if I wanted to be totally selfish. Everything has so many sides to it. So many consequences. Like throwing a single stone into the water, the circles get wider and wider. . . . But at least now I think I know what my choices are . . . what's important to me. I think I understand myself a little better. Good-bye, Hadassah. And thank you. I probably won't be seeing you again. Sorry I ruined your evening."

Hadassah walked over to her and slipped her arms around her back, hugging her gently. "Don't pick through your life, Tamar. You're not being punished. Things just happen. Bad things to good people. And nobody deserves what happened to you."

Tamar felt her eyes well. "Hadassah?"

"Hmn?"

"Take care of yourself!"

"Oh, that's my specialty, as you well know." She smiled, patting Tamar's hat into place, tucking in the stray hairs. "You can call again, you know."

"No, I don't think so, but thanks."

Jenny tapped Hadassah lightly on the shoulder. "Do you want me to tell your parents anything, send regards?"

"Let the dead rest, Jen," Hadassah said, her voice weary. "They've got my brothers. Grandchildren. It's no good. Some things can't be fixed. Besides, he's got you. You're the daughter he really always wanted."

"That's silly!"

"He's got you," Hadassah repeated, nodding with a cryptic smile. "And it's okay with me, really." They looked at each other for a long time. Then they hugged, a swift, hard, reluctantly parted hug.

Hadassah waited for the elevator to take them down. She waved. And then the door slid shut and took them away.

Hadassah walked into the bedroom, kicking off her shoes and peeling off one earring. Then she picked up the phone and dialed the airport. It rang and rang, but no one picked up. She looked at her watch. Five A.M. She'd try again at nine. They might even have a flight to Maui the same day. She closed her eyes and mentally packed a suitcase.

Choices.

❖19❖

Out in the street in front of Hadassah's apartment house, they watched a gossamer thread of light trail through the night sky, lost in the artificial light of office buildings.

"It's already dawn." Jenny breathed deeply, searching for more evidence of the coming light. "Misery never lasts, Tamar. You'll look back and see that it could have been worse. You'll forget the pain."

"Do you really think so?" Tamar said with strange hopefulness. "I can't imagine ever forgetting. Ever feeling ordinary again. Ever feeling at peace. Wherever I am, whatever I'm doing, I have this terrible feeling, this terror in my stomach. I keep thinking: Will G-d's hand hold me tonight? Or will *he*—some anonymous, hard, sickening *he*—be there?

"*Hashem ori veyishi, me me efchad?* The Lord is my light and my salvation, whom shall I fear?"

"G-d is the refuge of my life, of whom shall I be afraid?" Jenny whispered, her lips brushing Tamar's forehead.

They sat together silently in Jenny's old car, watching the city lose its vivid darkness to a pale, almost ghostly dawn.

"We learned in seminary last week that evil has no real existence. It's a parasite, like a virus, living off good. It can't do anything on its own. It can only attach itself to something good and distort it or destroy it. There is always a little bit of good even in the most evil thing. . . . You just have to find it and extract it. Then the evil just sloughs away like dead skin. It loses its power to exist."

Tamar listened, wondering if it could be true. What possible good could come from any of this?

"Come, I'll drive you home."

Tamar watched her enviously as she put the key into the ignition and backed out. "I think it's so great you can drive. I'd like to learn one day. We have a car. It's just an old Buick. But it's good enough for us."

"I'm wild about driving. It makes me feel like an adult. Like I'm in control and not dependent on anyone else."

"I don't think we were brought up to feel that was a good thing. Girls were supposed to go from their father's house to their husband's house. They were always under some man's protection and control. I always used to think it was strange that even though our school was all girls, and almost all women teachers, that we always had a male principal. I guess that's one of the reasons I don't want to go to a rabbi now. I don't want another man telling me what to do. None of them were there to protect me when I needed them. I want to make this decision myself."

"Will you be able to?" Jenny asked her gently.

"The only reason I think I can is because even if I do nothing, if I just let it happen, that's also a decision. It's going to be made. It's not something you can avoid."

"Tamar, one thing: Don't just let it happen. Even if you do decide to do nothing, at least let that be a conscious decision, a choice that satisfies some desire, that gives you some knowledge. . . . Whatever happens to us, G-d means us to grow, to learn. Otherwise it's just a meaningless horror, a waste. Try to get something of value out of this. . . ."

It's so easy to talk and be pious when the horror has happened to someone else! It's so easy to be smart when your body is still yours, your lips still yours, Tamar thought, looking at Jenny.

When would this endless night be over? These endless words, meaningless, flung back and forth? Friends. They visited you when you were sick, fed you when you were hungry, gave you a hand when you were tired. But also, they judged you when you strayed, persecuted you when you faltered. They were hasty to judge and incredibly slow to forgive. And they could not, for the life of them, ever really feel what you were feeling, ever really put themselves in your place. Which is all we really want, isn't it? More than help, more than pep talks, more than anything. Simply understanding. And that was the one thing rarer than platinum. A commodity that could not be found anywhere, except, perhaps, in the heart of another Ohel Sara girl who had been raped in her sister's house by a black man with a knife. Even if such a person existed, she too must be hiding. She too must be too mortified to share her experiences and feelings, imprisoned and isolated by walls made up of the yellowing parchment of holy books, the thick red flesh of wagging tongues, and the cold sterling of pious reputations.

Had it been any help, this marathon with old friends? She honestly didn't know. But somehow she did feel she had inched closer to some decision simply by a process of elimination.

She began to understand what it was she didn't want.

She didn't want Josh or her mother or sister or community or friends to know anything about what had happened. She didn't want their startled, pitying eyes, their gasps of horror, their hugs of comfort. She didn't want to take Hadassah Mandlebright's place as community pariah. It was too high a price to pay for understanding.

She didn't want to kill Josh's baby. Her own baby.

"Tamar?"

She looked up. The car was already parked in front of her apartment house. She was back in Orchard Park.

"Home already."

"You sound sad."

"Josh will just be getting up. He'll be full of complaints and hard questions. I better hurry. I'll see you in shul this Shabbos. Don't worry. And please, not a word to anyone—you promised, remember?"

"Tamar, forgive me!"

"For what? You've been so kind."

"For not being better. For not really understanding. . . ."

Tamar reached out to her, touching her smooth skin, searching her face. "I love you. It's not your fault. You tried."

"Take care, my dear friend."

"I will. Good-bye."

She waved, watching the car disappear around the corner. She was glad to see her go. Glad to be alone.

She didn't go home. Instead she crossed the street, walked around the corner, and waited. She saw his familiar brisk stride in the distance, his impeccable black suit and regal bearing.

Josh.

His step had not slowed. There was no trouble on his mind.

She waited for him to turn the corner toward the yeshiva, then wound her way slowly home.

She locked the door and its five latches and checked all the windows in her now familiar ritual. She threw off all her dampish sweat-salty clothes and stepped into the shower, turning the water on full blast. She scrubbed her white fragile breasts and still flat stomach, her firm and pliant thighs. This was her life, this white body. She was not just a thought, a feeling, a spirit. She was also this white flesh. The spirit and the body intermingled irrevocably.

If only they didn't have to be!!

She had, even at the time, removed her mind, her spirit, from the act of rape. She, the real she, had not been there. But this flesh she carried with her, it had been. She could not forgive it for that. For dragging her down in its humiliation, for not escaping. For compromising her.

She wrapped herself in clean, thick towels, patting her body, hugging the person she was, someone she had once liked and valued. My body, she mourned.

If she was not going to tell anyone what had happened, if she was not going to kill Josh's baby, then it meant she was not going to get an abortion. It meant she had decided to go through with the pregnancy.

But what, what if . . . The terror that dwelt in her stomach flashed through her, sharp as a glinting blade, tearing at her heart.

But it won't be. G-d wouldn't do that to me. I have to have faith. G-d is good. He wouldn't punish me like that. G-d is good. I must believe that. I must have faith. . . .

But what . . . what if?

A tiny face, dark, cocoa colored; small black eyes stared up at her from the depths of her horror.

She closed her eyes and clenched her fist. She would not look at it. That image was just a nightmare, just a simple scary nightmare. It would go away. G-d would make it go away. He would have mercy. She would simply pray it away, that tiny cocoa-colored face, those dark black eyes. . . .

But what . . . what if? The question persisted, more forcefully.

Then there is no mercy. There is no faith. There is no joy. No reward.

Then there is no G-d.

And if there are none of these things, I do not choose to live.

She felt she had tumbled somehow unexpectedly through a crack that led to the center of the universe, a dark pit of howling winds, the very black depths of her soul which she had always thought to be so light-filled and perfumed, so full of beauty. But she did not try to climb back up. She felt strangely at home, at peace there.

I will carry this child. I will nourish it. I will keep the laws of kashruth. Attend the synagogue. Support my husband when he learns Torah. And then I will give birth.

And if the child is black, I will kill myself.

❖20❖

"Mazel tov! Oy, mamaleh, mamaleh, mazel tov, mazel tov!" Tamar looked at her mother's beaming face, the two wrinkled, aging hands clasped together jubilantly, the wet shining eyes.

"When, mamaleh?"

"I'm right at the beginning, Mameh."

"Does Josh know?"

"Of course, Mameh." Josh, the staid scholar, the respectable rabbi and talmid chachom, had jumped up and clicked his heels together in the middle of the living room, like some young lad on the Highlands of Scotland.

"Was he happy?"

"Yes, Mameh. Very happy."

"Something's the matter? Nu, tell?"

"Nothing. What's the matter?"

"Should I know? I'm asking."

"So I'm telling. Nothing, Mameh. Really."

"It'll be healthy, beautiful. My beautiful daughter. What else could it be? If only Tateh . . ."

"Mameh." She hugged her as always, shocked at her smallness. Where was the mother who had towered over her like some shady tree, who needed to bend down to her to help her tie her laces, button her blouses? Where was that mother of the wide lap and comforting bosom where you could hide your face and find comfort for any tragedy? The mother who could solve all problems, prevent all harm? Strong as a lioness, powerful.

"You must go to the rebbe and get a blessing."

220

Josh had also said this. The thought made her sick. Surely a wise rebbe would see through the facade; surely with his otherworldly powers he would divine the truth. . . .

"Well, it's very early. . . ."

"It's never too early to be blessed!"

"I told Josh I'd go if he could find a rebbe who will agree to be in the same room with me. Some of them won't even talk to a woman! You have to write things down and send it through an assistant. I'm not going to do that. I'm not going to be invisible. . . ."

"What are you getting excited? *Mamaleh,* this is not like you. But *nu,* pregnant. We always get a little crazy when we're pregnant. Are you throwing up?"

"A little."

"Good. That's good. It's good to throw up. It means the pregnancy is healthy. But not to throw up too much. You're eating, I hope. *Oy,* don't tell me you're not eating! Tell me what you ate for breakfast," she interrogated.

"*Mameh,* I'm fine. I'm eating. Look at me. Do I look like I'm wasting away?"

Mrs. Gottlieb looked over her daughter's pretty round figure, her pink, lovely full cheeks, and shrugged, satisfied. "It should be in a *mazaldiga shur!*"

It should be in a good hour. "Thank you, *Mameh.* Now I have to go. You'll remember to take the medicine? And Thursday at nine-thirty you have your doctor's appointment. Do you want me to pick you up?"

"Pick me up, pick me up? What is this? Who's the *mameh* here?"

Tamar looked at her mother, fragile, gray, and small as a child. "You are, *Mameh.* You are."

"I'll be on time, don't worry, he'll get his money, I'll get my pills—green ones, blue ones. Everybody will be happy. Did you call Rivkie?"

"Not yet. I wanted to wait. You know how she talks. I don't want the whole world to know. It's too early yet."

"This is true, G-d bless her! So I shouldn't say anything? Of course. Right. I won't say a nothing, not a word. Just be well, *mamaleh*. So happy, you made your mother. So happy . . ." She sighed.

"Good-bye, *Mameh*," Tamar said huskily, uncertain of how long she could keep her voice steady, her eyes dry.

She wanted so badly to cry.

She felt so alone. Amid all the good wishes, the happiness, she felt lost, a bad actress in a part she had neglected to learn the lines for. What should she say? How should she feel? How would it be if there had only been the prayers, the mikvah night, and then the joyous day when the menstrual blood stopped flowing?

And how would it be if Eve had not wandered over to the snake and taken a bite from the fruit of the tree of knowledge? We would all still be in paradise, instead of east of Eden. What was the point of imagining?

But she had no choice. She had to play the part she had cast herself in. Joyous, first-time pregnant Ohel Sara girl, wife of the great hope of the yeshiva world. Look in the mirror. Arrange your features, the way you make your bed. Smooth down the wrinkled worry lines, fluff up the depressed corners of your mouth. Make it look nice. Make it look real.

How was she going to get through the next seven months?

One day at a time. One day at a time.

But the days, she realized very quickly, were not the problem. The days were light-filled and voice-filled. People she loved coming over, happy. Acquaintances stopping you in the afternoon on the bustling, safe streets of Orchard Park, out in the open air where nothing could touch you because there were so many people to see. . . . The days had activities, and chores, and plans. Teaching small children, lesson plans, dentist's appointments, buying a new wig, looking at baby clothes.

The days could be endured.

But what was she to do with the nights? They began pleasantly enough. She and Josh would talk over the events of the day quietly, cheerfully. And then they would go to bed. There were no separations between them now, no counting of days, no mikvah nights. He could be with her as much as he wanted, and he was very loving. They fell asleep cradled in each other's arms.

But then, a few hours later, when the world slept, she would give up the struggle with the night and extract herself from his embrace. Shivering, she would put on the table lamp in the deadly quiet living room and try, again, to read. Often, she found the tears clouding her reading glasses, making the nose bridge slippery so that it slid down her cheeks, making reading impossible. So she put down her book, and just sat there, staring into the darkness of the ill-lit room.

I must have sleep, she told herself. I can't go on like this night after night. So much anger, so much pain! And no place to put it! No place to let it seep out, harmlessly, like heat from a pressure cooker.

"You look terrible," Josh told her one morning. "What's the matter with you?"

"Nothing . . . just . . ." She had never been an imaginative person; concocting plausible lies came slowly and hard. "My legs hurt me. I have headaches."

He was immediately all concern. "What did the doctor say?"

"He said it was normal, that I'd get over it. I guess I think too much about things going wrong," she let slip.

"You have too much time on your hands!"

Why, why had she said it? "Maybe," she replied, flustered.

"Then you must use it to do *chesed*. Join a women's charity group. Or the Bikur Cholim committee. They do such a big mitzvah visiting people in the hospital, cheering them up. It would be good for you to get out, not to think about yourself so much."

Hospitals, she thought, cringing. The sick, the injured . . ."I don't know. I really hate hospitals," she pleaded, but already she glimpsed the concern fading from his eyes, the stern, uncompromising glare of judgment taking its place.

"*Chesed, chesed teardof,*" he said with an edge of sanctimony she couldn't stand. Kindness, kindness pursue. "Call them. Promise me! You'll see. You'll get more out of it than you give. Call them today."

It wasn't an inquiry, it was a command. He had the moral upper hand. She was helpless.

The hospital, built by Jewish philanthropists at the turn of the century, smelled of strong disinfectants that try as they might did nothing to hide the smell of poverty that rose up from its emergency wards and corridors.

"We'll just divide up the floors," Mrs. Geller said, smiling. She was the head of the Bikur Cholim committee, a heavy, beaming grandmother in a short gray wig. She handed sheets listing the Jewish patients to Tamar and two other young women.

Tamar took hers wordlessly, scanning the unfamiliar names. She walked quickly through the cheerless corridors, into the rooms of old men and old women with tubes in their arms and noses. Most of them smiled when they saw her and tried to sit up. Their efforts to be hospitable shamed her. So much suffering in the world, and still people smiled, they made an effort to go on, to think of others, to make each moment worthwhile.

Why can't you? she asked herself. Why can't you just try to forget? Give up your right to hate. Give it up unconditionally. Give up your anger, your right to avenge, to punish, to destroy.

She smiled at the old woman whose body was as faded and delicate as dried dandelions. "And how are you feeling, *bubbe?*" she asked, giving her a package of sweets.

"Oh, thank G-d, a little better today. Maybe they will do the operation on my hip tomorrow. I would like to get it over with, to go home. . . ." She smiled, nodding. "I bought so many new outfits just before I fell. I'd like to wear them. Such nice clothes," she said cheerfully.

"May *Hashem* give you a *refuah shelamah,* a full recovery," Tamar whispered, wondering at the woman's smile, at her optimism.

The children's ward was next. A tonsillectomy. A broken arm. She gave them chocolates and a coloring book with pictures of dreidels and Chanukah menorahs, shofars and willow branches. They seemed very pleased.

"Does it hurt very much?" she asked them.

"It hurts," the little boy without the tonsils whispered hoarsely, "but I get to eat ice cream. And that's good."

It hurts, but there is also ice cream, she thought, patting his head. Simple, good things. A small child's silky head, his smile. Simply live. Simply love. Simply, simply.

She took the elevator down to the first floor to wait at the entrance for the others so that they could walk home together in the gathering shadows. She passed by the emergency ward. A black man lay moaning on a gurney, his face wrapped in stained red bandages, his arm torn at the wrist. She looked at him with a growing fascination, a tiny, shameful blossom of hatred sprouting in her chest.

Just the hint of going back in time, of reliving and trans-forming the moment, made her happier than she imagined possible. She would fire six bullets into his woolly black head. She would stab him a hundred times. She would see him bleed and die and beg and suffer. . . . I did it! she imagined herself saying and feeling glad, smiling triumphantly at her friends. He raped me and I killed him and I'm glad. The image of his dead body made her happy.

Only, what would she do with it, such a heavy immovable object? She glanced at the moaning man on the gurney, looking at his heavy arms, his long legs.

I'd slash it to bits, she thought.

I'd burn it.

I'd throw it down the elevator shaft.

She could almost hear the thud. It was beautiful. Beautiful music.

"So, did you get to everyone?" Mrs. Geller said with her kind, cheerful smile.

Tamar nodded. "Yes, everyone."

"Don't you find yourself full of beautiful feelings? I always do. Whenever I do this, I'm so grateful to *Hashem* for every-thing I have, my health, my family's health. You can have everything, but if you don't have your health . . ."

"Yes, a beautiful feeling," Tamar agreed, feeling as if she were in the midst of a frightfully potent nightmare, yet one full of thrilling possibilities she was reluctant to relinquish.

She walked home quietly, the other women's chatter like the sound of far-off sparrows in her ears.

When would it be over? she wondered. When terrible people

touched your life, were they always a part of it? Or just until some kind of reckoning?

"And when is your little blessing due?" Mrs. Geller was asking her. She looked at the woman's placid, gentle face, the face of an innocent matron of sixty-five, who had known only the purity of the mikvah waters, the gentle embrace of a dignified husband.

Why didn't I scream? Why didn't I run? Why didn't I kill him?

"I'm due after Chanukah."

"Will you give birth at Beth Shalom?"

"Yes, in Beth Shalom."

"My daughter had all her babies there. The nurses all know me. Your first baby! What a beautiful blessing! What a beautiful experience you have waiting for you. I'll never forget my first. . . ," the woman chattered on, her voice light and unbearably sweet.

Why doesn't G-d punish him? Why doesn't G-d stop punishing me?

"Well, good night and bless you! Will you be coming next week?"

"Oh, yes, of course," Tamar murmured, turning into her apartment house. "Of course. I'll see you next week."

The apartment was dark and cold. Josh was not yet back from his evening *shiur* at the yeshiva. She went into the kitchen and lit the stove, warming a pot of soup. She stirred it, watching the vortex form and then dissipate. What was the answer to death? To hatred? What was the answer to sleepless nights? And debilitating fear?

Josh walked in, his step cheerful, enlivening the lifeless rooms. "How was it?" he asked her, his lips grazing hers, his arms warm around her shoulders.

"It was wonderful. You were so right," she told him, happy at the sight of his approving, pleasant face, his accepting smile.

"Are you feeling better now?"

"Yes, Josh. Much better. I have so much to be grateful for," she said, her heart weighted down, aching.

What is the answer? she thought as she sat later that night in the living room, sleepless.

"What, headaches again? Come to bed, my love. Come, try to sleep, my love. Lie in my arms," Josh said, tired but compassionate, pulling her up, leading her gently back to their bedroom.

The answer is, she thought, your husband who loves you, coming to find you as you sit alone in the dark room. It is your kind husband who wakes because he's stretched out his hand beneath the warm covers and your absence is a disturbance to him in the warm bed, in the sleeping house.

And what is the answer when he does not come?

Don't ask. It will not happen. His kind, warm arm will always find you in the night as you sit alone with the couch pillows and a simple glaring light in the silence of the satisfied, all sleeping, indifferent world. His warm arm will always guide you safely back to bed, past the night terrors, the cynically jubilating roaches in the wall. You will turn your head and pretend you've never seen them.

And some time, some day, you might even sleep.

❧21❧

The pains were starting, but somehow they didn't hurt, not really. They were like rolling waves, big and daunting but ultimately harmless. At least that was how she felt. They didn't hurt.

She was surprised.

It went very quickly. And there was a confusion, a gray rush mixed with red and green. Cars speeding past streetlights. Big green buses. And then the white of the hospital.

White and surgical steel gray. And she was rushing forward on something wheeled, but the wheels made no sound. She thought that was odd, the soundlessness. The only thing she heard was the pounding, like warning drums, beating in her ears. Like the pulse of the fetal heart.

She felt helpless and wanted it all to stop. She felt happy and wanted it all to be over, finally over.

But there were the doors of the delivery room, two big mint green doors slammed back against the walls, her rolling bed smashing through.

Still, there was no sound.

Where was the doctor?

Where was Josh? And her *mameh?* And Rivkie?

And suddenly she was lying on her back and looking up at strange faces of people in white masks.

Push, they urged her.

She pushed. It did not hurt. No. It felt good to participate. To push. She wanted this with all her heart, to push this child from her body, her womb. To see it.

Push.

The sound began. A few whispered words, then louder, a human sound of many voices joined in cacophonous horror, then suddenly inhuman, something monstrous and mechanical, a freakish machine, bellowing and dangerous, mercilessly rolling downhill toward her.

The faces looked down at her, their eyes wide with horror and suspicion. They held the child up.

Black dark skin, like a burnt thing. A foreign, burnt thing she did not recognize. Monstrous. Its dark fists, big as a man's, flailed violently, the small baby face suddenly grown large. A dark man's strange face, threatening her life.

We must tell your husband! they screamed at her, like some Greek chorus, many voices one. Your husband, they screamed and screamed. He has a right. Your husband has a right, every right.

Then suddenly the room was full of rabbis. Bearded, humorless, and smelling of old books. Men she had never seen and men she had known all her life. Her principal at Ohel Sara, Hadassah's father, Josh's friends, Josh's rebbe.

Josh.

Who is the father? they threatened her.

Who is the father of this cocoa-colored baby? Who?

Zonah!

Pritza!

Adulteress.

Harlot.

What shall be done?

Divorce.

Disgrace.

All of it. All of it shall be done.

She looked for her husband, wildly. He must protect her. But he is too far away, standing behind the inner circle of doctors and rabbis. She motioned him to come closer, but he made no move to join her. His face was closed, set, fixed. He had no love. It was he shouting the words at her. He who had thrown the first stone.

"*Bogedes,*" he spat at her. Traitor. And the spit separated into drops, each one a sharp knife hailing down. A thousand knives found her flesh, each sharpened to small murderous points, glinting dangerously as they fell.

"Hold your baby," the nurse said, her face disgusted, her fingers recoiling from the strange, small creature. "Here it is. Yours. Hold it."

"*No,* I don't want it. *No!*" Its dark head pressed into her arms. Its lips attached themselves to hers with the kiss of a succubus. She twisted her head, but could not remove it.

She was suffocating, her body bludgeoned, the hateful small creature taking away her breath.

I am dying, she realized. And it was not what she wanted.

"Josh!" she screamed.

"Tamar, Tamar, wake up, wake up, darling."

Daylight. Home. Awake. A dream. Nothing more.

The child, still cradled in her womb, moved within her. Josh's warm hand cradled her large stomach.

"I feel it. My child." He laughed. "Wait!"

He ran and brought back a little blue rattle, shaking it in front of her stomach.

She smiled, the tears of terror drying on her cheeks. She reached out for Josh, and he held her, his arms calm and reassuring, the stroke of his hand down her back a fatherly stroke of love and comfort.

"What is it? What's wrong?"

She searched his blue eyes so filled with sincere concern, and then her eyes caught the impeccable gleam of his black wool suit hanging in the closet, worn on the hottest summer days in strict adherence to custom. Worn because pious Polish ancestors had worn the clothes of the Polish nobleman of the village to show a Jew's respectability. And generations later, out of love for G-d, for custom, for the holiness of tradition, still worn. Because new ideas bring dangers. Because straying off the familiar path leads to the slippery slope. . . .

Can't take the chance.

"I'm afraid."

"Of what?"

"Of the pain. Of something being wrong with the baby."

This was plausible. Why should he question it? It is his first wife, his first child. How was he to know that endless, sleepless nights were not what happened to pregnant women? That crying out nightmares, dark circles under terrified eyes, were not normal for pregnant women?

"Come to the rebbe. Come get his blessing. Then you will have a *segula*, you will be protected from any harm. . . . Come, darling, for me. For my sake."

Maybe, she thought. Maybe it will help. The hand that is forming this child inside me, this blessed hand over which I have no control, I will kiss that hand. I will implore that hand to keep the nightmare far from me. A *segula*. A blessing.

"Which rebbe?"

"Why, whoever you want, Tamar. Whoever you would feel most comfortable with. What about the Kovnitzer Rebbe? You know him, don't you?"

"Yes, I know him. Knew him. I was a child. His daughter's friend."

"The daughter who . . ." His face went rigid.

She noted the hardening of his features. A small, joyous comfort flowed through her knowing it was Hadassah he thought of, her sins, as his kind face froze into the supercilious, judgmental lines of a petty tyrant. "Yes, that one. He has . . . had only one daughter."

"You'll come?"

Why not? she thought. The Kovnitzer Rebbe never blamed me. He knew it was his precious daughter all along egging me on, leading me astray. In a way, she almost felt he owed her something. "If he agrees to see me, I'll come."

"Agrees?"

"If . . . if he has time, that is."

Hadassah's house. The same polished mahogany gleam. The same sparkling silver behind tall glass doors. The same noise- and people-filled rooms. But it had lost something, Tamar thought. That air of splendid perfection, of almost holy order- liness. It seemed less cold, more human. And Hadassah's mother, the rebbetzin, her beauty long faded into a pale, aggrieved middle age, looked strangely kinder now.

"Rebbetzin . . . "

"Tamar!" Her face lit up for a moment, then faded, resigned. "It's been a long time." She nodded, sighing. "Come in, come in. Rabbi Finegold." She nodded to Josh courteously, giving his Torah knowledge its due.

They stood in the hallway. The rebbetzin seemed lost in thought. "A long time," she mused. "It was Purim, that first time? Remember? And I was angry about the sticky hands on the . . . I shouldn't have been angry. What difference does it make? You clean it up. So? And the dress. She . . . wanted blue and we made it brown. Do you remember?" she asked with odd impatience.

"I remember, Rebbetzin. It was the most beautiful costume in Orchard Park," Tamar said kindly.

"I still have it, you know. It's up in the attic in tissue paper, along with . . ."

Josh cleared his throat.

She stopped suddenly and looked at them in alarm. "*Oy,* I don't know when to stop! What does it matter now, anyway, tell me that, will you? Come. The Rebbe is expecting you?"

"I think so," Josh said politely, feeling uncomfortable. He disliked talking to other men's wives. To women in general. The Talmud was full of admonitions to avoid lightheaded and frivolous talk. The idea of socializing was a very American one. Religious Jews, especially Torah scholars, did not socialize. And if they were at a family celebration, or otherwise unavoidably involved in social contact, the only acceptable topic of conversation had to do with Torah and had some instructive or moralistic purpose. He stood silent and uncomfortable.

"We don't see the girls from Ohel Sara very much nowadays. Maybe it's a blessing, although who can tell, who can say. . . . Well, come, the Rebbe is probably waiting," Rebbetzin Mandlebright finally said, her face closed and inscrutable.

About a dozen Hasidim waited outside the closed door of the Rebbe's study. They looked up enviously as Tamar and Josh passed through, escorted by the rebbetzin, who did not knock but simply opened the door and ushered them in.

The Rebbe of Kovnitz looked smaller than she'd remembered. Frailer. And yet there was a certain sorrowful majesty about him. It reminded her of the story of Moses led to the mountaintop to survey the beloved promised land from a distance, forever forbidden to enter. His white, thick brows lifted in surprise as he looked at her, and he stroked his graying beard thoughtfully.

"Sit, sit," he said with affable authority, waving them onto the two armchairs facing his Talmud-laden desk.

"Please, Rebbe, we couldn't possibly!" Josh entreated. To sit in the presence of such a *gadol hador*, such a luminary of the Jewish world, was like asking a peasant to sit down next to a king.

"You could and you will," he insisted calmly. "Your wife has a big enough burden to carry without making it any heavier, my son," he added a bit severely.

Tamar looked up sharply at his wise face, a strange foreboding filling her heart. She shouldn't have come, she suddenly thought. The Rebbe had that sixth sense, that ability to know the past and the future that came from being so close to G-d. He would know everything just by looking at her! She panicked.

"Thank you, Rebbe," Josh murmured, chastised, pulling out a seat for Tamar and sitting down quickly. "We have come for your blessing, Rebbe. As the Rebbe can see, my wife is expecting. We ask that you bless us with an easy birth and a healthy child."

"I have no powers. But if you would be enriched by my blessing, I am happy to give it. May G-d grant you a healthy child and an easy birth," he answered. "How is your mother, Tamar?"

"She is as well as can be expected, Rebbe." Tamar looked up, touched.

"Please send her my blessings for a long, good life full of mitzvos and much *nachas* from her children." The Rebbe nodded.

"Thank you." Tamar swallowed hard, imagining her mother's joy at the Rebbe's words. But she had no satisfaction from the blessing he had just given her. She was not worried about a painful delivery or a child full of disabilities . . . she could manage both, if only she could be sure it was Josh's child.

She sat gripping the sides of her chair tensely, trying to think of some inconspicuous way to ask the Rebbe to peel away the mask of the future, revealing it to her.

"Will the child look like its mother or its father, Rebbe?" she asked.

The old man looked at her, his eyes burning with a sudden intensity. "How the child looks and who it takes after is G-d's will. May G-d grant you the ability to love this child with all your heart, to recognize in its creation G-d's infinite wisdom and divine will. . . ."

"Rebbe, we both want this child! It is our first. We have prayed so long and hard for it. Of course we will both love it no matter what!" Josh exclaimed, scandalized that the Rebbe should misinterpret their concerns as shallow and fatuous. He shot Tamar a warning look. "We came because my wife has been having nightmares and sleepless nights worrying about the child's well-being. . . ."

Tamar stared at her lap, at her fingers weaving complicated, torturous designs with each other. "Rebbe, I'm afraid," she whispered.

"Of what, Tamar?"

"Of . . . of . . . being punished. I am not such a good person. I'm afraid I will not have the *zchus* to give birth to my husband's child," she said, choosing each word the way a girl chooses her engagement ring, knowing she will live with it for a very long time.

The Rebbe stroked his beard and closed his eyes. "Pick up your arm," he commanded her suddenly.

She looked at Josh in shock.

"Can you?" the Rebbe asked again.

"Of course, Rebbe." She lifted her arm.

"Can you leave it there, up like that? Can you also put it down?"

"Of course, Rebbe!"

"Who controls you, Tamar? No one. You control yourself. Your own actions. You are never judged on what is done to you, forced on you. But only on your own free choices. And the beautiful thing that G-d has done is to let us start over again when we choose wrong. Again and again and again.

"You say you are not such a good person. But I know differently. You judge yourself too hard. Don't be afraid to fail at things. Nothing you ever did wrong has to hold you back from being better in the future. Have a *passion* to be a good person. Even if you only have the chance once in your life to do a certain mitzvah, it's worth preparing all your life to do it.

"Never envision the worst. Envision the best. G-d is with you. He watches over you. He will take away your nightmares, take away your fears. I see His love covering you like sunlight. Go home, child. Sleep, eat, take care of yourself. You have nothing to fear. Everything will be as G-d wills it in His goodness. Everything will be all right."

"Thank you, Rebbe," she whispered, and her heart, so long imprisoned and afraid, felt a sudden flood of new oxygen, springing up in her chest, young, alive. She believed in him. In his ability to know the future. And from all the complicated things he had said, she gleaned one thing that mattered to her: he had promised her she had nothing to fear. That everything would be all right.

They got up to go, Josh thanking him profusely and hurrying to leave so as to not take up any more of the Rebbe's precious time.

Unexpectedly, the Rebbe stopped them. "Wait a minute. I have something I want to ask your wife, if you don't mind. Tamar, I ask your *mechilah*," the Rebbe suddenly said.

"Rebbe!" Josh was flabbergasted at this show of incredible modesty. What possible reason would the great Rebbe have to ask forgiveness? He who learned all day, who did only good deeds, kindnesses? He who had helped so many, performed so many miraculous deeds of kindness with his blessings? And from Tamar?

"You understand me, Tamar?" the Rebbe persisted. "I tried to do the right thing, but perhaps it was misinterpreted. Please tell your mother I ask her *mechilah* also."

"Rebbe—" Her throat was thick and painfully hoarse with emotion. "I give you my *mechilah* with all my heart, and I ask you to forgive me for anything I might have thought or said . . ."

"I grant you mine with happiness," the Rebbe answered, a flicker of pained recognition crossing his features.

Josh, bewildered and anxious to question Tamar privately, edged toward the door. "Thank you so much, Rebbe, for your help. If it is a boy, will the Rebbe honor us with his presence at the *bris*?"

"I always come to a *bris* with great joy." He nodded, suddenly weary, dismissing them.

"What does it mean, his asking your forgiveness?"

"Josh, don't ask me!"

"Why?"

She thought fast. The trip to the Met. The call at the bar. She knew what Josh would make of it. "Because it was long ago, and if I tell you, it will be *loshen hara*."

Almost consumed by curiosity, he nevertheless did not pursue it because it was wrong to encourage his wife to speak *loshen hara*. That was the *halacha*.

❖22❖

The words of the Kovnitzer Rebbe acted like a magic elixir. Tamar felt a bubble as thin as sunlight, as impenetrable as steel, surround her. Nothing could harm her. Once, she even forgot to latch all of the windows. And at night, sleep again became that soft blanket of restful forgetfulness. Her dreams were oddly mild, forgotten as soon as she woke.

She went looking at baby clothes with Rivkie, fingering the soft pastel jumpsuits with their little snaps and embroideries, wondering at their tininess. Could a human being fit into that? A whole human being?

Jenny called frequently, but their conversations were short and strained. All the important things were avoided, all the trivial belabored until, bored and uncomfortable, they both found some reason to hang up.

The doctor's appointments grew more frequent. And in the pristine, white waiting room with the lovely pictures of healthy, smiling babies and their healthy, smiling mothers, she felt herself lulled into forgetfulness. She began to think in terms of a baby, a longed-for little child. As she flipped through *Family Circle* and the *Ladies' Home Journal*, she lingered over crochet patterns for crib blankets and darling little sweater sets, going so far as to write down the directions and buy the wool.

It was going to be all right, she strengthened herself, praying with extra diligence, saying the Book of Psalms until she was hoarse. But it was not a real prayer, she knew. Because it was forbidden to ask G-d for something that was already decided.

You could not ask for a boy or a girl once you were pregnant. Your prayers were foolish, meaningless. So she could not really ask G-d to make this child the union of her egg and her husband's sperm. It was what it was. But still, she prayed all the same. She prayed and prayed and prayed for this thing, knowing it was wrong and useless.

It was inhuman to ask her not to pray, she thought.

The elixir lasted until she entered her ninth month. And then, for no reason, its potency suddenly failed her.

The dream was red this time, all shades of red, brick and blood and rust and wine. She woke up like a diver who has swum desperately to the top with empty oxygen tanks, gasping for breath. She did not remember the details, only the color: red, splashed over everything. Horrible pain. Tremendous fear, hot red, heavy red. She put on her robe and walked into the bathroom.

There was blood, real blood. Her panties were wet with it.
"Josh!!"
"What?"
"I'm bleeding," she whispered, panic-stricken.
"Sit down. I'll call the doctor," he said with cold fear.

She lay on the examining table in the cold hospital room, the light shining in her eyes, blinding her. She heard the doctors conferring, snatches of words: ". . . irregularity . . . better to go in . . . first pregnancy . . ." The soft flow of distant words from strangers hovered over her life and body.

"Tamar, darling. The doctor thinks we shouldn't wait. The placenta may have detached. He wants to do a cesarean right away. But it's up to you. We can still wait, get another opinion . . ."
"It's too soon, too early!"
"You're almost at the end of your ninth month. The doctor says the baby is big enough, it won't be premature. Tamar, we have to, or the baby might die."

It might die, she thought, wondering at the strange mixture of emotions. Did she want that? Her baby, she thought. Black or white or green or yellow. Her baby. Her mind couldn't go beyond that. It was too late. She had made the choice to give it life. To trade its life for her own if need be. She had spent nine months giving it life. She wanted that work to bear fruit. Living fruit. There wasn't room for any other emotion.

"I don't want to wait. Tell them to do it."

The rolling bed, the slam of mint green doors, the masked faces looking down at her. The old nightmare come alive.

No!! she began to scream, but her mouth was smothered by the anesthesia mask, and mercifully blessed darkness, like the best night's sleep in the world, enveloped her.

"Tamar, wake up!"

Her eyelids fluttered. She tried to move, but her body felt horribly bruised, as if someone had cut her in half.

She was afraid to open her eyes. Afraid to face what had happened.

"Tamar!"

"Look!"

It was not the voice of the nightmare, but a friendly, warm sound. The babble of happy people involved in something they liked.

She looked up.

Josh stood at the head of her bed, a small blanket in his arms, a tiny warm, small blanket. Her mother's arms went around her shoulders. Rivkie was smiling ear to ear.

"Look at your son!" her mother commanded, her eyes wet.

Josh bent down. Painfully, she pushed her body off the pillows. She pulled back the blanket. Her fingers trembled.

A face, white and pink and perfect, looked back at her.

She closed her eyes and wept.

"Crying?" Her *mameh* laughed. "Tamar, you're all finished! It's over. The baby's fine. You're fine. I mean"—her mother winced at her daughter's painful movements—"you will be fine after you rest up." She hugged Tamar as if she were a small child. "You've made me so happy. Given me such *nachas*. You will call him Aaron, after your father?"

"Of course, *Mameh*," Josh said without hesitation.

"A namesake for your father." She glanced at Rivkie, who lowered her gaze guiltily. Rivkie had named her baby after her husband's grandfather. "It would have made him so happy. A beautiful little grandson. Tamar, Tamar, you've made us all so happy!"

"My dear wife," Josh whispered, taking the baby from her. "A little kaddishul. A son, *baruch Hashem, baruch Hashem,*" and she could see his knuckles whiten as they gripped the precious package, guarding it.

It's all over, she thought.

"Look, he's waking up!" Rivkie exclaimed. "Look at his eyes!"

"What color are they?" Tamar asked.

"They're that baby color—bluish gook. You can't really tell. They might be Josh's blue, or your gray. But look how dark the hair is!" Rivkie exclaimed. "That's strange. You're both blond."

Tamar felt a sudden sick jolt tear into her stomach, leaving her breathless.

"That's nothing. That hair always falls out, and then the blond grows in. Tamar was the same way. So much black hair, and then it all fell out and grew in blond," Mrs. Gottlieb said offhandedly, examining the baby with great joy. "And if it doesn't . . . black hair is beautiful on a boy. Handsome. Your grandfather had the blackest hair, like coal it was, and black eyes. My beautiful little Aaron, my beautiful boy, we won't let them say anything about you that's not nice, will we?" she cooed to the infant.

Tamar sank back onto the pillows.

"Visiting hours are over," a nurse told them. "Do you want the baby in here, or should I take him?" she asked Tamar.

"Leave him, please."

"Good-bye, darling. I love you," Josh mouthed voicelessly, embarrassed to make such a declaration out loud in front of the others.

"I love you, Josh." She smiled up at him. He looked happy, oh so happy! Had anyone since the creation of the world ever looked as happy? she wondered.

"Mazel tov, my little Tamar. Be well, eat, rest," her mother murmured, kissing her cheek, rubbing a finger over the baby's smooth little chin.

"Good job, Tamar." Rivkie laughed. "Now you can open a day-care center, and I can bring Shlomie over every morning. . . ."

"Or you could baby-sit for your sister, it wouldn't kill you," *Mameh* said dryly.

"Well, sure, I suppose." Rivkie smiled wanly. "Be well. I'll come tomorrow."

Tamar waved to them tiredly, relieved to see the door close behind them.

She laid the baby on the bed and opened his blanket, the way a married woman would open a secret letter from a lover. She undid his soft cotton undershirt and opened the diaper, her heart beating with guilt and dread and excitement. With one finger, she traced the lines of his tiny body, from his small, smooth forehead to the tips of his tiny perfect pink toes. He had her own mouth, well shaped and vulnerable, her father's big ears, and her mother's high cheekbones. The eyes were small but with thick dark lashes, almost too pretty for a boy's, the color a newborn's indistinct motley blue. She studied them and thought she glimpsed a darker blue beneath. Josh's blue.

Or was it wishful thinking?

She laid her hand over his chest, her fingers spanning his entire body.

White and pink and beautiful, she thought.

Why should you worry anymore? White and pink and perfect. Mazel tovs. Smiling eyes. I love yous. Perfect.

Everyone was happy.

Everything was perfect.

Thank you, G-d, for this child. Thank you for doing what I asked of you. Thank you, oh, thank you!

She touched his head, smoothing down the dark black curly strands.

❧PART TWO❧

❖23❖

July 10, 1971
With G-d's help.

Dear Tamar,

The plane took off and I shut my eyes, wondering if I would turn out to be one of those people who are petrified of flying. Guess what? I love flying! I like it better than driving any day. I think I know the reason why. In a car you have some illusion of being in control so you're always tense and worried about the car behind you or the car coming toward you, your imagination working overtime. . . . But on a plane, you are up there in G-d's hands, completely helpless. Nothing you do matters. I'm one of those that feels a whole lot safer that way (considering the way I drive!). I figure, I'm on my way to Israel, to do this great good deed, to start this beautiful good life, G-d will carry me there safely.

The plane was jammed, packed, loaded, engorged. And everybody was so up, so happy. Lots of students with backpacks, lots of Hasidic families and little kids, lots of good-hearted Jews from Detroit and Chicago and Denver all fingering their little cameras and Mogen Dovids. In the middle of the trip the Hasidim got up, gathered in the back, and started praying. If I didn't feel safe before, I certainly felt safe after that! Imagine, thousands of feet in the air, and all these black-and-white prayer shawls, and tefillin. . . . I mean, how many commercial airlines are also flying shteibels? I love Shalom Airlines! Even though everything you've heard is true: they pack you in like sardines, the bathrooms are feculent (look it up!), the stewardesses are nasty and unhelpful and throw the food at you if you're not a handsome man in your thirties. But they speak Hebrew, and they're from Israel, and I love them anyway. I loved every single person on that plane. And I loved them even more when the plane swooped out of the clouds and we looked down and saw the coastline of Israel, blue and fair. I really felt like that old prophecy was coming true: "And I shall carry you on the backs of eagle's wings . . ."

When I think of how many Jews spent their whole lives dreaming about seeing this place and that I actually have the privilege of fulfilling that dream . . . shivers. I almost feel sad, in a way, as if I don't deserve it. Why me? Why not all the great rabbis who lived and died in Polish ghettos, or in Spanish or Portuguese auto-da-fés? Or those who died on those long treacherous sea–land journeys through Arabia before ever achieving their dreams? Or the Jews in Russia and Syria who are virtual prisoners? Why am I privileged to have been born at this time, in this place, to pay my ticket and come so easily?

Anyway, the plane landed and everyone, but everyone, sang that Naomi Shemer song "Jerusalem of Gold," and as corny as it all was, I felt the tears pouring down my cheeks (this will be a frequent phrase in this letter, so I'll just abbreviate it from now on—TPDMC).

Something very strange happened to me when I got off the plane. I saw people actually bend down and kiss the earth. I wanted so much to do it, but I felt paralyzed. I am just such an American. I wish I could let myself go. I wonder if a person can really change countries, or do you carry your birthplace and culture with you always? And is American culture really stronger than anything we learned in Ohel Sara?

I got my passport checked. Got my immigrant card. Picked up my luggage. And then, total panic!

My Ohel Sara Hebrew is just about worthless. My HIF Hebrew slightly better, but too slow. Everyone speaks so quickly, the way the Puerto Ricans speak Spanish. But the real problem is I don't know how to say anything. I mean, if I wanted to negotiate for a burial cave, or warn the Jews to break all their idols, I could probably manage with the Hebrew we learned in chumash class. But trying to hail a taxi left me speechless.

Somehow I managed to locate a taxi going to Jerusalem. Not a private cab, which costs a fortune, but this thing called a "sherut," sort of a shuttle service. There was only one problem: the driver needed six passengers to make it worth his while and there were only four of us. We waited and waited. I got to feeling I'd be ready to shanghai someone just to get us moving (and some air circulating) until finally an old gentleman and his wife turned up. I had to restrain myself from hugging them.

The car started moving and all the way I kept thinking: I've really done it, I'm here!! I looked out the back window and saw the airport fading in the distance, and this lump came to my throat. It wasn't the same type of lump I had when I kissed my mother and brother good-bye, or when I hugged you. I knew what was in that lump: nostalgia, parting, when will I see you again, don't let me leave the familiar, all my good friends, my dear family. . . . Looking out that back window, I felt the lump was hard and small and full of one feeling: fear. I never want to leave. I never want to come back to the airport and take a plane out. On the other hand, I was feeling: I don't want to be here, I'm afraid of the unknown. Take me back.

Aren't human beings strange?

That ride up to Jerusalem I will never forget as long as I live. It was level at first, and surprisingly green. We passed orange orchards and men in horse-drawn wagons. I pinched myself and thought: I don't think I'm in Kansas anymore! Or Orchard Park for that matter.

But then the car started climbing. I could feel my whole body straining, as if I'd been walking up a mountain and suddenly reached the top. In the distance I could see this shining white vision, sparkling like some marble sculpture rising out of the ground, a mirage of something too perfect, too lovely to be real.

"Will you look at that?" the nice touristy lady in the polyester pants suit nudged me.

But I couldn't answer her.

Jerusalem.

TPDMC.

With a vengeance.

The cab let me off at the absorption center. (I immediately, first night, had a nightmare in which sinister characters sidled up to me and said: Being absorbed, like a sponge.) Actually, it is just a residence hotel with studio apartments that new immigrants can use for a few months. The hostel managers were pleasant but offhand. My quarters were clean, plain and very Israeli. The bed

*was a thin slab of wood covered by an even thinner slab of foam
rubber. (Good for your back, right? Almost as good for you as
sleeping on the floor!)*

*There was orange juice in the fridge and a box of crackers. I
ate the bagel and lox from the plane, drank some juice, and then
fell asleep on my foam rubber torture chamber.*

*I don't know how long I slept, but this knock on my door must
have been going on for some time. Why do I think that? Because
later the people knocking told me, "We thought Shalom Airlines
had finally killed one. We weren't surprised."*

*The people knocking turned out to be my neighbors. Ariela, a
postdoc candidate at Hebrew U in chemistry. Wild, curly black
hair, Indian cotton skirts and the loveliest voice. Pure Boston.
Joseph, a distant cousin of Golda Meir, who is going to "farm
the land" just as soon as he learns something about farming. And
right after he does three years as a commando or a paratrooper—
that is, if he can convince the Israeli army to take him at all, with
his eyesight and back problems. . . . Tall, feather thin, with cute
glasses and shoulder-length brown hair that the Israeli army will
have lots of fun cutting. His parents back in Detroit—who I
understand paid for four years of CPA training at Brandeis—are,
he claims, heartbroken but proud.*

They dragged me off to meet Joseph's roommate.

*He was sitting there shyly minding his own business when the
three of us barged in on him. He wouldn't shake hands (too
religious to touch a woman), and he wears a big black skullcap.
His name is Marc (Menashe) Halpern. He's a Californian.
Actually, San Franciscan. Thick dark hair cut like a nice Jewish
boy's, a broad face that I think I might call very handsome if I
wasn't afraid you'd start up the "nu, nu's" and pick the wedding
date. Greenish eyes (I think—I didn't get close enough to actually
check it out). He seemed quiet and basically unfriendly, or was
that shyness masquerading as aloofness? Or was he really that
absorbed in Maimonides' "Guide to the Perplexed"? Go tell.
Anyhow, Ariela told me later he has a law degree from Stanford
and will be studying in one of those baal teshuva yeshivas for the
newly religious until he decides what else to do. Another Jewish
American mother's nightmare.*

Why have we all wasted our expensive educations and broken our mothers' hearts by leaving them?!

I wonder what father Abraham's mother said to him when he told her Ur of Chaldees wasn't where he wanted to spend his life, and he refused to go into the family's idol-selling business? What can we do? It's in our genes!

I start my master's degree in English next month. In the meantime, I have to a) find a job b) find an affordable apartment c) buy a bed with two more inches of mattress d) pray at the kotel and e) stop TPDMCing all over the place every time I walk down the street.

It is so beautiful here, so exciting.

So far away from home. . . .

Kiss Aaron for me. Seven months old already and trying to stand! A genius. We always knew it, didn't we?

> *Much love,*
> *Jenny*

P.S. I got a long letter from Hadassah just before I left. She's leaving Hawaii for San Diego. She's doing some modeling and a few commercials. There's a new man. Much older. Very, very, very rich. She says she was happy to hear all went well with the baby and sends you . . . No I won't lie. She doesn't send regards. But you know Hadassah. She means it anyway.

October 30, 1971
With G-d's help.

Dear Tamar,

I am a terrible person for not answering you sooner! I will list my excuses:

1. *No time*

2. *No time*

3. *No time*

4. *Lazy*

5. *Marc*

If I didn't know you were very careful about keeping all the laws that prevent a person from taking revenge and holding a grudge, I might beg you to please not punish me by waiting three months to answer me. But I know you won't do that.

The picture of little Aaron is wonderful! Handsomest little boy in the world. Maybe someday by me, as they say in Orchard Park.

I can't believe it's autumn already. I miss the paper crinkle of old brown leaves crushing underfoot that there would be in New York. But here there is the compensating soft bounce of the greenest grass. There is still that lingering scent of summer dust not yet washed fully away by rain. I sat on campus yesterday just looking at the coolish stretch of autumn sky, listening to the eager keening of new birds readying for their first long winter flight. I guess I feel sort of up there with them. I've never been on my own this long.

Everywhere I look there are so many role models, so many different kinds of inspirations. The young soldiers going back to their bases, front lines with Syria, Lebanon, Jordan, or Egypt. Young yeshiva boys returning to their studies, all serious and pale. Then there was this woman I saw sitting in front of me on a bus. She was dressed in severe modesty, her hair completely covered with a kerchief, her dress clean and pressed and covering her calves and wrists and neck. A new baby was resting on her chest, and you could see by the way he was dressed, he was loved and scrupulously cared for. With one hand she patted the sleeping infant, and with the other she held a little book of psalms. She spent the whole bus ride murmuring them. I could just envision her life: the tiny apartment immaculately clean. The chicken cut into twelve pieces every Sabbath. The bare living room, the big bookcase full of Talmuds. Her bearded, yeshiva student husband making kiddush Friday night. A pure life, full of strictness and denials, full of satisfaction and fulfillment. And at first I thought: This must be it! This is what G-d wants of me! What I should want of myself. What a good person! I mean, what else could G-d want?

The sun was just going down, and I was looking out over Jerusalem's hills. It was magnificent: magenta, purple, shades of gold and blue and orange. I felt my throat contract in this little

*prayer of thanksgiving for being alive in such a world. For having
eyes to see it and a heart to feel such beauty. And when it was
over, I turned back and noticed the woman hadn't even looked
up! She had let the sunset pass her by! And I thought: No. This
is not it. Or at least you couldn't really tell by looking at her if
she'd faced all the challenges in her life, if she'd wrested whatever
happiness was due her. You couldn't tell if she'd the courage to
seek and experience joy. I think we are also accountable for these
failures. Not just for denials, for strict adherence, for sidestepping
evil, but also for not appreciating good. For not living richly,
savoring the beautiful earth, its colors, its light; the spring, the
golden autumn . . .*

*School began right after the holidays. What a pleasure to be in
a Jewish country where instead of taking off for your weird New
Year in September, you are just normal, celebrating with everyone
else as the whole country shuts down. That's the most wonderful
thing of all: feeling normal. Going into a greasy spoon for a
hamburger, fries, and Coke and knowing it's all under rabbinical
supervision. So what if the hamburger is paper thin and inedible!
So what if the fries are half soggy and half raw! You can eat it!
It's all kosher!*

*In that old, tired debate that's been going on forever among
religious Jews on where you should live—in Israel or the diaspora—I think I'm convinced Israel is best. I went to the Old City
the other day. . . . What can I say? How can I describe to you
how it feels to touch the Wall? I think, for the first time, I
understand the way Americans feel when they visit Gettysburg,
or the Alamo, or Valley Forge, or the way the French feel about
the Bastille. It's so meaningful to me. Everything. I feel so
connected to the people, the streets, the language. And it's not this
artificial little world, like Disneyland, all make-believe, the way
Orchard Park is, that has no roots, no connection with its
surroundings.*

*It's all so phony, the way we grew up in Orchard Park. All those
Hebrew words we wrote in English: malach, tzadik, frumkeit . . .
All the pretense about living this Glatt kosher Jewish life steeped
in pious values, when the truth is, most of the people around us
were as American as kosher pizza. Their values were American*

values, climbing the ladder of business success, getting the kids into law school or medical school. So they bought their take-home from Kosher Corner instead of Gristede's. Did that make them so different?

I know you and Josh are not like that. That's why I think you belong here. I know you'd feel the same way I do once you got here and checked it out.

I went to the Israel Museum the other day and saw this earthenware jar holding oil they found in a cave filled with Jewish coins and manuscripts. It's about 1,500 years old. And I stood in front of it and I thought: Those hard, stubborn ancestors of mine really had guts. They didn't marry out or get lazy and forget. They didn't get fed up or choose to hide in some easier guise: Canaanite, Philistine, Greek, Roman . . . They didn't let the majority win. I am standing here, in Israel, a Jewish woman, because nobody in my family in those 2000 or so years gave up.

As you can tell, I'm having a ball. School is interesting. But it seems rather a cop-out to be learning English literature at Hebrew University. I have no real career plans. You know how I love to read, and this way I can read as much as I like and make believe I'm a serious person. Maybe I'll teach, or write. I've already got a part-time job working for some subsidiary of the Jewish Agency, writing little feature articles about all the nice things they're doing on the kibbutzim, and on the farms . . . nice little pleasant, cheerful aren't-the-Israelis-terrific propaganda. They pay me by the piece, and so far I haven't earned enough to be able to afford another inch of foam rubber for my mattress, which should indicate the pay scale! But guess what? I'm actually getting used to it. The mattress, that is. It is actually starting to feel . . . gulp . . . comfortable!

This is a bad sign.

Absorbed. Like a sponge.

On the personal front, remember that guy I told you about? Marc? Well, he isn't so shy after all. Just very sincere and in the first throes of religious conversion. You remember what you once told me about how the newly religious tend to go overboard? Well, that is what we are seeing here. He's afraid to talk to a woman, to sit down next to her . . .

But nevertheless, we have managed to have some interesting talks. He went through so much of what I did in college, the same questioning, the same revelation. If only he would find some equilibrium and stop lecturing me all the time! He is so hard on himself. He's never good enough, never religious enough . . .

I keep telling him all this sadness and self-loathing is the opposite of serving G-d. I remember Hadassah's father sitting at his tisch, his hand slapping the table, singing with closed eyes, the whole room rocking with joy. . . . I'm trying to tell him about that, about the joy.

Yesterday he came by with his toolkit and spent the whole afternoon fixing all leaking faucets. He sprayed for spiders in the bathroom. And he brought me fresh oranges from the shuk.

I hear the "nu, nu's" all the way across the oceans and continents that divide us. Powerful stuff, that Jewish telepathy! I have a revelation for you, my dear friend. I'll admit, I wouldn't mind.

It gets kind of lonely at night.

Love you. Kisses for your darling little boy. Regards to Josh.

Jenny

P.S. Hadassah's doing a movie in London. She may be getting married to one of the actors. Or was it the director? Anyhow. A blond Viking warrior. Not of the people of the book, I might add. Following Hadassah's adventures makes me feel as if I'm looking at a trapeze artist flying through the air with no net below. Hadassah is so brave, it's scary! I miss her.

July 15, 1972
With G-d's help

Dearest Tamar,

It is very hard for me to write this letter. As you can imagine, your last letter broke my heart. It was so unlike you, Tamar, to be so unkind. Okay, I deserved it. I had no business shooting off my mouth about the phoniness of Orchard Park. . . .

I have been racking my brain about what to write you. You know how dear you are to me. You're my sister in every way. I

253

want so much to undo the harm, to take back the hurt. But what can I do? If I forced myself to lie, it would lie beneath our friendship like some wound, festering and festering, an infection that would invade the bloodstream of our lives and poison everything between us.

So I'll tell the truth. You and Josh don't belong in Brooklyn. You, both of you, who believe in the Torah, in the prophecies, who try to live lives devoid of any connection to American culture and history, what are you still doing there?

Hadassah's father was right. America is just too powerful for anyone to resist. It is too beckoning with its luxuries, its easy life, its cornucopia of opportunities and chances for good times. Sooner or later American Jews—even dedicated, sincere ones—are going to get absorbed. Like a sponge. They are going over the mountain.

And the attempts to preserve our religion and values by keeping congregations huddled together in the decaying pockets of inner cities, places like Orchard Park and Williamsburg, Borough Park and Crown Heights, is just becoming too dangerous. When will our religious leaders finally realize it isn't right to bring more daughters and wives into these violent streets?

Please forgive me for hurting you. I'm just trying to be a good friend.

Now, I'll take a deep breath and turn from all these painful subjects to a glorious one: Marc and me.

We're in love.

And this is the way it happened:

About a month ago I moved into my own little place. It's a second-floor walk-up in this charming, quaint (you'd say it was a slum) area near the shuk called Nachlaot. I have high, domed ceilings, green shutters, and lovely black iron grillwork. I also have outdoor plumbing, pipes dating from the Ottoman empire, and lovely green mold around the sinks. I painted the walls a light rose and bought a mint rose chintz fabric for curtains and bedspreads. (I'm sure it's not real chintz, it was much too cheap. I bought the last ten meters on a roll at the shuk and bargained for an excellent price.)

When I moved in, I decided to invite all my absorption center friends over for a Friday night dinner. I went all out. I spent hours shopping at the shuk: the house smelled of lovely ripe peaches, cantaloupe, nectarines, fresh coriander, and parsley.

It was a very hot day. The air was full of that desert dust that sometimes settles on everything like a thin layer of white scum on the top of boiled milk. But toward the evening, as always, the fresh breezes came up out of the Judean hills and blew through the windows. I remember sitting by the open window, opening some buttons on my blouse, letting the coolness wash over me like a waterfall in some desert oasis. I think it was only my third Shabbat at home, and I was feeling excited and jittery about how everything looked. And pleased, too. All my things were where I wanted them. All the food crisp and hot and tender, waiting on the hot plate. The table was blooming with vases of tea roses and carnations in pretty shades of red and peach and pink with lots of baby's breath. And I remember thinking: Almost, almost perfect.

And then Marc knocked on the door.

He was dressed in a clean, new white shirt and dark pants. His dark hair was still wet, combed so carefully, the way a mother combs a little boy's. His arms were strong and tan and his fingers long and tender somehow. He had brought a bottle of wine.

We sat down on my awful straw-filled Jewish Agency mattress on my awful Jewish Agency metal bed frame, which I use for a living room couch and then he said, sort of offhandedly, that he had been looking forward to seeing me again. That the absorption center had never been the same after I left. And I sort of looked down and said: "Marc." And then we looked at each other and at that moment, I had this sense of wholeness: Him in the living room. The cool breeze from the hills of Judea. The fresh peaches from Mahane Yehudah shuk. The Sabbath. It was all one perfect thing. Had any thread been missing, the whole fabric would have unraveled completely.

I was terrified to look into his eyes. I was hoping and praying the others would show up soon and rescue me.

And then he said: "It's not good for a man to be alone."

And I looked up and felt this crazy urge to cry. Quotes from Genesis! This is what I was going to get in the way of romance! But he looked so sincere and so shy and so utterly lost. And there was just so much boyish yearning in his eyes. And so much kindness and a sort of uncertain, quivering expectation.

"We could live a good life together, Yehudit," he whispered. "We believe in the same things, we want the same kind of life. We could have lots of kids, and lots of guests, and . . ."

"And who would diaper them and who would do all the cooking and cleaning?" I said sternly. "I am not the pushover you think I am."

"Well, I'd do anything for you. Anything," Marc said to me.

The truth was, it was almost enough. But not quite.

"But what about love?" I asked him.

"Our sages teach us love is divine, that it grows from compassion and understanding. From being kind and sensitive to another's needs. . . ."

I blush to tell you what happened next. I just slipped my arms up his back and shamelessly kissed him until I was sure if I stopped, he would not have another thing to say.

But I didn't figure on his response.

There is something to be said for repression of carnal feelings among yeshiva men. Once they unrepress . . . well.

It was a good thing Ariela and Joseph turned up.

We made kiddush and announced our engagement.

The wedding will be in Jerusalem!

You must come!

> *Love and kisses,*
> *Jenny*

Tamar folded the letter carefully. The paper was yellowing and crisp, like dead leaves. She placed it carefully back into the shoebox along with all the other letters, invitations, birthday cards and pictures she had especially treasured for the last twenty years.

Why had she never answered it?

Vaguely, she remembered her fury. She'd been insulted—no! More. Outraged! She tried to call some of it back, to remember exactly what it was that had so upset her. How dare Jenny say all those things about Orchard Park? Who does she think she is to give me *mussar?* To imply that my husband is a hypocrite, that I am putting my children at risk! . . . How dare she tell me what to do? Why, my husband is a respected rebbe. . . . I am Rebbetzin Finegold . . .

But now, so many years later, the fury seemed inconsequential and meaningless, like a rusty warning bell on an old beached ship rung without conviction, just to see if it still worked. Had she ever really been angry? she wondered. Or simply looking for an excuse to break off contact with the last person who knew her secret?

She thumbed through the box. Jenny's wedding invitation, the picture of the slim, serene bride, the tall, gentle groom.

Jenny's wedding.

She had not responded to the invitation. She had never even sent a gift. She felt the hollow thud at the bottom of her heart echo. And even so, Jenny had sent the picture with her love.

Her heart contracted with loss. Twenty years. A whole lifetime of friendship. No one had ever taken Jenny's place. There was just a blank, an empty space. Like that religious custom of leaving part of a wall in a new home deliberately unfinished as *zachar lechorban,* a reminder of Jerusalem's destruction, of exile.

She got up, restless, her eyes roaming the room. There were the photographs of the family on the walls, smiling, filled with self-satisfaction and pleasure; sunny bright pictures, chronicling the milestones of a blessed, calm, untroubled life. Aaron's first day in heder. *Mameh,* may her memory be blessed, holding two-year-old Sara, the child's wild blond hair futilely restrained by ribbons, her blue eyes sparkling with mischief. Malka in her playpen, her gray-green eyes serene and smiling, her light brown hair a silky scarf down her back, so fine it outlined the delicate shape of her ears.

Twenty years had passed so swiftly. Good years, rich years, where there had always been something happy to occupy her time. Preparations for Rosh Hashanah—the honey and apples, the festive meals, the circular twisted challah with raisins. Gathering willow and myrtle branches for Succoth. Making flags for Simchat Torah. Getting the bags of candy together for the children of the synagogue. Purim costumes. Passover cleaning . . . And always the poor brides who needed help with trousseaus, sick congregants to be visited, charity drives to organize. Prayers to say. Dinner to make. A husband and children to care for. Religious obligations that gave form and content to her days, filling them like harvest baskets with good and more good, packed tightly, filled to the brim, so that there was no room for idle speculation and dreams. So that there was no room for thoughts to roll about to the past or the future or into speculation about what it would have been like to live a different kind of life.

She rummaged through the shoebox, picking out the family photograph from Aaron's Bar Mitzvah. She sat down with it, scrutinizing it.

Aaron. Small, pale, unsmiling, with serious black eyes and short cropped black hair beneath a large black silk skullcap, an exclamation point between his smiling blond parents and sisters. How well he had read not only the haftorah, but the whole Torah reading! How beautifully he had delivered the *pilpul* on the Talmud before the entire congregation!

"You must be so proud, Rebbetzin Finegold, so very proud!"

"Mazel tov! May he continue to give you *nachas!* Such a fine boy! So intelligent, so learned. Like his father."

He was the joy of her life. She thought of his childhood, the pages of droll stories and clever drawings that always littered his room; the glass jars full of convalescing insects being nursed to health with lettuce leaves that always lined his windowsill; the precious cards: "Dearest Ima, I love you, from your son Aaron. . . ."

He had grown from a beautiful active baby to a sweet, curious, affectionate toddler to a diligent schoolchild who worked hard to fill report cards with A's and B's, and paeans of praise to his good character. His teachers always said the same things about him: that he made up with hard work for any lack in his natural ability. That he was helpful to others, respectful and diligent.

He did not have Josh's easy brilliance. But he was climbing

up the same mountainside of accomplishment with endless toil and dogged determination. And Josh was always there beside him, helping him up. The two were inseparable, bonded together by such love and mutual admiration, Tamar often felt left out. But somehow she didn't really mind. Each time she looked at him, something bright and warm flashed secretly inside her. Her tall, handsome, affectionate, respectful boy. Her Aaron. A son like his father.

Blessed child, she thought. Blessed, blessed child.

She touched the photograph's frayed edges. It was seven years old. Could it actually be fading, like those yellowing portraits of girls in bottle curls and mididresses in her mother's album? She looked at Aaron, short compared with the tall young man he had become, his face wreathed in an uncertain smile, proud and full of childish dignity, his shoulders rubbing against his father's arm; Sara, petite and golden; and little Malka, the fuzz of light brown hair, the little gold earrings. And there was Josh, straight backed and youthfully slim, yet somehow making her think of the word *venerable*. And there was herself, the white expanse of her neck rising out of the festive, flowered dress, the skin so smooth and firm—so young. Not that she was old now, she comforted herself. But that woman in the photograph was a young mother, flowing with baby milk and hormones that made her skin glisten with health, elastic over her bones. Her young arms, white and full and proud, lightly touched the shoulders of her young son, the Bar Mitzvah boy.

And now her young son was a young man who wanted a wife like that, a young woman with smooth, elastic skin. And she would become like her mother before her, a woman with faded photographs and dull flesh through which the sap of young life no longer flowed.

She would become a grandmother.

She cringed.

A grandmother . . . She mouthed the word. Your little babies grew up and turned into handsome young men and women and married and had babies, making you a grandmother.

That was the very best thing that could happen. That was what happened if you were very, very lucky.

The best thing that could happen was that you got to fade, to grow old.

That was life.

She wasn't ready. But Aaron was. He had been for two years. He was twenty years old. Many of his friends already had two small children, having married at eighteen. The matchmakers were banging loudly on her door. And why not? He was the son of Reb Joshua Finegold, head of Yeshiva Mesifta Kavod ha-Makom in Orchard Park, a Talmudical academy rivaled only by places like Lonovitch in B'nai Brak or Chafetz Chaim in Jerusalem. Josh had turned it into one of the most respected and influential Talmudical academies in America, she thought, allowing the idea to fill her with a brief but heady sense of pleasure.

And Aaron was such a promising scholar, such a handsome bridegroom-to-be: dark, broad-shouldered, with a physique that made the other yeshiva boys seem puny and unhealthy in comparison. Such a fine boy, such a loving son, she thought, her eyes misting. Everyone knew how good he was! The diligent hours he spent in the study hall conquering the thousand-page books of Talmud, the hours he spent on the Sabbath visiting the sick in local hospitals, making sure they heard kiddush and had a proper Sabbath meal.

But oddly enough, it was not his good qualities, but his failures that gave her the most pleasure. His arrogance, his unforgiving intolerance for backsliding or sloppy religious observance. His proud confidence in himself, in his knowledge, in his position in life, which gave him an unpleasant streak of haughtiness and bad temper. For in these things, he was really just like his father. Just like Josh, she repeated to herself in a way that had now become familiar.

She ran her hand through her hair. It was never uncovered now. Even in the house. Only sometimes, at night, when Josh and Aaron slept, did she allow the walls their eyes. She touched the long, thick curls sadly. She was graying by the day it seemed—those horrid stiff gray hairs. Dry and ugly, they seemed to sprout up like weeds from her aching brain, manifestations of her aging soul.

Could life ever again be a gay summer evening on Thirteenth Avenue, with your pretty new summer dress swishing and your gleaming bright hair spilling gaily down your shoulders? Her eyes moved restlessly. There were her husband's religious books—tomes and tomes filled with knowledge. Be kind. Be good. Obey. And there was the oil painting of a flower she had bought as a young girl, its captured bloom going a bit plastic in the bad light. The closed, well-dusted piano. The black synagogue hat and veil she had left on the dining room table since last Shabbas. Everything so calm and familiar and reassuring. There were no dangers here. No threats of any kind.

Then why couldn't she sleep?

She looked out the window. A light snow had begun to fall, and in the morning the whole world would be strange and beautiful, all the trees sculpted in sparkling sugar coating, the garbage cans and fire hydrants beautiful new creations. Even the sky would be new, white, clean, and somber, turning the falling light into long, purple shadows. All the familiar darkness of the city would bleach white. She would see it in the morning. But for now, it was so terribly dark, the light of the moon and stars blotted out by the pregnant dark clouds.

She was so tired. So very tired. But she knew better than to try to go back to sleep. From long experience she was intimately aware of the nuances of her life and had grown wise in the ways of survival. To go back to bed now would be to stare at the dark ceiling, the shadows of the chest of drawers, the dark eyeless socket of the window. It would mean battering away furiously at the night terrors, trying to keep their heavy bodies from sitting heavily on her face and chest like little mythic animals with sneering grins. She would lie there tense, willing the night away, tossing in exhaustion, afraid to close her eyes, afraid of that sinking feeling as she edged into the horror that awaited her the moment she succumbed.

All these years. She had been all right for most of them. She had slept, her belly swelling blessedly with her baby girls, her arms tired from the baking of challah, the making of hamantaschen, the Shabbos meals, the festive meals. . . . For years she had allowed herself the luxury of some modicum of peace.

But now, Aaron's search for a bride . . . something was happening to her again. She didn't know what.

She started to cry, pressing her hands over her mouth to keep the sound from waking her family. I'm sorry, so sorry, she thought. My whole life, never any end, never any relief.

It doesn't matter how much love I get, how much respect and honor. The whole surface of my life, so perfect. But the real life underneath, never any real happiness, never any real, untainted joy. Never, never. He is always there, always just about to rip my clothes. His kiss still poisons me, a rotten fruit I've bitten into whose taste never leaves me, no matter how much good food I swallow, no matter how much fine wine I swirl and swirl over my tongue.

I can't get him out of my life.

She sat alone in the dark room, her glasses misted from tears. She was so alone. She thought of her husband deep in peaceful sleep, a few footsteps away. At the end of the universe.

Not like the days when she was a young bride and he reached for her, her absence changing the very air so that he had to wake and search for her; like the days he had to find her and put his arm around her and lead her back to bed. . . .

He was older now. He snored. He did not wake easily. He did not even know she was not there beside him. Her life was separate from his. It had happened gradually. Too much he didn't know. Too much she didn't dare tell him. And now, so long after, did not wish to tell him.

How I begrudge his snoring, heavy-lidded sleep-filled nights! His righteous, thoughtless, peaceful, heavy sleep.

She could not forgive him for not knowing intuitively. Magically. Why doesn't he know? If he was a better man, a bigger man, he would rescue me from myself, my sleepless nights, she thought unreasonably. She was cruel in her senseless antagonism. She hated her creation, the marriage she had built and designed after her own will. A marriage with so many dark corners, so many attics and basements where you had to be careful never to go.

An old rabbi, founder of the yeshiva, had died, and out of respect Josh had flown with the casket to Jerusalem to be at the burial on the Mount of Olives. It was bitter cold and pouring rain when they buried him, he told her later. Why didn't you wait? she'd asked him. For another day, for better weather? That is the law, he'd answered. The dead must be buried. To leave them even a day is an abomination. If I die and it is pouring rain, don't bury me, she'd suddenly begged. Wait for the sun to come out. And he had answered patiently that it was the law to bury the dead the same day.

And she had thought: He would not say yes to a dying wish. He would bury me in the cold night, in the freezing rain, because a dead body is an abomination to G-d and must be buried. Even on a cold night. Even in the icy rain.

He was not a cruel man, not unfeeling. But he was principled. He did what he learned was right, though it might tear his insides. But somehow, though she tried to see him in a kinder light, a softening pinkish glow of goodness, she found his righteousness appalling. Perhaps, she thought, because I am weak and emotional I cannot really appreciate his strength. Perhaps it is simply Eve's old wish to involve Adam in her desire for the forbidden. To get him to side with her against the Law, the Word.

And what was the Law when it came to adultery? To rape? To illegitimate children? She would never ask. She did not want to know. It was safer not to know.

Tomorrow she would get up and wash her face and start fielding the calls from the matchmakers. She would have to start visiting the young girls and their parents. Nothing could happen until the mother of the boy got involved and gave the green light.

How she hated the idea of it! The prospective mother-in-law lumbering up the steps to the scrupulously scrubbed house of strangers, making some poor sweet young girl tremble in her room at the coming inspection! She didn't want that role! She sided too much with the girl! Besides, who was she to judge? What right did she have to decide? And yet it was her duty. Her son was counting on her. It was the way their world worked. Aaron would never have a bride if she did not lumber up those steps and terrify that young girl.

And she could not tell them, tell anyone, that beneath that heavy flesh, that graying hair, was also a young girl, trembling too. She went back to bed and reached for her husband's inert hand. She put it under her cheek. And then she slept.

❖24❖

The pattern was always the same: The matchmaker's phone call. The pious sales pitch: "Such a fine family!" "Such a lovely, pretty, friendly girl!" "So smart!" "Whoever knows her, loves her!" "Such a distinguished father!" And more rarely: "Such a well-to-do *mishpachah!* Such a generous dowry."

Tamar had been through this five times before. The matchmaker did not always have the same taste in beauty she did. Nor the same view of what friendly meant. To the matchmaker, "lovely" meant a good, healthy appetite, a fine, ruddy complexion; "friendly" meant that her eyes were open and she didn't immediately turn white when the prospective mother-in-law said hello.

This time it was a little girl, barely seventeen, named Fruma Devorah. Josh had already made discreet inquiries about the family and found nothing amiss. Fruma Devorah's father, Rabbi Engel, had already visited Aaron at his yeshiva and questioned him on the finer points of Talmudical intricacies. The prospective father-in-law and the prospective son-in-law had waxed enthusiastic over each other.

"Too bad you can't marry the father," Tamar finally said.

"*Ima*, really!" Aaron had protested touchily. "I don't think you're taking this seriously enough. I mean, my whole future is at stake. I would like it to be finished already. I want to get back to learning."

"So what is the next step, Aaron?"

"Why, you know. . . . You have to go see the girl. Nothing can happen until you see the girl."

"But why can't *you* go see the girl? I mean, why do I have to decide? Since when is the future mother-in-law allowed to choose?"

"*Ima*, I can't understand you," Aaron said with that foreboding, humorless stiffness that she knew so well. He was offended, shocked at her lack of *frumkeit*. At her questioning the strict social conventions that had wound its relentless tentacles around Orchard Park and Williamsburg, B'nai Brak and Jerusalem, over the past twenty years, tightening up what the new generation viewed as the shocking slackness of their parents' world. Educated by old European rabbis, the young men and women of Orchard Park yearned to return to the unbending, almost wrenching purity of their self-sacrificing European grandparents and great-grandparents.

"In my day, your father came to me," Tamar protested. "Only then did I meet his parents. Afterward, when we'd already decided."

"But this is not the way it's done now, *Ima*. At least not among real B'nai Torah," he said stiffly.

She bit her lip, chastised and resentful. How she had come to resent that term, used whenever one group wanted to brag how many miles nearer the intersection of G-d and His divine will they were than another group! She was reminded sorrowfully once again of how much the community of her childhood had changed.

Though outwardly the grid of streets and avenues, the little one- and two-family homes of Orchard Park had remained the same, socially the community had undergone a drastic transformation. Gone were the relatively easygoing Orthodox American families that once dominated the streets, replaced by the devout Hasidim, mostly imports from Hungary and Russia and Poland. The influx of the Hasidim, especially the devout Hungarians, had changed the community's standards with amazing swiftness.

Ruach Chaim Yeshiva was gone, its standards no longer living up to those of the newcomers. Indeed, the rumors that the boys had sometimes crossed the street to talk to girls had invoked such wrath that the Hasidim had not only closed it

266

down, but actually demolished the building and plowed under the earth with a team of oxen! (Where had they gotten oxen? she still wondered. New Jersey?) It was the only way, they insisted, to remove the impurity from the neighborhood.

Sometimes she wondered if people had really become *frumer*—sincerely more religiously observant—or simply more *farchnyokt*, outlandishly obsessed with making up new strictures that helped them showily display their superior piety, similar to the way people had once bought cars with bigger and bigger tail fins. Would the Jews of Orchard Park ever decide that less was more, the way people had concerning their cars? She somehow doubted it.

It seemed that you proved your status by denying yourself. The foods that were kosher enough for your parents and grandparents (and everybody else's parents and grandparents) were no longer kosher enough for you—or anyone you'd allow your children to play with. So now, even canned peaches in sugar syrup needed rabbinical supervision, a stamp of approval. Even salt, even sugar! Not to mention the hysterical lengths people went to about meat—which really did need strict supervision to see it was ritually slaughtered so no pain was felt by the animal and salted and soaked to remove the blood. Butchers who wanted to make a living had to know the right rabbis, pray in the correct synagogues, and probably pay off the right kashruth supervisor. It was getting so ridiculous that no one would be allowed to eat anything at all very soon!

She bit her lip, surprised at the heretical train of her thoughts, feeling disloyal. After all, wasn't Josh one of those people? Every week there was something else he warned her to avoid buying, saying, or doing because it was no longer acceptable to "B'nai Torah." But wasn't it just snobbery? A way to exclude those who didn't think and behave exactly as you thought they were supposed to?

"*Ima!*" Aaron implored with a touch of despair.

"All right, all right. I'll go see her."

Friday night. She lit the candles and left Sara and Malka to fend for themselves as their father and brother went to shul. It was a cold night. She pulled her coat around her, barely able to button it. I have to lose some weight, she told herself, appalled at her own girth.

She'd mourned her lost figure after each pregnancy and vowed to regain it. But like some unstoppable gushing of molten lava flowing up from the center of the earth, her body had continued to add the unsightly layers, hoarding the stores it was sure it might need when the impending famine arrived. Except there had been no famine. And the storerooms were seriously overstocked. Ridiculously overstocked, she mourned, hurrying, glancing at herself in anger and despair in the windows of stores already closed for the Sabbath. I look like one of the matrons, she thought. One of those women who used to make faces at me and Jenny and Hadassah when we skipped down the streets or ran to hide from the boys.

How had that happened?

And now her son was looking for a bride. And she would be a mother-in-law.

Awful name! One of those heavy, disapproving women with aggrieved expressions who roamed the world in search of aggravation. More often than not, they found it. The kind of older woman no one really liked, but everyone tried to be nice to in a phony, plastic way, just waiting for her to leave her gift offerings and go home.

She found the Engels' house and looked it over. A neat, if not lovely, little garden, watered and pruned. A respectable two-family brick on a good street. She walked slowly up the steps, her heart beating from exertion and nervousness and dread. She knocked softly, hoping no one would hear and she could go home.

But already the door was opening. The woman on the other side was smiling. Her brown wig was newly set and smelled of heavy hairspray. The dining room table was also set for Sabbath dinner, awaiting the men's return from Friday night prayers.

The girl sat on the sofa, drenched in the pale Sabbath candlelight. She is paler still, Tamar thought, and so young! Her hair was still in braids! And her simple skirt and blouse looked childishly loose and shapeless over her thin body.

The girl nodded but did not speak. Her mother, on the other hand, did not shut up; did not stop smiling and pressuring her white, trembling daughter to join in the conversation. The girl spoke only when spoken to and was brief to the point of rudeness.

"Well," Tamar said, feeling the time pass with excruciating slowness, desperate to remove herself before the young girl fainted altogether. "Well, it was a pleasure to meet you. And of course we will be in touch. A *guten Shabbos*."

"A *guten Shabbos, Rebbetzin*," the girl's mother boomed out with desperate friendliness. Tamar saw the woman's elbow dig deep into her daughter's stiff arm.

"A *guten Shabbos, Rebbetzin*," the young girl finally piped up, looking at her with the startled eyes of a doe caught in the headlights of a speeding car.

"Well?" Aaron asked with burning impatience.

"Well. . .," Tamar hedged. "I think she is very young. Maybe too young."

"But all the girls who have been suggested are young!" Aaron exploded with annoyance. "Of course they are. They must be. All the 'good' girls are married by twenty!"

"There is something to that, my dear," Josh agreed mildly.

"So then, whatever you decide!" She threw up her hands in exasperation. "I told you I don't know, I can't decide these things."

"*Aba* . . .," Aaron implored.

"We will go see her again. This time together, Tamar. All right? Now, let's not ruin Shabbos with any more of this. . . ."

The next time there was no candlelight, only the clear harsh overhead glare of a good, fake crystal chandelier. But the girl still looked pale. She still had braids. She still twitched her fingers in her lap. And her eyes still looked up with the fear of a trapped little night creature.

Tamar found herself cornered in the living room with the parents, who were already beginning the negotiations. How much each would give for the wedding? What kind of furniture would be purchased? Who would give what and how much for support while the *chasan* continued his yeshiva studies? And most important of all, where would Aaron continue learning? A lively discussion ensued between Josh and Rabbi Engel on the various merits of big yeshivas versus small *kollelim*, America versus Israel. . . .

Having nothing to contribute, Tamar sank back uncomfortably into the cushions of the plastic-covered couch, her back beginning to sweat. She kept smiling, all the while her eyes wandering to the girl, who sat in the corner. She seemed . . . resigned. She had no spirit, not a word to say for herself, Tamar thought with annoyance. Already she imagined how her son would boss her around. She began to feel sorry for the little creature. She shrugged. Out of my hands, she thought. Completely, completely, out of my hands.

"A little mouse," she whispered to Josh on the way home.

"That is *loshen hara*. She is very young and shy. But she will make a good wife, I think. A pious one."

"She dresses like a child, not a *kallah moide*," Tamar pointed out.

"She dresses modestly and without pretension," Josh chided her.

"Well?" Aaron said when they got home. "When do I meet her?"

"Whenever you wish, my son," Josh said placidly.

"Yes, whenever you wish," Tamar repeated wearily.

Early Sunday morning mother and son walked back to the Engels. How nice Aaron looks, she thought. He'd spent all Saturday night brushing off the lint from his new black Fedora, polishing his shoes, bathing.

They went into the living room. The mother, as usual, did not close her mouth for two seconds. The girl was ushered in. Now two very red spots burned into the paleness of her cheeks. Now her fingers kept each other company, her whole body trembling, Tamar observed with alarm.

But somehow the two young people made their way to a quiet corner of the room. Aaron began to speak to her in determined low tones, doggedly going through the list of questions he had prepared beforehand: Did she understand what it meant to be a *kollel* wife? To help support a Torah scholar for years? Did she understand that they would live wherever his studies took him, even if it was very far from Orchard Park and her parents?

The girl nodded and nodded. Surprisingly, she seemed to be answering him in sentences, for Tamar could see Aaron focusing on her lips and face with the utmost interest.

"Well, my son knows his way home, so I think I'll just be getting back," Tamar excused herself, wanting to flee.

All the way home, she did not understand why she felt like crying.

The phone rang. It was the matchmaker. *"Nu?"*

"Well, they are talking. I'll let you know."

A disappointed clearing of the throat.

"Soon as possible," she conciliated.

Aaron arrived. He seemed elated. But then moments later the phone rang again.

It was Mrs. Engel. "I'm very embarrassed, but Fruma Devorah . . ." She hesitated. "She kept saying she didn't want to get married. That she was not even seventeen, and what does she need it for? She sees how hard married women work. . . . We thought it was *narishkeit,* that it would pass once she met your son. We didn't want to pass up such a fine opportunity. . . . But she doesn't want. She doesn't want. It's nothing personal, believe me. She says she still feels too young. . . ." The voice was abject with apology and slightly hoarse, as if her vocal chords had been strained to the breaking point.

"Well," Tamar said with almost breathtaking relief, "that is perfectly understandable."

Aaron was devastated. "So many weeks wasted on this, with nothing to show for it!" he fumed.

"Would you rather marry a frightened rabbit? Be grateful she called it off."

"I knew you didn't like her!" he accused.

"What was there to like?" Tamar admitted. "Like gefilte fish without horseradish. Bland, tasteless."

"All of that time and effort, wasted. Well, I have no intention of waiting around for her to grow up. I'm going back to yeshiva."

The phone kept ringing. More prospects. More enthusiastic sales pitches.

"I need a rest from all this, Josh. I mean, it's making me crazy!"

He looked at her curiously. "You don't want him to get married, do you?"

"Why, that's unfair! Haven't I kept going, kept looking? Haven't I done whatever I was told?"

"But you always find something wrong."

"Is that my fault? What can I do if they are pale and rabbity and loud-mouthed and materialistic? Is that my doing? Blame the messenger," she said, wounded.

Of course, he was absolutely right. She didn't want to find a bride for Aaron.

She wasn't ready yet, she thought, terrified at what lay beneath the surface of her reluctance. Everyone just assumed it was the usual selfishness of the mother who was unwilling to part with her child, unwilling to share his affection and attention with a stranger. That it was the usual fear of the empty nest. She longed for it to be true, to be able to crawl into the niche of cliché as one crawls into the restful comfort of a big old blanket that has gone soft from many washings and much use. But as much as she tried to cover herself with it, it brought no warmth or comfort.

There was something more.

Something too terrible, too terrifying, to look in the face.

"But if you're not ready for him to get married, that is your privilege as his mother. He'll have to respect that. He'll just have to wait," Josh said calmly.

The blatant unfairness of her right to sabotage her son's life left her breathless with self-recrimination. She was ruining his chances, getting him a reputation as a difficult match. Instead of helping him, of cooperating, she was taking away his chance for happiness, his right to join his peers as a husband and a father.

Silent tears fell down her cheeks.

"Aach," Josh said, wiping them away. "This is . . ." He sighed. "We all need a vacation from this. I have had an invitation from the Yeshiva of Lonovitch in B'nai Brak for Aaron to learn there. He was so busy with *shidduchim* I didn't even mention it to him. Let him go for a few months. Let everything cool down a bit. It would be a vacation for you, too. . . ."

"Well, if he wants to. I wouldn't want to force him," she said cautiously, but then as the wonderful vision of several months off from the torture of matchmaking took hold, her enthusiasm could not be held back. "I mean, it sounds like a wonderful idea. If Aaron agrees . . ."

Aaron was thrilled.

"Lonovitch!" he exulted, the way a college hopeful might say: Harvard! or Stanford! or Oxford! It was the pinnacle of serious learning, producing the leaders of the *haredi* Jewish world. "I will learn so much!"

His bags were packed. He waved good-bye from the airport shuttle taxi.

Tamar exulted. No more phone calls, at least for a while. No more young women to look over and terrify. She took a long bath. And that night she slept like a baby.

Three weeks later Josh came home early, his face beaming. "I got a letter from Reb Asher Lehman, one of my old classmates who now lives in B'nai Brak. He has found the perfect *shidduch* for Aaron. Her name is Gitta Chana Kleinman. Her father is the mashgiach of Lonovitch!" His voice rose triumphantly.

"The mashgiach!" Tamar repeated with dread and awe and a sense of panic. The job of mashgiach was one of the most esteemed positions in any Talmudical academy. The person who filled it was responsible for the spiritual and physical comfort of the boys in the yeshiva. Though not necessarily a rabbi himself, he was a friend and confidant of the rabbis who taught there. And he had the final say on many administrative and financial matters. The person who held such a position was usually the most pious and respected person the community knew, a serious *talmid chachom*. His children were considered very lofty matches. And this was the daughter of the mashgiach of Lonovitch!

"I have heard of Reb Kleinman. A real tzadik. A man who

wakes up at four every morning and walks to the Kotel to pray. A man who is in the Beit Medrash learning until midnight every night. . . . Wise, compassionate, generous!"

She had never seen Josh so excited.

"So, what happens now?" Tamar asked, trying to be helpful and upbeat, trying to ignore the thudding of her reluctant, panic-stricken heart.

"I will write my friend Rabbi Lehman back to handle the entire matter as he sees best!"

"Yes, that is a good idea," Tamar murmured, thinking it was a terrible idea. Almost as terrible as Aaron meeting some Israeli girl and settling in Israel, far away from his parents. Almost as terrible as Aaron getting married.

A few weeks later the phone rang. It was long distance. A Reb Asher Lehman for Rabbi Finegold.

"Josh! It's him! Rabbi Lehman!"

She watched her husband's face as it registered excitement, satisfaction, and then a rare pride.

Josh rubbed his hands together. "Reb Asher says Aaron and the girl have met. Things are going fast. He wants one of us to come!"

"You go." Tamar shook her head, a queasiness in the pit of her stomach. Aaron had met her! It was going well!

"No. It's not my place to go. You have to go. This is the mother's job, to find a wife for her son."

"You don't want this responsibility any more than I do," she accused. "You're just making up excuses! Look, why do either of us have to go? Why can't Aaron make up his own mind? I mean, he's got Reb Lehman there, and we could ask your cousin Velvel to take a look," she said, beginning to feel as if some heavenly reprieve might be in the wings for her, sparing her.

"So don't go," Josh said levelly. "So let Aaron feel like some motherless child who has only strangers and distant relatives to help him with the most important decision of his life. . . ."

El Al flight number 401 from Kennedy Airport gained speed rapidly. Tamar gripped the armrest, her neck stiff with tension, her body vibrating to the accelerating wheels of the lumbering machine as it propelled its giant carcass forward. And then, suddenly, the lift. A sense of lightness, of surging wildly upward. A feeling of release.

She felt an inexplicable rush of joy that made her want to laugh out loud. It was a feeling of bursting through some underground, oxygen-poor mine shaft, having been buried there for countless hours; a feeling of swimming up and breaking the surface of the sea after having lain on the bottom, drowning.

The overpowering, dangerous labyrinth of New York City, transformed into a harmless Legoland! And the higher she rose, the more the city continued to shrink beneath her, taking with it all of its dark threat, its frightening chaos, its indecipherable, sinister landmarks. After all these years, she thought. Finally, finally free! After all this time. And I never knew it, never understood it was possible. That it was possible to simply leave, to go away. To leave behind her sister's apartment. The window. The bed. The back alley and fire escape. The dark, wretched stranger who still walked the streets, still ate his breakfast, still slept in a bed, like a real human being. Who was still out there somewhere. Close by.

Can't change that it happened, where it happened, how it happened. But can simply go away and never see those places again. Go away and never, ever come back!

She unlocked her seat belt and lurched forward, groping the backs of the aisle seats, making her way to the bathroom. There, in the tiny, uncomfortable cubbyhole, sitting on the toilet seat, the smell of chemical wash and soap bars filling her nostrils, she wept.

Finally gone, she thought. Finally left behind! The shadow-filled, cavernous darkness of the never-ending jungle. . . .

She had never realized how much she hated it!—all of it, all of these years! Her whole body rose up in racking, silent sobs until she felt raw and fragile and clean, like a woman taking her first bath after giving birth.

She wiped her eyes, straightened her wig, and splashed some water on her face. Then, carefully, she made her way back to her seat. Her step was light.

It was a wonderful flight. She emptied the little Styrofoam food trays with appetite; she watched the foolish movie with pleasure. She chatted with the young girls sitting next to her and even with an elderly, bearded man across the aisle.

She chatted and laughed and ate and felt dizzy with freedom, like a helium-filled balloon slipped out of a child's grasp, making its way, up, up into the stratosphere. The ten hours passed like ten minutes. She saw people looking out the windows at the first glimpse of the Israeli coastline, but she made no move to see. She didn't want to land, she realized. She was happy just as she was. She didn't want to put her feet on anything as real and incontrovertible as concrete. She didn't join in the singing, the hand clapping. Her euphoria left her, smokelike. She was suddenly afraid.

Where am I? she wondered, thinking not of a place, but of an inner landscape gone fuzzy now, like the scenery through a windshield battered by rain. Was she in another place, really? Had the past faded behind her as easily as the solid ground? She stepped out into the mild November sunlight of a perfect Indian summer day.

Israel. The Middle East. Thousands of miles away, she told herself. But it didn't seem that way. It felt so familiar. As if she had always lived here and was simply coming home. But to a different home. There didn't seem to be any darkness, anything to fear.

"*Ima!*"

"Aaron!" His handsome face was warm with pleasure. He wiped his sweating forehead, pushing his dark hair beneath his black Fedora. She wanted so much to embrace him, but it would not have been seemly for a bewigged matron to publicly caress a young yeshiva boy. Even if she was his mother. So she satisfied herself with a long, caressing look.

"Thank you so much for coming! I can't wait for you to meet Gitta Chana. . . ."

"Gitta Chana! So, we're on a first-name basis already," she teased him. But he blushed so furiously, she stopped. This was serious business, she thought, her stomach beginning to churn

with tension. "So when are we going to see this lovely girl?"
she added with the utmost seriousness.

"Reb Lehman has set it up for Sunday morning. Cousin
Velvel and Cousin Drora apologize for not coming to the
airport. She's expecting the new baby any minute."

The short ride from the airport to B'nai Brak was filled with
Aaron's excited whispers. How much he was learning! How
wonderful his *chavrusa*—his learning partner—was . . . what
a fine man Reb Lehman was . . . what a fine man the girl's
father, Reb Kleinman, was . . . what an important man . . .

"And Gitta?" Tamar laughed.

"Oh, *Ima*, you'll meet her. You'll see!" His eyes glowed.

Her eyes misted. Maybe it would all be fine in the end, she
thought, her own heart growing warm and light, like the air
in early morning filled with clean, fresh sunlight. Maybe that
fear too would be washed clean, that fear that hid in the dark
place of her soul, afraid to say its name.

Out of the windows of the taxi she glimpsed the palm trees,
the first she had ever seen. She smelled the orange groves'
strong perfume and saw the green, healthy fields. Only then did
she allow herself to connect time and place. This was not around
the corner from Fourteenth Avenue. It was the land of the Bible,
where David fought Goliath, where Saul chased the Philistines.
. . . Jewish beyond the black clothes of sad European ghettos.
Jewish, in the way that Joshua and the twelve tribes were
Jewish: hard, spare farmers and shepherds, lean warriors. . . .

"The land into which you cross over is not like Egypt. . . . It is
a land of hills and valleys. . . ." She remembered the words of
the *posuk*, as Moses described the land to the tribes. She didn't
have an ounce of Zionist blood in her veins. For her, Israel
wasn't a political entity, forged by an army, by international
treaties. For her, Herzl had been an ignorant semigoy, his vision
of a secular homeland a simple travesty that discounted the
holiness of the land. In her mind, the two thousand years of
Diaspora was simply erased, a blip on a screen. For her it was
simply Joshua back again, the land divided into *nachalot*, each
piece of land farmed by a tribe member.

And she was a member of the tribe.

And then, suddenly, they reached B'nai Brak, and she was back on Fourteenth Avenue. The same kerchiefed women pushing baby carriages; the same black-garbed yeshiva students; the same bustling streets with food and clothing stores filled with Hasidim. Her heart sank. It was too familiar.

Velvel and his wife, Drora, were the warmest of hosts. They plied her with cakes and drinks and enveloped her in family conviviality. People she had met only once, twenty years before, at her wedding. Drora insisted on going with her to meet the girl on Sunday, even though the conversation with the parents would take place in Yiddish and there would be no language barrier. Tamar was grateful for the company. It was still a different country, with different ideas of etiquette. She didn't want to hurt Aaron or disgrace Josh.

It was a beautiful sunny day, but not the sun of summer—that burning, pitiless heater that scorched foreheads and singed eyelashes—but a friendly bulb that lightly warmed their clothes as they walked down the main avenue, Rechov Rabbi Akiva. Aaron's face as he said good-bye before leaving for the yeshiva haunted her. It was so aglow, so wretched with hope, so anxious that she be pleased, that everything go well. . . .

"Don't be so nervous! I won't eat her! I'm sure she's a lovely girl, I'm sure it will be fine," she'd told him.

Now, she hoped it would be true.

She was happy for the constant chatter of Cousin Drora, her easy small talk. How much does a skirt cost in America? How much a lighting fixture? How much curtains? . . . She seemed fascinated by the answers. "So cheap! And how much does rent cost? . . . And how much salary does a *kollel* student make?"

The apartment was in a modest, older building on the third floor. There was no elevator. Tamar felt her face flushing red and her armpits drenched by the time she stood at the front door. She felt so sorry for Drora, so heavy with child. But Drora was used to steps. Hardly any of the older buildings in B'nai Brak had elevators.

The door opened wide and beaming faces rose to greet her. A short man with a vigorous black beard and an even smaller wife, her head done up in an elaborate conical headdress known as a *shvis*. Two older, married sisters, each wearing a pretty wig in shades of ash blond, reached warmly for her hands.

The sisters were small and round and gentle looking.

Ah, Tamar breathed out. It will be all right, then. This is not so hard to do. She looked over the table. Great trouble had been taken. There were platters of delicacies: herring, knishes, meatballs, pastry-wrapped chopped liver. Trays of cakes and marzipan fruits had been set out, enough for a dozen guests. She envisioned meeting the girl, loving her, and sitting down to eat in peace.

And then they ushered in Gitta Chana. Tamar looked up with an expectant smile, and then her heart suddenly gave her an enormous *clop*, a blow that made her ears ring.

She sat down a little too abruptly, aware that the girl's mother was eyeing her strangely. "All the steps," Tamar excused herself lamely. The mother and sisters rushed to bring her a drink.

She couldn't stand her.

What's the matter with you? a voice inside her complained bitterly. *There is nothing wrong with this girl! She is gentle and sweet looking, with thick, dark hair and pretty brown eyes. Her fingers are smooth and well cared for. Her body slim and charmingly petite in her well-made, sophisticated suit of lavender crepe. What don't you like?*

But there was nothing she could do. Her spontaneous, overwhelming rejection of the girl was so enormous that she could not even begin to bargain with herself. She wiped her forehead wretchedly.

The girl's expression didn't change. She seemed unconcerned, as enthralled with Tamar as Tamar was with her.

Tamar added this to her list of complaints.

"Well, I understand you have met my son. It is very important to get a few conditions settled. I hope Reb Lehman discussed them with you."

"What conditions?" the girl demanded.

She isn't fragile and shy, I'll give her that much. Tamar

breathed out. "One, that Aaron continues to live in Orchard Park. And two, that he continues his studies. We, of course, will contribute to his support for at least two years . . . then, hopefully, he will leave the yeshiva and get a job. . . ."

"What!" The young lady exploded into a heated Hebrew debate with her parents, which was so fast that Tamar could hardly make out more than every tenth word. The parents wrung their hands. "I absolutely refuse to leave B'nai Brak! That is no life for religious Jews, in America. Even the food is not kosher, at least not to our standards. . . . As for Aaron leaving the yeshiva, I would not consent to marry a man whose life is not Torah. I don't want a *balabos*, a businessman. I want to be the wife of a *talmid chachom*," Gitta Chana said in a big voice, enunciating the Yiddish words with absolute clarity so that Tamar should have no doubt as to what she was saying.

Ah, Tamar sighed. Good. She doesn't want. She refuses. It gets me off the hook. Obviously she hasn't been told the two main conditions of this match, conditions Aaron would never forgo. He is adamant about remaining with his rebbe in Orchard Park, at least for the next two years. And he has often said that the life of poverty of a perpetual yeshiva student is not for him. That he expects to work and support his family. . . . "Well, there must be some mistake," Tamar said, looking at the young woman with something akin to kindness.

She's got a pretty little face, but there's a little shrewdness around the eyes, and her mouth is wide and aggressive looking. She is also very petite. Maybe that was it. The incongruity between her delicate appearance and the aggressiveness in her manner. . . . Her dogmatic, aggressive goodness. Her rock-hard piety. Maybe that was it. (But you disliked her before she even opened her mouth! she reminded herself, trying to be fair.) Never mind. What difference did it make now? So they would part company, polite strangers, never to cause each other aggravation again.

Tamar looked out the window. The sun was still shining. It was still a lovely day. Soon this would be over and she would enjoy herself. Shop for Chanukah menorahs in Tel Aviv, pray in Jerusalem. . . .

"Something to eat?" the mother interrupted, her gentle face confused, disturbed.

"How can I refuse?" Tamar smiled graciously. They would find another boy for their daughter. An Israeli yeshiva bochur, a perpetual student who would be content to live on family handouts and community dole to buy his one chicken a week, his two challah breads, sliced into twenty-five small pieces when guests came. . . .

"You know, Rebbetzin Finegold, I am very confused," the other woman said mildly, pouring her a cup of tea. "When your son was here, Gitta told him exactly the same things she is telling you, and he was most enthusiastic. In fact, he *kvelled*. He said he wanted just such a life. . . ."

Tamar slowly put down the fork of chopped liver–filled pastry, pushing herself slightly away from the table. "My son, Aaron, said this? He said he would move here and spend his life in *kollel?*"

"He did!" little Gitta exclaimed, her little jaws slammed together unforgivingly.

Cousin Drora frantically waved her hands, throwing out compliments like confetti. "Such a beautiful dress, Gitta! Did you buy it or have it made? And where did you get it? Uhm, these mandlebrot are delicious, Rebbetzin, you must give me the recipe. Not that I need more cake, I mean, just look at me. . . ."

"When are you due, may *Hashem* watch over you?" Gitta's mother asked, glad for the distraction.

"Any minute, *shyehiyeh b'shaah tova.*" She smiled.

"Amen, may it be in a fortunate hour," the women chorused.

"I think I should go. I will talk to Aaron. Perhaps some mistake? . . ."

"That's what he said," Gitta repeated charmlessly.

A block away she already spied Aaron leaning over the porch railing, his hand shading his eyes like some picture of an Indian scout. He looked so anxious and childishly hopeful. Her heart sank.

She repeated the girl's story. "Is it true, did you tell them it was what you wanted?"

"Yes!" he said defiantly.

"But we discussed just the opposite!"

"I know. But that was before I came here. I'm just so happy here. I see the lives of the rebbes in the yeshiva, so involved in learning, in charity and kindness. . . . Of course I have to talk it over with you and *Aba* first, but I would be happy to stay on here. . . . As for learning, I know I agreed to get a job in a few years. But it's not what I really want. I want to learn, to teach. I want to follow in *Aba's* footsteps. It's just so hard to find a girl in America who would agree to live such a hard, simple life. I thought I needed to compromise. But Gitta, she's everything I want! She would help me live the kind of life I want. A life of *kedushah*."

Tamar stared at him. *Kedushah*. Holiness. Sincerity strained his brows, wrinkling his high, smooth forehead. His stiff collar was dazzlingly white, his brand-new black suit immaculate. Only his black, curly hair remained outside his perfectly maintained and disciplined appearance, wandering across his forehead like a stranger who'd lost his way. It gave him the look of an American teenager, she thought, undermining all his efforts to resemble a serious young sage. She brushed the hair out of his eyes, tucking it lovingly beneath his dark skullcap.

The girl had been telling the truth! He had agreed. Her two main, objective, impersonal arguments had now been thrown out the window, forcing her to deal with the very personal nastiness of her irrational dislike.

"But what did you think of her otherwise?"

"Otherwise," she hemmed. "Otherwise . . . she's got nice hair and eyes. She knows her mind."

"Yes, I know." He nodded enthusiastically. "I realize now how childish the other girl was. You were so right. I didn't realize it at the time. . . ."

"That doesn't mean we shouldn't discuss it with your father," she hedged, grabbing on to small roots on the smooth mountain wall, trying not to slip into the chasm. "In fact, I have very serious doubts about . . ." She saw his face fall alarmingly.

And it suddenly struck her that she was a character in a farce. The mother has to meet the girl! The mother has the right to choose her son's wife, to approve or disapprove! Looking at his face, she understood that the choice had been made and that the only way she could change it would be to break Aaron's heart.

"... serious doubts about staying in Brooklyn if you decide to move to Israel! I would have to talk *Aba* into coming, too. She's a special girl, I can see that."

"Really, *Ima?* And you do like her, don't you?"

"My future daughter-in-law? I know I will learn to love her, the way I love you, my son."

He took her in his arms for a grateful embrace, and the strong bones of his slim young man's body surprised and embarrassed her. Her little boy. A tall, handsome young man. What a blessing he had been to them, all these years! Blessed child! Blessed, blessed child. Never anything but good had come from him. She smoothed the black unruly curls from his forehead. Her fingers trembled.

❧25❧

"They want to make the wedding at the end of the month," Tamar shouted into the phone. Josh sounded a million miles away.

"So, tell me about Gitta Chana. . . ."

"Your son Aaron has chosen her for a wife, what's to tell?"

There was a pause. "And what is that supposed to mean?"

"It means that it's probably *beshert*. That a *bas kol* went out of heaven forty days before Aaron's conception announcing Gitta Chana was waiting for him when the time came. . . ."

"Probably *beshert?* Only that?"

"Josh, please don't push me. I've never married off a son before. I'm doing my best," she yelled with something like desperation.

"So, that bad," his faraway voice resounded with displeasure. "I'm surprised."

"The first time I looked at her, I just had this feeling, I don't know, like something hard had gotten stuck in my throat. She wants to live in Israel, to be a *kollel* wife. . . ."

"This is not a reason to dislike a person! We should all be lucky enough to live in *Eretz Hakodesh*, we should all be lucky enough to find pious, hardworking women for our sons to marry, women who will help them grow in Torah," he chastised her. "*Die kallah ist zu shoen?* Is that your complaint?" He sounded impatient.

The bride is too pretty, a perfect Yiddish expression defining complaints such as hers! She felt the fight drain out of her.

"If you could just give me some normal idea, some objective

problem we could discuss, maybe I could try to talk Aaron out of it. . . ."

"I don't want you to talk him out of it! This makes him happy! She's a very nice girl from a very nice family. You know I didn't like the others, either. I'll probably never find one I like enough for my son. Let him be happy!" she finally capitulated, acknowledging defeat. Her objection was not reasonable or rational. It was something she just couldn't put her finger on.

This was what her son wanted. This was something her husband approved of. What difference did it make that the girl set her teeth on edge? The son had to live with her, not the mother.

"Anyway, Josh, *you'll* like her."

"If this is the case, if it's settled, then let's make the wedding at the end of next month. You better stay there and make the arrangements."

"But how will you and the girls manage?"

"It's too expensive to fly back and forth. Better use the money to help Aaron get settled. My mother will help. We'll manage."

"I miss you," she whispered.

"And I miss you. *Tzchi le mitzvos.* Stay there and settle everything."

She hung up, forlorn. She hadn't realized how much the separation from Josh had bothered her. But now, hearing his voice fade in the rasping echo of underwater cables stretching beneath vast seas, she realized how much she needed him.

Not that he would actually do anything, take care of anything, if he was with her, she tried to comfort herself. The engagement party, the wedding, Aaron's apartment, it would all fall on her shoulders either way. She would do the talking, the negotiating, the shopping. He would sit back and approve or disapprove of the results, giving his opinion on the spiritual level of her decisions. Had she bargained too hard, offending the merchants? Had she been honest enough in the terms she laid down? If, for example, she contracted a carpenter to build kitchen cabinets, had she insisted on a deadline with monetary penalties if he failed to finish on time, and might this not encourage the carpenter to desecrate the Sabbath in order to meet it? Josh would smooth his beard down and consider, perhaps making her call back the wily tradesmen and renegotiate, giving him numerous ways to rob them blind.

But still, he was her husband. She loved him.

The bride is too pretty.

Somehow, she didn't think so.

She rented a small apartment in Sanhedria, one of Jerusalem's most religious neighborhoods, and spent her days like a business tycoon, phone in hand, finding Aaron an apartment with a reasonable rent (later they would help him buy something), arranging for furniture and appliances, negotiating with the caterers over the menu, the photographer, the band. Buying the bride her wedding gifts. . . .

She tried to feel a little more kindly toward her future daughter-in-law, softening at the many lovely reminders of her own happy days as a bride-to-be. She could see the girl's delight, which rose from her like an almost visible cloudy essence, warm breath exhaled on a winter night. But shopping with her, she felt the renewed nudge of the little hard rock that lay in her throat and wouldn't budge. Gitta Chana went from store to store looking at engagement rings, trying to find the one with the smallest diamond, proof of her spiritual loftiness, of her dedication to her future calling as the tight-fisted, practical helpmate who would allow her husband to support his family on a *kollel* man's stingy stipend. But she would have liked her more if she had taken a bigger stone and if she had not asked that the gold bracelet Tamar selected for her be exchanged for a clothes dryer. ("With many children, I will have no time to wear gold," the girl had loftily informed her.)

Still, she kept trying. She acknowledged Gitta Chana's piety, her strong, consistent virtues. She worked hard to convince herself such things deserved her love, admiration, and attention.

But mostly she tried to keep busy.

It was not good, she found, to think too much.

Only at night, she would sometimes wake and walk to the window of the little rented apartment in Sanhedria, looking out at the dark rolling hills of Judea, the dark overarching sky whose small lights, like knowing eyes, blinked at her in amazement.

The days went quickly. And then, suddenly, the wedding was only eight days away. Josh and the girls were to arrive in four days. Her outfit, a simple suit of pink and cream, custom made by a local seamstress, had already been taken in twice, as the pounds dropped away from sheer excited exertion.

It was midafternoon. She had spent the day shopping for a good set of china in B'nai Brak with Gitta Chana and her mother, a wedding gift from the groom's parents. The bride, as usual, had selected a local product that was highly unbreakable, inexpensive, and ugly.

As she got out of the taxi that had returned her to Jerusalem, Tamar felt exhausted from the failed effort to convince the girl to buy the imported china from Germany or Japan, with its lovely translucence and delicate gold edging. She felt sad she had spent so little on the dishes; sad she'd failed to convince Gitta Chana to splurge foolishly and smile about it with a bride's unbridled joy.

As she walked toward the bus stop on Straus Street to get the bus home, the vision of cooking dinner on the simple gas burners in the rented apartment was suddenly too much to deal with. Besides, she told herself with no small degree of irony, you saved so much money on the dishes. You can afford to buy take-out food.

There was a long line at Chaim's Glatt Kosher Home-Cooked Take-Out. There was always a long line. Not because of the gourmet quality of the pale chickens and thick, brown kugels, but because Chaim, a Belzer Hasid with a long gray beard, was universally trusted by even the most exacting *haredim* to adhere strictly to the laws of kashruth.

She shifted from foot to foot as the long line wound slowly toward the counter. She thought she imagined the tap on her shoulder. But then it happened again.

She turned.

At first she thought it might be one of Gitta Chana's friends she had met briefly at the engagement party or one of the other family celebrations. But then she looked closer. It was a woman her own age, her limbs lean and shapely, with hardly an ounce of extra padding. Only the little lines around the lively green eyes, the soft folds of skin above the eyelids, betrayed the two decades her body hid so gracefully. She wore a long black wig that looked almost exactly as her hair had when she was in high school. She had hardly changed at all.

Tamar felt her throat suddenly cake dry, tears stinging her eyes. She stood there, frozen for a moment in stupid loyalty to the stance of anger she had maintained but had never really felt. But the pretense of coldness was impossible to sustain. She hung her head, her eyes overflowing, her heart filled with longing and shame for having treated a dear, loyal friend so badly.

"Jenny," she whispered finally, crashing through the barrier and finding, to her surprise, no obstruction.

Jenny's familiar soft cheek pressed against her own. "Come, let's get out of here." She took Tamar by the hand, tugging her out of the store. Wordlessly they walked up Straus Street toward the bustling center of modern Jerusalem. They walked past the elaborate facade of the old Bikur Cholim Hospital, up King George Street, turning down the Ben Yehudah pedestrian mall with its colorful gift shops and open-air cafes. It was crowded with unemployed Russian immigrants playing violins and accordions, with street vendors selling jewelry and oil paintings of the Western Wall. It had the atmosphere of muted celebration. They said nothing, but they gripped each other's hands with a kind of fearful love, as if afraid of being torn apart at any moment.

"Someplace quiet," Tamar said hoarsely, not trusting her voice.

Jenny took her down a small side street and inside a quiet indoor coffeehouse. They made their way to the back. It was empty and cool and quiet, smelling of wood and fresh tomatoes. They ordered warm drinks and held the cups with one hand, the other hand still gripped in an entreating handshake. Tamar looked down into her cup. She felt so ashamed.

"You look so pretty. The same pretty little girl," Jenny told her.

She looked up, startled, and laughed. "About twenty pounds heavier!"

"The face is the same. A good girl's pretty face." Jenny smiled.

"I've had a good life. Blessing after blessing," Tamar said with a shock of recognition at having voiced some deep truth. A good life, despite it all. Husband, children, a position of respect in the community. Blessing after blessing. "And now my son, Aaron, is getting married."

"Mazel tov!" Jenny said.

Tamar looked at her, her eyes welling with tears. "And if it hadn't been for you, there wouldn't have been an Aaron. If I had listened to Hadassah . . . if I had done what I wanted to do . . ." She shuddered. "My fine, precious son. Never to have known him. To have killed him because of my fears. . . ."

"Your memory is not good! You were the one who decided to go through with it! Hadassah and I didn't give you any help at all. So it's worked out for you?"

"*Baruch Hashem!*"

"Thank G-d!"

The two sat silently, searching through their memories like a beacon of light searching out ghostly ships on the dark horizon.

"And you never told?"

Tamar shook her head. "It was pointless. I saved them all such trouble and worry. My husband, my family. And of course now there is nothing left to tell."

Jenny's eyebrows pinched together unhappily. She started to say something and then stopped. She squeezed Tamar's hand. "It's so *good* to see you! I've missed you."

"I don't deserve it. I treated you so badly. I just couldn't stand the idea . . . the idea of someone knowing. Can you understand that? It was nothing you did."

"I figured that out long ago. That's why I stopped writing. But I always asked about you. I knew you had two beautiful daughters. You're very famous in Orchard Park, Rebbetzin Finegold, you know! Considered a real *tzdakis!*"

Tamar blushed, pleased. "And what about you? Do you have a family?"

"I have the best husband and three great kids!"

"How wonderful! My children are also wonderful. . . ."

Invite her back home! Tamar thought. And then the image of Jenny meeting Aaron, the long, slow searching glance and perhaps those thoughts—those same, inevitable, heartbreaking thoughts that had kept her up for the last twenty years—stopped her. So instead she asked: "And what do you hear of Hadassah? Are you still in touch?"

"I get postcards every Rosh Hashanah. Sometimes from Venice or Greece or Istanbul. . . . And we speak on the phone a few times a year. She is married again, you know. Number three. Or is it four? I forget. Someone younger this time. A set designer . . . producer . . . something. I think this one might even be Jewish. She is trying to have another child. She had one, a boy, years ago. He's all grown up and lives with his father and stepmother in Los Angeles. She's taking hormone treatments, shots, holistic therapy. You name it. She sent me some pictures of her gorgeous house in La Jolla—it looks like some lush tropical island. Hadassah! I'll always love her! And I guess I'll always worry about her, too. Her life has been so exciting, so full of adventure. She'll never give up or give in to anybody else's vision of her. I imagine it must be a hard, lonely struggle sometimes. . . .

"Giving in to everyone's expectations is not any easier, believe me. It's the opposite side of the same coin. The older I get, the more I admire her guts. But her choices have taken a terrible toll on her family. Her mother died before her time, and her father is old and ill when many other men his age are still full of life. . . . You must know that. He spends about half the year in Israel these days. I don't think either one ever really recovered from the disgrace, her leaving. . . .

"I know she tried to see her mother right before she died. Somehow, it didn't work out. I see her father whenever I can. We're very close. I tell him what I know about his daughter." She shrugged sadly. "He's never stopped caring. He's never stopped blaming himself."

"And what about you, Jen. Are you happy?"

She hesitated. "Yes," she said slowly, thoughtfully, "I think

I can honestly say I am. I have so much love from my husband and kids. I feel so connected. . . . Everything I know and believe in and care about, it's all right here. I just look down the street and I see the patriarchs standing there." She laughed and then was suddenly serious. "I can't imagine being anywhere else. But it hasn't been easy. . . . There was a time some years ago when I felt a certain panic, as if every decision I'd ever made was based on the wrong information. I felt maybe G-d didn't care about me after all. And that I'd been wrong to marry Marc, wrong to move to Israel. . . ."

"I'm really surprised!"

"After all my first euphoria wore off, I felt I was never going to fit into this strange, foreign country. I'd look at all the newscasters on TV and think: They were born here. They've been in the army. They go to the beach on Shabbat and discos Friday night. They'll never accept me as one of them. . . . And then I'd look at the people in Meah Shearim, the Hasidim, and think: They were born here, or in Poland or in Hungary. They speak Yiddish and think I should be wearing seamed stockings and shaving my head. They'll never accept me, either. At least in Orchard Park the Hasidim spoke English. They were Americans. But these guys . . . It was a whole different ball game.

"And then I had all this guilt about abandoning my family. My mother was getting on in years and was all by herself with nobody to care for her. My brother was out in California. I tried to keep in touch, but writing isn't a substitute for touching, for sharing birthdays and holidays.

"And then"—she hesitated—"there were all kinds of other problems. Starting a family . . ." She stopped. "So many times I wanted to call you, just to ask your advice!"

Tamar reached out to her impulsively: "I wish you had! It's so hard for me to imagine you needing help, though. You always seemed to have all the answers."

"I did, when it came to everyone else's life. With my own, it was a little bit harder. . . ." She smiled.

"What got you through it?"

"My old *chumash* notebooks. Just reading over the lives of

the patriarchs. Sara's childlessness. Jacob's having to run away from home so his evil brother Esau wouldn't kill him. Isaac's losing his son and going blind. You couldn't say any of them had easy lives, even though G-d loved them and they were considered tzadikim. They never really fit in anywhere, either. So I stopped looking at my difficulties as a sign I was on the wrong track. I simply plowed ahead. It's worked out, thank G-d."

"I imagine life in Israel has never been easy. And now with the *intifada* and terrorist attacks all the time . . . How you must hate the Arabs!"

Jenny rubbed her mouth thoughtfully. "I'll tell you a story. When we moved into our first apartment, we were the only ones in the building because the other apartments weren't yet sold or finished. Living right next door to us was the Arab watchman whose job it was to see nothing got stolen from the building site. He was a thin fellow with a bright, sunny smile. Very religious. His name was Mansour. He prayed six times a day and believed that the Koran preached tolerance and love for all men. He was very handy and helped us with all kinds of problems we had in the house: broken tiles, leaky faucets . . . you name it!

"My husband and I got to really like Mansour. We'd invite him in for tea. He liked that. Tea with about two cups of sugar in it! Not so much the tea, as being served it in a clean cup on a tray. The courtesy of it. He began bringing us these large bunches of grapes from his vineyard in some village in Samaria. Biggest grapes you ever saw! And so sweet.

"Well, just about the same time, the son of a friend of ours was murdered by terrorists. He was on the road hitching a ride home from his army base, and these animals grabbed him and pushed him into their car. They found his body mutilated, burned, stabbed twenty times. He was nineteen years old, a gentle yeshiva boy with glasses. . . ." She paused, swallowing hard. "Well, one Shabbat afternoon I was getting ready to walk over to see this boy's mother, my friend, to comfort her, and when I passed my kitchen, I saw my husband sitting there drinking tea with Mansour. And then I realized that there isn't any simple solution. Why should we hate Mansour? Because some other Arab is a murderer? Yet how can I drink tea with someone who lives with these people, who rejoices with them, who identifies with them?

"I believe there is going to be peace here one day. And it's going to start with us giving Mansour tea and him bringing us grapes. It's going to start when Mansour can get up and tell his family and friends in the village: 'What our brothers did, what those terrorists did, to murder Eliezer Cohen, it's wrong. It's against the teachings of our Koran. G-d, the same G-d Mohammed and Abraham believed in, wouldn't want that!' It's going to start when I have the guts to stand up in shul and say: 'Hating the Arabs is against the Torah. The Torah teaches us to pursue peace, brotherhood.'

"You can sign any peace treaty you want, give back this piece of land and that piece of land, but peace is never going to happen until those things do. It's got to start with us learning each other's names. With us feeling responsible for each other's fates."

"I don't agree with you, Jen. You are never going to have peace with the Arabs or any other goyim, period. Because they all hate Jews! Some hide it better than others, but deep down, they can't stand us because we're not one of them. An enemy is still an enemy. It doesn't matter if you invite them to tea and find out their names," Tamar said bitterly.

Jenny sighed, thinking of Mr. Adams, principal of the Head Start program in Brooklyn where she'd been a teacher's assistant. Good, kind Mr. Adams, who'd done so much for those kids, who'd kept the black teaching assistants from Harlem and the white teaching assistants from the Upper East Side from eating each other alive. And Lawrence, the handsome clarinetist she had gone to college with. . . . Just as Mansour was never "an Arab," Mr. Adams and Lawrence had never been blacks. They had names. Had Tamar ever even met a black person or a gentile, except for that one time?

"After what the goyim did to my parents in the war . . . I have no use for any of them," Tamar continued.

"I understand how you feel. But what do we do about the

Torah, then? I mean, being religious means accepting the whole Torah, not just the parts they emphasize in Orchard Park. It means being part of the world, a 'light unto the nations.' How can we be a light if we shut ourselves off behind lead partitions? 'Goy' means a people. Jews are also goyim. We're part of the world. Part of mankind, Tamar. That's G-d's will. . . ."

"The same discussions we had in Ohel Sara," Tamar said, wondering. "You haven't changed a bit."

This was surprising. The newly religious always took things too far, going off on tangents. But eventually they became part of the community; they understood all the unspoken feelings, the rules. Antagonism toward the gentile world was part of that. Jenny had been religious for more than twenty years now, and her opinions still had not fallen into line. . . . Somehow Tamar found that genuinely refreshing, if a little frightening. No one she knew ever questioned anything. Their religious lives were all so neatly packaged, no one ever bothered checking the contents. . . .

"I'm sorry for running on. . . . What about you, Tamar? How have the last twenty years treated you?"

"I'm the most respectable matron on Twelfth Avenue and Forty-eighth Street," she said, smiling brightly. "I mean, my house teems the way Hadassah's used to, people coming to ask my husband questions. . . . I'm the rebbetzin . . . and now I finally understand Hadassah's poor mother. We used to think she was such a snob, remember? But she was just overworked and constantly interrupted, that poor woman. She had no private life. She had to share everything, even her husband and children. I'm not that bad off. I mean, Josh is the *rosh yeshiva*, not the *rav* of Kovnitz. But I've had a taste of it. Still, I can't complain, I have everything—fine husband, beautiful children, a lovely home, respect . . ." She stopped, the flow of clichés suddenly going unbearably sour in her mouth. After all these years, finally someone to talk to. Someone who would understand. She looked into Jenny's eyes, her smile suddenly gone: "I've been miserable for twenty years."

There was a shocked silence. "Why?"

She shook her head. "Because it's all a lie. Nothing about

my life is real. My husband doesn't know anything about me. And I don't really know him. I love him, but I don't really trust him, not enough to tell him the truth. I guess that means I don't really trust his piety or his goodness. Oh, he gives charity and visits the sick, and helps the mourners . . . but how would he feel about me if I told him the truth? How deep does his compassion really run? I wish I knew. But I can never risk finding out. The past isn't over. Nothing has been resolved. All these years I've pushed it away, vacuumed it, flushed it, and swept it, and it just keeps coming back. Like dust on windowsills. It's like I've been building this sand castle at the water's edge. No matter how beautiful it is, I keep feeling it can just be washed away with the first big wave. I guess I just keep waiting for that wave to come along."

Jenny reached out and touched her cheek. Her eyes were full of compassion. "Still rosy, like that little girl's on that cold Purim day rushing to school."

"It's makeup, Jen. I lost my color long ago. I still remember that Purim, though. It started out so happy. I felt so beautiful and loved. And then it was all shattered. I guess that's the way I see life. All our happiness is simply temporary. Only the bad things last and last and last. . . ."

"I feel just the opposite. All the bad things are temporary. And the good things last and last. Like love. Like children. Like a home, and a country and a people and G-d. . . . You've got to meet my family! We're moving soon. To a settlement in Samaria. A place called Beit El. Built on the same spot as the biblical Beit El, you remember, from our class in prophets? Where they set up an altar and kept the Ten Commandments before King Solomon built the Temple in Jerusalem?"

"But that's over the Green Line! Aren't you afraid to live out there? I mean with the stone throwing, the Molotov cocktails, the shootings on the roads?"

"Hey—" Jenny grinned. "I'm a New Yorker. Remember? It's not more dangerous than navigating your way around the Bronx. . . ." Then she turned serious. "I'm afraid. Sure. I'm not stupid." She shrugged. "We're always in G-d's hands."

Tamar played with her spoon. "No place is really safe, is

it? It's just an illusion, being able to control what happens to you."

"In some ways. But I want to tell you something else. Once at the university, I saw this little sparrow swoop down to eat something. And as soon as she landed, ten other sparrows flew over, pecking her. She gave up and moved out of their way, trying to find a quiet spot, but it didn't help. Wherever she went, they went after her, pecking at her, screaming at her. I remember thinking: Sometimes you just have to take a stand. You have to say: This far and no farther.

"Wherever Jews have lived, there has always been someone who didn't think they had any right to be there. Cossacks, Nazis, Klu Klux Klanners . . . Beit El is an ancient Jewish city. Every time you stick a shovel in the ground, you come up with Jewish graves, synagogue remains, Jewish artifacts . . . Mansour understood that. He really did. He respected the ties of culture, history, religion. 'It's just the troublemakers,' he'd tell me. . . . Well, it feels like we've never been apart." Jenny laughed. "Same old arguments, same old questions. . . ."

"Except now . . ." Tamar stopped herself.

"What were you going to say?"

"Except now, we've got so much less time to figure it all out. When I was sixteen I was sure that by the time I'd reach forty I'd know everything."

"Only now it's even foggier, right?"

"Right. Except now I understand that friendship is precious. You don't just throw it away. At twenty, I thought I could replace you. Now I know I can't." She reached across the table and felt the warm contact of Jenny's hand, the hand of a dear girlfriend, dearer in some ways than a husband or mother or sister, or even a child. The hand of one who really helped you get through life's crises. Who didn't lie or butter you up. Who helped you grow honestly and with some insight.

"I've got to go." Impulsively Tamar took out a piece of paper and wrote down the date, time and place of Aaron's wedding. She handed it to Jenny. "Please come with your husband."

"I wouldn't miss it for the world."

❧26❧

T he girls came out of the terminal first, their blond heads bobbing like dandelions in the wind.

"*Ima!*" They ran to her, throwing their arms around her.

"My little *shefelehs*, my dear treasures! How I've missed you both." Tamar knelt, gathering them into her arms, their warm cheeks pressing against hers. Flesh of my flesh, I would give my *neshamah* to keep anything bad from touching them, she thought with odd, misplaced ferocity. "Where's *Aba?*"

"Oh, he's waiting for the suitcases. . . ."

She bit her lip, wondering if he would get through the Green Line safely or if they would make him open the suitcases and boxes. If he brought only half the electrical appliances, towels and sheets she'd told him to. . . ! She wondered how her dignified, scholarly husband would react to being caught by customs!

But a moment later he was by her side with two filled carts.

"No trouble?" She smiled.

"I told them the truth." He shrugged. "They have Jewish hearts."

She was happy to see him. They didn't touch—no physical contact was allowed in public between religious couples scrupulously concerned with modest behavior—but his eyes caressed hers.

"How is our son and his *beshert?*" he asked.

"May the *Abeisha* give us *nachas* from them both." She sighed. "You'll like your daughter-in-law very much. Come, let's find a taxi."

Of course, Josh liked Gitta Chana very, very much. More important, he liked Gitta Chana's father very much. The two men had an immediate rapport that surprised even Tamar in its unending enthusiasm. Josh spent the days before the wedding learning with Reb Kleinman in Lonovitch, exploring the classrooms, the dormitories, listening to lectures in the big study halls by distinguished, elderly scholars who had earned the lofty honorific of "Admor," an acronym from the Hebrew words meaning: Our Master, Our Teacher, Our Rabbi.

Busy though she was with wedding arrangements, Tamar nevertheless could not help but notice the profound change that was coming over her husband. He was suddenly as excited and happy as a young boy, the somber dignity of his appearance altering subtly. He lost his strained respectability, his body relaxing, the lines of his forehead and around his eyes melting away.

"Do you feel lighter? Like you've lost weight or something?" he asked her, shocking her with his odd tone of strange gaiety. She was not used to having such lightheaded conversations with Josh.

She thought about it. "It's not being light as much as it is not being weighted down. Not struggling. In America, I always feel as if I'm walking against this terrific wind which is trying to push me in another direction. And here, the wind is simply gone."

"That's a perfect way to put it! Like a wind. Only now I feel as if the wind is at my back, pushing me forward to where I've always wanted to go. Our sages tell us living in the land of Israel is equal to doing all the six hundred thirteen mitzvos in the Torah."

"Josh, would you consider it? Moving here?"

He rubbed his hands together and looked down at his shoes, thinking. "I'm not sure. I've never given the idea much thought. Until now. I mean the first time I was here, it was just for a few days, and all I saw was the cemetery. . . ."

"I don't want to go back to Orchard Park! In fact, I never want to see Brooklyn again as long as I live!" she blurted out shockingly.

"What!?"

"Uhm . . . I don't . . . I'm not . . . it's . . . I just like it here so much," she said weakly, frightened.

"I do, too." He shrugged. "But to say you never want to see your home again. . . ."

"No, not that I don't want to see the family, friends . . . just, it's gotten so dangerous, and there's no way to really protect yourself," she said carefully. "Every day you read about the worst tragedies. Why, just last month, just before I came . . . that poor, poor girl!" Her eyes welled.

A beautiful young religious woman in her early twenties, eight months pregnant with her first child, had been attacked on her way home from a bargain clothing factory in a Brooklyn apartment building. The rapist had murdered her and stuffed her body into a garbage can.

"I just keep thinking of her parents. Such fine religious people, waiting for their first grandchild. Instead they went to a funeral. I just keep thinking about our own daughters, Saraleh, Malkaleh!"

"Shhh. Don't even say such a thing! How can you?"

"I think about it all the time. I mean, sure, bad things happen in Israel. Arab maniacs stab innocent old ladies standing at bus stops. Small girls are abused by their fathers. Young women are molested. But that kind of thing—Josh, she was so pregnant and so young! And why did he have to leave her that way . . . in a garbage can? It's just so savage. I mean, it could only have been done by someone who grew up without any normal human feelings. It could only have happened in a big, cruel place that somehow manages to squeeze out the last drop of goodness from a person. I don't know! Josh, those things just don't happen in Israel! Not those things. It's a more human place, somehow. If you fall down, five people help to pick you up. I just feel safer here."

"This is the first I've heard about you not feeling safe," he said, his brows arching.

"Well, it's true. I have my certain places that I can go. I never wander off into side streets, or even take the subway into Manhattan anymore. And even so, I'm afraid. I'm afraid, Josh, all the time, that . . ." She stopped, not trusting herself to say another word.

"Would you really be prepared to live here? To leave your sister behind, the graves of your parents?"

"Rivkie and I have never been that close," she admitted. "As for my parents, I carry them with me."

"Well, you'll have to go back to pack." He smiled, suddenly finding her enthusiasm amusing.

"Not even for that." She shook her head. "A moving company can do that without me."

"You know, our sages tell us that the day of the Ingathering of the Exiles will be as great as the day heaven and earth were created." He grinned. "They also say it will come about with just as much difficulty and that G-d himself will have to grasp each Jew personally by the hand. It won't be so easy for you to leave. You'll see!"

"You have no idea how easy it will be," she said grimly.

He gave her a strange look but said nothing.

❖❖❖

On the wedding day, Tamar woke up late with a weird queasiness that was somehow strangely familiar. It was, she finally understood, the same feeling she'd had on the day her daughters were born: a feeling of anxious excitement, happiness, fear, regret and joy. A feeling of glad anticipation, fright and impatience; a desire for it to be over already.

As she dressed for Aaron's wedding, she looked at her matronly body, searching for some physical remnant of the young woman she had been, pregnant with her first child, a child now grown who was getting married. It was unbelievable. Her little boy, her little Aaron of the small, soft knees and shiny dark hair, a man! Getting married! Another woman would cook his food, iron his shirts. Another woman, younger and more beautiful, would love him, and he would return that love. And his mother would be irrelevant to his life.

On the other hand, she cheered herself, it would be the good ending. The very ending you prayed for at the very beginning when they were only eight days old about to enter the covenant through circumcision. "May we live to raise him to Torah, to the marriage canopy, and to good deeds!" The time had come for her to give up her place in his life, which, she now realized, had only been temporary. Oh, she would always be his mother. But an adult didn't really need a mother. She'd be like some old-fashioned piece of porcelain that everyone was careful with and respectful of, but no one really had much use for.

She felt resigned.

The girls looked beautiful, she thought. Thirteen-year-old Sara, slim and fine in a lovely blue satin dress with silk bows and lace that made her blue eyes sparkle like a clear lake; and eleven-year-old Malka, *zaftig* and charming in a lighter shade of sapphire that turned her gray-green eyes into little jades. And Aaron, tall and darkly handsome in his fine new suit of black wool with tiny gray pinstripes. He was pale with fasting, his hair still wet from the immersion in the men's mikvah in which he had purified himself for the holy union he was about to enter.

The wedding hall was crowded, noisy, and charged with a heady excitement, rollicking with happy voices. The whole yeshiva had turned out to dance to their mashgiach's good fortune in finding such a fine *talmid chachom* for a son-in-law. A long procession of distinguished *admorim* dropped by, their elbows supported by young grandsons as they made their slow, painful progress to pay their respects to the two fathers and the groom. The most respected Talmud teachers and scholars of B'nai Brak and Jerusalem, the elite of the yeshiva world of Orchard Park and Lakewood, brushed elbows and shoulders, jockeying for a better view of the pale, sweating bridegroom.

In a completely separate women's hall, the bride, her relatives, the wives and daughters of the important *roshei yeshivot*, and the wives of yeshiva *kollel* students stood around chattering like a flock of colorful birds, their head coverings like exotic plumage. The more important rebbetzins wore the turbanlike *shvis* (the higher the turban, the more important the rebbetzin, at least in her own eyes), while more modern women had doll-like human hair wigs or elaborate new hats that covered all their hair. Unmarried girls of marriageable age, their uncovered hair smoothed back and shiny, looked joyously at the bride, their eyes filled with delicious anticipation. They chattered like happy little sparrows, smiling and talking innocently, catching up on each other's lives.

Tamar, in a lovely new wig, stood in a place of honor beside the bride's elaborately decorated chair. She felt her head swim, as if she were in some kind of trance. It was almost a nightmare, she thought, with no reason she could point to. There, everyone was so happy, so happy! Why should she feel it was a nightmare?

With relief she spied Jenny and waved to her. She was by her side a moment later, bringing with her a strange sense of serenity.

"A beautiful mitzvah. G-d's will," she said.

Or a terrible mistake. Man's will, Tamar thought, shocking herself. How could you tell?

The bride, in a dress of heavy, opaque satin borrowed from a fund for religious girls, a dress that had to be returned in the morning and cost almost nothing, smiled smugly. Her figure was small and shapely in the pretty folds, her hands long and delicate. Only her eyes seemed hard to Tamar. Like a determined businesswoman's rather than a delicate, quivering bride's.

The groom-to-be, slender and pale, sat at the long table with the important rabbis and his father and father-in-law, looking as if he would prefer to remain that way, expounding on a problem of Talmudical interpretation rather than joining the bride in the next room. But, finally, the singing began.

"Ay ya ya ya, yaya, yaya ya," the room resounded, all voices raised. And Aaron rose, supported by his father and father-in-law, both carrying candles to light his way to joy. Closing his eyes, he silently mouthed psalms, allowing himself to be ushered to his waiting bride. Before him, dozens of yeshiva boys danced wildly, waving their arms and kicking, sending their round black hats flying. Tamar watched Aaron and Josh approach the bridal chair.

My son, my husband.

My son, his father.

She felt the tears of happiness and gratitude choke her.

The fear was weak now, the happiness and optimism strong. If ever two men were father and son, it was these two. How close they were in mind and spirit. They believed in the same things, loved the same things. They had the same values. They even walked the same way, she thought, smiling, that loping gait of great decision. Only now, each walked with identical, deliberate slowness, solemnly.

The yeshiva boys moved to the sides, leaving the way open for the groom to approach the bride. Aaron opened his eyes, looking down at the bride, smiling into her face. Only then did he grasp the ends of Gitta Chana's thick veil, bringing it down to cover her face, a Jewish custom ever since the patriarch Jacob married a heavily veiled bride only to find the next morning he'd been tricked into taking the wrong sister—Leah instead of his beloved Rachel.

Tamar took up her candle and looped her arm through the arm of the young woman who would become part of her family, the mother of her grandchildren. Flesh of her flesh. The time was past for regret. It was time to love, she considered. She would love Gitta Chana, her son's soon-to-be wife. Or, at least, she would do her no harm. Leading the girl down the aisle with careful, measured steps, she brought her to Aaron.

❖27❖

Of course, she went back to live in Brooklyn after the wedding. Was there ever any doubt that she wouldn't? she thought. The idea of great changes, monumental upheavals, life-altering choices, at their age was silly. Josh was settled, the revered head of Yeshiva Mesifta Kavod ha-Makom in Orchard Park. The girls were in Bais Yaakov of Williamsburg. They had their friends. She had her neighbors, her respectful congregants, her butcher, her take-out food place. She knew where to buy gifts and linens and wigs. To move across continents, to a place where you would have to replace your butcher and your wig maker, this seemed so impossible. It was no wonder that most human beings lived and died within twenty-five miles of where they were born. Ingathering of the Exiles. Josh was right. G-d was certainly going to have to reach out and grab each Jew to get them to leave America, England, Brazil, Australia . . . to get them to pull up stakes and move to the Land of the Jews.

Oddly, it was Josh who didn't give up on the idea.

He seemed sadder when he returned. He was still the Prussian officer, straight-backed and meticulous in word and deed, but there was a certain softening in his staunch pose. Often Tamar would find him on his favorite chair Friday night, the open Talmud in his lap, his eyes gazing unseeingly toward some far corner of the room. The wasting of time, the nemesis of every yeshiva boy and man, the enemy that blocked the narrow mountain passes upward toward the vast, high peaks of Torah greatness, was winning the battle more and more often in recent combat. Josh's piercing, intelligent eyes seemed to be losing some of their determined, hard shine, becoming soft and dreamy and gently apathetic.

He missed Aaron. He missed his son.

Ever since he had been old enough to read, and even before, Aaron had been his learning partner. Sitting side by side in the living room on winter evenings and long Sabbath afternoons, they had bounced questions off each other, sharpening their wits. He missed his son's quick cleverness, the physical presence of his young man's fine strong body, his face, his voice . . .

He also missed Israel, the brief but heady joy of participating in the workings of a yeshiva of Lonovitch's standing, the interaction with hundreds of bright students, hearing the lessons of venerable old *admorim* . . . His own yeshiva seemed puny and lifeless and somehow artificial, as if they were playing some strange game in the hostile, foreign streets of Brooklyn.

The letters and phone calls from Israel were the only bright spots in his week. He read them over and over again, chuckling at one of Aaron's droll descriptions: how a burly Jewish truck driver stopped on the road to tell a mother her child had thrown his bottle out of the baby carriage; how a group of rabbis in the Galilee had performed the kabalistic prayer for rain amid the laughter of scoffing newsmen, and how the rain had soaked the TV cameras. He read again and again the passages in which Aaron described the gist of lectures given by venerable scholars who crowded the narrow, modest streets of Jerusalem and B'nai Brak. There was so much he still wanted to learn, so much! And so few to teach it to him. And the challenge of meeting the standards of a place like Lonovitch . . .

As always, he sought the answer in the *halacha*. What was the law? Was it a mitzvah to live in Israel, a religious obligation? He took out volume after volume, probing the issues, finding obscure commentaries from famous *poskim* from the Middle Ages onward who addressed the issue, until finally he came to a clear conclusion that, once reached, could be ignored only at the peril of his own soul.

His life was the *halacha*. Nothing he did, from the way he tied his shoelaces to the way he had married and loved a woman, was outside its noble steel embrace. And the law to him at once seemed clear.

"And you shall inherit the land and live in it." Numbers 33:53. Ramban even numbered living in Israel as one of the sacred 613 basic commandments of the Torah. There were only four reasons a Jew was allowed to live outside of *Eretz Yisroel*: if he endangered his life by embarking on the trip there; if he could not assure his children a religious education there; if he could find no way to support himself and would become a charity case there; or if he was the sole caretaker of elderly parents who refused to move there with him.

Certainly the trip there was no longer dangerous. A pleasant flight, a few hours of bad food and silly movies. He could more than amply assure the continuation of his children's religious education. His parents were well and self-supporting. Besides, his sister and brothers would be left behind to care for them. As for earning a living . . . it might be harder, but he would not starve. Perhaps, through his connections, he might even be offered a position at Lonovitch's. . . .

But still, he hesitated. How could he abandon his congregants, his community, his students? He was keeping his little ship afloat in the vast sea of assimilation. In the last twenty years, half the Jewish people in America had already jumped or been swept overboard. Half! And now there were Jews for Jesus, made up of the spiritually undernourished children of assimilated Jews, denied by their ignorant and foolish parents their own faith, come to proselytize in another's. . . .

Could he abandon ship and swim to shore? Or should he stay on and keep rowing, keeping as many people afloat as he could?

Tamar, in the meantime, found herself happier than she had ever been in the last twenty years. At home with her daughters, she found herself humming all day, much as she remembered her own mother doing when she was a little girl. From all accounts, Aaron seemed very happy with his Gitta Chana. Not that he would ever have the audacity to say so directly! But his letters were lively and happy, full of interesting stories, the letters of a man with peace of mind and security. She'd been right to go along with the *shidduch,* she congratulated herself.

She thought about her son often but did not really miss him. She had done her job, her mother's work. He was grown with a woman of his own to cook his chulent and bleach his tallis and tzitzis white. In a way she did not like to admit to herself very often, it was almost a relief to have him living so far away, safe and happy, leaving her with her two blond daughters and the rest of her life to live in tranquillity.

And then the letter came that secretly they had all been waiting for: Gitta Chana was, G-d willing, expecting.

Josh took it as a sign from heaven. "Tamar," he told her solemnly, "it is time to pack."

❖❖

To her unending shock and amazement, he meant it.

"We will be there in time for the birth. Our first grandchild, born in *Eretz Hakodesh.* It is a great *zchus.*"

"You can't mean it, Josh!"

"But it was your idea! Don't you remember? And you were right. Women are always intuitively closer to G-d. Remember how Sarah wanted to get Ishmael and Hagar to leave because they were corrupting Isaac, and Abraham didn't want to listen to her? G-d tells him: Do exactly as your wife says. I should have listened to you when we were in Israel and never come back! But it isn't too late. I've written to my friend Reb Asher Lehman, and to Reb Kleinman. There is a job. In Lonovitch."

"But the girls . . ."

"They'll make new friends. They will be better off there."

"The Arabs?"

"Where is a man safe? We are always in G-d's hands."

Jenny's words. The echo resounded in her ears, a thump, a slap. Her own words, just a few short months back! And now, perversely, she felt stubbornly opposed. All my friends, all the women who know and respect me . . . all my familiar landscapes, the places that feel like home . . . She mourned. And Macy's and Bloomingdale's and Loehmann's! And designer towels and sheets half price with the labels cut out! Bargains!

And hard stringy Israeli beef, and pale Israeli chickens not properly plucked . . .

Things were so comfortable in America.

"And what if I refuse?"

"My dear Tamar, this was your idea! It's so hard to keep up with you!" He sighed, stroking his beard thoughtfully. "The *halacha* requires a husband to move to Israel if his wife wishes it, and a wife to move to Israel if her husband wishes it. Neither is allowed to prevent the other from performing the mitzvah. . . ."

She saw in his face a sudden rigidness, the look she feared. He would move. With her. Or without her. It was the *halacha*.

"We will find a nice, big apartment and take all of our furniture. We will be near our son and his wife and the baby, please G-d!" he said soothingly, putting his arms around her shoulders.

The warmth and intimacy of the sudden gesture startled and moved her. She always felt so distant from him these days. She leaned her head against his broad shoulder and closed her eyes. In the distance, she heard a siren wail. But whether it was a police van rounding up criminals, an ambulance saving a life, or simply some malfunctioning car alarm, she couldn't tell.

❖28❖

"Put that in the bedroom," she told the movers in halting Hebrew and then English. They stared at her, their eyes puzzled, uncomprehending. What language did they understand? she wondered, looking on in resignation as they set the chest of drawers in the middle of the living room. But no matter. The entire bedroom set would never fit into the bedroom anyway. The rooms were so much smaller than those in Orchard Park. And instead of closets, there were boxy cupboards built up against the walls, with five or six doors that gave little hanging space and lots of shelf space. It would mean ironing and folding almost everything.

But she liked the apartment. It had a clean, airy feel to it, washed with sunlight and sweet breezes. Outside her window, she could see the heavy green branches of Aleppo pines, laurels and silk oaks, their forest smell mingling with the tantalizing scent of orange blossoms in nearby orchards. She had wanted to be in Jerusalem, but the yeshiva was in B'nai Brak, just outside of Tel Aviv, and Josh felt commuting would take too much time. The truth was, of course, he wanted to be near Aaron.

Not that she didn't, she assured herself. It was just such a tricky relationship with a married child. Slight distance was not such a terrible idea. At least until they got settled and stopped feeling threatened by any suggestion you made, stopped reading criticism into every twitch of your eyebrows. . . . She sighed. Gitta Chana was very, very touchy. But at least this way, she thought, her grandchild would always be just

309

around the corner. With any luck, she'd be able to prove her generosity and goodwill over time, earning her right to live nearby.

Gitta Chana was enormous, poor thing, suffering from swollen ankles and a weight gain that was nearing thirty-five pounds. She bore it all stoically, although just recently she had begun replacing her habitual *Baruch Hashem*'s, when asked about her health, with complete, exhaustive details of the cataclysmic upheavals taking place in her gastrointestinal tract.

"Can I go outside to play?" Malka asked breathlessly, excited. Tamar looked at her slim, pretty young daughter, soothed by the sight of her silky hair, flat stomach, and slim ankles. That was the age, she remembered. Twelve years old. It was all fire and joy, all discovery, all passionate friendships, your body a fresh new instrument you hugged to yourself in secret joy. Why did little girls rush to grow up and get married and have babies? She thought of the girl who had called off the *shidduch* because she felt too young. Smart girl. What, after all, was the rush?

"Go. But don't get lost," she said, planting a soft kiss on the child's shiny, moist forehead. To be young and carefree and happy! She turned her attention to her older daughter. "You go, too, Saraleh. You've been cooped up all morning."

"But I want to help you, *Ima*! Besides, I'm too old to play silly games." She frowned, creasing the bridge between her eyebrows like an old lady.

"Don't do that to yourself. You'll get wrinkles by the time you're fifteen!" She rubbed her knuckles softly across her daughter's smooth forehead. She had the face of a goyisha icon, Tamar thought. One of those medieval pictures at the Metropolitan Museum. Light blond with little wisps of platinum low on the forehead. Eyes as blue as peacock feathers. Oh, in a few years—oh, how the phone would ring and ring with *shadchens*, with *shidduchim!* Oh, the mothers-in-law who would crowd the living room with orthopedic shoes and ready smiles. Beautiful, modest, intelligent, pious Sara Finegold! the matchmakers would sing to the finest young yeshiva men in the country. The lovely sister of Aaron Finegold, the brilliant scholar married to the mashgiach of Lonovitch's daughter. The gentle, good-hearted daughter of Rabbi Finegold himself, a rebbe at Lonovitch!

She clutched her hands together in joy. She had achieved the dream of every *haredi* mother: both her daughters were princesses, assured by their illustrious family achievements and reputation of the best matches available and thus the brightest futures imaginable within their narrow, charmed circle.

It was Josh's doing, of course. The credit all went to him. He had gone on ahead, arranging things, beginning his work in the yeshiva. It had not taken the yeshiva long to recognize Josh's outstanding abilities, she thought proudly, as well as his true piety. There was no pinnacle he would not be able to reach, including, she thought secretly, *rosh yeshiva* of Lonovitch. The highest prize in the yeshiva world.

Invitations had been piling up like cans on a supermarket shelf. They'd been to lunch at all the top *rabbaim's* homes, been invited to spend time with the families of several *admorim.* Her spirit soared.

There was another knock on the door: "Rebbetzin Finegold, welcome, welcome." It was yet another kind neighbor, one of an endless stream of bright-cheeked matrons bearing cloth-covered delicacies. Cakes, pies, casseroles, roast chickens, salads. She would not have to cook for a month.

Tamar wiped her hands and took the offering. It was a potato kugel, fresh, crisp, and hot with the most tantalizing smell!

"I know how it is to move. So you shouldn't have to cook for Shabbos." The woman smiled, adjusting the kerchief wound around her bare scalp and looking curiously around the room. Tamar smiled her thanks. The neighbors were friendly and unbelievably nosy, she thought without rancor. But they all meant well. And the respect in which they said her name was a balm to her spirit.

"*Tzchi le mitzvos,*" Tamar said, the familiar way to acknowledge any kind deed. May you have the merit to do more kind deeds. There was never any end. And virtue was its own reward. If only the woman did not stare so, cataloging with hungry interest every single scrap of their personal belongings. If only she would look up admiringly and walk out deferentially . . . But she stayed, despite the fact that she was obviously in the way.

"That's a very nice wig. It must be American. It must cost a fortune. Here in B'nai Brak the *rabbaim* have forbidden women to wear long wigs. They say it leads to *pritzus*."

Tamar felt her insides tighten in fear. She had left her friends and neighbors behind. The people who knew her. And now she had to start all over again, proving who she was. More than losing her home, her family, her familiar stores and comforts, losing her status had bothered her most about the move to Israel.

"My husband allows it," she said with what she hoped was full confidence, smoothing down the flip on the shoulder-length hair. "He says the *halacha* makes no stipulations about such things. That it is just a *minhag*, a custom."

"Well, yes, a different *minhag*, and if your husband allows it . . . My husband, of course, would *never* permit such things." She touched her hairless forehead, adjusting the scarf that made her look like a nun before Vatican IV. "And I agree with my husband. It's wasteful, frivolous. Married women walking around in ponytails like little girls! You can't tell the virgins from the matrons in B'nai Brak anymore. Maybe you need some help to unpack?" she pursued.

"Oh, thank you so much. But my girls will help," Tamar said rather desperately.

"But I just saw them both outside. Delicate-looking girls. Pale and thin. I hope they like my kugel. It'll fatten them up a little. Shouldn't they be in here, though, helping their mother instead of playing? My girls wouldn't dream of not being up in the house helping. With ten children, they learn to help. This is G-d's wish. They play too much in America, I hear. Here we teach them they never have free time. They can always be doing something useful. The boys learn. The girls are at home helping their mothers. . . ."

"They wanted to stay and help, but I sent them out. I think

I'd rather unpack myself, in peace and quiet," she said pointedly.

Like most tactless and offensive people, the woman was also very touchy and sensitive, Tamar could see. Her face registered immediate offense.

"They're my husband's *sifre kodesh* mostly," Tamar apologized. Neighbors. No point in starting out so badly. "He trusts hardly anyone to arrange his library. Even when we packed, he did most of it himself."

This was true. Josh had given her a long lecture about the subject, instructing her in what the *halacha* said about which books could be placed on the bottom and which on the top, the efficiency of packing giving way before gradations of holiness. It took many more boxes that way.

"So many boxes of books!" the woman said with new respect. "And where is your husband learning?"

Tamar was surprised. She assumed everyone automatically knew. "He is teaching in Lonovitch. He is the new rebbe there."

"Lonovitch! A rebbe in Lonovitch!"

"My son is also learning there. He is married to the mashgiach's daughter." Tamar smiled, feeling wicked as the woman's eyes continued widening in awestruck misery and respect.

"I didn't know. They said you were Americans," she mumbled, her face a bright pink deepening to mauve. "May you have only health and good fortune in your new home," she gushed. "And please call on me if I can help you with anything," she fawned, almost bowing out the door.

Tamar nodded pleasantly. After closing the door, she laughed to herself in sheer relief. It had disturbed her more than she cared to think that the grapevine and rumor mill had not prepared this woman for her coming. She did not want to start all over again. Bless the grapevine. Bless the rumor mill. . . . Most people knew all about them. But even those who did not know, all she needed to do was tell them.

Tamar felt a little bird of happiness fly up and sing in her heart.

She unpacked as much as she could and then decided to explore. It was four o'clock, time for stores to reopen following the afternoon siesta taken year round by merchants, come rain or shine. She felt happy as she wandered through the tree-lined streets bereft of threat, cleansed of all dark memories. A clean slate. Streets and alleys and roads without history. Even the shadows of the apartment buildings were benign, she thought, devoid of secrets. They were simple plays of light, cooling and dappling. They hid no potential horrors.

She felt almost giddy with freedom. To walk down any street! To make any turn you wished without the threat of death or violation hanging over you if you made the wrong one! How had she endured the life in New York City? How? It seemed like some dark labyrinthine jungle to her now. But when you were in it, you just didn't realize you had a choice. That there really was a way out.

She took Sara and Malka by the hand, and had it not been for passersby, she would have skipped down the street as she once had with Jenny and Hadassah so many years ago.

The shine, she thought, the shine. G-d is back in His Heaven. He is back ruling the world, she thought exultantly.

Everything gave her pleasure. Even the street names. Instead of the grid of numbers, there were thrilling reminders of Jewish history. Rabbi Akiva Street. Just a street name! Yet what worlds of meaning it held. Jenny had once written her something to that effect. It was all meaningful. You were connected to everything around you. It was your history. Your culture. Your people.

The stores were bustling and crowded. She stopped at a few dress stores and came out with a look of shock on her face: a hundred and fifty shekels for a house coat! Why, that was seventy-five dollars! Seventy-five dollars. For a house coat. Why, in Orchard Park, there was a store where you could get such a thing for nine dollars. . . . Maybe the storekeeper was crazy. There were always a few like that around. She went into another store. The same house coat, only it was ten shekels more! Maybe it was clothes. Something about fabrics being imported, or something. . . ? But then she went into a store and saw a baby carriage. And it was six hundred shekels. She blinked, not believing her eyes. Why, that was three hundred dollars! For a locally made baby carriage with plastic sides and plastic upholstery.

Were they insane?

Who bought this stuff? Certainly not rich American tourists, who knew what to do with a dollar. It must be Israelis, who made about one-fourth the salary Americans did. She was beginning to understand Gitta Chana's frugalness, her insistence that they would get the baby equipment from relatives and friends instead of buying it. Shopping, she could see, was not going to be the fun-filled hobby it had been in New York. In fact, it wasn't going to be a hobby at all.

She was never going to shop again.

Next time she needed a house coat, she'd write Rivkie to buy her one on Thirteenth Avenue. She could mail it—or better yet, give it to someone who was coming to Israel. Someone was always coming, she comforted herself.

That wasn't a bad idea, she thought. Rivkie could shop in Orchard Park and send her packages of things she could sell to Israelis from her living room. Maybe she could even open a little store of her own!

Her mind was suddenly awash with possibilities.

As they said: Change your place, change your luck.

A new *mazel*.

She passed a fruit stall. Luscious apples from the Golan, beautiful oranges from nearby orchards, and carrots and potatoes from kibbutzim in the south. They even smelled differently from the fruits and vegetables in America. Earth fresh, instead of deep-storage chemical, the produce shipped in open trucks straight from nearby farms to local open-air markets. And everything was so cheap and abundant and good! A land flowing with oranges and apples, potatoes and carrots, strawberries and mangoes. . . . She bought as much as she and the girls could carry.

Besides, she already had ten house coats.

❖29❖

The phone rang. Josh mumbled in the dark. The light went on.

"What is it?" she sat up, alarmed.

"Gitta Chana. The baby. Aaron thinks it's time. I'm going to bring around the car and take her."

"I'm going with you." She threw off the covers.

"Do you think. . . ?"

"Don't say another word. Do you think I could stay here while my first grandchild is being born?"

"You'll just sit in the hall on those chairs and drink bad coffee in paper cups."

"And you'll sit next to me, so what?" She smiled into his eyes.

He smiled back. *Uray vanim lebanecha.* And you will see your children's children. The ultimate blessing.

Gitta Chana was calm, but clearly in pain. Aaron was hysterical.

"Hurry, hurry! Why did you take so long?" he agonized.

"Calm down. A first baby takes a while. You have hours yet. How do you feel, Gitta Chana?"

"*Baruch Hashem,*" came the weak reply.

Tamar turned around and patted the girl's limp white arm. "It will all be over soon. How close are your contractions?"

But Gitta Chana didn't answer. She just held her stomach as her cheeks filled with air.

"It's her breathing. She's breathing through the pain," Aaron explained. He had also been to the hospital's childbirth class.

A little while later, it happened again. Tamar looked at her watch. Only five minutes between them. This might go faster than they expected.

"When did they start?"

"She got up last night and kept going to the bathroom. But she thought it was a stomachache. We'd been eating sunflower seeds all evening, and she thought her stomach was just upset. But this morning she saw some . . . something red," Aaron said, embarrassed.

The show. The plug was out and she was ready to go, Tamar thought, getting excited. My grandchild.

She couldn't wait!

The private maternity hospital was the most beautiful one she had ever seen. Built for the religious women of B'nai Brak by a wealthy, *haredi* Swiss obstetrician with eighteen children of his own, it looked like an expensive hotel.

"It's to encourage our women to have many children," Aaron said proprietarily as he hurried to register his wife. Tamar looked around. The colorful ethnic mix so common in Israeli streets and public institutions was dramatically absent. There were no black Ethiopians or blond Russian Jews. No dark Yemenites or Indian Jews. All one saw were pale, bearded Ashkenazi men with their white-faced pregnant wives. Even the doctors looked like Talmud scholars in their beards and black skullcaps. And the older nurses all covered their hair with the pious married woman's *tichel.* It seemed more like a synagogue than a hospital.

The waiting rooms were lovely, too: well lit, clean, and cheerful. She walked over to the window where the newborns lay. Maternity hospitals were so wonderful. Not sickness and death, but birth and life. She looked longingly at the tiny human creatures in their plastic cradles, her eyes resting on one. A little boy, for sure. No need to even bother taking off the diaper to check! A strong face with much character and lots of silky dark hair. Tiny, flailing fists and a pair of lungs, G-d bless him. Healthy and lusty and hungry. A little boy to love and take home and raise. And then when you were all finished, and the little boy was gone and only the man was left, with broad shoulders and enough height to look down at his mother, he'd get married and start the story all over again, atoning for his crime of growing up by producing a little one for you to cuddle again. A grandchild.

She looked at the clock. An hour had passed.

Josh sat in the waiting room, reading. She looked over his shoulder. He was reading psalms.

This surprised her. Of course, things went wrong in births. But she felt strangely confident about this birth, about the health of the baby, so that she really didn't feel the need to whisper *tehillim* begging for G-d's salvation in times of trouble. Perhaps because she'd experienced three healthy pregnancies, three normal births. The baby was full term. And even if there were complications, they were surrounded by doctors and the most modern equipment. Worse came to worst, they could always do a cesarean. Not, G-d forbid, that she wanted that! She just thought that as a worst-case scenario, it was not particularly frightening. At least not enough to send her mouthing psalms.

It would be different if it was Sara or Malka giving birth, she realized. With her own daughters she would feel every contraction, agonize over every pain. She wouldn't care at all about the baby, who'd be a little interloper that had invaded her own darling child's body, bringing her pain.

But this girl was not of her flesh. Her suffering didn't enter into her imagination the way her own daughters' would. Was that cruel, wrong? No, she decided. It was just natural.

She bought the paper and leafed through the pages calmly.

Suddenly there was a great deal of activity in the hall: A sound of controlled shouting. Doors rapidly opening and shutting. Doctors' and nurses' hurried footsteps.

Tamar looked up. Josh stood, his prayer book clasped in his palm.

"What?" she said to a passing nurse, who stopped for a moment but did not answer her. The woman's face was as white as her uniform. Her arms trembled.

"What is happening?"

Now all the other couples in the waiting room stood and looked around, a feeling of alarm filling the pleasant space with suffocating rapidity. Grandparents like her and Josh, prospective fathers, sisters, older children. Everyone stood with a look of fright on their faces.

"Doctor, please. . . ," one of the other men in the waiting room pleaded with a young intern, grabbing his arm. "Please, my wife?"

"Your name?" the young man asked cautiously.

"Engel," the man half sobbed.

The doctor shook his head. "She is fine. She hasn't given birth yet." The man released the doctor's arm, sinking with stupefied relief back onto his chair.

"And what about our daughter?" someone else shouted.

"Name?" the intern said wearily.

"Goldberg."

"I think a girl. Healthy fine," he answered, his steps picking up speed as he attempted to flee the crowd.

But Josh blocked his way. "Excuse me, Doctor. Our daughter-in-law, Mrs. Finegold . . ."

"Yes, our daughter-in-law," Tamar repeated, on the verge of hysteria, rushing over to help her husband corner the fidgeting doctor, who by now sincerely regretted the momentary compassion that had made him stop and get involved. "Our name, her name . . ."

"Finegold," the young man said, giving her and Josh a swift, curiously embarrassed look, then lowering his head and hurrying through the doors.

"G-d!" Tamar sobbed.

"Stop it!" Josh shook her. "We don't know anything yet. He didn't say anything was wrong."

Just then Aaron came through the doors.

He staggered like a drunk, lurching, holding on to the walls. Josh ran to him, opening his hands instinctively. The book of psalms fell to the floor.

Tamar bent and picked it up, kissing it, wishing now she had said every prayer, that she had been sitting here praying and praying. . . .

Aaron looked at his parents like a man woken from a deep nightmare, the horror still lingering over him.

"Have you lost the baby, son?" Josh asked gently.

"Lost? You mean dead?" Aaron asked almost brutally, with a cold fury.

"Aaron, is the baby all right, is Gitta Chana all right? What is the matter? What is happening?" Josh shook him softly.

"Do not say her name. She is not my wife."

"Gitta Chana?" Tamar said in deep shock.

"You're talking crazy, Aaron. *Meshugga,*" his father whispered, gripping his son's shoulders. "Come, sit down. Take a drink."

"Why won't anyone tell us what is happening?" Tamar said frantically. Then louder, not realizing she was screaming: *"Tell me if my grandchild is dead! Tell me!!"*

The room suddenly filled with doctors and nurses. Tamar felt herself hustled down through the delivery room doors, down long corridors, the pressure on her arms gentle but insistent. She looked over her shoulder. Josh was close behind her, his arm around Aaron's shoulder.

They stood before a closed door. Tamar held back, suddenly terrified. *"No,* I don't want to go in. Just tell me if it is dead, just tell me . . ."

But the doctor put his hand on the doorknob and turned it.

There was Gitta Chana in bed, her face hidden in the pillow, her sobs heartbreaking. Tamar looked around the room for the baby. There was the bassinet. There was a round form hidden beneath a swaddling cloth. The cloth moved. Was it the wind? No, it was really moving. It was *crying! Thank G-d! Alive.* But why did no one go to it? Why did no one go to comfort it?

What was the matter with it? The idea washed over her with horror. There was something the matter with it. It was alive. But something was horribly, horribly wrong. Monstrously wrong.

But it was a baby. Her grandchild. Even if it was physically deformed. She would help it. Her heart swam out to the forlorn, crying child that lay alone, untouched in the room full of people. Would no one go to it? No one?

She stepped forward to pick it up, swiftly, before anyone could stop her. And as she touched it, the swaddling cloth fell back.

The baby was black.

❊30❊

Everyone waited patiently for the hoarse screams of the mother-in-law to die down. They were not interested in the mother-in-law, in the heavy American woman who now screamed in horror and betrayal, as they would expect any mother-in-law to scream under the circumstances. They waited for her husband to put a steadying arm around her, to quiet her. And then they turned their attention once again where it belonged.

All eyes were on Gitta Chana. The doctors, nurses, and close relatives encircled her bed like a noose. The girl lay there forlorn, reaching out, calling her husband's name. Aaron stood there, unmoving, unmoved, staring with the others, part of the noose, his eyes the most accusing of all.

Even Gitta Chana's own parents stood at the foot of the bed, not the head, unwilling to face the battery of accusing eyes. They too stood with the accusers.

The girl, alone, sobbed softly into her outstretched palms.

The dream, Tamar thought. The monstrous machine steam-rolling down. The circle of accusers. The black, burnt thing that is the child. But the eyes that hate and accuse are not directed at me. They are directed at my daughter-in-law, at Gitta Chana of the pale lashes and righteous jaw, at Gitta Chana, whom I have never liked.

A nurse came and carried the baby from the room. She did not cradle it in her arms. She held it at arm's length, her elbows barely bent.

It was clear what needed to be done. The very air shouted it.

There had to be a sacrifice.

Someone, something, had to be sacrificed. There was a child, a black child, when it should have been white. The community would not stand for it. The whole religious world would not stand for it. Such a terrible disorder had to be corrected, because people could not be expected to live with such disorder. The seas would churn and rage until the guilty one, or at least someone who accepted guilt, was thrown overboard. The throbbing grapevine had to be calmed. The right message had to be sent through its complex, far-reaching tentacles that wound around the hearts of community members, keeping them in line with the right endings to all tales. The endings that would educate, moralize and discipline. Endings that would frighten the uncertain into compliance, reinforcing the unassailability of their vision of life. There had to be a sacrifice to bring back peace. To bring back the status quo.

Someone had to be punished.

But what if no one was guilty? What if husband and wife were married by rabbis? If they were pious, faithful to each other and to G-d, and the result had still been a black baby? Could you not accept that the black baby was simply G-d's will, his choice? The great disorder, G-d's will, his choice, like volcanoes, or mudslides, or monsoon rains that wrecked the fragile lives of millions? Could you not accept then, this black baby, the way one accepted a lava flow? As an act of G-d to be accepted unconditionally, blamelessly? More, could you not love this black baby, because you loved G-d, who had willed its birth? Because a righteous, beloved, compassionate G-d had wanted its birth?

Such an idea was far from everyone's mind.

And even if they had thought of it, it would not have been a good ending. It left too much open. Too many frightening possibilities that messed up the careful quilt pattern design, putting in the wrong shapes, the wrong colors. Such things could not happen to the pious, to the strictly religious,

G-d-fearing. It was the wrong ending, the wrong message. All disorder had to be the result of man's bad choice, his backsliding evil, his selection of wrong over right. All evil, all suffering, came into the world as recompense. An eye for an eye. A tooth for a tooth.

And then what of Job? The blameless good man? Must you find some way to blame Job?

Most would.

Most had.

Look at Job's friends.

But G-d had not sided with the friends. He'd sided with Job, in all his pain and misery and blamelessness. . . .

But the people in the room at the hospital in B'nai Brak were not thinking of Job as they looked at the cringing, sobbing, red-faced girl. They were thinking of the black man who had been able to seduce the mashgiach of Lonovitch's daughter right under her husband's nose. They were thinking of how the mashgiach's carefully brought up daughter had managed to commit adultery. They were thinking about how they were going to get her to tell the truth.

They were getting ready to bind her up and put her and her black baby on the sacrificial altar.

❊31❊

A aron went home with them that evening.
Sara and Malka stared at their parents and brother, their excited, girlish shouts of "Is it a boy or girl?" shoved back into their throats by the terrifying blank silences of the adults.

For a long time, no one spoke at all. They ate simple, ready foods—yogurts and bread with butter—in the inappetent way of mourners. Aaron paced and paced, a caged tiger, hungry for some kind of resolution, feeling cruel and reckless.

"We will get the truth out of her, *Aba*. I will call for a delegation of the Beit Din to meet with her tomorrow, to force the truth from her." He slapped his fist into his open palm. "How could she betray me like this?!" he cried with the pain of a wounded animal, hurt not only by falling into the trap, but by the humiliation of it. It was his pride that roared, Tamar saw. Not just his heart.

"We shall do what needs to be done. But don't be hasty to judge, Aaron. I can't believe it of Gitta Chana," Josh said quietly.

"What do you think, *Ima?*" Aaron suddenly turned to his mother. "You're a woman. I know you never had . . . that you had your doubts about the *shidduch* from the beginning. Do you think she's guilty?" he pleaded wildly, his eyes begging for her support.

Tamar stood by the sink, her back bent over the dishes. She wiped her hands and turned to face her son and husband.

Aaron. She could hardly stand to look at him. The hair, the eyes. It all made sense now. She looked at him, suddenly seeing his face turn black and menacing. The face of her enemy.

Aaron, Aaron.

She put her hands over her temples, ripping at her hair, covering her eyes and ears.

"It's not right to ask your mother such a thing!" Josh said, coming to comfort her.

His arms were warm. Protective. He loved her.

And she needed love. She had always needed it. Always did what she had to do to earn it. Not to lose it.

"I'm sorry, *Ima.* I didn't mean. . . ," Aaron apologized roughly. He was angry at himself, upset and puzzled she wouldn't answer, that she wouldn't take his side unconditionally, especially since he had expected to elicit her support so easily. She and Gitta Chana had not exactly been warm toward each other. He wanted a team on his side.

Disappointed, he turned from his parents. He would go to the yeshiva. Speak to the *rabbaim.* Even if his father-in-law was the mashgiach . . . still, there was proof too solid and real to be ignored.

There was the black baby.

He did not think of it as his son. Or even as a child. It was simply living evidence of sin. A curse. An abomination. He would enlist the support of the pious men he knew, who would have no choice but to uphold the law. He would divorce the wanton. He would remarry quickly. No one would hold anything against the wronged husband, the badly betrayed *talmid chachom.* Whereas she, she would live out the rest of her life in hell—husbandless, friendless, an outcast from the community. Not welcome in any G-d-fearing home. She would be shunned by her disgraced and ruined family, who because of her would find no decent *shidduch* for any of their other children. Once a family's reputation was tainted, it was outcast forever from the world of prestigious matches, worthy brides and bridegrooms. Her father would lose his job. Her mother would be ostracized. He had no pity. After all, hadn't they brought Gitta Chana into the world and raised her? Were they not responsible?

Her devastation would be total.

He envisioned it.

And it made him glad.

The next day, Aaron returned to the hospital with four rabbis from the yeshiva. Waiting outside the door as they went in to speak to Gitta Chana, he listened to the inquisition.

Denials. Tears. More denials. The pious mouthings of a young woman of blameless past fell from her throat so easily, he thought with venom.

And then the gentle questioning getting stronger. Did she know the punishment for adultery? Did she know it was the loss of her life everlasting, her World-to-Come? That G-d himself would visit the death sentence upon the adulteress? And the child, her baby, would be a *mamzer*, shunned forever, forbidden to marry into the Jewish people forever? He and his offspring. But if the father was a non-Jew, then some leniency could be found; the child would not be a *mamzer*, an ignominy reserved by *halacha* exclusively for the offspring of two Jews involved in an adulterous relationship. The child would be an untainted Jew. Wouldn't she tell them the father's name so they could help her poor child?

Aaron! she screamed at them. His father's name is Aaron, Aaron, Aaron. . . . my husband.

He pressed his back against the wall, stirred by the vehemence of her denials. But soon his heart hardened. Why should he be surprised? She had committed adultery beneath his nose with all the trappings of a great *tzdakis*. Why should the supreme cleverness of her acting surprise him now?

They emerged, sweating.

"Go in. Talk to her. Perhaps you, her husband. . . ," they told him.

He went in reluctantly. Only because the men, his teachers, asked him to.

"Aaron," she cried piteously, holding out her arms to him. "Aaron, I am innocent. I never so much as talked to another man who wasn't a relative. You must know that!"

His face was stiff, unforgiving, as he looked at his bride of one year, the girl he had loved from the moment he saw her. Or had it been her he loved? Or simply what she represented? The piety and self-sacrifice of a truly virtuous woman. Had he loved her or an idea?

"Please, Aaron. Don't punish me. Believe me. My husband. Isn't there any love left in your heart? I love you so," she said with heartbreaking sincerity, her whole soul yearning toward him.

Slowly he clapped his hands together, again and again, then faster and louder.

She watched him, fascinated and horrified. "What. . . ? What are you doing?"

"I'm applauding. Applauding a great performance. The 'filthiness is in her skirts,' and yet she speaks of love, forgiveness." Suddenly, his attitude underwent a change. He softened. He smiled sadly. "Gitta Chana. It is not for me to exact judgment. But for your own sake, the sake of your own *neshamah,* you should tell the truth. Why should the man get off free?"

"You don't believe me, nothing I've said . . ." She was shocked, finally realizing with whom she dealt. He was her enemy.

She stopped crying. "There is a G-d," she said with a little of her old strength. "And He is just. I put my faith in Him. One day, you, Aaron Finegold, will come on your knees and beg me to grant you *mechilah* for what you've done. You will come three times, with witnesses. You will beg me again and again. But I will never, ever forgive you." She lay down in bed and covered her face with a pillow.

He walked out of the room, his confidence oddly shaken. The faces of the rabbis restored it. *"Nu?"* they asked him.

He shook his head. "She is intractable in her sin. You must talk to her again. Tomorrow."

They nodded in agreement. The matter had to be settled. For the good of the religious community. The obligation lay on their shoulders to calm the hurricane tides engulfing the streets of Jerusalem and B'nai Brak. The grapevine had done its work. The story was now common knowledge in almost every *haredi* home in the country. People wanted an ending. They had to have an ending.

❧32❧

"Today it will be settled, I know it will." Aaron rubbed his hands together excitedly.

In all her life, she had never seen him like this. All his righteousness, his single-minded devotion to the law, to goodness, to G-d, suddenly transformed into this ferocious, almost deadly drive to destroy his young wife. To her horror, she saw his pleasure in it.

He was wrapped in some evil, dark embrace, almost in love with the frenzied desire to destroy. And when she peered into his gentle, kind eyes, she saw the dark shine of a stranger she had once met briefly, amused and elated at his own power, the power to destroy another human being. She was horrified.

Yetzar Hatov . . . Yetzar Harah. The drive to goodness . . . The drive to evil.

Locked in a wrestler's embrace within him, within herself. Within her black rapist. Within every man and woman who lived. A saint could act like an animal; the most bestial of humans act like a saint. Each human being was capable of anything. It was a choice, she thought, not a destiny. It was human accomplishment, not some G-d-ordained fate.

I too, she thought, badly frightened. I too am capable of anything.

He had just finished saying his morning prayers and still wore his prayer shawl. Its white gleamed distinctly against the deep black stripes. Black and white, Tamar thought. The white so pure, so immaculately, perfectly untainted. And the black so dark, with no hint of light. Simple, clear. A prayer shawl to wrap around yourself when you prayed clean, pure, good prayers to a perfectly understood G-d.

"The *rabbaim* of the Beit Din tell me in such a case I don't need my wife's consent for a divorce. The evidence of what she did is so strong. . . . I'll do it! I'll divorce her. I'll remarry. Start my life over," he said with enthusiastic bitterness, almost madly.

Start his life over, Tamar thought, a shock wave going through her. Another bride. Another child with the genes of his half-black father, his black grandfather, and somewhere along the line, sooner or later, another black baby. And what then? More lies? More tales of adultery? Never any end to it, the lying, the deception? Never any end to the hatred.

G-d, she thought. G-d. G-d.

"Aaron, Aaron, why such a rush?" Josh said desperately. "Why can't you investigate first? Perhaps there is a skin disorder, or some . . ."

"You, my own father, take her side? Why, *Aba?* Why?! It isn't right. You are *my* family. I need your support! . . ." Aaron shouted.

"Stop shouting at me! Have you no respect?" Josh shouted back.

The doorbell rang. On the threshold stood Gitta Chana's parents, the Kleinmans.

"Don't let them come in! I don't want to see them!" Aaron screamed.

"Rebbetzin . . ." Gitta Chana's mother began to sob softly as she addressed herself imploringly to Tamar.

"Aaron, stop!" Josh warned him, mortified, leading the Kleinmans into the living room.

"You don't believe it of my Gitta Chana, Rebbetzin Finegold? Do you?" the woman wept.

She looked at Rebbetzin Kleinman, a stranger who had never harmed her in any way. I have to tell the truth, she thought. I can't let an innocent girl's life be ruined. Her good parents lives be ruined. And yet, to tell the truth . . . What of my own innocent children? What of Aaron, Malkaleh, Saraleh? Utterly, utterly ruined. No one will want to marry them. My beautiful children . . . my innocent, beautiful children. And what of Josh? His place at the yeshiva? His chance to rise to its head? It would all be lost.

I was also once an innocent girl. Who says the innocent do not suffer? Who says life is fair?

The thoughts drummed hard, sometimes this thought, sometimes the other, two sounds of equal loudness, equal weight. Was she capable of it? she wondered. Capable of letting her daughter-in-law be convicted of adultery? Divorced, disgraced? Could she stand by and say nothing?

"Don't answer her! They want to talk us into accepting their wanton, their disgusting *zonah*. . . . I will never accept her back!" Aaron's voice rose shrilly.

"There has to be another reason. My daughter is pure. She is innocent," Rabbi Kleinman said, his voice rising.

"She is a sweet, good girl!" Rebbetzin Kleinman pleaded.

"She is a *zonah*, a *pritza!*" Aaron proclaimed pitilessly.

"How dare you say that about our daughter, about your own wife!" the Kleinmans screamed hysterically.

"Aaron, stop!" Tamar begged him, her eyes wide with horror, as if she were watching him dig his own grave.

"No! I will not. Never. Until she is divorced and in hell!!" He banged on the table. *"Get out of here!"* Aaron thundered at his startled, humiliated in-laws. "You raised a daughter who disgraces the whole Jewish people. You foisted her off on me, tricked me! You should be ashamed! Get out, I tell you, or I'll throw you out!"

Tamar heard the doors of neighboring apartments open and close. She heard windows slamming shut. And from the bedroom, she heard the sobbing of her two daughters. She pressed her hands savagely over her ears, willing the noise to stop. I have to leave here, she suddenly realized. I have to go away or I'll begin to scream. I will begin, and I will not be able to stop. I will scream and scream and scream until my lungs burst and my heart simply shrivels, like grapes set out in the sun.

She grabbed her purse and ran out of the house and down the street.

Beit El. How did one get to Beit El? It was past Jerusalem, on one of those dangerous *intifada* roads. Maybe, she thought, a rock would hit her in the head, cracking it open, letting all the thoughts, the drumming, simply spill out like coffee from a tipped-over cup, leaving her clean and quietly dead. The thought did not frighten her. On the contrary.

She took a bus to Jerusalem and got off at the Central Bus Station. The neon destination board flashed the information that a bus was leaving for Beit El in a half hour. She bought the ticket and waited by the bus stop, the sounds in her head never stopping, a cacophonous chorus of bad sounds—desperately sad, angry, unforgiving sounds. The images of the cowering Kleinmans; of Aaron, his immaculate white shirt damp with sweat circles under his armpits; of Josh, helpless in the midst of it—they made her sick.

She tried to distract herself by looking around at the people waiting with her. There were young soldiers holding incongruously clean rifles in dusty, begrimed hands, their eyes weary in their young faces. Every day another tragedy. Boys Aaron's age getting blown up by bombs in Lebanon; their heads split by concrete blocks thrown down at them by other young boys standing on rooftops in Arab villages. Aaron at least was safe in the yeshiva. She thanked G-d for that. And then she thought about the word *safe*. Safe? What did it mean? Protected from harm, from disgrace, from discomfort? A word that described something fleeting, temporary, a momentary state of grace, reversible any moment. Who could really be called safe?

She looked at the women waiting for the bus to Beit El: Orthodox, married, dressed in modest long jeans skirts and inexpensive head scarves, their bare feet in sandals. Their modesty was amazingly different from the bewigged, designer-label *tznius* of B'nai Brak and Orchard Park, which invited envious attention. Pioneers, she thought. They lived in Beit El and traveled to Tel Aviv and Jerusalem to study or work. They traveled these dangerous roads every day. They did not look particularly brave. But inside, they must be. Not like me, she thought. I'm afraid of everything.

The bus filled and the ride began. Slowly, the soft hum of

the engine, the gentle chant of pleasant conversations, began to work, lulling the noise in her head. She looked out at the tranquil landscape: olive trees, gnarled and ancient looking, planted neatly on the rolling hillsides; twining grapevines that created lovely shady arbors against the harsh Mediterranean sunlight; small flocks of grazing sheep led gently by old men and children, the lambs softly jumping after their mothers, who grazed with unhurried grace among the abundant green pastures.

Judea and Samaria. The place where the patriarchs had lived and died. Historically, the biblical land of Israel. It was so beautiful, she thought. And there was so much open space, acre after acre of uncultivated land. Why, she wondered, need anyone fight over land when there was so much of it no one was using?

Ahead, she saw an Arab village. And even though it seemed bucolic and pleasantly sleepy from a distance, still her heart contracted as they drew closer. At first the villagers didn't seem to pay attention to the bus. But then she saw it: little boys staring, almost palpable hatred in their small, wary eyes; older women who looked up from their work with dull, malicious stares. And as the bus made a turn, a hail of rocks battered its side. Passengers crouched, moving away from the windows. The bus driver speeded up. And then the village was behind them.

"Not too bad," one of the women said. "This time, they didn't break the glass."

Tamar wiped the sweat from her forehead. That's where it all begins, she thought. In a small child's eyes.

Hate everyone who is not from your country. Hate everyone who is not from your part of the country. Hate them if they come into your neighborhood from a different neighborhood. Hate them if they pray too much, or too little, or to the wrong G-d. Hate them if their hair is a different texture, if they eat meat from a different butcher. Hate them if their skin is too dark or too light, too yellow or not yellow enough. Hate them if they don't belong to your family. And hate your own family if they aren't exactly like you.

She thought of her grandson lying alone in his cradle while

his pious parents tore each other to bits. While his pious grandparents dithered and traded accusations. While the pious community frothed and rose like boiling milk, getting ready to scald and punish, destroy and shun.

While she herself watched and said nothing.

Hate, she thought. Hate, hate, and then hate some more.

The bus rolled through the barbed-wire fences, stopping at a checkpoint guarded by a bearded, scholarly looking soldier with tzitzis hanging out and a big black skullcap. He waved them through.

The last stop.

She got off and looked around, breathing in the fresh air of the mountainsides, the blossoming almond trees. She didn't know where to go. She had no address.

"You look lost," said a pretty young married woman in a jeans skirt and a warm, unfashionable army-style winter jacket. Her tone was friendly, her English halting.

"I am lost," Tamar admitted, wiping a tear from the corner of her eye.

There was a pause as the young woman looked at her, puzzled and sympathetic. "Maybe I can help you?"

"I'm looking for Jenny. . . ." She couldn't think of her married name. "Or maybe you know her as Yehudit. She's an American, about my age. . . ."

"Oh, Yehudit! Sure. I'm walking that way anyhow. Follow me."

They'd spoken on the phone several times, but had not seen each other again. They were both busy and the roads were dangerous and Jenny didn't get into Tel Aviv that often Tamar had often excused herself. But the truth was, by moving to Beit El, Jenny had left the *haredi* world, the world of black-suited men and bewigged matrons. The world of Orchard Park. Oh, there was a yeshiva in Beit El, too, but its bearded *rabbaim* wore knitted skullcaps, not black cloth ones. And on their feet they wore sandals, not heavy, black laced-up shoes. No one in Beit El wore black suits or hats. And no self-respecting, *haredi* B'nai Torah would be caught dead learning in a yeshiva in Beit El. She'd felt uncomfortable about inviting them to visit her in B'nai Brak, concerned about Aaron and the girls' reaction. What would they think? What would the neighbors think?

Her heart ached for her snobbery.

The *yishuv* was very attractive. Large private homes with lots of flowers and grass and trees. A feeling of safety and suburbs and rioting, happy, undisciplined kids enjoying childhood to the hilt.

"Over there—" The woman pointed. Tamar thanked her and walked in that direction.

It was a pretty house, maybe the prettiest one of all, she thought, built of rosy Jerusalem stone with a red-tiled roof and dark wooden shutters that reminded her of pictures of chalets in Switzerland. The garden was laid out in dreamy exuberance that even in March more than hinted at the glory it would be in June. She saw a red ball whiz its way in a happy arc and heard the shouting of playing children. She smiled, walking up the steps and opening the garden door.

The lawn was full of children. As she stepped inside, she saw one of them was in a wheelchair. He was about thirteen, a skinny child with a big, toothy smile and oversize glasses. There was a girl about twelve, a pretty dark-complexioned beauty, and a little stocky redheaded boy about seven.

"*Eeeeemmmmmahhh!*" the girl screamed. "It's your turn!" Jenny laughed, picking up the ball and throwing it to the boy in the wheelchair, who reached up and caught it with one hand.

"Menachem, have mercy. Let your sister catch one. Just one," Jenny's voice rang out, teasing.

"I don't want him to let me. I can do it," the girl protested.

"No, you can't. Girls can't," the redhead assured her. His words had a strange lilt, almost too carefully enunciated. He sounded, Tamar realized, like Zissel.

"*Ima's* a girl," she informed him flatly, putting her face strangely close to his.

"No she's not! She's a woman," he countered.

"Jenny."

"Tamar!"

They walked toward each other quickly, embracing.

"I've been meaning to call you," they both said, guilty, then laughed. "Come, meet the children.

"This is Menachem, my eldest," Jenny said, ducking as he leaned out of his wheelchair and reached above her head to snatch the ball. She gave him a friendly punch on the shoulder. "Never stops showing off. And this is Ilana." The little girl smiled shyly. "And this is Jesse." She tapped the child on the shoulder and looked into his face in the odd way the little girl had. "This is my friend, Tamar, from America." The boy shrugged and ran away.

"Terrible manners. A real Sabra. Come in, have a drink."

The house was a mess. But it was warm and basically clean, with the pleasant smell of cookies baking in the oven.

"Tamar, I didn't know . . ."

"You mean Menachem. He was born that way. Something with the spine. I don't know all the medical terms. But he's still the best catcher we've got in this family." She smiled.

"And the redhead? He's deaf, isn't he?"

"He's deaf," she said matter-of-factly. "And Ilana was born premature with a heart murmur. But the doctors have fixed that. Four operations. But it's over now. She's perfectly fine."

"All of your children? How could that be?" She sat down and gulped from the glass Jenny offered her. "When I was here last year, you said your life was so wonderful. That you had been so blessed with everything. . . ."

"But my life is wonderful! I am blessed. The kids are great."

"But it's not fair. In one family, so much tragedy. . . ."

"Tamar," she said quietly, "there isn't any tragedy. They're adopted. All of them. I chose them."

There was a long shocked silence.

"Come out to the patio. It's quiet there, and the view is beautiful."

Jenny carried a tray of coffee cups and cake through the living room out to the tiled veranda.

"This is such a pretty room!" Tamar murmured, admiring the stonework around the fireplace, the colorful hand-hooked rugs on the walls, the collection of Hebron glass with its sea blue sparkle. Everywhere things were growing, sprouting green from hand-turned clay pots, cans, wooden buckets, and old bowls. She saw geraniums, African violets, lobelia, and thick-leaved succulents with dazzling red flowers that seemed almost too strange to be real. In the corner was a desk and a word processor. The whitewashed walls were lined with oak bookcases holding hundreds of volumes in English and Hebrew. More books were laid in neat piles all over the floor and coffee table. Children's toys were strewn on the rug. Worn, hand-knitted children's sweaters hung on the backs of chairs.

"You've kept up with your reading, I see." Tamar smiled, feeling better seeing the evidence of a life full of many indulgent pleasures. There was nothing monastic about the place, nothing clinical or fanatically self-sacrificing. Just a family, she thought, breathing easier.

"You might say! Except it's such a hassle to get books. There are so few libraries with anything decent in English, and new books cost a fortune. . . . But I scrounge around in old bookstores and get best-sellers from five years ago. . . . It doesn't matter. Good books don't age."

"And the wall hangings?"

"I do them in the winter in front of the fireplace when the kids are sitting around doing their homework. They complain Ohel Sara didn't teach me anything because I can never help them with their lessons in *chumash* and *navi*. I don't know if I forgot this stuff, or just never learned it properly. At least, I never learned it the way they do here, with maps and pictures. It's so alive for them. Everything the Bible talks about happened just around the corner!"

They went through the patio doors and sat on big comfortable lawn chairs. The wind whipped through the pine trees, making them rustle with a sound like the tinkling of tiny bells.

Tamar leaned back, listening to the silence, the peace of playing children, of calm weather. The sky was water clear, stretching blue until the explosion of white that was the sun. Even now she could see its blinding power diminishing as it receded into the pink-and-mauve-and-violet shadows that came up from the hills to meet it. She closed her eyes, blurred and blinded by trying to take in all that vivid light.

"The hills are blue today. They aren't always," Jenny commented. "Sometimes they're green or purple, or even gray. I think I like this color best. This midnight blue."

Tamar nodded, looking at the little white stone houses outlined in the distance, little starbursts in the blue vapors of the hillsides. She heard the birds but did not see them. The sound of a mule braying came from far off.

"He sounds tired today. Usually he's much louder." Jenny smiled. "Today he sounds bored. Poor old mule. I'd like to meet him someday."

The air was so clear, the breeze gentle and cold and crisp. Tamar hugged herself.

"Are you cold, do you want to go in?"

Tamar shook her head. It was cold, but so clear and clean and beautiful. So very, very quiet. They sat drinking hot coffee, the steam warming their cool faces as they watched long shadows bisect the lawn. They talked in gentle, nostalgic, unhurried tones of Orchard Park and subway rides; Italian ices and Thirteenth Avenue on a summer's day; of Mrs. Kravitz and the boy with the bad complexion who had chased them into Temple Emanuel.

And then they sat in companionable silence, watching the sun slowly lose its height, shrinking, compensating in beauty for what it had lost in stunning power, becoming bronze and then copper, sending dark purple shadows flowing like a river along the horizon.

Soon it would be dark. The mule brayed. It sounded like farewell. A flock of birds rose up from the valley floor, startling in their easy freedom.

"We tried for so many years to have a child," Jenny said softly. "Everything. I was living in Geulah then. Even more pious than Orchard Park. I mean, people were so careful about every tiny thing they ate or wore or read or thought. . . . I had a neighbor who was a teacher in Bais Yaakov. She had three perfect children. Blond, blue-eyed, bright. Gorgeous. And she was always smiling, always happy. She kept telling me to have faith, that a child was a reward from G-d for keeping His laws. She would tell me about how she never used cabbage because

337

it might have worms in it. And how she always wore the thickest stockings in summer because it was an extra show of *mesiras nefesh;* and how she wouldn't let her children eat local ice cream even though it had a rabbinical stamp because they used powdered milk, which might be imported and might come from cows not owned by Jews. . . .

"And then she got pregnant and had her fourth. She came home and I saw right away something was funny. She didn't have a baby with her. I asked one of the neighbors what the problem was, and she told me the child had Down's syndrome and the mother had just abandoned it in the hospital. Just refused to take it home.

"I know you shouldn't judge someone until you're standing in their shoes, but this made me crazy. I felt like going in to her, shouting at her: 'You're so religious. You try in every small way possible to please *Hashem.* So how can it be a child that He's created, and He's entrusted to you, you're throwing away like so much garbage? You know what I would give to have a child of my own? Any child?'

"But of course I didn't. I just kept smiling when we met. I never mentioned the baby. A few months later, I saw she was pregnant again.

"But the worst part of all wasn't the woman, the mother. Maybe it's even wrong to pass judgment or condemn her without knowing all the facts. . . . Maybe, if you try very hard, you could even understand her. The worst part for me was the neighbors—all super-*frum* people, women who covered every inch of their hair, or shaved their heads so G-d forbid a hair wouldn't escape; men who bought exactly the right length black overcoat to wear in summer and had the right length beards and *payess*—all of them, they all accepted this. No one said: Let's not let our children play with hers. Let's fire her from teaching in Bais Yaakov. No. It was perfectly acceptable to them that she leave this baby in the hospital to be given away to strangers. It was perfectly okay for her to say: I reject G-d's will in giving me this child to raise. If she had taken off her wig, or bought a television set, these same people would have been outraged. She would have been ostracized, fired, her kids would probably never find *shidduchim*. . . . But this, giving away this baby, this G-d-created human being, this little soul, that was okay with them. It made me sick. They made me sick. I moved out of the neighborhood.

"Afterward I did a lot of thinking. All those religious people, all that carefully measured out adherence to minute details of minute laws . . . And then they just miss the big, enormous challenges of their lives, their opportunities to show G-d, to show themselves, how much they love, how much they believe. And I decided that maybe I wasn't any better. Maybe I was also refusing to accept *Hashem's* will. And I decided to adopt."

"But why crippled, deaf . . . Why not a healthy baby?"

"We were on a waiting list for a healthy child for two years with no end in sight. And then the adoption service called us about Menachem. They said he might have some handicap, but they weren't sure of the extent. His parents had just left him in the hospital and gone home. Marc and I saw him lying in his bassinet in the nursery, so tiny and alone. His hair was so long and silky, and his cheeks so soft. He looked up at us and started to cry—you know, that frantic newborn cry—like the world is coming to an end. I just picked him up and put him on my shoulder. His head grazed my cheek. And that was it. ·　．

"A year later, the call came in about Ilana. And a few years after that, they called us about Jesse. Somewhere along the line, I guess I figured out that maybe this was G-d's plan for me. That He was saving me to take the ones He can't quite place. To help Him out."

"And your husband, didn't he ever want one of his own . . . didn't he ever feel cheated?"

Jenny looked at her strangely. "My husband is the one who can't have children. Not me. Oh, yes . . . I thought about . . . divorce. Believe me, I considered every possible choice. I felt angry and hurt and cheated. . . . But what can I do? I love him." She shrugged. "He's a wonderful husband, a fantastic, loving father. And the kids . . . the kids are . . . I don't know how to express it. They're gifts, each and every one. Oh, I won't lie. I won't say I never ache for a child of my own, or dream about what it would have looked like, been like. I'm normal," she admitted. "But I've made my choices and I'm proud to live with them. And most of the time, not only isn't the cup half full, it runs over. Most of the time, I can't imagine our family any differently. I look at my husband and my kids and I just *oohf* them, like that girl I went to college with, remember? I simply *oohf* them. Can't you tell?"

She did look happy. And young and slim and pretty as ever in her soft white sweater and flowing pine green skirt, her dark hair tied back with a pretty silk scarf. Not like a martyr or a Mother Theresa at all. Just a healthy, happy, pretty, busy, normal mom.

"How do you do it, Jen? Tell me. What's the answer?"

"I have no idea most of the time, either, believe me! And I change my mind again and again. But one thing I do know: Love is better than hate. I could have chosen to hate. My fate. My husband. G-d. Life. Even when I was a little girl, my father died so suddenly, my life was so messed up. But I think even back then, I decided to love instead." She shrugged. " 'And you shall love your neighbor as yourself.' 'And you shall love the L-rd thy G-d with all your heart and soul and strength.' We say it three times a day, don't we?"

"We mouth the words three times a day," Tamar said bitterly. "It's so much easier to hate. To want revenge. So much more satisfying somehow."

"It only seems that way because most people don't really experience unconditional love. We think of it as tit for tat. You did this nice thing for me—my husband, G-d, my child—so I'll do this nice thing for you. I'm not talking about that measured-out-in-coffee-spoons kind of love, that professional kind you see in ads in women's magazines, where the mother's making cookies and smiling. I mean something a lot stronger and in a way much more dangerous. Because you have to let go of yourself. You have to stop keeping score. You have to take a chance on giving more than you get, or getting more than you give. I know I have with these kids." She grinned. "A *lot* more than I bargained for."

"But what if you have to choose? If love for one person makes you destroy another? Which love do you choose?"

"That's hard. But I only know one answer: You go with the *halacha*. It's not your choice, but G-d's. You do what you're supposed to do and hope for the best."

"Even if it seems cruel, or wrong?"

"Even then. That's where faith comes in."

Tamar nodded. It was so simple put that way. So easy. Go with the law. Don't lie anymore. Just tell the truth.

"My son and daughter-in-law had a baby. A boy. Three days ago."

"Mazel tov! Your first grandchild!"

"Jen. He's black. My grandson was born black."

Jenny's face froze, her eyes welling. And then she got up and gathered Tamar into her arms. She didn't pat her, or hug her or try to be motherly. She just stood there, her body connected and undemanding. Tamar leaned against her and they rocked together for a moment, supporting each other as if braced against some great wind. Then, slowly, Jenny pulled back, looking deeply into her friend's troubled eyes. "And when is the bris?"

Tamar blinked.

The bris. The circumcision ceremony that must take place when a male child is eight days old. The big, public celebration welcoming a manchild into the congregation. A celebration of parents, grandparents, friends, and family, where the child is publicly displayed, handed from mother to father, from father to the honored grandparent. A time for rejoicing, for family, for public acknowledgment of G-d's gift of a new member to the Jewish people.

She had not even thought of it. No one had.

She had not thought of it, because it was unthinkable.

It was also, she realized, the *halacha*. Her grandson was the blameless, legitimate child of two Jews, married with all the meticulous caution of those who love the law. He had to have a bris.

She tried to envision it. The large hall. Long tables set with wine and challah. The venerable *admorim*. The *roshei yeshivot*.

The yeshiva boys. The rebbetzins. The friends, relatives, and neighbors. And in the middle of it all, the black baby.

Her whole body heaved in revulsion.

It was impossible.

"*Ima,* can we take some more cookies? They've cooled off!"

It was Menachem. He roared in on his wheelchair, playing tricks with the wheels the way boys on dirt bikes did in America. Tamar looked at him and thought of the others: the little girl with the patched-up hole in her heart, the little redheaded boy who could not hear. Adopted by kind strangers, who were not even flesh of their flesh, loved by strangers, cared for by strangers. With such kindness. Deformed of limb, tainted with illness, nevertheless called blessings, acknowledged publicly as belonging. Called "my children" to the world.

She thought of her tiny grandson, alone in his hospital bassinet, fed by nurses.

My grandson, she suddenly realized.

She would prepare the celebration herself. She would take him from his lonely cradle with bent elbows, cuddle him against her grandmother's breasts, and hold him out to her son, her daughter-in-law, her husband, her in-laws. She would hold him out to the community, this blameless child, her grandson, and insist they accept him into the congregation. She would try love. Finally. She would test its strength.

"The bris will be on the eighth day. Tuesday. But I don't know how many people will come. Will you?"

"I'll bring my husband and the children. You know what else? Hadassah's in Cyprus doing a documentary on antiquities. I got a call from her last night. That's only an hour away by plane. Shall I call and invite her, too?"

"Why not? And is the Rebbe of Kovnitz in Israel?"

"He's always here this time of year. But I don't know. Do you think it's a good idea to invite them both? After all these years . . ."

"Yes. I do. Especially after all these years. . . ." Why not invite them both? Why not invite everyone and just put an end to the hatred, the lies, once and for all? Just refuse to go on with it. Insist the community live up to its own ideals of piety and compassion. Insist they accept her blameless son and daughters; her blameless grandson. She would do it! she suddenly thought. Yes, I have the strength. It would be all right.

I will make it be all right.

❈33❈

"We were worried about you!"
"Where did you go?"
"Really, Tamar!"

She walked into the maelstrom and closed the door behind her. She looked them over, her husband, her handsome son, her two golden daughters. All she loved in the world.

She sat down by the kitchen table and wiped a few crumbs off with her pinkie, trying to clean away one small spot on which she could focus. There was a coffee stain. She rubbed at it.

How to begin? she wondered. How to find the right sentence to begin? Would it be better to ramble, to talk in soft, roundabout sentences that would slip over the truth and mask it for a while, dulling its sharp edge? Or would it be better to plunge in with it, like a scalpel, cutting away the lies and illusions like a surgeon going after a cancerous growth in the hope that the patient would somehow survive the pain and violation, would somehow heal?

But she didn't feel like a surgeon. She felt like an intruder who had sneaked into the home of innocent strangers and was now about to murder them.

She cleared her throat.

"Saraleh, Malkaleh, I have to talk to your father and your brother. Please go to bed now." She kissed each of them on their fragrant, warm foreheads.

"Please, we want to hear also!" Malka pleaded.

"It's not fair! Everyone's so angry, and we can't see the baby, and no one talks to us about anything!" Sara wept.

Tamar looked at them helplessly. She had tried lies, silence. And the cancer had responded by spreading its tentacles farther into the living flesh of her family. Now she would try truth, words. She looked at Josh. Perhaps she should have taken him outside and walked the dark streets, telling him alone, letting him decide how to tell the others. But now it was too late. She didn't have the strength to walk out the door, down the stairs. To be alone with her husband.

Josh shrugged as he met her glance. "If it concerns them . . ."

She felt a sudden pity for him, for the decision he had now made in such ignorance. They were still so young. Tender young girls. He would be sorry.

She looked at her fingers rubbing away the stains on the table. The work of my hands, she thought as she studied the clipped nails, the torn cuticles. The work of my hands. She began.

"When I was twenty-one years old, I went to baby-sit for your aunt Rivkie because she had a driving lesson. Your cousin Shlomie was less than a month old. I heard a noise and I went into the living room. There was a man standing there, a black man, a stranger. He had come through the window and he stood there looking at me. At first I thought, A mistake. But then I saw the knife. He held it over Shlomie's head. He told me that he would kill the baby if I didn't do exactly what he wanted."

She couldn't even hear what she was saying; her heart suddenly filled with the unspoken sounds coming from the eyes, the mouths, the eyebrows, the skin of the people around her. There was a tension like electricity, a reaction of sympathy, of pain and compassion. The girls reached out to her, hugging her. Josh and Aaron looked at her in shock and pity.

"All I could think about was the baby. And I didn't want to die. I prayed for life, for both of us. He took me into the other room. The bedroom."

How was she going to tell them this, her family, her pretty young daughers, her pious son and husband?

"And he did . . . he did what Shechem did to Dina," she said, using the ancient tool of the Talmud to discuss any unpleasant subject, couching the language in words of Torah that would fall more smoothly on their ears. "What Amnon did . . ."

"To Tamar," Sara finished for her in a voice of astonishment.

"To Tamar," Tamar repeated, nodding. Be careful what you name your children, she thought. Be very, very careful.

The room went suddenly white with the crackle of tension. Limbs and muscles tensed, eyes filled with tears.

"I felt like an animal going to the *shochet*. I felt as low and filthy as a person can feel. And when it was over, he told me to count to ten and he would be gone. I counted. And when I opened my eyes, I did not see him. But he wasn't really gone. Not really. In all these years, he's never really been gone, never really left my life for a moment.

"I didn't know what to do. You can understand that, can't you? I wanted to scream and scream and scream. But I didn't. I thought of my family. My mother, my sister. And most of all, of you, Josh. Of how angry and ashamed it would make you all. Of how it would hurt you. And I didn't want to hurt you. To hurt anyone."

She wiped a single tear from her eye, rubbing it into the now clean spot on the kitchen table. "I decided to hold it all in. To keep all the pain to myself. I decided not to tell anyone, ever. And so I went to the mikvah. I purified myself. I washed it all off. And then I went home. I went home to your father and tried to begin my life again."

Their compassion was so palpable. If only she could stop now. If she could leave the story at this point, where she was the only victim. The heroine, the martyr.

"A month later, I found out I was expecting a child."

She stopped, letting the simple words sink in. Letting them do their savage work.

"I prayed it would be your father's child, and not the child of the other. For nine months, I prayed. I couldn't sleep. I kept having a nightmare that the baby would be born black and everyone would yell terrible accusations at me, blaming me. And when Aaron was born, I thanked *Hashem* for answering my prayers."

Now the dawn of understanding. She could see it, the tiny

flickering light of horror suddenly ignited in Aaron's eyes, the responding reflection in her husband's eyes. The slow, excruciating dawning of terrifying knowledge.

Aaron stood as stiff as a corpse, his face white, his proud back curved as though someone had whipped it raw.

"Aaron!" Josh reached for him. At Josh's touch, his rigid posture dissolved. He groped his way into the living room. He sat on the couch. He did not turn on the light.

Josh's eyes lost their alertness, going wild and undirected. She saw his strong chin, his distinct jawline, quiver. He looked like a man coming home from war to find his home in ruins, his loved ones corpses.

Sara began to weep, throwing her arms around her mother. Tamar held her.

"Does that mean that Aaron is not our brother?" Malka wanted to know.

A small, strangled sob came out of Aaron's throat.

"Don't you ever say that! He is your brother!" Josh exploded.

Aaron didn't look up.

Josh turned to her. She saw something in his eyes, his face, she could not name, something threatening and primitive and without a clear boundary. More complex, she saw, than hatred. More boundless and perhaps more praiseworthy.

Who was this person? she wondered. What was her connection to him?

He had missed his opportunities, those moments when her life seemed to totter in the balance, abandoned to the dark forces, those moments when his love could have become her true home. He had simply slept through them.

Was it her own fault? For not having wakened him?

And did it matter?

Would the measuring out of blame, the careful, chemical analysis of the elements that had produced this brew, change the brew? Would it change that they had been strangers for twenty years? Would it redeem what had been sacrificed?

And what exactly had she laid down upon the altar?

Her chance for real happiness.

Her chance for true goodness.

Her chance to know a real G-d who was complex and difficult and compassionate, rather than the cardboard image of a deity who responded to human obedience with divine gifts. Some idol as greedy and cruel and unpredictable as the people who created him.

She had lived a perfect picture of a life, a perfect imitation, perfectly lighted, with everyone wearing the perfect outfit, the perfect expression. She felt a desire to weep for all the lost years, the real feelings, the real life she had given up with such simple-minded cheerfulness.

She had not made the sacrifice for Josh, or Aaron, or her girls, she finally understood. She had made it for all the narrow, attached houses. What's not nice, we don't show. Because it's not nice to make people feel uncomfortable, not nice to show them things they can't reconcile in their easy, predictable version of a complex faith. Keep it hidden, keep it quiet, so they can go on without questioning or working, without challenges. . . . You create a perfect world by denying the imperfection in it, by forcing the misfits to hide. There are no wife-beaters or adulteresses; no deformed, or mentally unbalanced, or crippled, or retarded, or deaf, or blind among our kind! None of our women are raped, none of our children abused or molested. No one commits suicide. Not on our streets. Not among our kind.

Our world, our grid, is perfect.

She had hidden what was not nice. She had kept the knowledge from him. In this Josh was blameless. But the question that had held her all these years, like some instrument of torture, was this: If she had told him, what would he have done?

She put the girls to bed and then returned to the kitchen to find her husband, to find the answer.

But when she got there, he was gone.

❧34❧

Aaron had fallen asleep on the couch. She took off his stiff black shoes, loosening the laces, easing them soundlessly to the floor. She put a pillow beneath his head and covered him with a thick blanket, tucking it under his shoulders. She let her hand rest there a moment, feeling grateful to be able to touch him with such simplicity, knowing that awake, it would be difficult and fraught with meaning. Awake, she would need his permission. He might not grant it.

She went into her bedroom and got ready for bed, washing her face and hands and slipping a clean, warm nightgown over her head. Its old flannel was soft and homey and comforting against her skin.

I should feel sad or abandoned or ashamed, she thought. But I don't. I feel very calm, almost grateful.

This surprised her. Like someone who has watched a loved one die slowly and painfully of some terminal illness, the tragedy was also a relief, she realized. The waiting was over. The worst had happened. The mourning would come later, she imagined. The heartbreaking loneliness of separation from the old life.

For she didn't doubt that her old life was over.

Josh, Aaron, the girls . . . all of them. Their old lives were gone. There was a black baby, and they were responsible. The seas would calm again only when they were all thrown overboard out of the ship.

She looked out of the window, watching the breeze lift the branches in the tarnished light of street lamps, listening to the sound of footsteps on the street grow louder and then softer until they faded away into a heartbreaking silence. And then she listened to the gentle, even breathing of the human beings asleep close all around her.

G-d bless my family. My good mother and good father. Cast your shadow over them, O L-rd, in the valley of the shadow. And bless my husband, wherever he is. And bless my sleeping son, my Aaron. And my innocent sleeping daughters. And Gitta Chana. Bless my little grandson, nameless, alone in his crib. In this time of trouble. Bless them all. All of them that are alive and struggling and wounded.

And bless me. Not most of all. But just. If you can. That I might forget the shame of my youth. That I might not have to feel ashamed anymore. Anymore.

She lay down in bed, her arms at her sides, her palms turned upward in supplication. The room seemed empty without her husband. And peaceful, too. She was still awake at dawn when Josh walked into the bedroom.

He looked familiar and dear in the room they shared. And frighteningly large.

"Where did you go?"

"I went to see the Kleinmans. To see Gitta Chana."

She had not thought of that. The hardest, most humiliating task of all. And he had taken it on without discussion. He had spared her that, she thought gratefully.

"What. . . ?"

He shook his head. "She is leaving the hospital tomorrow without the baby. She wants a divorce." He looked toward the living room, toward Aaron.

"Joshua . . ."

He held up his hand to stop her explanations, her words, to shield himself from them. "I want you to know something. The only thing that is important to me right now is Aaron. Nothing and no one else. He is my son! I have no other! I want him to know that, to understand that, despite everything. My son, mine. . . ." His voice grew less angry, the timbre dissolving into a soft moan of despair. "We will both have to leave the yeshiva. Probably the country. . . ."

She was not surprised, but the reality of the destruction, the splitting apart of her life, was stunning. "But where will we go? Back to Orchard Park?"

He shook his head. "That is impossible. You know this story will spread like wildfire. Has already spread. Aaron needs to be able to start a new life. We will find some town in California or Michigan or the West that needs teachers of Hebrew. . . ."

She stared at him. His whole brilliant future . . . A teacher of the Hebrew alphabet to children in some tiny assimilated Jewish community! . . . He, who had been a candidate to head the most prestigious house of Jewish learning in the world.

"But why? Your whole future . . . you had such good prospects at the yeshiva. . . . Why does it have to be this way? Surely no one will force you out. They are all pious men."

What, after all, had Josh done? She had been raped and borne another man's child. Her son had the genes of a black rapist. But what had Josh done? What was the unforgivable taint that would force him out of the world he loved, destroy his future prospects, his whole life?

He had simply associated with the wrong people.

His wife and son.

"Of course no one would force *me* out! But Aaron . . . he's lost everything. The way he treated his wife and the Kleinmans . . . The accusations he made, the things he said. Now that the tables are turned, they will crucify him! Do you understand that? And on top of it all, he has to deal with losing everything he thought he was, or wanted to be. . . . I'm afraid of what he might do. . . . I have to be with him."

He stood by the window. Pushing aside the curtain, he stared into the dark, empty streets, the dark inscrutable heavens. "If he were sick, I would gladly give him my kidney, my bone marrow, anything," he said quietly. "But this, this . . . thing is, you see, worse. I want him to know whatever happens, he has not lost me. He has not lost his father."

She felt breathless.

She had lain beside him for over twenty-two years, and she had never understood him. The blow that would have turned a lesser man into a beast, roaring with betrayal and lost pride, had simply etched his best qualities into fine relief. He would give up everything he had worked for, everything that was most precious to him, for Aaron. How many men would feel this way? she wondered. And how many would simply reject the son, the mother? Wash themselves clean in the mikvah and go on living their blameless lives in their comfortable niche?

He is a good man. The best. It gave her courage. "And what," she said softly, "about us?"

He turned to her, his back against the cold window glass. "All those years we lived together . . . a lie."

"What else could I do? I looked up the *halacha* in the Mishnah. It said that if a married woman was raped in the city and didn't cry out, if there were no witnesses that the rapist had a knife and threatened to kill her, then she was considered an adulteress. That meant you'd have to divorce me, didn't it? Even though I knew I had been raped. . . . But I had no witnesses."

"Tamar, Tamar . . ." He shook his head, holding his face in both hands, bent over in shock. "That is not the law. There is a well-known principle in *halacha* that says: 'The same mouth that accuses her, acquits her.' In any case where there are no witnesses, then the woman's own testimony is believed."

"But I didn't see it. It wasn't written. . . ."

"It's not written anywhere. But every rabbi, every Talmud scholar, knows that. If you had just asked . . . Why didn't you ask? All these years, you were blameless. A married woman who is raped by force is blameless. She is not divorced, she is not punished. She is without taint. That is the *halacha*. And even the pregnancy, going through with it, that, too, was the right decision. That, too, was the *halacha*. When a married woman has a child, her husband is considered the father, no matter what. There would have been no reason to abort the child.

"I would have helped you, brought you some comfort, given you strength. But you didn't trust me. You didn't trust G-d. You never gave either one of us a chance. . . ."

It was true. She had judged him by her fears. Judged the *halacha* by her fears, not trusting in either one's justice or compassion. In fact, she had judged and condemned the whole society in which she lived by her fears, not giving them a chance to show they could rise to the occasion, that they could become the compassionate people the law was trying to make them with all its constant demands.

"If you see a mother bird sitting on hatchlings, send the mother away before you take the young." "Do not harvest the corners of your fields. Do not denude the fruit tree of its fruit. Leave these things for the poor, the orphan, the widow."

Compassion. The whole Torah was filled with compassion, with love for the misfit, the stranger. How could a society built on that Torah, on those laws, be unjust, unfeeling? Perhaps there was more love there, more justice, than she had given Orchard Park and B'nai Brak credit for. Perhaps they would rise to this occasion. It was time to find out.

"What about us, Josh?" she repeated. And then, breathlessly, "Do you want a divorce?"

He looked at the floor. "I think this family has had enough disgrace without adding another, don't you?"

She felt suddenly very cold. "You mean, to keep up appearances?"

"Tamar, it is very late. I am very tired."

"Not yet, Josh, there is something else. . . . I want to make Aaron's son a bris. I want to hire a catering hall. To invite the yeshiva, the *admorim*, our relatives. . . . And then, if Gitta Chana goes through with her plan, I want to take the baby home with us."

He stared at her. "Are you crazy?" he exploded. "You can't do that to Aaron! You can't humiliate him like that, showing the whole world that child!"

"He is my grandson. He is a Jewish child! Where is your compassion?"

"My compassion is for Aaron! You can't do this to him, I tell you! Hold up that child in front of the community! Rub their faces in it! And why, Tamar? Not for the child's sake. He won't know the difference. But for yourself! All these years when it suited you, got you what you wanted, you hid, and now you want to make a big party? For whom? To wipe the slate clean? To atone for yourself?"

She swallowed hard at the wounding accuracy of his words. "Perhaps. But also for us, for our family. Why should we be thrown out, ostracized? Why should my girls become damaged goods, bad matches, my lovely, innocent girls! I will make them accept us!! I will—"

"Tamar, it's over. Nothing you do now matters! Don't you understand that?" His voice was gentle, almost comforting. "These ideas will only lead to more humiliation, not less! I won't let you do this, not at Aaron's expense! Find your peace another way!"

"He is our grandchild, part of our family! He deserves a normal bris."

"You can't make Aaron stand there in front of everyone as that child is passed around, everyone looking and whispering."

"But the father must be present at the bris. Isn't that also the *halacha?!*"

Josh suddenly sat down heavily on the bed. "Yes," he admitted. "That is the *halacha*. The father of the child must be there. But it can be done discreetly. In the hospital. With only the immediate family—you, me, Aaron, and the *mohel* who does the circumcision. And afterward, let them put the child up for adoption. It will be easier for Aaron that way."

"No," she said with quiet decision. "No, Josh, it won't. I tried it that way. It isn't easier. It might be easier for B'nai Brak or Orchard Park, you mean. For the yeshiva. For the Kleinmans and their daughter. But it won't be easier for Aaron, or for me or you or the girls in the long run. There's been enough lying, enough hiding. Not me. Not me anymore. I have nothing to be ashamed of. I won't be part of it! If people are truly G-d-fearing, if they love the *halacha*, they will come, they will accept this child, the blameless, legitimate child of two pious, married people. . . . They will accept me and you and Aaron, Malka and Sara. . . ."

"You are dreaming." He shook his head in quiet defeat. "And

what makes you think Aaron will come? Have you thought of that? What if he continues to insist the child is not his?"

"Then you must convince him, Josh."

"And what am I to him, that I will be able to convince him?" he said with sudden bitterness. "You have seen to that."

She winced, the tears stinging her eyes. "No. G-d has seen to that."

For a long time, no one spoke.

"I will talk to Aaron," he said. And in the darkness, his expression was inscrutable.

❊35❊

"A public ceremony? A public execution," was Aaron's immediate reaction.

"It is your son. You must!" Tamar demanded.

"No! He is not my son!" he said, walking out and slamming the door.

"I warned you, Tamar," Josh said quietly.

She ignored him. Aaron would change his mind, she thought doggedly.

She hired the catering hall. She began making phone calls, inviting people. Everyone who had come to the wedding. All the people who had invited them over, all the neighbors, all the relatives. Everyone took her calls but were brief to the point of rudeness. The people she stopped in the street were polite but suddenly very late to be somewhere. And then, some simply crossed the street when they saw her coming.

I don't see you, she told herself. I don't see you crossing the street.

She put up notices in the halls of the Beit Medrash in Lonovitch, inviting all the boys, all the rebbes, all the married teachers and their wives and children. She even went to the doctors and nurses in the hospital, to merchants with whom she had struck up a casual acquaintance, telling them the time and date. She tried calling Gitta Chana, but Rebbetzin Kleinman politely but firmly told her Gitta Chana wasn't going to any bris, and neither were they. It turned out to be the last time she ever spoke to Rebbetzin Kleinman.

She did not really blame her.

And how many people should we prepare for? the caterers wanted to know.

She thought about it, trying to estimate how many boys there were in the yeshiva of Lonovitch. How many sons each of the rebbes had. Trying to estimate how many people who had been invited would actually come. But it was impossible. It could be a thousand, it could be half that. And if Josh was right, it could be barely the quorum of ten men needed to say the prayers.

"Four hundred," she said, writing out a check. Her hand shook. She was in the middle of a dream, coasting on sheer will. There was no way to estimate, no way to predict.

And then, a day before the bris, the *mohel*, the most respected *mohel* in B'nai Brak, a dark-bearded Hasid of excellent reputation both for his surgical skill and his piety, called to ask them to find someone else to perform the bris.

"You can't do this to me," she said.

"You didn't tell me the details," he defended himself. "I do every bris in Lonovitch. Rabbi Kleinman is like my brother. He wants the bris done privately, at the hospital. He won't agree to come to the hall. I'm sorry. Try to understand my position. . . ."

She had a hall for four hundred people. And no *mohel*.

She called Jenny. "I'm lost."

"No, you're not. We have a *mohel* who does all the babies in our *yishuv*. I'm sure he'll do it. I'll take care of everything."

G-d bless Jenny, she thought.

On the day of the bris, she woke up at dawn.

It was a lovely day, she saw. Cloudless, with a bright, clean feeling to it. She dressed quietly, not wanting to wake Josh, who was still deep in enviously heavy slumber. Men, she thought. Nothing stops men from sleeping. She shook her head with a little smile of wonderment. She said her prayers, the words falling thick and sweet from her lips, heavy with meaning. She felt happy, almost blissful. The girls got up, and the house was suddenly alive with movement and a natural kind of cheer. Almost normal again, she thought.

Then the caterer called. He wanted a final count.

"Four hundred," she told him, her throat constricting a little with sudden panic as she began to understand the enormity of the risk she was taking. Full, the hall would be a celebration of life. Empty, it would provide the perfect backdrop for their ultimate humiliation.

She began to wonder if Josh had not been right. . . .

Would anyone come except her, the girls, Josh and Aaron, Jenny and her family, and the baby?

Then she began to wonder. Would Josh come? Would Aaron come? And if Aaron didn't come, how would she get the baby? The hospital wouldn't release the baby without Aaron or Gitta Chana.

She had a hall for four hundred people. She had a *mohel*. But now she wasn't sure she had a baby.

Even though she and Josh continued to share the same bedroom, they hardly spoke and were careful not to touch each other. She kept waiting for him to tell her how it was going with Aaron. She wasn't even sure where Aaron was. She kept telling herself that if there was a problem, Josh would tell her. But now the bris was hours away.

She woke him up. "Josh, is Aaron going to come? He's got to bring the baby, to bring it to the hall. Otherwise . . ."

"I don't know, Tamar. I don't know. I'm trying."

"Trying!"

He looked at her levelly. "I'm doing the best that I can under the circumstances," he said with almost belligerent calmness, immovable.

"Then I'll go. Tell me, where is he?"

He swung his feet off the bed, his fingertips lodging in the bridge above his eye sockets, his palms meeting, closing over his suddenly lined and sagging face. "No. I'll go." And something in the way he said it made her understand this was how it had to be.

He washed, he dressed, and then he prayed in the little *shteibel* around the corner. He folded his prayer shawl and put his tefillin back into a little velvet bag, kissing them, the same as every morning of his life as far back as he could remember. He tried not to let his thoughts interfere with his devotions, his heartfelt words of praise and supplication. He tried not to notice the faces of people gone suddenly aloof and distant. He smiled at friends and acquaintances, and for the most part, they nodded and smiled back in respectful, friendly acknowledgment that had, he saw, a touch of compassion.

The streets still had that early morning serenity. He found it helpful as he walked down the block to Aaron's apartment building, to the home his son had once shared with Gitta Chana. She had gone home to her parents, Josh knew. Aaron was alone.

The steps up seemed higher to him, the floor more distant. He felt his heart pumping wildly, straining with the effort to reach Aaron's door. And then it was in front of him. He looked at the little wooden plaque he himself had fastened to the front of it: "The Finegold Family." His own name. His father's name. He was glad the sign was still up, that Aaron had not taken it down.

He knocked.

A hard, brief shuffling sound came through the door, and then silence.

"Aaron! Please! Open the door for me."

Soft footfalls, and then the lock turning.

Aaron stood there, shockingly pale, his dark hair matted, his clothes wrinkled and stained with coffee and perspiration, smelling of something gone rancid. His small dark eyes looked at the floor.

"You shouldn't be here, *Aba!* Go home, please!"

"I'm not going home," Josh said quietly, firmly. "What are you doing to yourself? Just look . . . look at yourself. What's going to be with you? Aaron . . ."

"*Aba* . . ." His voice caught in his throat. "If it's about the bris, I already told you. *Ima* can't do this . . . not only to me, but to you. . . . You don't owe me anything. . . . Please, *Aba*, go home! I don't want anyone to see you here!"

"Why didn't you come to shul this morning? Have you washed, prayed? And when was the last time you put something into your mouth to eat?" Josh continued, ignoring his entreaties.

Aaron shook his head dumbly.

Josh took him by the shoulders, steering him toward the bedroom as he would a small, reluctant child. "Go, son. Wash, change, pray. I'll make you something to eat. And then we'll talk."

Aaron walked away slowly, with strange obedience. Josh went into the kitchen, looking around at the foreign territory, not knowing where to begin. He found eggs and margarine and a frying pan. As the eggs sizzled, he heard the reassuring sound of splashing water, of shoes scuffing against the floor and closet doors opening and closing. He heard the sound of prayer: short, bitter, muffled.

The eggs browned at the edges and stuck to the pan. He scraped them into a plate and put up water to boil.

Aaron stood in front of him, his hair wet, his clothes clean. Only the look on his face of accident and mourning had not washed away.

"I can't find the coffee cups. . . ."

"I'm not hungry, *Aba*."

"But I am. Come, sit and eat with me a minute."

Aaron got the cups and made coffee, splashing the milk in a little pool around the saucers.

They sat in silence, looking at each other across the bad, hastily prepared meal. Aaron took a few obligatory mouthfuls, then sat with his hands gripped hard around the hot cup.

"*Ima* is pressuring you, isn't she? Why can't she leave me alone? I can't take it anymore—"

"Aaron, come sit and learn with me a little bit," Josh suddenly interrupted him. "The way we always did, remember? In the mornings, before you went to school?" He didn't wait for an answer, but walked into the living room and reached up to the large volumes of Talmud that dominated the room. He took one down and sat on the couch, opening it.

Aaron stood in a corner, watching him.

"Come, son." He beckoned him. "Come, sit." He patted the space next to him. "*Talmud chullin, Resh Pay Heh*," Josh began in the lovely singsong of learning so dear to them both. " 'An ox or a sheep, you shall not slaughter father and son on the same day. How do we know who is the father? And who is called a son? He who clings to his father, who walks in his footsteps. . . .' " He felt the sudden weight of Aaron's shoulder pressing into his.

"Now, let us look at another *sugiya. Chullin Yod Aleph.* 'A son is born to a man and his wife. And we shall nor harbor any suspicions that the woman has strayed and borne to another. Her husband is the father of the child. . . . And even if evil gossip slanders the woman, and everyone speaks vilely of her, still, the husband is the father of the child. . . . And even if the woman is the most promiscuous of all women, still her husband is considered the father of the child. . . ."

"*Aba. . . ,*" Aaron whispered, choking.

"This is the *halacha,* Aaron. You are my son. Mine. I will never give you up, I will never turn my back on you or pretend otherwise."

"Why didn't she just get rid of me? Why did she let me be born? I'm a monster. I had no right to be born! Why did G-d let me be born? Why did He let me have a child, another monster?"

"Do you remember the story of Ruth?" Josh interrupted him, his hand on his shoulder.

Aaron looked up, confused. Every little child knew the story. How Elimelech the rich farmer from Bethlehem had left Israel during the famine so as not to share his wealth with the many poor. How he and his wife, Naomi, and two sons had settled in Sodom. How the boys had intermarried with girls from the hated Moabites, the people G-d had told the Israelites never to marry because they'd denied them bread and water when they were hungry and thirsty in the desert. How Eli and his two sons had died, and how Ruth, the Moabite daughter-in-law, daughter of the king of Moab himself, refused to leave the widowed Naomi, declaring: Wherever you go, I'll go. Your people will be my people. Your G-d my G-d. . . . How Ruth had married Boaz, Naomi's relative, and became King David's grandmother. . . .

"I remember once asking my own rebbe why King David had to have a grandmother who was not only a convert, but the daughter of the hated king of Moab himself, known for his selfishness and cruelty? Why had G-d arranged it that way? And my rebbe told me this: Even in the cruel king of Moab there was a small spark of kindness, of goodness. G-d had wanted to redeem that spark, to carry it on before it was extinguished completely, by bringing it into a people known for their compassion. Ruth carried that spark, that gene. She brought it into the Jewish people, she passed it on to her children, and their children. That spark gave us King David, the psalms, King Solomon. And one day it will bring the Messiah himself. It was all G-d's will."

"*Aba* . . . the *rabbaim* at Lonovitch are good people. No one will ask you to leave. As long as I go away, your life doesn't have to change. . . . Why should it change? I have to go anyway. There is nothing left for me here . . . nothing. . . . Gitta Chana . . . after the way I acted . . . she'll never . . . And even if I hadn't been so cruel, such an idiot, I could still only give her more children like the one she has and doesn't want. . . . I'll never find another wife among B'nai Torah. . . . I can never have more children. . . . I'll never be allowed to teach. . . . It'll be better for everyone if you all just forget about me. I'll go to some town in America. I'll get a job. I'll be like everybody else. . . ."

"You can do that," Josh admitted. "But I think . . . I really think . . . it would kill me."

Aaron stared at him hard, astonished.

"All my life I have spent teaching Torah. But only one student ever took all I was able to give. Ever lived up to my highest ideals. That's you, Aaron. You've acted foolishly. You've made some mistakes. But if you abandon everything I taught you, if you choose to live a faithless life without purpose, without family, without Torah, without mitzvot . . . if you disappear, it will kill me," he repeated with simple honesty that couldn't be doubted.

"*Aba*, what else can I do?"

"You can be yourself! You can keep learning. You can find work teaching. You can find your *beshert*, a truly G-d-fearing woman, you can have more children. . . ."

"Black children!"

"Good children, the children of their good parents . . . who will be any color G-d chooses to make them."

Like a breakwater giving way before the tremendous force of nature, something broke inside Aaron Finegold. He sobbed, the big, gulping, strangled sobs of a man who does not cry. "*Aba* . . ."

Josh held him tight. They sat there for a long time.

Then Josh released him. "Come now. It's time for you to fulfill your obligations to your son. Come. Your mother and sisters are waiting. Come now, my son. Whatever has to be done, we'll do it together."

In the hospital, Aaron signed the papers. The nurse wheeled the baby out in its bassinet.

"You take it, *Ima*. I don't know anything about babies," Aaron said.

Tamar looked down at the small, swathed creature and suddenly froze.

She had gotten caught up in the beauty of the deed, the feeling behind it. All the right feelings. And on the wave of that good feeling, she had done everything she was supposed to. But she had never considered the details, the actual, practical physical details of accomplishing what she wanted to. It had been an idea, a righteous, compassionate idea. And now it was real, a deed. Now, she had to hold this baby. She had to look at this baby. She wanted to. She wanted to be the kind of person who would be able to love it, no matter what.

But would she succeed? After talking everyone else into love, into tolerance, into being open and kind and compassionate . . . would she herself be able to reach out to this child, to look into his strange, foreign-looking face, his small dark eyes? Or would it forever remind her of another face, another stranger, no kin? She reached down to lift it, trying to see past its differentness, to the softness of its skin, its small perfect limbs, its perfect baby's head. But as hard as she tried, she could see nothing but its color.

She cringed.

"Saraleh, take it!" she begged her daughter.

Sara reached into the bassinet without hesitation, tenderly lifting the sleeping infant.

"Can I see him?" Malka asked.

Tamar nodded uneasily, her whole body inflexible with tension as they folded back the blanket.

She watched their soft, pretty blond heads hover over the infant.

Saraleh and Malkaleh, she thought, her heart aching. Princesses dethroned. Did they understand as they looked at the small, sleeping infant, their little nephew, that he had destroyed their world, their future, like a bomb? They were now grade B, grade C, on the *shidduch* lists? Who would want them now? Widowers, divorced men with bad histories? The newly observant from irreligious families? Nobodies. The finest families, the most educated and promising boys, were forever beyond their reach.

"He has Aaron's eyes," Sara said, letting the baby's fist clutch her finger.

"And a small chin, like Rebbetzin Kleinman." Malka giggled, touching the baby's chin. "And your cheekbones, *Ima*, look! And a dimple just like Sara's." She laughed.

How was it possible for them to accept this child so easily? Tamar wondered. What magic lens had made their vision so kind? Youth, perhaps, or innocence. Or simply good, kind hearts that saw nothing bad in a good world, a world still full of that precious shine.

And then, for no reason at all, she felt sudden hope. Her beautiful daughters! Perhaps it was not over. Perhaps something magical would happen, some lovely transformation outside the realm of predictability and understanding. A miracle.

She walked behind them out to the waiting taxi.

❧36❧

The cab let them off in front of the hall.

Malka ran happily inside and then back out. It was ten o'clock. Tamar was afraid to ask how many people were already inside.

"The *mohel's* inside. And a friend of yours, and a few kids," Malka informed her.

Her heart sank. She was afraid to walk into the hall and see all its vast array of food, all the vast long empty tables.

"People are always late," a familiar voice soothed, as if reading her mind.

"Jen! Thanks for coming. For everything."

A small wheelchair whizzed past them. Jenny grabbed the handles, laughing. "Menachem, this is not a playground!" she said with her best try at severity. "Come, where are your manners. Stop a minute on your journeys and wish Tamar mazel tov."

The boy, dressed in a new white shirt and his nicest Sabbath pants, his hair neatly combed, sat up with new dignity. "Mazel tov!" he said with hearty cheer, his smile mischievous. "Now can I go?" he begged his mother.

"Go," Jenny sighed, "and no hit and runs, please, Menachem!" she smiled, watching him careen away. "Honestly, if they issued licenses to operate those things, his would have been revoked long ago! You remember Jesse and Ilana . . ." The children clung to her skirts, poking their heads out briefly to reveal shy smiles. "And this is my husband, Marc," Jenny smiled proudly, turning to a tall, handsome man, clean shaven, with steady, warm green eyes.

Tamar nodded and smiled, noticing his arm draped affectionately around Jenny's shoulder, something very unusual
among religious couples in public places. At another time it
would have shocked her. But somehow, now, the gesture
warmed her.

"Can I hold the baby?" Marc asked.

"You're lucky he asked your permission!" Jenny laughed.
"Usually he just snatches babies right out of our friends' arms."
Jenny punched him affectionately on his shoulder.

Tamar nodded, pleased, watching as Sara transferred the
baby to Marc.

" 'I am dark, but I am comely,' Song of Songs, remember?
They say King Solomon was black, and Moses' wife, Tziporah
. . . little fellow," he said softly. "All your toes, all your fingers,
sight, hearing, sturdy little legs. G-d blessed him!" he said,
nodding solemnly at Jenny.

That was one way of looking at it, Tamar thought, the words,
the sight of the baby cradled in the big, handsome man's arms,
somehow giving her hope. "Where is everybody?" she said
lightly, trying to keep the panic from her voice.

"You called it for ten. Ten Jewish time, remember?" Jenny
calmed her. "That's good for at least another half hour. He
looks so peaceful, poor thing. Little do you know what you're
in for, child." She smiled sadly, leaning against Marc's arm.
"Is his mother here?"

Tamar shook her head. "Not yet."

"I see. He will cry afterward. He'll need some comforting . . . Do
you have a bottle?"

"I think the hospital sent a bottle of formula with him."

"Marc will put it in the fridge so we don't have to plow
through all those Hasidim in the kitchen. You better give
Tamar back the baby first, though," Jenny suggested.

He leaned toward Tamar with the baby.

She backed off, dropping her hands quickly to her sides. "Oh,
better give him to Sara."

Marc gave Jenny a quick, questioning glance, then gave the
baby to Sara.

"I'm sorry. I just can't . . ."

"It will be all right. You'll see," Marc said compassionately, with a confidence she found infinitely comforting.

The *mohel* had already laid out all his surgical equipment on a long, sterile white table. The chair of Elijah the prophet was readied for the *sandak*—the godfather—who would hold the child as the *mohel* did his work. Usually, families fought over who would have the honor to be *sandak*. Now, Tamar wasn't even sure anyone could be persuaded to accept the honored position.

She looked at the long tables that held bottles of wine, glistening cold with moisture, and egg-glazed twisted challah breads. Plates and cups and forks were already set out for the banquet. Four hundred place settings.

At ten past ten, a couple from their apartment building turned up. And then one of the rebbes from the yeshiva came with five students. The greengrocer came with his wife. And the man who sold her fish. Cousins Velvel and Drora came. The trickle continued. Not hundreds, but dozens. As each one entered, she felt a sudden surge of hope. A trickle now, and then the river, the hall filling, she thought. By ten-thirty there were about eighty people in the hall. By ten forty-five she realized even the trickle had stopped.

The only ugly Queen Esther, she thought. All my life. . . . All the outer trappings, yet underneath, it was never right. She wanted to weep for each empty chair, for each unoccupied foot of space, for the silence, the scattered whispers. For her son and husband and for the poor guest of honor, tiny and oblivious of insult, about to be humiliated.

This must be the way G-d feels, she thought, when He looks into the synagogues on Rosh Hashanah and Yom Kippur, counting the number of sincere worshipers. A few good people here and a few there. Not as many as there should be. But not completely empty either, she tried to comfort herself.

"Hello, Tamar."

She was a striking woman, tall and slim with tangled curls the color of honey, beautifully dressed in an expensive turquoise silk suit with a scarf of apple green, mauve, and gold. Tamar's heart lurched.

The face was the same, its youthfulness a bit strained now, speaking of expensive skin care and excellent makeup. Only the eyes seemed changed: eyes that did not match the beautiful young-looking figure, the perfect bouncy hair. They were not unhappy eyes. Just eyes that had seen and experienced more than their share of everything, good and bad. They looked tired. And bored.

"Hadassah!"

"Mazel tov, Tamar."

"You saw the baby?"

She nodded, giving Tamar a gentle hug that was more than polite. "He's a healthy, beautiful baby. You know what I'd give for a healthy, beautiful baby? Any color, any sex?" She shook her head. "I'm not going to stay long. I've just done yet another *in vitro*." She shrugged. "I've got to get back into bed. Doctor's orders."

"Where are you living now?"

"I've got a house in St. John's Wood in London. And a small beach house in Kauai. Jack, my husband, has an apartment in Manhattan on the Upper East Side. And then there's my house in La Jolla. We're frequent fliers."

She looked at Hadassah, wondering why she was so happy to see her. The friends of our youth. They brought back a whiff of silly pranks and harmless laughter, of hope and great expectations. "Slim and beautiful as ever, Hadassah."

"Please. I'm as fat as a cow." She plucked at her suit. "Size twelve. I wore a six forever, and then two years ago I gained all this weight, and nothing, absolutely nothing, helps."

"I haven't seen the inside of a twelve since tenth grade," Tamar laughed. "You look gorgeous."

Hadassah was very pleased. "You think so?"

"Yes. I do."

"Well, then it was worth it to come just for that!"

"What are you doing now?"

"I have a film company. We make documentaries. Mostly nature films. My husband is a nature photographer. We met in Hawaii. We've done specials on whales and sharks and coral reefs. Very environmental. We spent the whole month of September on this little island in the Galápagos filming seals."

"Rosh Hashanah and Yom Kippur on Galápagos with the seals," Tamar said absently, looking over the crowd, not really paying attention to what she was saying.

"Well, right, it was great seeing you. And if I get lost in the . . . crowd . . . afterward, just let me say good-bye now. And good luck, really," she said stiffly.

"Look, Hadassah, I'm not thinking straight. I didn't mean to be self-righteous, to hurt your feelings . . . it was stupid of me. Thanks for coming. I really appreciate it."

"Okay, okay. I'm too damn touchy on this subject. Let's call a truce, shall we?"

"I certainly don't need any more enemies. That's for sure. Look at this place." She bit her lip, her throat contracting. And then, Josh was at her side.

"There's no point in waiting any longer, Tamar," Josh told her, his face a mask.

"No! Wait just a few more minutes! Maybe traffic . . ."

Jenny held her hand. "It's all right, Tamar. You did your best. You tried. Now just go on from here."

Tamar wiped her eyes and nodded.

Josh told the *mohel* to begin. Sara handed the baby to Josh, and then Josh handed him to Aaron, and Aaron handed him to the *mohel*.

"*Baruch habah!*" the *mohel* sang, holding up the child so all could see him.

There was a small gasp.

Blessed are you who comes.

The *mohel* laid the baby on the empty ceremonial chair, murmuring the prayers:

In your salvation do I trust, G-d,
For your salvation do I hope.
. . . I rejoice at your Word, as at finding a great treasure.
Great peace comes to the lovers of your Torah
For them there will be no impediment
Happy are those that choose their dwelling close to Yours.

Tamar let the words fill her mouth, nourishing her. She looked around the almost empty hall, trying to imagine it filled to the doorposts. She tried to imagine Rabbi Kleinman and his wife and Gitta Chana standing in the front row smiling, all their friends and relatives around them, their faces wreathed in delight. She tried to imagine all the yeshiva boys in their dark suits and white shirts clapping and singing, their eyes closed in the joy of doing a mitzvah. She tried to imagine the wives and daughters of the *admorim* crowding around behind the pious partition. She tried to imagine the head of the yeshiva sitting on the chair of Elijah the prophet, holding the baby in his arms.

She tried to imagine a different world.

She was imagining so hard that she almost thought she had imagined the doors of the hall suddenly opening and the hundreds of Hasidim who started pouring through, packing the room. And then she saw the sea of black part and an old rabbi with a long white beard walk through. Rabbi Mandlebright. The old Rebbe of Kovnitz. Someone ran to bring him a chair, but he shook his head, his once large, imposing frame now bent as if under a heavy load. Slowly, with dignity, he moved toward the front of the room. The Hasidim parted like the waters of the Red Sea to let him through. Josh hurried back to greet him.

"*Nisbe-ah be-toov baytecha, Kadosh hay-challecha,*" all the assembled guests shouted joyfully, the noise exploding like thunder through the suddenly packed room.

"Who is the child's *sandak?*" the Rebbe inquired, looking at the empty chair.

No one answered him.

"Then perhaps I may have that great honor," he said quietly.

"Who is the *sandak?*" Tamar heard people whispering to each other, wondering. "The Rebbe himself. The great Rebbe of Kovnitz!" came the awed reply, whispered again and again and again with great emotion. People who had come out of obligation or kindness or pity, hoping their presence would not be noticed, felt a sudden surge of unexpected pride. This would be something to brag about! "You know where I was yesterday? At the bris of the Finegold baby. Yes, yes that one! The black baby. But do you know who the *sandak* was? The Rebbe of Kovnitz himself! I couldn't believe it! I was standing right next to him!" To be in the same room with the Rebbe of Kovnitz! They had all heard of him, the great *tzadik* and scholar. The guests suddenly looked at the child and his father and grandparents with a puzzled sense of new respect.

The *mohel* waited for the Rebbe to be seated then handed him the child. The old Rebbe laid him lovingly across his knees.

"Blessed are you, King of the Universe, who sanctifies us with His commandments and commands us to perform circumcision."

He looked at Aaron. "Are you the father of this child?"

Tamar watched her son, a sharp twinge twisting her heart. She saw his slow nod of affirmation. "Yes. I am this child's father," he answered.

Her eyes welled.

The Rebbe nodded to Aaron, handing him the siddur.

"Blessed are you, G-d, King of the Universe, that has sanctified us with His mitzvos and commanded us to bring this child into the covenant of Abraham our father." Aaron read.

"And as you bring him into the covenant, so may he be brought to Torah, to the marriage canopy, and to good deeds!" the assembled guests shouted with joy, as was the custom.

The *mohel* cut the foreskin.

"*Mazel tov!!*" hundreds of voices shouted, the words slamming into the walls of the packed room, bouncing off the ceiling like confetti.

Through the shouting, Tamar heard it: the cry of the newborn! That insistent, demanding, amazed, forlorn, terrified, helpless, desperate sound! A cry like no other, not sad, not hurt, but reckless, tortured, a sound that pierces the heart like surgical steel. Tamar held her breath, her whole motherly being suddenly yearning toward it with an instinct beyond control.

Someone has to hold him, she thought. Sara did not know how to hold a crying baby. Nor did Malka. But she did. She leaned over, lifting the screaming child from the pillow, hugging him to her breast, pacifying him with cotton dipped in sweet wine. He sucked, his sobs quieting, his eyes closing drowsily.

She looked at him. He was yawning, his nose wrinkling, disturbed. She studied his features. He looked, she realized, like a baby. A beautiful little baby. Not a miniature hundred-and-seventy-pound black rapist. But he did not look like *her* baby, or any baby that had ever been born into her family, her people. He looked like a stranger.

The guests made their way to the tables. Not a seat was empty. The Rebbe crossed the hall to a place of honor beside Aaron and Josh. Jenny walked quickly toward the Rebbe, Jesse and Ilana clinging to her arms, Menachem propelling his wheelchair forward with gay recklessness. The Rebbe nodded and smiled at Jenny, bending down to talk to Menachem.

From across the room, Hadassah watched, almost hypnotized, as her father laid his hands in turn on the heads of Jenny's children, blessing them. Slowly, almost like a sleepwalker, she walked toward him.

The Rebbe watched her moving closer, the bright colors of her dress, the gold of her hair hurting his eyes like a glare of concentrated light.

Shayne maidel. Shayne, shayne maidel, voices long silent shouted inside him, hands clapping, feet stamping the floor in joy. He closed his eyes and saw her again in the beaded russet velvet. A beautiful little queen, he remembered, his chest growing warm as if somehow, once again, a little girl's light, graceful body was leaning back into his arms . . .

"*Tateh* . . ."

He was her father. G-d had entrusted him with guiding her pure soul through this dark, false world and he had failed utterly. She had wandered off the only chosen path, disappearing over the mountain. A whole world had been lost—a loss incalculable and completely without replacement. And he was responsible.

"*Tateh,*" she repeated, her voice strangely young, pleaded. "Is there a blessing left for me?"

He looked up at her, startled, his old, sharp eyes going pale and liquid, moisture gathering at the corners. He tried to read in her face those chapters of her life unknown to him. In the soft creases near her eyes, the downward pull around her mouth, he learned of passion and happiness, betrayal and bitter disappointment. And in her eyes, he saw a need still unsatisfied, and a stubborn, unrelinquished glow of hope.

Something told him, he would never see her again.

"Please, *Tateh*. Even Esau got a blessing," she begged, her voice finally cracking.

Esau, Isaac's wicked son, who had forfeited his birthright and blessing to his pious twin, Jacob. But Isaac had loved Esau. He had saved him a blessing.

He moved toward her painfully, laying his hands on her warm, bent head. "May G-d grant you what you pray for, my daughter," he told her, wondering what that could be and why it was she wept.

Sitting in a corner of the hall, Tamar watched Hadassah and her father slowly part, each going in their own direction. And then she glanced at Jenny, kneeling in front of Menachem, tying his shoelaces.

Raising a child was such a mystery, she realized. There were no neat formulas, no guarantees. And it really didn't matter if you started out with the longed-for, perfect child of your womb, or with the adopted, handicapped offspring of strangers. There was no predicting if in the end you'd wind up polite acquaintances, enemies, or lifelong partners in the most powerful bond of love human beings can know.

She looked down at the little stranger, the cocoa-colored baby sleeping peacefully in her arms. Already his eyes, the shape of his mouth were growing familiar to her. Soon he would wake up, she thought. She didn't know how much he ate or how often. If he suffered from colic or slept peacefully through from feeding to feeding. It would take time, she realized, until she knew all of these things. Until she recognized the meaning of each cry, understood what would make him happy. And each day, something would become a little more familiar, a little less strange. And in the end, you just had to hope there would be love.

She waited for Josh, wanting to share this with him, feeling suddenly full of hope, and almost girlishly anxious. The whole bris, they had said hardly a word to one another. But that wasn't important, she told herself. Hadn't he done what she asked of him, despite his own objections? Hadn't he brought Aaron to the bris and stood by his side before the whole community?

It had all worked out, she thought, almost happily. Everything would be all right now. Their lives would simply continue, flowing over this hump, like a river flows over rocks in its path.

She waited and waited. But still, he did not come.

She watched the hall empty out, the catering staff gather the soiled tablecloths and fold up the chairs. When they took away the long partition separating the men from the women, she saw Josh standing there at the other end of the hall. She lifted her hand in a small, shy greeting.

She saw him look toward her, and then she saw the unmistakable, deliberate movement of his head as he turned away.

Her heart did a sickening somersault. She felt giddy, almost faint as she realized how thoroughly and profoundly she had misunderstood. "Sara, tell *Aba* to come over. I need to speak to him." Her voice was weak with fear.

And suddenly there he was, towering over her, blocking out the light. His face told her everything: that he was full of hurt pride, loss, and shock; that the bris, which she had found so beautiful and life-affirming, had for him been a public humiliation; that he had lost his status, his ability to fulfill his dream in the yeshiva world; that his whole marriage had been a lie; and that his pure wife was unbearably tainted.

Like the terrifying beat of tribal drums, her heart tattooed the message into her mind. Their marriage was over. Her position in the community was over. Life as she knew it, was over.

"Thank you for bringing Aaron. For being so kind to Aaron," she whispered hoarsely. "Thank you for coming to the bris."

"Kindness had nothing to do with it!" he said brusquely.

"Aaron is my son—that is the Law. This baby"—he looked away—"had to have a bris. That too is the Law."

She saw through his gruffness. No law in the world could make Aaron his son. And even if Aaron had been his natural offspring, even then, no Law required a father to give up everything he had loved and worked for to help a son. And no Law demanded that a bris be performed in front of four hundred people when a quorum of ten men would have sufficed.

She loved him. She wondered if everything that was to come would change that, and whether his love for her had been pulled out by the roots or simply cut down to the ground, awaiting a simple change of season to sprout again. "Then I wish there was a Law that said you had to forgive me," she whispered.

"It's not a question of forgiveness, Tamar! You are just not the woman I thought you were."

She felt the words flash through her like a surgical laser, leaving a deep and bloodless wound.

She swallowed hard.

"We will go away, Aaron and I. I've made inquiries. There are positions for both of us at a small day school in Detroit. There's some money in our account here. I'll send you more. I don't know yet about the girls. Maybe . . . later . . ."

Her whole life—everything that was dear to her, that she had built up over so many, many years—she could almost smell the smoke, see the flames of the great conflagration leaping up and consuming it all, like some offering on the Temple altar.

Where would she go, a religious woman with no husband, two blond daughters and a black baby? She could not think of a single place she had ever lived where such a woman would not be an outcast. What would happen to her, to her daughters? What had happened to Hadassah, she thought with cold fear.

Here was the end of the story, then, happening as she had always known and feared it would from the moment her hands had reached through the dustballs beneath her sister's bed, desperate to find and hide the flotsam of her ravaged life.

She closed her eyes and trembled, waiting for that knowledge, for the hardness in his eyes, the unforgiving tightness around his mouth, to annihilate her. And then a sudden vision came to her: *Tateh*, beaten down, humiliated because the wallpaper could not be replaced. Because appearances could not be kept up. She felt a hard kernel push up out of her soul like the cutting edge of some early spring bulb. She examined it, and found it to be indifference.

She did not share his ideas, nor his pain. Neither did she feel humiliated by the beautiful ceremony she had just witnessed or by the child in her arms. Her life was separate from his, and had been for a long time, she realized. His judgement of her was no longer her judgment of herself.

She felt a sudden, inexplicable relief.

"I'd like to speak to Aaron now."

She could tell the words surprised him. He had expected her to plead, perhaps, or simply to prolong their parting. He seemed disappointed, almost deprived, as if he had been watching a play whose final act did not live up to his expectations.

She would not agree to let him take the girls. But somehow, she felt it would not come to that. He did not realize it now, but he would miss her. He was a married man, used to his comforts. There would be no one to warm his bed, to bake his challah, to light the Shabbos candles, she comforted herself. He would soon enough find life without her unendurable.

Unless, unless . . . he could always divorce her and find another woman to marry. The pious widow of some *talmid chachom.* She thought of the nameless, faceless woman who might take her place and hated her.

She looked up and Aaron stood over her, much as Josh had. But unlike her husband's, his face was pale and soft and without anger.

"I don't want to wake the baby, so you'll have to bend down," she told him, her eyes wet. This was going to be harder, much harder, she realized.

"Aaron . . ." She could think of so many things to say, but

nothing that really needed saying. "Take care of your father," she finally whispered, wiping a stray eyelash off his cheek with her thumb. "You know he can't cook. He'll forget to eat. And it's cold in Detroit. Make sure he dresses warmly . . ."

She felt his arms clasp around her, around his son, his head hiding itself in her shoulder, like a little boy's.

❖37❖

June 17, 1993

Dear Josh,

I got your letter and was happy to learn that you and Aaron have decided to come back to Israel for a visit this summer and look around for possible teaching positions. As I said, there is a yeshiva here in Beit El where I think you might both find your place.

Winter in Detroit must have been cold. I am glad the people you met there were so warm. Still, I am not sorry that you write you miss me. I don't know what will happen between us. You were right. I'm not the woman you thought. You'd have to accept that—even like it. I do.

Can our long exile from each other be coming to an end at last?

Malka and Sara are happy in Beit El. The sunshine, the being constantly outdoors with a million girlfriends, agree with them. They have become very Israeli. Sandals and no stockings. Jeans skirts. They felt very strange at first, it was so different from Beit Yaakov. But they are learning so much. Most of all, they are learning how to think, how to question. They are not afraid to ask questions.

They miss their father, their brother.

I am glad Aaron is anxious to see his son. Little Duvid grows taller each day and smarter. My little wise man, I call him. My little King Solomon. . . .

She sat in the garden of her rented house in Beit El, writing. She put down the pen a moment and looked at the baby taking some drunken steps around the grass, falling as much as he stood. "Very good, darling. Again, *matok sheli*," she called out to him. He giggled and crawled very fast toward her, laying his soft head of dark wooly curls in her lap. She laid her chin on his fragrant head, nuzzling him.

It was late afternoon, and wonderfully cool. She looked up at the sky and saw some beautiful light pouring down on the earth through the clouds. The sound of birds mingled with the triumphant call of the rooster and the braying of some far-off mule.

She felt a peace descend on her that she couldn't explain or understand. Not the peace of resolution, but of transcendence. The sense of sitting in the spot G-d chose for her, the perfect place for her to be alive. Everything that had happened to her, everything that she had done, all of it together, had brought her here. There was nothing to regret or mourn. All of it, like the symbolic steps and gestures of some strange modern dance, had led her to this place, to the sense that the light pouring down was meant for her alone, to warm her heart, bleaching out all the bitterness, the darkness; lightening her soul.

It was a gift unearned, this sense of peace, of fulfillment, she thought. For so much still had to be righted, so much could never change. The gift was that she could accept it, accept her life, all that had happened, all that was still to come; the confidence that the calm center of her life could not be touched. That finally, she'd claimed it.

She thought of her sister, Rivkie—of her soft comfortable existence that had never been disturbed; her pale, bloated faith that had never known the rough tear of calamity, the piercing of tragedy. She thought of it and found there was no anger or envy in her heart.

She thought of her son, of Aaron. G-d had given him his life, with all its difficulties and challenges. She did not hope to understand why. He would have to find answers for himself or live with the silences when there were none. As she had, as every human creature born in any time and place in human history must. She was not responsible.

She had a simple faith, but real and deep, that G-d's

goodness was like the sun pouring down, touching every human creature. And it didn't matter if you had all your limbs, or a perfect brain, or a wonderful home, or the envy and respect of others. . . . That sun poured down on you equally, making you grow, warming your heart. It was like manna, she thought, landing all around you, lying there waiting to be gathered. Waiting to nourish you.

Aaron's portion was there, too. He would have to look around for it, open his eyes to see it and his arms to gather it. She could not do this for him or even imagine it for him. But the manna was there, for her, for Josh, for Aaron, her daughters, her grandson. . . . For everyone who lived.

The stones of some ancient cemetery gleamed calmly in the distance. But I am still alive, still warm, she thought. My eyes still see, my ears still hear. And every day I taste the sweetness of small victories—a bird I never saw before, the smile of a friend, an unknown plant growing in my garden.

Until she lay beneath those cold, white stones, she would not deny that unearned joy growing inside, spilling over, taking wings and flying above her, like some strange new bird. She would try to follow it as it spread its wings and flew effortlessly, wind carried, circling, around and around, filling itself with sunlight and fresh blue skies.

She felt alone in the world. Happily alone. And safer than she had ever felt. And all over, she saw green sprouting, even over the hard rocks. New growth. Everywhere. Flowers, vines, twining around the old altars, covering them, so that they could never be used again. So that even the archaeologists would not be able to find them.

She wove her fingers through the baby's warm hair. She was part of him and he of her. Through him she felt a strange, tenuous connection to a whole new world, vast and incomprehensible, that overflowed the boundaries of the neat grid in which she had grown up; a world in which you could not be certain that if you walked down Fourteenth Avenue, you would reach Fifteenth Avenue; in which you could not be certain you would not find yourself instead in some jungle or some tropical paradise—a place with new landscapes, new rules, and new ways of adding up good and evil on the ledger of Judgment Day.

In the stillness of her waiting soul, she felt a small movement toward the redeeming chaos of some hard-earned knowledge she knew must be wisdom. It allowed her to see beyond the small apartments, the narrow alleyways, the dark streets overshadowed by ugly man-made barriers to the soaring, shining glory of what was possible on this earth among all human creatures.